MIDNIGHT'S SMILING

Alexandra Connor was born in Oldham, and still has strong connections to Lancashire. Apart from being a writer she is also a presenter on radio and television.

ALEXANDRA CONNOR

Midnight's Smiling

HarperCollins*Publishers*

HarperCollins*Publishers*
77–85 Fulham Palace Road
Hammersmith, London W6 8JB

A paperback Original 1998
3 5 7 9 8 6 4 2

Copyright © Alexandra Connor 1998

The Author asserts the moral right to
be identified as the author of this work

A catalogue record for this book is
available from the British Library

ISBN 0 00 649842 6

Set in PostScript Sabon by
Rowland Phototypesetting Ltd,
Bury St Edmunds, Suffolk

Printed and bound in Great Britain by
Caledonian International Book Manufacturing Ltd, Glasgow

*This book is dedicated to my niece,
Daniella Brierley-Jones, who holds
a special corner of my heart.*

PART ONE

The venal city soon to perish.

Sallust, 86–34 BC

Prologue One

*Look at the moon. Look at the clouds across its face.
They make it look like the man in the moon's smiling.* She
paused, watched the night clouds pass over in the bitter
wind and then her eyes fixed on the face of the moon once
more. *It's midnight and the man in the moon's smiling.
Tomorrow will be a lucky day.*

Prologue Two

Lice smell of onions. Strange that, Michael thought, but it was true. The room in which he stood housed a cramped bed, and a chair beside it, the chamber pot under it giving off a foul odour. The woman on the bed was past caring; sores around her mouth, the greasy blanket which covered her mottled with stains. The fire had long since gone out. In the dimmed light Michael could see something scuttling into a corner and from behind the curtain partition came the sound of a child whimpering.

She wouldn't see the night out; he knew that, just as he knew that the man she lived with wouldn't come back. He'd gone off when she took sick. It was amazing, some said, that he had stayed so long. The woman had been on the game for years, walking the Salford streets, known as Pearl Lizzie because of the cheap necklace she always wore. She swore blind it had come from some rich admirer, but the pearls were fake and yellow with age. She had, as far as Michael knew, four children, the eldest following her mother into prostitution, the two teenage boys in and out of trouble, the baby – the one crying behind the curtain – too young to get into anything. Except bed sores from lying too long in unchanged nappy cloths.

Pearl Lizzie, Michael thought grimly, sitting down on the chair next to her. He would stay until she died, not just because he was her doctor, but because no one else would. And he didn't like to think of anyone dying alone.

Outside, the Salford night came down, hard rain like stair rods banging on the cobbles. The pub across the road was loud with noise, a horse stamping its hoofs as it waited for its master outside. Someone suddenly called out on the street under the window; someone asking Pearl Lizzie if she was working tonight ... Michael looked over to the woman's face. She'd never work again.

Closing his eyes, Dr Michael Cochrane tried to ignore the smell and the shuffle of the cockroaches whilst the damp seeped into his clothes and his breathing fell into step with that of the dying woman. The moon – waxy and blind – rose over the dark streets and made faces in the puddles, the pub finally emptying, the baby in the curtained-off room falling into a damp sleep, as Michael, cold to the bone, stared at his patient and thought of his father.

He remembered the first time he had watched someone die, only minutes after someone else had been born, and recalled only too easily how his father had reacted.

'They go out like a candle, if they're lucky.' He had made a snuffing motion with his fingers. It wasn't particularly cruel, only honest.

'Is that it?' Michael had responded.

His father had been bemused, a weighty man in his shirt-sleeves, impatient with sentiment.

'What else is there? It doesn't pay to be fanciful,' he'd replied shortly. 'If you want to believe in God, you can. I don't, but I've no objection to your saying a few words over her.'

Startled, Michael had looked back to the dead woman. He was only fourteen, and in awe of his father. What was he supposed to do? Refuse? How could he? So, slowly, uncertainly, he said the Lord's Prayer, George Cochrane watching him intently. When he had finished, Michael swore that he would never pray for the dead again. Instead he would look after them and nurse them, but pray for them, no.

In 1910, God had no place in Salford.

Chapter One

The first thing Michael Fields Cochrane remembered was the cat climbing into his pram. He couldn't have been more than eighteen months old, the sky was unendingly wide and blue above him, the sounds of birds and far-off voices soothing. And then suddenly there was a violent rocking of the pram, a shape jumping across his sky view and settling heavily against his feet. He could hear loud purring, and feel the warm heat of the animal's body pressing against him. He felt no panic, only wonder.

His second memory was of his father, Dr George Cochrane, massive and loud-voiced, flying a kite he had made for his son. It was a skilful affair, with the painted face of a dragon on it, and all the other children were envious, gaping open-mouthed, as it rode the summer air tides. Then – on the very first occasion four-year-old Michael was allowed to hold the cord – the string slid from his grasp and the kite sailed away, its dragon's face leering at him from a high cloud.

Michael didn't remember what happened after that, but the look of exasperation on his father's face never left him.

Michael was, like so many others, and like all the servants, in awe of George Cochrane. It wasn't surprising – most people were, except his mother. Thinking of Abigail, Michael relaxed, soothed instantly. She, of course, always saw his father's best side and never felt the pounding terror he did. It wasn't that he was afraid of his father in a physical way, it was more that he felt out of place when he was around. Even before he was six, Michael knew enough to slip away when his father came home. He would be with his mother and then, when George entered, he would go upstairs, reducing the number back to the complete and magical two.

He knew he was an interloper, long before he knew what the word meant. He sensed it; and all the loving attention his mother gave him could not compensate for the fact that his father resented him. What made the situation worse was that George tried so hard to cover his feelings: extra smiles; extra loud laughter at one of his son's jokes; extra attentiveness. It was hollow and felt sour to both of them.

Unfortunately Michael not only played second fiddle to his mother, but to his mother's health. His life had been punctuated by periods of panic, times when Abigail Cochrane was confined to bed, curtains drawn, George deep in conversation with other doctors.

'She's my wife, I know what's best for her!' he'd bellow. 'Haven't I got her well before?'

But Michael wondered about that. Wondered why it was that his brilliant father couldn't cure his mother, and he judged him inadequate because of it. Not that the boy dared mention it, of course, and it didn't help matters that as he grew older George's temper shortened. His work exhausted him, but he rarely took on help. '*It's my patch, no one else would touch it with a bargepole,*' he said repeatedly, and it was true.

No other doctor *did* want to work in Greengate, the worst part of Salford, amongst the slums and the unemployed, the drunk, the feckless. Prostitution and incest were rife there, the slatternly terraces pressed up against each other, windows broken, the gates of the backyards tied with string or left hanging, mongrel dogs barking hoarsely on the ends of chains. Once George had visited a house to find an Alsatian hanged. It had jumped over the gate and accidentally strangled itself. That wasn't the worst of it. The dog had been left hanging for more than a week. Some of the houses – only two-ups and two-downs –

housed as many as four families, although there was no running water, no toilet, the night soil men coming quiet after dark.

Fights were frequent. Religion fanatically observed by some, sneered at by others, each street boasting the odd family who tried, against depressing odds, to make something of their home. Others let time and poverty take their gloomy course; brown paper tacked over burst windows; as many as four to a single bed; illness rife, passed as it was, from one to the other without pause. There was no hygiene, no proper food and no birth control.

No other doctor wanted to know; certainly none wanted to walk the Salford streets after dark – except George Cochrane. Physically imposing, he had come from money; from a rich father who had added to his family's existing wealth by specializing in rubber and who had then built the fabulous Aynhams as a monument to his success. She, above all the other grand houses on Buile Hill, Pendleton, was the greatest. An Italianate villa which had taken thirteen years to build; a galleried, muralled, terraced talisman to ward off the industrial mire of Manchester, lurking just over the River Irwell.

From the first, George had adored Aynhams, but he never once considered going into his father's business. He wanted, he told his parents flatly, to be a doctor. Well, they thought he would grow out of it, and his father took George to the factory and showed him how they made rubber, and how they used it for wheels and mackintoshes, and the more that he showed his son, the more George wanted to be a doctor.

Why? . . . Because I'd be a good doctor . . . How d'you know? . . . I just do, that's all. Besides, I hate rubber.

Stung, his father then decided that if he couldn't persuade his obdurate son to change his mind, George would be set up in a spectacular practice in Deansgate, Manchester. But George had other ideas. He wanted to do what *he* wanted, in *his* own way. So when he qualified and heard of a slum practice in Greengate, Salford, George went to work there as a junior partner.

There was hell to pay. His parents couldn't make enough excuses. *George is just making a point . . . you know how young men are – he'll come to his senses . . . No one stays in the slums for long . . . He'll be out of there within months* . . . And everyone believed it – except George. He clung on to the practice and became a full partner in time – and his father ignored his son's medical career as though it didn't exist, his mother referring to it as 'George's little obsession'. But by the time his parents died during the following decade, George's little obsession was in his full control. He was in sole charge of the practice, his junior partner the evangelical, malign, Dr Tudge.

So when George inherited Aynhams the paradox was not lost on anyone. Here was one of the richest men in Salford, in the finest house in the area, working as a slum doctor for the poor. And the villa *was* magnificent, impressing everyone who saw it. Built on a slow hill, miles from the squalor of Salford, with its alien terracotta walls and water gardens running down to an old stream, peopled by a silent army of servants, it was vast, unwieldy, as opulent as his patients' homes were squalid.

Of course his patients knew about George's background, but no one resented his wealth. He was helping them, after all, getting his hands dirty when few other doctors would. And in response George was abrupt and bullying: if they argued, he argued back; if they threatened him, he stood up to them; if they dared to ignore his advice, he castigated them. He was aware of everything which went on in his patch, took issue with every wife beater, and child batterer. He had, in his time, moved daughters from fathers whom he suspected of incest, and given evidence in cases no one else would have brought to court.

Then suddenly an accident in his thirty-ninth year left

George blind in his left eye; he had had a fall riding and no amount of treatment could save his sight. For a while afterwards he was even more irascible than usual, his head turned to the left so that his good eye was trained on whoever he was looking at. It made him awkward, stiff, his big frame more unwieldy than ever. Only gradually did he adjust, Abigail soothing away the rough edges as she had always done. But there was another reason why the patients weren't envious of George Cochrane – because for all his money and his sumptuous house he went home daily to a sick wife.

Michael stared at his mother and wondered for the thousandth time why his father couldn't make her well. He was supposed to be so caring, so determined, but she was ill. She was nearly *always* ill.

'Stop worrying, Michael. I'll be better soon,' Abigail said to him as he sat on her bed, his beloved toy train in his hand. 'You mustn't worry.'

Oh, but he did. He worried all the time because his father had told him that 'overtaxing' his mother was dangerous. No one told him what overtaxing was, so he stayed very quiet – just to be on the safe side.

'Why can't Father make you well?'

Abigail stared at her son in amazement. 'But he does, Michael –'

'Not all the time. You're sick now.'

She stared at the sober little boy and laughed. Michael flinched. Would laughing overtax her? Would it kill her? Take her away for ever? And where would that leave him? Alone in Aynhams, with his father?

'Mother –'

Tiny in a cream dressing gown, she stared at him, and then she winked, mocking his solemnity.

'You do worry!' she said lightly. 'I'm fine. I'm just a bit under the weather, that's all.'

The drapes were in place around the bed as Michael laid his head down on the coverlet, his gaze moving upwards to the silk rosette overhead. It was like a faded red eye watching them. Slowly he ran the train over the counterpane, making train noises under his breath. Soon the train was real to him, the mounds where his mother's legs were, hills and valleys.

'Hooe, hooe!' he said softly under his breath. 'Hooe, hooe . . . Here comes the station and the passengers, here's the station master's dog, and the man with the flag . . .' He barked loudly, carried away, making his mother laugh again, the make-believe train waiting for her as she pretended to run down the platform.

'. . . Look, there's a tree fallen on the line!' Michael shouted suddenly, his voice rising excitedly as he tipped over the train, making a crashing sound, Abigail laughing as the bedroom door opened.

'You're just in time to prevent a fatal accident,' she said lightly as George walked in. 'We were in the middle of a terrible train crash, weren't we, Michael?'

But the boy was no longer excited and was now silent, sitting rigidly with the toy train in his hand, staring at his father.

'You shouldn't overtax your mother,' George said, his tone kindly.

So he had done the very thing he had tried to avoid! He had overtaxed his mother. *Now* what followed? Michael wondered. More illness, or worse . . . ? Silently, he watched his father sit down, his mother turning to him, and just as silently he slipped out of the bedroom, before his nanny came to claim him, running to the forbidden east tower, his special, secret place, and sliding under the rope which cordoned off the unsafe steps.

Unaware that his son had gone, George turned his whole attention on his wife.

'You look better.'

'Michael made me laugh,' she said happily. 'Have you finished for today?'

'Not quite, but I'll be back soon. About seven thirty, with any luck.'

'George, I was wondering about Michael –'

But he was still occupied with his own thoughts.

'. . . I should go out and see Clem Willis later. It's getting cold again and his place isn't fit for an animal to live in – especially now that winter's coming.'

He stopped, suddenly remembering the previous winter. Soon after Christmas the frosts had come, the house chilled, the treacherous stone tower on the east wing shrouded in snow, fires in every room making little impression on the overwhelming gloom of thunderous skies. There were gales too, some so fierce that they lifted the trees from their roots, one falling across the stable roof and spooking the horses. And, night after night, the temperature kept dropping. And, night after night, the simple chest cold which had first confined Abigail worsened.

George had insisted that she go to bed at once and had rung for her maid. Abigail had been reasonably well for a while, but the failure of her health was like a temperamental ghost: something unexpected and peevish in its attack. Naturally George thought that he could contain her sickness this time as he had done so many times before. But he was wrong. The infection spiralled out of control, George seeking advice from London, fear making him nervy, panicked.

Relentlessly, Abigail's cold intensified. She coughed incessantly, then developed a fever and needed constant nursing. Impatiently dismissing all other help – and reluctantly relying on the morose Dr Tudge to take care of his practice – George nursed his wife alone. But nothing seemed to help her; nothing brought down her temperature or steadied her pulse.

I'm a doctor, for God's sake! George thought wildly. I have to know how to help her.

But he didn't, and finally, defeated and afraid, he suggested that she be hospitalized in the Salford Royal – something Abigail flatly refused to do.

'No. I'll stay at home.'

'I think it would be better –'

'No!' she said firmly. 'You look after me, just as you always do.' Her hand fixed around his. 'I'll be all right, George.'

But with the onset of winter her health had failed again, and by the next day Abigail had dipped into semi-consciousness. On the second night, Michael crept into her room and lay down next to his mother, his head against her chest. When George found him he carried his son to his own room, but later, clutching his train for comfort, Michael sneaked back. His father, having dismissed the servants, was dozing in a chair by Abigail's bed. Michael stared anxiously at him as he crept across the room.

George stirred. Michael froze. After a moment, George slid off to sleep again . . . Cautiously the boy inched forwards then looked down into his mother's face. She was very still. *Overtaxed*, Michael thought blindly, turning the word repeatedly in his brain. Had he been responsible? Had *he* done something to overtax her? To make her sick?

Gingerly, Abigail stirred, the candle flickering, George breathing heavily, as Michael, afraid of discovery, slid under his mother's bed, his toy train grasped tightly in his right hand.

For the remainder of the night he stayed there, dozing intermittently on the floor. Sometimes he woke to see his father's feet move past the bed, or to hear his mother mumble in her sleep, but after a while it would be quiet again. In silence, Michael listened for some signal of the thing he feared most – the death of her. George, not realizing that his son was in the room, murmured diffident prayers whilst the night darkened and his anxiety crawled the walls. Then, just after one, the bedside candle blew out.

The dark was sudden and terrifying under the bed. Yet only feet from where Michael crouched, his father slept, breathing heavily, his mother hardly making a sound as she breathed. Unable to see anything, scared and alone, Michael stared into the dark. He thought then that the goblins might get him, drag him away, take him somewhere foul from which he could never escape, away from his home, his mother . . .

Silent and dry-mouthed, the child Michael stared into the darkness, then slowly and deliberately he began to run his toy train along the floor under the bed to comfort himself. Gradually he created an imaginary world in his head; a world of daylight, filled with healthy people. Above him, his mother idled in and out of consciousness while Michael played silently in the dark, and listened, on and off, throughout the night.

Having finally fallen asleep in the early hours, Michael woke suddenly with the dawn. He thought at first that it was the light which had disturbed him, but it wasn't. There was something wrong. Terribly wrong. Still holding his beloved train, Michael crawled out from under the bed and stared at his mother.

She was very still. Her lips seemed dark. Too dark. And her hand, resting on the pillow, looked like someone else's. Someone he didn't know. Close to panic, Michael leaned towards his mother.

'Wake up!' he whispered. 'Wake up!'

She didn't stir.

Hurriedly he caught hold of her hand and then dropped it. It was cold, without life. Michael screamed insensibly as his father snapped awake. First staring incredulously at his son, George then glanced over to his wife and leaned forwards, his expression dazed.

'She's dead! And you let her die!' Michael shouted,

running round the bed and pounding his fists against his father's stomach. 'You let her die! I hate you! I hate you!'

Feeling frantically for his wife's pulse, George blustered, 'Stop it! Stop it! Calm down!'

'I hate you! You let my mother die!' Michael repeated blindly. 'I hate you!'

His fists were flailing, his face distorted with panic and distress. George, looking frantically at his wife, faltered, then in exasperation picked up Michael's toy train and hurled it out of his way.

It flew in an arc before it landed, the bright green and red paintwork finally striking the bedroom wall, the engine crashing to the ground as the carriages splintered in pieces.

Chapter Two

Michael shook his head, his thoughts returning to the present. His mother's death had been a long time ago, but that night any true sympathy between himself and his father had been as thoroughly smashed as the toy train. They both knew it, the repeated accusation resounding over and over. *I hate you, I hate you. You let my mother die . . .*

It was no good either of them being rational: saying that the words had just been a terrified response from a grief-stricken child; the syllables had inflicted a wound which would never heal.

The accusation had left George Cochrane rigid with guilt. He had prided himself on being a good doctor, but his son had accused him of the thing he most feared – his own limitations. He should have been able to save his wife, but he hadn't. He had promised himself that he would keep Abigail alive and he had failed both her and their son. He was a tyro, a fake, an amateur. His own son had told him so.

And both of them knew it was something from which George would never truly recover. Over the years which followed, every time Michael caught his father looking at him he heard the words repeated between them. They became an invisible barrier; a fence cemented high and wide separating them, a hurdle which could never be scaled. Dr George Cochrane might walk the streets of Salford and treat the untreatable, but he had let his wife die.

It was only days after Abigail's death that George suddenly and unexpectedly lumbered headlong into depression. It caught him out as abruptly as a tidal wave would wash a swimmer into the depths. He was engulfed in grief; sodden with remorse; unnerved by the house and every corner and cushion which reminded him of his wife. And of his failure.

He blundered round the rooms; smoked his pipe unceasingly, his weight peeling off him as the days passed. He felt, in his soul, abandoned, with only the company of his resentful child left. The servants moved as shadows through the house – more discreet, more distant, more silent than ever. Aynhams – once so much the haven – became the torture chamber to which George was inescapably tied. He was scalded by the memory of Abigail and burned by his guilt, so much so that two weeks after her death he temporarily gave up the practice and left the dour Dr Tudge in charge.

Tudge was a thin man who had once been handsome, but whose bitterness had narrowed the good looks unflatteringly. His teeth were long in the gum, his hair too thick over the prominent forehead, his eyes judgemental. He was a Christian and his duty dictated that he work the slums. There was no pity or humour in it. At any other time George had little patience with Tudge, but now he no longer cared, no longer wanted to be faced with the daily reminder of his failure. The truth was that he no longer wanted to save *anyone*.

Staring fixedly out of the window, the adult Michael let his thoughts drift, his mind ambling back into the past. He thought of his upbringing at Aynhams after his mother's death, of the chill between him and his father and then he thought of the day he had decided to become a doctor. A number of years had passed since Abigail had died, George now practising intermittently again. William Tudge had just finished that morning's surgery in Greengate.

He had ridden back to Aynhams to report to George

18

and was cold, his face bloodless, his left hand clutching his medical bag fiercely.

Michael was standing by the back door, watching him.

'What do you want?' Tudge asked, his voice ponderous and slow.

'I want to be a doctor.'

Unsettled, Tudge looked at him.

'Why?'

Michael had surprised himself by the admission and merely shrugged.

'You must have a reason, a vocation,' Tudge told the fourteen-year-old boy. 'Did God tell you what to do?'

'God doesn't talk to me,' Michael replied honestly.

Letting out a brief exclamation of irritation, Tudge moved past the boy and walked into the morning room. His thin body hurried towards the fire and once there he lifted the tails of his coat to warm himself.

'I want to be a doctor.'

'You said,' Tudge replied shortly, uncertain of what to say next. He was unmarried, with no children of his own, and disliked confidences.

'I would be a good doctor.'

Steam was rising from Tudge's damp clothes.

'God only loves the humble, boy. You should remember that and mind your arrogance.'

Michael was impervious to the warning tone. He had finally articulated his dream and was eager to pursue the matter.

'What's it like, being a doctor?'

'I do the Lord's work,' Tudge replied, shifting his position and silently cursing the boy in front of him.

He was even more irritable than usual, a patient having died that morning and another having thrown a bucket of slops over him. George Cochrane, Tudge thought bitterly, might have been respected by the Salford scum, but they loathed him.

'Please,' Michael persisted, 'tell me what it's like.'

Tudge hesitated. What was he supposed to tell the boy – the truth? That the patients stank and were sometimes covered in vomit when he examined them? That two girls had died within the week from botched abortions? *Go and see Professor Lyne*, the word went round Salford. *He lives up Gillon Street, in the house with the medical specimen in the window in a glass jar*. The 'specimen' was a snake, long bleached white in formalin, and all the women who were pregnant and didn't want to be visited the crank Lyne.

He wasn't even a good abortionist, Tudge thought grimly. Last month a woman had come to him grey-skinned with pain. When he examined her, her vagina was stuffed with wadding to stop the bleeding. She fainted when he pulled out the engorged cloth.

'So, what's it like being a doctor?' The child was persistent.

'Ask your father.'

Michael stared at the man in front of him. Tudge had been around long enough to know that Michael couldn't ask his father anything.

'You tell me.'

Annoyed, Tudge let go of his coat-tails and walked away from the fire, snatching up his medical bag as he passed.

'If you want to be a doctor, boy, do your lessons and work hard and then you can inherit your father's practice,' he said coldly. 'How many other boys can say the same? I had no advantages – no home like this.' He glanced round, his envy making him momentarily hoarse. 'It's all waiting for you, all waiting for you to claim it. All you have to do is follow your father's footsteps.'

'I don't want to be like my father,' Michael said coldly.

'But you want to be a doctor –'

'I want to save people.'

'Your father's saved many people.'

'But not my mother.'

Oh, thought Tudge, so that was it. Michael Cochrane would become a doctor not to impress his father, but to spite him. The thought was an uncomfortable one: another man might have tried reasoning with the boy, but Tudge was too envious and too bitter to concern himself any further.

'God knows what is truly in your heart,' he said finally.

'God,' Michael replied without malice, 'knows nothing.'

Stiffly Michael stood up and walked over to the fire, the wind was gathering strength, smoke suddenly choking the chimney and making unwelcome inroads into the consulting room. He was aware that the patients were already arriving for afternoon surgery, but for once Michael was unwilling to follow his normal routine. Memory, slow in coming, had suddenly engulfed him.

When he had told his father about his ambition to go into medicine, George had tried to be enthusiastic but he couldn't help wonder at the motive, and was only grudgingly proud.

'Of course I'm pleased,' he said, his weight restored, his suit tight around his corpulent frame, his one good eye turned to his son. 'But do you *really* want to be a doctor?'

'Of course –'

'Why?'

Michael blinked. 'Because I just do.'

'Because you think you'd make a better doctor than I am, you mean.'

'I didn't say that!' Michael snapped.

'You didn't have to!' George snapped back.

The depression from which he had suffered since his wife's death had never totally left him; he found at times a sodden blanket of despair smothering him, and only work could lift it. And only work reminded him of the *reason* he was depressed.

'We shouldn't fight,' George said at last. His tone was

almost hopeless. 'I want us to be friends, Michael. We *should* be friends.'

But we never will be, his son thought, we never will be.

Michael had been very young to enlist when war first broke out, but when it continued he volunteered, abandoning his studies at medical school to the greater cause, hoping instead to find a purpose in the army. He saw action in France but was soon wounded, one of the uncomfortable heroes shipped back home in 1917 – to the relief of George.

Hospitalized at the Salford Royal Infirmary, Michael was remote and listless when he first met Sylvia; very young, very pretty, very different. Nothing like the few girls Michael had met through friends of his father, embarrassed offspring set up for inspection by the future heir of Aynhams. They had all been given the same message: *Charm him, he's going to come into money and besides, he's an attractive young man.* They were right, Michael Cochrane *was* attractive – if you could get past the chill of his reserve – something no English girl ever had.

So when Sylvia first came upon Michael he was lying flat out in bed, his broken ribs bandaged, his left leg in plaster. His eyes were closed.

'Mr Cochrane?'

He had looked up at her and his eyes had been bright blue – clearer and stronger than any other colour Sylvia had seen since coming to England.

'Yes?'

'You have a visitor.'

He stared at her a moment too long before nodding, but he was at once fascinated, sucked out of his despondency by this dark-skinned, oval-faced girl.

'Who is it?' Michael asked her, not really wanting to know the answer, in a way hoping that the visitor might suddenly vanish and leave them alone.

'Your father,' she said simply, then smiled, white teeth

against the tinted skin, a smile as natural and giving as anything Michael had ever seen.

'Oh, my father, I see . . .' he replied simply, but he didn't want to talk to his father, didn't want to be subjected to the bluster of his forced concern.

'May I show him in?'

'Where do you come from?'

She smiled again; Michael felt suddenly light-headed.

'India. Bombay.'

'Are both your parents foreign?' he asked, amazed that he could be so straightforward, so direct.

'My mother's English, but my father's Indian – a doctor.' Sylvia paused; she too wanted to extend the moment. 'I came here to finish my nurse's training. My father says that it's better to train in England than anywhere else.'

Her voice betrayed nothing of her parentage; it was, in fact, impeccably English, precisely modelled in every syllable and vowel. It was the voice, Michael decided there and then, that he wanted to hear every day for the rest of his life.

'So,' George said moments later as he sat down by his son's bed. 'You turned out to be a bit of a hero.'

A bit of a hero. Michael winced inwardly.

'I broke some ribs and a leg, hardly heroic.'

'You know what I mean,' George replied, his tone steely as he leaned back in his chair and glanced around the ward. 'Good-looking nurse that. Striking girl. Not English, can't be.'

'Half Indian.'

George turned back to his son, amused. 'You must be feeling better if you're chatting up the nurses.'

'I wasn't chatting her up,' Michael replied defensively, 'I was just talking to her.'

If this man had been anyone other than my son, George thought angrily, *I would give him a piece of my mind. When the hell did he get so stiff, so prickly?* He had hoped

23

that Michael might have changed when he returned from the war, but he was even less forthcoming, almost aggressive.

Sighing, George turned back to his son.

'You'll be out of here in a few weeks. I had a word with the doctor looking after you.'

'Fine.'

'It'll be good to have you back in Aynhams.' George paused, struggling to find conversation. 'Tudge is taking on some more work for me now. He was bitten last week, came in clutching his hand, bleeding like a stuck pig.' He laughed, shaking his head. 'I thought it was a dog, but no, some kid had taken a dislike to being examined. Poor Tudge, so very righteous and so very unpopular.' George's one good eye trained on his son. 'Have you thought about what you want to do when you qualify? I'd like you to take on my practice. I've always hoped you would. Father to son, you know how it goes.' Silence. 'But it's up to you, Michael, you know that. Aynhams will be yours when I die, and I'd like to pass the practice on to you as well, but –'

'Can I get you anything?'

Startled, both men glanced at Sylvia, standing by the bed. She seemed so young that all thoughts of death and inheritance were blown to smithereens simply by her presence.

'No, I'm fine. How about the patient?' George asked, with forced professional jocularity. He was, Michael thought with uncharacteristic peevishness, becoming a parody of himself.

'I'd like some tea.'

'Tea it is,' Sylvia replied simply, the two men watching her as she walked off.

Abigail was about her age when we met, George thought idly, young and well then. She came to Aynhams and stood in the hall and laughed, *laughed* at the house. *It's so grand, so frightening, George. It's a beautiful old tomb* . . . Well, it was your tomb, wasn't it? George thought despairingly. You saw in that first moment – without realizing it – what the future was for you there.

'Here's your tea,' Sylvia said a few moments later, breaking into George's thoughts as she leaned over his son.

The older man's gaze fixed on her steadily, on the slim arms, the fine dark down at her temples, the mole on the left side of her neck. She shimmered in his sight, her energy and youth taking him back to the memory of his own young wife, Abigail's fairness mingling with the dark opulence of the woman in front of him . . .

'. . . Father? . . . Father?'

George blinked, hauled suddenly back to the present. 'What is it?'

'I said that I'd like to take over the practice when I qualify.'

'It's not an easy job, but you know that,' George answered warily. 'Not many doctors want the kind of patients I have. You don't have to accept because you're worried about hurting my feelings.'

Michael held his father's gaze. 'I'm not, I want to do it for my own reasons.'

'Yes,' George said wryly. 'I thought you might.'

A pause settled between them. For once Michael wanted to reach out and touch his father's hand, to forgive him – but he couldn't make the move and instead he said quietly, 'I won't let you down.'

Unable to respond, George stared numbly at his hands whilst between them Sylvia stood perfectly still.

Strange, but it was as though she already belonged there.

Chapter Three

It was the end of November 1918 when Sylvia came to visit Aynhams for the first time, arriving with Michael just after ten at night. The arched windows were lamp-lighted, throwing illumination onto the gravel driveway outside, the house an immense shape against the winter sky. Silently she stared at the building; her parents were comfortably off, but this was something different, this was *real* money, old money. Power money.

After receiving her invitation to Aynhams, she had written home to her father the previous week:

Dearest Poopa,

I have met a wonderful man – no, you mustn't worry, he is very proper and is training to be a doctor. His name is Michael, Michael Fields Cochrane. Grand sounding, isn't it? I so wish you and Mother could meet him. Mr and Mrs Lomax are guarding me like the Crown Jewels and nothing improper is going on! They send their love and say I can stay with them for as long as I wish.

I am working hard and doing fine. The hospital is very cold, very grim – you would think they charged for smiles. I still smile, though – for free!

My love to you and to Mother – I will write to her separately.

Sylvia.

Dark and sensual, she attracted comment on her unusual beauty everywhere. Yet she had no arrogance, laughed at flattery, pulled faces at the silliness of the men who ran after her. But she never belittled Michael, never undermined him, or hurt him and slowly she had broken down his reserve.

I want you, only you. You, Michael, just you . . .

He had been giddy with delight, then suspicious, resuming working his way through medical school, wondering why this glossy hybrid should choose him.

But what Michael didn't know was that Sylvia had seen in him something she wanted badly – something she saw in no other man – vulnerability. He didn't want her for his own ego, or simply to possess her; he wanted her simply to belong to him – and she wanted that more than anything. For all her swooping charm, Sylvia never forgot that she was an outcast. The Great War was over, but nothing had really changed: she was of mixed race, mixed blood, someone to be desired, but not accepted.

And oh, how she *craved* acceptance. Just as Michael did, lonely and cut off from his father and remote from his peers. She had watched him for some time, as his medical studies brought him back to the hospital where he had been nursed, and daydreamed about him, finally confiding in her father when Michael, who sought out her company whenever he could, had told her he loved her.

Yet strangely when she wrote to her mother, Sylvia said nothing about Michael. Instead the pages were full of the hospital and the kind of news Sylvia knew her mother wanted to hear. News about England, the weather, the shops. The food – hard bread and strong tea. Her attention to detail was incredible, because she knew her mother would read and re-read the letters avidly, remembering her homeland and what she had left behind. Because by marrying Tariq Dhahani she had lost everything. Lost her status, her good name, her social standing – and her family. When they knew of her love for an Indian, they cut her off without a moment's hesitation. She was marrying a native. She was a disgrace. No matter that he was a doctor: he was an Indian first and foremost in their eyes.

So all the time that Sylvia was growing up she watched her mother pore over the London papers and beg her few remaining English friends for news. Then sometimes she would just stand for a long while looking out at Bombay, her pale skin skimmed with perspiration. It seemed, at those times, that she was sad, longing, but then she would pull herself together and walk away from the window and carry on.

Then, one night when Sylvia was ten, she overheard a conversation between her parents. It was a steaming night before the monsoon and no one could sleep, the mosquito net over the bed making a false moonlight above Sylvia's head. Silently she ducked under the net and crept to the window for some air – but instead she found herself unexpectedly eavesdropping on her parents in the garden below.

'Do you *want* to go home?' her father had asked help-lessly, his voice hoarse.

'No . . . no.'

A rustle in the darkness: a sob coming from one of them.

'I would understand – you gave up everything for me.'

Straining to listen, Sylvia struggled to make out her mother's next words.

'. . . I don't care for myself. I don't regret what I did and I would do it again – I just worry about Sylvia. What kind of life will it be for her, half Indian, half English?' She paused in the darkness. Far away an animal made a startled night call. 'Who will marry her? No Englishman.'

Sylvia had stood rigid, listening. What was wrong with her? Was she ill? *Why* wouldn't an Englishman marry her? Panic made her pulse speed, her ears straining to hear the next words.

'We should never have had children. We should never have had her.'

Who will marry her? No Englishman. The words echoed inside Sylvia's head long after her parents had left the garden, long after the dawn rose and the Bombay streets started to pound with feet. She had never felt that she was different before; had only known love from her parents, but now she had uncovered the knowledge which would change her life – *she was different*. She was somehow faulted.

And so the process began – not that Sylvia realized it then – but gradually she became more and more Anglicized. Her English was immaculate because she had listened to her mother and perfected it, just as she copied her mother's mannerisms and expressions. She grilled her for news too, English stories, English customs. Amused, and frequently homesick, her mother encouraged her, thinking it only a whim which would pass in time.

But it didn't. Sylvia had decided that she was not going to be second rate, someone who was a social outcast. So she watched the English expats and heard their tales, and slowly she realized that she was expected to live in India and marry an Indian. She would have no other choice; no other life was to be open to her. Or so *they* thought. But as Sylvia grew up she visualized herself triumphant. Not cowed – as her mother sometimes was – not resigned. No, she was going places – she was going to England to do the impossible – she was going to marry an Englishman.

She didn't know *which* Englishman she was going to marry – until she met Michael Cochrane. Until then, her ambition had never taken her any further than the image of some phantom suitor. She had never thought about her feelings, or what he would be like, but when she saw Michael Cochrane, that was it.

Not that she was the only woman who had designs on him. Michael Cochrane was a catch – a young trainee doctor who had had to postpone his training until after the war. A man who had volunteered to fight for his country and who had been invalided home as a hero. Many of the other nurses had tried to effect some response in him, with no luck. *Don't go pining away, Sylvia,* they told her. *We've all had our eye on him, but he's not interested. Don't go holding out any hopes* ... Oh, but she *did* hold out hopes for the reserved Michael Cochrane; grand hopes, long-distance hopes. Unending hopes.

Hopes which had finally begun to materialize when he told her he loved her, and which had grown with the invitation to Aynhams.

When they arrived, servants spilled out to take the luggage, and George was waiting for them in the hall. He looked very much at ease; in control, waiting to greet his guest.

'Sylvia, welcome,' he said generously, taking her hand. 'It's good to see you again.'

She smiled in return, dazzled by the house and the sound of horses whinnying in the stables beyond.

'D'you ride?'

'Only on buses,' she replied drily.

Laughing, George turned to his son and clapped him on the shoulder. 'Grand girl,' he said cheerfully. 'Are you two serious about each other?'

Sylvia could feel Michael tense beside her, but the old man's bluntness didn't disconcert her for an instant.

'Yes,' she said, answering for Michael. 'We're serious.'

Thoughtfully George regarded her. Yes, he reflected, she'll do. She's ambitious, cheerful and good-looking.

Her foreignness amused him – he wondered what the patients would make of her and knew instinctively that she would be able to cope with anything – either the slums of Greengate, or the small industrial community of Pendleton which bordered Buile Hill. For all her delicacy, her slight frame and light manner, it was obvious that Sylvia was tough – tough enough to stand up to him, and tough enough to love his son.

Because it *would* be tough, George thought. Any woman loving Michael would be sure to encounter reticence, anger and unexpressed emotion. He wondered then if Michael had confided in Sylvia, told her about the death of his mother and his father's shortcomings – explained the real reason why he had decided to become a doctor.

'Tomorrow, will you show me around, Dr Cochrane?' Sylvia asked, breaking into his thoughts.

'Call me George,' he replied easily, taking her arm. 'I've missed feminine company for too long. Far too long.'

Only weeks after that visit George would joke that he had fallen in love again, teasing Sylvia and baffling Michael. She, for her part, cajoled the old man and listened, and walked the grounds of Aynhams with him, realizing from the beginning that understanding the relationship between Michael and his father was crucial to her own happiness. The George Cochrane she knew bore no resemblance to the one-eyed, shouting ogre of Michael's childhood, he was simply a lonely, ageing man, eager to have a family around him again – which was exactly what she wanted.

And so George and Sylvia worked together in unspoken unison, both aiming to achieve each other's dream.

'Apparently Michael wants to take on my practice when he qualifies,' George said simply, waiting for her response.

'I know.'

'It's a Salford slum practice, rough. The Greengate area. D'you know it?'

'I've passed through.'

He laughed. 'That's what most people do – pass through as quickly as they can. There's nothing glamorous about it, Sylvia. No new innovations. Nothing like the Manchester Infirmary, or even the Salford Infirmary come to that. Medicine here is about as basic as it gets.'

She pulled a face at him. 'I know that too.'

'Salford's an ugly place,' George went on, then added,

'I want to take you there, show you what to expect.'

They were walking past the stables, Sylvia wrapped up against the cold, George bare-headed as snow began to fall.

'Michael's told me about it.'

'Michael doesn't know the half of it,' George replied, walking on for a moment in silence. 'The death of his mother hit him very hard, you know. He thinks I failed her. He thinks he could have done better – maybe he could, at that.'

Head bowed, Sylvia walked beside him. 'What was Abigail like?'

Taking a deep breath, George stared across the lawn. 'Beautiful, loving, frail. My wife had tuberculosis. She was never fit, never robust. I was treating some of my patients for TB at the time – I think I passed the infection on to her.'

Pausing, Sylvia glanced over to him. The snow had fallen on her black hair and on her cheeks. She looked an alluring outcast.

'It wasn't your fault.'

'No one knows that for sure,' George replied, then glanced down at his hands, embarrassed. 'What does my son say about me?'

The question hummed on the air.

'Nothing,' Sylvia replied at last.

'"*Nothing?*"' George repeated, considering the word and then turning back to her. 'He hates me, you know.'

'No,' she replied quietly, brushing the snow away from her eyes. 'No, Michael doesn't *hate* you.'

Sighing, George stared back down the snow-cuffed lawns. 'You know, I love it here. I love this house and these gardens – I love the time I had here when I was happy, when my wife was alive. I even love my work – not because I feel I'm doing something worthy, but because working the slums reminds me how lucky I am to have

Aynhams. My practice stops me from being arrogant.'

He blew on his hands to warm them. 'My patients don't confide in me, they have to work too bloody hard at staying alive – they don't share their births and deaths, they don't even thank me half the time. They live and they die in conditions most people wouldn't believe exist. I've delivered idiot children born as a result of incest, seen babies smothered at birth because the family couldn't afford to keep them. I've even known a man kill his wife for drink money. It doesn't get any worse than this, Sylvia, and no doctor could bear it unless they had a good home to return to.' He studied her. 'Michael wants to save people to show me what a fine doctor he is – how much better he is than me. He may not realize it, but that's what motivates him.'

The snow was falling heavily, rapidly whitening the garden and the two disparate figures who faced each other in silence.

Sylvia was the first to speak again.

'I can make him happy.'

'I don't doubt it,' George replied, 'but will he return the compliment?'

Without answering, George moved on, Sylvia dropping into step beside him. Images floated in the air before her: the little white pavilion at the bottom of the lawn; the cool, high rooms, the furniture, the paintings, the carpets . . . She thought of the brass plate on the side door – 'Dr George Cochrane' – soon it would have Michael's name underneath. And then she thought, *Mrs Cochrane* . . .

Breathing in slowly to steady herself, Sylvia looked round. She could make a life here, she could make Michael happy here, she could *be* someone here. Have a name, status. She, a half-caste from Bombay, could marry her Englishman.

Then she felt a sudden unexpected panic. What did she really want? The house? The name? Or Michael?

'You'll get cold.'

She frowned. 'Pardon?'

'The snow's coming down hard, let's go in,' George said, moving on.

Silently Sylvia followed him into the house.

Look at me, look at me, the place seemed to whisper. *This could be yours. Yours* . . . Annoyed, Sylvia shook her head, but the windows still looked out to the immaculate winter gardens, and the brass plate still shone in her mind's eye like a beacon calling her home.

Chapter Four

His teachers could say what they bloody well liked, Harry Chadwick thought angrily. What the hell did they know? Snobs, thinking they were somebody, trying to make him grovel, trying to pretend that they were better than him. Couldn't wait to bring up his family, could they? Mother long gone, father a docker, causing plenty of trouble in Chapel Street during the dock strike, marked out by the police, collar felt, the name Chadwick engraved in their little black book for all time. A hothead, a bastard.

Tom Chadwick, red-haired, vicious-tongued, take on all comers. Didn't drink, didn't womanize, didn't thieve, but by God did he fight. Bare-fisted for half a crown off St Stephen's Street, in the alley behind the family's two-up and two-down on Gladstone Row. Gladstone Row: a block of ten houses, by 1904 six boarded up, the other four classed as uninhabitable by the council. No sanitation, no proper kitchens, just a slop stone stained and cracked. Conditions so bad the cockroaches moved on, the streetlamps long smashed, police coming infrequently, and always in twos. Gladstone Row, Salford, where no one spoke and on steaming summer nights the smell of old fat and dog muck could make you retch.

If you came from Gladstone Row you were the poorest of the poor. Likely an immigrant, or a thief, always a loser. No one who ever ended up in those squat dark houses – overshadowed by St Stephen's Street so that they never caught the sun – no one who ended up there ever left.

Harry would never forget their house. He would never forget his father's fights either. It would be night, Harry and his sister, Molly, sitting in the dark to save candles. The voices would come from a long way off, getting closer, and closer, to the sound of hurrying feet. Then the men would turn into the alleyway off St Stephen's Street, behind Gladstone Row, and the bets would go down.

Once Harry had gone out to watch, saw his father strip down to his trousers and then spit on his knuckles before standing up to his opponent. Perched up on the back gate Harry could see the two fighters in the middle of a circle of watching men, eagerly egging their favourite on. The noise was thunderous; but all that Harry could really remember was the sound of bare fist on flesh. The thump, thump, or the occasional dull, hollow sound when someone took it on the ribcage.

His father saw him watching when they stopped to take a breather, went over and belted Harry round the ear.

'Get in and stop there!' Tom snapped. 'And no more bloody spying on me.'

But the following day he bought Harry some sherbet, and a peg doll for Molly with his winnings.

Other times he didn't win. Sometimes Harry got up to the sight of bloodied water on the slop stone and a soaked rag in the grate, his father disorientated and thick-lipped for days. When there had been a particularly rough fight Harry would go out into the alley and see – amongst the scuffed earth where the men had fought – spittle and blood clots spat out against the rough, uncobbled dirtway. Once he found a tooth and kept it, wrapped it in a piece of rag and hid it in the lining of his coat. Why, he couldn't have said.

Harry's childhood went by not in years, but in fights. Bouts, not months. Money was won, or it wasn't. When it wasn't his father took on other work, providing muscle for God knows who – Harry didn't. Gossip had it that Tom Chadwick could be hired to sort out late payers, but Harry was never sure what was rumour and what was truth, he just knew that his father had the reputation for being a hard man. And no one could argue with that.

Naturally Harry suffered for it at school; being short and red-haired, the butt of jokes. He wasn't feisty like Tom Chadwick, wasn't able to provoke fear, only ridicule. Until the run-in with Cailey's dog.

Old man Cailey had a dog – no name – some son-of-a-bitch animal which its former owner had tried to drown with its peers in the River Irwell. Well, this dog got out of the weighted sack somehow and swam to the shore and then it bit every bugger it came across until old man Cailey took it in. Cailey never touched the dog. Just fed it, leaving the back door open so that the animal could come in and leave as it wanted.

That dog grew into the darkest, biggest mammal ever seen in Salford – and the meanest. Old man Cailey, who fenced stolen goods, never had to worry about being ripped off. The dog slept on the doorstep and kept its white-rimmed pale blue eyes fixed on anyone who came up St Stephen's Street. It never barked, just snarled under its breath and on the few occasions it moved, the street emptied.

Red-haired Harry, too bright for the local council school, had no friends. He wanted – and had wanted since he could think – to get out of Gladstone Row. He kept cuttings of the city of Manchester and of the great houses on Buile Hill, and he had a new book (and two newspaper clippings) about the up-and-coming pathologist, Bernard Spilsbury – because *Harry was going to be a doctor*.

It was an unhealthy ambition in Gladstone Row. It made Harry picked on, laughed at, his incredulous father telling him to buck up his ideas and not get above his station. Of course the kids at school taunted Harry. When his trousers were patched they laughed at him, the rough material of the repair making his arse itch. It made his big ideas even more ridiculous to them. Then, at the age of twelve, Harry decided that he had to do something to get rid of his

Salford accent; so he sneaked into the pictures and watched the Pathe News and tried to emulate the newscaster's voice.

His peers were merciless.

'Hey, bloody Chadwick. Charlie Chadwick, with his arsey-tarty voice!' they called out after him.

Resolutely Harry walked on, a bunch of boys following him into Gladstone Row.

'Charlie Chadwick! Arsey Chadwick!' they parroted, Harry suddenly finding himself surrounded by hostile faces. They were all poor, but he was the poorest, and worst of all, he wanted out – and had made it all too obvious.

They scared him, not that Harry would have shown it. His trousers were scratching him as he sweated, his clogs making a quick getaway impossible. He hadn't got the hard fists of his father, and he knew all too well that you couldn't fight with an intellect.

So within seconds they had surrounded him, and when the first boy lashed out, he caught Harry a pearler on the right side of his head. Others followed, Harry stumbling, saying nothing, refusing to cry, only panicked and too outnumbered to duck the blows and escape.

Then suddenly from nowhere old man Cailey's dog came into view, Harry looking straight into its pale blue eyes and thinking about angels ... But the dog wasn't about to bite Harry; it simply moved between him and the crowd of boys and *snarled*. Its hackles went up, its teeth bared, a clammy rumble emanating from its throat as the boys backed off.

When the street was empty, Harry looked at the dog.

The dog looked at Harry.

The boy didn't attempt to thank the animal.

The dog didn't expect it.

But from then onwards old man Cailey's dog walked to school with Harry and arrived in time to walk him home. And whenever the boy was under threat it appeared round the corner of Gladstone Row like it could smell trouble and was ready for it.

Time passed and Harry thankfully grew and filled out. He didn't get tall, but he got plenty broad. No one pushed him around any more, and besides, old man Cailey's dog – grey-muzzled and even nastier with age – was never that far away. Harry's sister, Molly, grew up and got out of Gladstone Row at the age of sixteen. Married the first boy who asked her. Stayed away from her father. Not because she was afraid of him, but because the rough Tom Chadwick, the ex-docker, the bruiser from Gladstone Row, was – at forty-nine – unsteady on his feet, shambling, with slurred speech and dilated pupils.

'Fucked up m' 'ead,' he'd explain. 'The fighting – it fucked up m' 'ead . . .'

That wasn't the hardest part to bear for Harry. Not the illness, but the way Tom's old cronies – the men who wouldn't have dared to *look* at him wrong in the old days – put money in his father's pocket when he wasn't looking. It was supposed to be a kindness, but Harry doubted that. Thought it was more like giving water to a lion once it had been caged. They were sorry, yes, but glad in a way to see Tom Chadwick brought down. In his prime, his father had scared the shit out of them.

Oddly enough, although Harry's mother had done a bunk it was two years before his aunt moved into Gladstone Row and took over Tom. She spent almost a week clearing out and washing the linoleum, the windows, and stoning the step, the neighbours watching her silently. And after all that cleaning the two-up and two-down looked as grim and unwelcoming as it had always done.

Undeterred, Gladys bought a couple of pot plants for the kitchen window, but they never got any sun and died within days. So the backyard, with its old pram, broken mangle and criss-cross of knotted washing lines, was cordoned off from the kitchen window by a net curtain from Salford market: because, if Gladys couldn't see it, it wasn't there. But Harry *knew* it was; knew that the outside lav was still there, with its gap under the door and cut-up newspaper to wipe your arse on. His father used to get the *Salford Gazette*. Not so he could read it, 'but so I can wipe my backside on the bloody rag.'

Harry had had enough of Gladys within days; Gladys had had enough of Harry within hours. She – a spinster and desperate – was more than willing to marry poor sick Tom Chadwick, and Harry knew it.

'Yer old cow. You'd marry old man Cailey's dog if it'd fetch you a house!'

She took a swing at him, but Harry was long gone, down to the River Irwell or over to Buile Hill, where he stared at the big houses and threw mud at the carriages which passed. Once he stole flowers from the garden of the grandest house, Aynhams, and took them to Gladys as a so-called gift. He hoped – not that it ever happened – that she would be arrested for theft and be taken away to the women's prison outside Manchester.

He liked to imagine her fate there; sewing mailbags or on the treadmill. He liked to imagine that his mother would end up next to her; the two sisters treading eternally, step after painful step. They deserved it; all women deserved what was coming to them, Harry decided, his mother, his aunt, and his sister who ducked out just as soon as she could.

Then one sodden March Tom Chadwick was taken into the Salford Infirmary and Harry went to visit him with a packet of cheap fags and a copy of the sports pages.

'Read 'em to me, lad,' Tom said with difficulty, his focus gone, his head rolling on the pillow. He had lost weight, the old fighter beaten down by sickness.

'It says here –'

'I've bin meaning to ask you where the bloody 'ell d'you git that voice, 'Arry?' his father said, almost laughing. 'Sound like a bleeding nancy.'

Harry continued unperturbed. '... the paper says that Pete Finnigan should win his fight on Saturday.'

'I could've beat that bugger once. When I were in m' prime ...' Tom said, waving for Harry to put down the paper, and adding curtly, 'I've left house to yer aunt. You'll meck yer own way, won't yer, lad? She's a poor old sow who's got naught else.'

Harry wanted to protest, but he hated Gladstone Row and when his father died there would be nothing to hold him there. So he kept his feelings to himself – even if he'd rather have seen the house burn than Gladys get it.

'You do what you like, Dad.'

'Oh, I will that. I will that,' Tom mumbled. Turning to look at his son he winked clumsily. 'Yer a bright sod, an' no mistake.'

'You're right there.'

Tom laughed hoarsely. 'Set on bein' a doctor then?'

Harry nodded. 'I'm staying on at school, like I said. I can manage – I do odd jobs to get by. You wait, I'll get to the top, you see if I don't.'

'Meck money?'

'Plenty.'

'Beats fist fights anyday.'

'You did your best.'

'Weren't much.'

'Were.'

Tom coughed twice then focused suddenly.

''Arry?'

'What?'

'Get out.'

His son blinked. 'You what?'

'I'm pegging out –'

'Nah.'

'I'm fucking dying!' Tom snapped. 'An' I don't want an audience. Go on, get out.'

Slowly Harry got to his feet. On his father's right a

yellow-faced old man lay motionless, smelling like all old people, and on his left a young boy stared blankly at the peeling ceiling overhead. The high windows behind the beds were uncurtained, the view bleak, overlooking buildings, the sky a slat of iron grey depressingly low over the hospital. There were no comforts, nothing to see a man sweetly to Heaven.

'Go on, 'Arry, there's a good lad.'

He still hesitated. 'Dad . . .'

Tom stared at his only son and nodded slowly.

'We've never said it, but I know what you think of me. Me too. Me too, lad.'

Only then did Harry turn and walk out.

He came back to Gladstone Row knowing that in the time it took him to return to the sour terrace his father would have died. Rain came down hard and low, the mean bank of houses damp, solemn in the half-light. At the end of the street Harry looked for old man Cailey's dog, but the animal was nowhere to be seen. Puzzled, he whistled. There was no response. Only a woman passed by, hurrying against the rain and pushing a baby in a battered pram. Somewhere a cat cried to be let in. But there was no sign of old man Cailey's dog.

As Harry paused by the front door of his house he stared at the broken knocker and the number 9, which had slipped loose off its nail to look like a 6. Absently he tried to prop up the numeral, but it fell back immediately, swinging against the damp wood. The afternoon was moving on fast, rain cheating the day, as he paused and again – more loudly this time – whistled for the dog. Then, baffled that there was still no response, Harry walked into the house and closed the door behind him.

It was past eleven that night when he found old man Cailey's dog. The animal was lying by the back door, its white-rimmed, pale blue eyes open, its massive body wet with rain. Kneeling, Harry felt for a pulse – the first time he had ever touched the dog – and then he went inside for a blanket. Upon the borders of Peel Park he buried the corpse of old man Cailey's dog and by the turning of midnight he had left his childhood behind him for ever.

After that Harry spent hardly any time at Gladstone Row and told everyone who would listen that he was going to be a doctor. He had promised his father, he said, and besides, he was smart enough to walk the bloody exams. It was true. Harry *was* profoundly gifted. Extraordinarily so. Beneath his truculence, his hardboiled ruthlessness, there was a brain which few could ever hope to match. His intelligence had been recognized early on, and although some of his teachers would have tried to help him, Harry would have none of it – 'I'll do it myself. I'll rely on no bugger.'

He wasn't going to be hurt like his father, no bloody way. Not by the world, or by fate, or by any bloody woman either. Instead he was going to rely on the one person who would never let him down – himself. So Harry grafted at school and won a scholarship, whilst his aunt kept on the mouldering house in Gladstone Row and grumbled about Tom having died before he could make an honest woman out of her.

'You got the house,' Harry countered, 'what more could you ask?'

'He could have made me his wife.'

'He died to get out of that one,' Harry replied smartly, eyeing Gladys and watching as she dusted the two brass medals his father had won. For fighting.

They weren't real medals, just tin ones off Tommy Fields market, bought for a bob, but she showed them off to everyone anyway, saying: 'That's what my late fiancé won. He was a famous boxer . . .'

Of course everyone laughed at her, and she knew it, but it was better to fantasize than admit the truth, to make more of the little status she had. So when Tom Chadwick was buried up in Broughton Copper, Gladys laid claim to the plot next to him although by rights it should have been her sister's. Not that anyone knew if Lilly Chadwick was alive or dead. In fact, no one round Gladstone Row had seen Lilly since she had left her family all those years earlier.

No one, that is, except Harry. Rumour had it that his mother had moved to Liverpool, but then, suddenly, long before Molly left home, and years before Tom died, there was gossip that Lilly had returned to Salford.

For weeks Harry waited for her to get in touch, but when she didn't his bitterness festered and then, one evening, quite by chance he met up with her. He had been up by Exchange Station, hanging about, knowing that he was in for the beating of his life when his father found him missing. So he hung around hoping that if he waited long enough Tom would be asleep when he got back.

The streets surrounding the station were ill lit, almost deserted, a couple of drunks sauntering past, a late tram making its rackety way up the steep slope when he saw her. His mother. Lilly Chadwick. Against his better judgement Harry wanted to run to her, to ask her to come home, to beg her to come back to Gladstone Row. He wanted to say that things were bad at home, that his sister still cried for her at night and that the fights were getting to his father. *He's getting beat more and more often*, Harry wanted to say. *They'll bloody kill him one day.*

His heart thumping, Harry followed his mother from a distance, smoothing his hair to tidy himself and walking slow so that his clogs wouldn't make too much noise and tip her off. Because if they did, she might turn, and run off like she had done before – and he couldn't risk that.

So he followed her warily up Salford Approach, struggling to think of what to say. What words *would* be clever enough to bring his mother back? It had to be something right, something which wouldn't spook her . . . She was dressed better than he remembered, quite smart really, but flash, even to a child's eyes.

Carefully Harry followed his mother, then suddenly there was someone else on the opposite side of the street and he was spotted, the man laughing and calling out to Lilly: 'Looks like you've got a customer, Lilly. Starting a bit young these days, aren't they?'

She turned, laughing, and stopped strolling when she saw Harry. And he *knew*, just knew, what she was. A streetwalker, a whore, a tupp'ny-ha'pn'y drab. Flushing scarlet, Harry stared at his mother, his mouth drying, shame making his hands moist and tears smart in his eyes. But that wasn't the worst of it. Nothing like the worst of it.

His mother didn't know him. His mother simply saw a kid and laughed at him.

'Off 'ome, lad, yer too young! Come back in about a year or so and I'll teck you on.'

She was wearing lipstick. Probably red, but it looked indigo in the night light. An indigo slat of a mouth pouring out muck. Then she turned, clip-clopping on stacked heels under the lamplight, and moved on, the darkness taking her God only knew where.

Chapter Five

He had to stop bloody daydreaming, Harry told himself irritably as he pushed open the doors of the Manchester Royal Infirmary and hurried past Reception, ignoring the interested look from the nurse stationed there. Now in his twenties, he was no beauty, hair a little too much on the sandy side, build too stocky, nose too broad for good looks, but the nurses were always ready to cry off another date if Harry asked them out. It was his personality, they said, and even if he didn't treat them well he was exciting.

Turning into the hospital canteen, Harry lit up a Capstan as he joined the queue for his bangers and mash, still seething from his earlier argument with the Principal, his annoyance obvious as he drummed his fingers on the counter. Behind him, Michael was also queuing, patiently reading a book as he waited.

'Could you pass me a fork?'

Silence.

'Could you pass me a fork?' Harry repeated, Michael finally glancing up from his book.

'Sorry,' he said, reaching for the cutlery and handing it over.

'Good book?'

'Venereal disease.'

'Over lunch?' Harry asked, smiling his lop-sided grin, his bad temper lifting.

'It doesn't bother me.'

'I wasn't thinking about you, I was thinking about your companions,' Harry replied, slipping into step with Michael as he moved over to a far table and sat down.

46

He would normally have been irritated, but Michael was curious instead, having heard plenty of gossip about his companion. A hothead, the story went, but bright. Terrifyingly so. Slopping two spoonfuls of sugar into his tea and dragging deeply on his cigarette, Harry leaned across the table.

'Why VD?'

Michael met his gaze evenly. 'I need to know about it for the practice I'm going to.'

'Jesus, you work fast! I've no idea where I'll end up.'

'It's my father's practice,' Michael explained, 'in Salford.'

The words were heard, that much was obvious, but Harry made no immediate response. Instead he inhaled again, getting the last fragment of tobacco from his cigarette before grinding it out in the tin ashtray in front of him.

'I want to be a surgeon – a plastic surgeon.'

Michael stared at him thoughtfully. 'Why?'

'*Why?* Because it's new, exciting,' Harry answered, putting out his hand. 'Incidentally, I'm Harry Chadwick.'

'Michael Cochrane.'

Harry's eyes quickened with interest and some envy. 'Cochrane ... I've heard about you. Your old man's a doctor and your family has that great pile up at Buile Hill.'

'Aynhams.'

Harry paused. 'I stole some flowers from your garden once ...'

Jolted, Michael said nothing.

'... I was only a kid. I wanted to get my aunt arrested.' Harry paused again. 'If your father's so rich why did he want to be a slum doctor?'

'I don't know, I've never asked him,' Michael answered cautiously.

'If I had money and a house like Aynhams I'd never go

near the bloody slums. But then I was born there – Gladstone Row. Not Aynhams, is it?' Harry drank from his cup, his hazel eyes watchful. 'Why d'you want to follow in your father's footsteps?'

'I don't want to emulate him, I just want to take over the practice,' Michael said with obvious coldness, which did not go unnoticed.

'I've said something tactless, haven't I?' Harry asked, hurriedly shovelling a spoonful of potato into his mouth, his bad temper forgotten.

He was curious about Michael Cochrane, fascinated to find himself sitting opposite the heir of one of the richest families in the county. He wanted to know what it was like to live in a house like Aynhams, to have running water and space. To have status.

'I'm always saying the wrong thing. Maybe I should get some water to wash down my foot.'

Michael glanced at him placidly. 'You didn't say anything tactless –'

'Oh, yes I did!' Harry carried on, swallowing. 'I always do.' He wiped his mouth with his handkerchief.

His voice was curious, Michael noticed, his accent indecipherable. Certainly not a slum accent, but unlike anything else he had ever heard. The vowels weren't flat, but the inflection was pure Salford.

'. . . Still, whilst I'm being so outspoken I should mention what else I heard about you – that you've a stunning wife.' Harry paused. 'Now, you can either smack me in the mouth or accept the compliment generously.'

Michael smiled at his companion. 'Sylvia *is* very beautiful –'

'But not English?'

'Half Indian.'

'Exotic.'

'Exotic,' Michael agreed.

'She's a nurse, isn't she?'

48

Michael nodded. 'Yes, she trained over here at Salford Royal.'

'Convenient, you'll be able to have your wife as your surgery nurse. Cheap too,' Harry said, lighting up again and staring at a passing nurse's legs.

'You married?'

'God, no. Never will be either.'

'You don't know that for sure.'

Harry's genial expression hardened. 'Yes, I do. I know I'll never marry.'

Silence fell between them awkwardly, Michael turning back to his book, Harry looking round the canteen. Idly, he nodded at a blonde nurse and then finished his tea, swallowing noisily before leaning across the table towards Michael again.

'Got any children?'

'No,' Michael replied, glancing up from his book, amused. 'How about you?'

Laughing, Harry pushed his cigarettes into his pocket. 'Not that I know of. Look, I don't fit in here, I'm the token upstart. I'm common, rough as a bear's arse, only acceptable because I'm smarter than anyone else.' He paused. 'I could do with a friend. Fancy a drink sometime?'

He was lonely, Michael realized with surprise. For all his reputation and arrogance, Harry Chadwick was friendless.

'I can do better than that – come for lunch on Sunday. At Aynhams. It won't be very exciting for you, but you're welcome.'

It was hard to say who was the more surprised by the invitation, Harry for receiving it or Michael for offering it. It was totally out of character, Sylvia said to her father-in-law that night; Michael had never made friends easily before. But perhaps that had something to do with the fact that he had been educated at home, away from his peers.

'Maybe it's because they're both doctors,' she suggested, glancing over to George.

Reluctantly, he turned to face her. 'Well, it can't be their backgrounds. Tom Chadwick was a bare-knuckle fighter, a real hard man, and that's saying something in Salford. But he took one fight too many and now he's dead. I attended him once after a bout down Garden Lane. Oh, it was years ago. God, what a bloodbath. I've never seen any man so injured recover. But Chadwick did. That time.' George shook his head. 'If his son's anything like him he'll be a hard case. Still, whatever he's like, it's about time Michael made some friends. He never had any as a boy. I used to wonder what the bloody hell was wrong with him.'

'He was shy.'

'God knows what he was – but forthcoming wasn't it.'

Sylvia had had many similar conversations since she had married Michael and moved into Aynhams. The dream she had so assiduously courted had come to fruition: she had her English husband; she had her English home; she had had the last laugh, after all. Unfortunately though her parents never made it to the wedding, and her mother's tone was odd when she wrote. Jealousy? No, Sylvia thought, it couldn't be. But there was *something*. As for her father, he was ecstatic, writing her new name at the bottom of his letter repeatedly.

Sylvia Cochrane, Sylvia Cochrane – how grand it sounds!

Then after the wedding – a very private affair at St Anne's Church, followed by a reception at Aynhams – Sylvia finally sat back and looked at what she had achieved, and realized with a pungent sense of guilt, that she didn't truly love Michael. He would never know, she promised herself, he would never even suspect, and God willing, nature might well take its own course and she might fall in love with him. She didn't know if that *would* come about, all she knew was a sense of uneasy contentment when she looked around Aynhams – followed immediately by a nudge of sticky guilt.

She would be the good wife, she told herself, she would look after her father-in-law and her husband, and when Michael was qualified she would work with him as his nurse. She would repay him for the status he had given her – and she would never let him know the truth.

So whilst Michael completed his training she continued nursing in the Salford Royal Infirmary – until the night that George asked her to assist him with a difficult delivery.

'I need help, Sylvia, and the midwife's off on another case.' He was checking his bag, preoccupied. 'You don't have to come, but I'd be grateful if you did.'

She was ready in an instant, running through a heavy wind to the car waiting in the drive. George was one of the first in Buile Hill to buy a car, although he sounded his horn too readily and frequently forgot to put on his headlights after dark. Hurriedly Sylvia slid into the leather passenger seat beside him and rubbed her gloved hands together to warm them.

The cold was frightening, George outside cranking the engine, his white hair whipped around his head by the wind, Sylvia flipping on the headlights and pulling out the choke as he shouted instructions. Finally the engine shuddered to life, George throwing himself into the driver's seat and turning onto the road.

'In the old days we had horses. You didn't have to bloody crank up a horse.'

'But they did go lame,' Sylvia said, smiling.

'I had the same hunter for nearly ten years,' George continued, banging the car seat, 'which I doubt I will say about this thing.'

Within minutes the benign country roads disappeared, the outskirts of the town coming into the headlights. Empty streets, boarded-up shops and rain-greased cobbles sat squat and sullen under gaslamps, a child standing in a doorway watching them as they passed. As they turned a corner into Garden Lane the only noise came from a pub and a bakery, the smell of bread coming unexpected and sweet in the hostile streets.

It suddenly reminded Sylvia of her childhood in Bombay; of the narrow poor streets where she had been forbidden to wander, her nanny hurrying her past them as though even to look and see the poverty could contaminate her.

'Where we're going is one of the worst parts of Salford,' George said evenly. 'Do as I say, nothing else, and don't touch anything unless I hand it to you. Don't pick up the children you see in the house, and when we come back to the car afterwards you rinse your hands in disinfectant.' He reached under the driver's seat and passed her a brown ribbed bottle. 'If anyone offers you food or drink – which isn't likely – don't take it.'

Beside him, Sylvia nodded.

'I suppose you think I'm being hard. Well, I am. I don't want you picking anything up in this place.'

'I'll do what you say.'

'You have to learn, Sylvia. If you want to work with Michael in the practice, you have to learn to take care of yourself now. You know I have a slum practice, well, this is Greengate and this is as bad as it gets.'

Squinting at a chipped signpost, George turned the car into a street without lights. On the left the houses were abandoned, on the right a few were still occupied, a rusted mangle left lying in the middle of the road. Turning off the engine, George got out and motioned for Sylvia to follow him. With the headlights turned off, only his torch gave any illumination as they walked along, its beam picking out the ironic name, Paradise Row.

With the uneasy feeling of being watched, Sylvia stayed close to her father-in-law, following George as he shone his torch up to read a sign on the next wall – Hayland's Row.

'This is it. Now remember what I told you.'

Sylvia nodded, her voice low. 'I remember.'

'Stay close by me now,' George said. 'Don't leave my sight for an instant.'

Hayland's Row consisted of a semicircle of slums, two storeys high and barely discernible in the darkness. In the window of one a dim lamp burned, a piece of brown paper tacked over a broken window. Knocking, George waited for a reply, then tried the lock. It was broken and the door opened without effort as he moved immediately into the room beyond.

The smell of urine and animals was so strong it made Sylvia's eyes water. A broken table in the middle of the room was stacked with newspapers – no towels. By the far wall lay a woman on a mattress on the floor, several small children huddled next to her. One was picking at the torn corner of a dirty pillow. None was fully dressed. The youngest was barely a year old.

On the other wall an oven grate – black with grease – sported a kettle of hot water, a piece of fat bacon hanging over the range to smoke. The stench was overpowering, Sylvia swallowing repeatedly.

''Lo there, Jeanie,' George said, squatting down beside the woman.

She said nothing, merely stared at Sylvia.

'Baby coming, is it?'

Still she said nothing, her eyes fixed on the dark-skinned stranger.

'Jeanie,' George repeated, 'let's have a look at you.'

'I want her out –'

'Hey now, Jeanie –'

'Get that fucking cow out!' she snapped, pushing away the child nearest to her.

Without altering his tone of voice, George said simply;

'Sylvia is a nurse, she's helping me, and she'll help you.'

'She's black,' Jeanie said, her voice thin with bitterness.

The word even stunned George for an instant.

'I'm half Indian,' Sylvia said at last, her pulse pounding with resentment. 'Which makes me half English too, and I'm not going anywhere, so you'd better get on with having your baby, hadn't you?'

It was a unpleasant moment of truth for Sylvia. She had thought she had escaped racism, but in the Salford slums she had faced it once again – insulted by a woman who had seen in her someone she felt was even lower than herself.

In silence, Sylvia assisted George, taking orders and following his instructions precisely. She touched nothing unnecessarily, and after the birth they returned to the car where she disinfected her hands as her father-in-law had told her.

Having more sense than to refer to the matter, George drove home in silence and only later did he sit in the study and allow himself to remember the look on Sylvia's face when she had been called black. Her beauty had faltered for an instant by the sheer fury the word aroused in her. In that split second George could see the two diverse aspects of her character at once, vulnerability and – he hated to admit it – rage.

Yet Sylvia never betrayed herself again in the two years which followed and when Michael qualified George formally made him a junior partner in the practice. Tudge, his face as sour as bile, shook Michael's hand grudgingly.

'Congratulations, the Lord works in mysterious ways His wonders to perform.'

'He's my son,' George said bemused. 'What the hell has it got to do with God?'

Tudge flinched. 'Everything concerns God,' he replied,

only wondering fleetingly why it was that God hadn't seen fit to let him become a partner.

After all, whilst that lucky brat had been growing up *he'd* been the one to keep the practice going; and whilst George Cochrane had been stewing in depression after his wife's death, *he'd* gone out and looked after his patients. It was enough to make anyone bitter . . .

Watching Tudge's face, Michael could almost read the thoughts on his once handsome face, and for an instant he could fully commiserate with him.

But after that one sour moment Tudge continued in much the same way as he always had, George gradually introducing his son to his patients, most of whom were indifferent to the newcomer.

'You can't expect gratitude from them. If you get it, fine, if not, accept the fact and get on with the doctoring,' George explained. 'The most important thing to know is what to tell them. If they're a family of six living in squalor in one room, don't talk about cleanliness and eating a lot of vegetables. They'll think you're a bloody idiot – like they do Tudge. Don't patronize and don't pity –'

Michael blustered at the word. 'I'm not supposed to feel pity?'

'You're not supposed to *show* it,' his father replied deftly. 'There is a difference.'

Gradually, and only after repeated requests, Michael was allowed to make calls on his own – but not in the roughest areas or to the most difficult families. He was allotted old people or the younger families who weren't yet embittered, cutting his medical teeth on the least troublesome. At that time in the North West the big problem was infectious diseases: pneumonia, TB, gastrointestinal infections and diphtheria sending many off to the graveyards of Salford. Public health was hampered not only by the lack of efficient drugs, but by the deficiency of knowledge as to how infections were spread. Even though news was coming of innovations there was little medical optimism, the gilded Harley Street in London being referred to as 'the valley of the shadow of death'. Even the spectacular discovery of blood grouping to aid successful transfusions was virtually ignored for decades. The black medical bag which George carried was more a reassurance than a cure all.

Michael regarded his father's attitude with sympathy but longed to bring to their patients the innovations he had found in the Manchester Infirmary. Insulin had not long been discovered, X-rays were now used for diagnosis, and ECGs could finally explain the workings of a defective heart. Not unnaturally he was keen to bring to the slums the techniques he had seen, but the poverty and reluctance of most of their patients tied his hands.

Then one morning, when George was occupied elsewhere, Michael was called out to a school. It was a council-run establishment, an offshoot from the poor house, all religion and discipline for the slum kids. There had been a sudden and unexpected death of one of the children, and now another was suffering from the same symptoms.

By this time fully recognized as the practice nurse, Sylvia attended with her husband, undressing the little girl they had been called to see and asking for a blanket.

'What for?' the headmistress replied shortly.

'For the child, she'll get cold otherwise.'

'We have no blankets,' the woman replied, turning to the door. 'Please let me know what you find when you've finished.'

Shaking his head Michael took off his overcoat and wrapped it round the little girl, drawing up a seat next to the school form on which she had been placed.

'What's her name?' he said, jerking his head to the door.

'Miss Stokes,' she whispered.

He pulled a face, the child smiling dimly, Sylvia watching her husband curiously. There was an ease about him she had never seen before, a relaxation which was altogether natural. His voice was instinctively pitched low to calm the child whilst he rubbed his hands together to warm them before he examined her, his smile easy and reassuring as he talked. He would, Sylvia realized suddenly, make a remarkable father.

'So, now, where is that pain of yours?'

Listlessly, the little girl touched her head.

'Oh, that's nasty,' Michael replied, feeling her forehead and around her neck.

She winced. Michael frowned, then glanced at the rash on her body. Worried, he looked up to his wife.

'Sally's not well,' he said, his tone easy although his expression was implying something very serious. 'We're going to give her a big present and pop her off to hospital for a couple of days –'

Immediately the little girl began to cry, Michael stroking her hair gently.

'Do you want your present?'

She nodded.

'Then you have to be very brave. It's a present for bravery, you see.'

Dumbly, Sally nodded, then winced with pain, Michael laying her down on the form and covering her with his coat.

Outside the door he looked at his wife.

'You know what it is, don't you?'

'Meningitis?'

He sighed, then glanced down the corridor.

'It's highly infectious. God knows how many other children have got it.' He tensed suddenly, hearing another cry from inside.

Before Sylvia could say a word Michael returned to his patient, rocking the child and telling her stories until the ambulance arrived.

Imagine this: an old brick construction on five storeys, the mortuary in a separate building below the main body of the hospital. The walls are blackened with Northern soot and decades' accumulation of rain and coal dirt. Although there is no garden attached to the hospital, a few recalcitrant weeds struggle between the cracks in the walls. The ward windows are high, but uncurtained and bare, divided into rectangular blank panes. All about the corridors are signs pointing to the various departments; one fairly new, marking the way to the X-ray Unit – something still regarded as innovative, a major breakthrough, a mechanical peek at illness.

The doctors at the Manchester Infirmary are trying to control illness, epidemics, outbreaks of diseases which the conditions in the slums exacerbate. They are struggling with the new innovations and trying to encourage the change in attitude after the end of the war. There is optimism. There is change. There is hope.

Slowly the hostility towards the medical profession and the hospital is fading; patients diffidently come for help. But not the poorest; they still huddle together, amongst their own, have their children and keep to the tenements. The mortality rate for childbirth and infant deaths is fading elsewhere, but in the poorest areas nothing changes. Child funerals are commonplace.

Although aware that his son doubts it, George knows his limitations but is forced to make allowances. He works to accommodate his patients and never expects them to accommodate him. He even tolerates Mrs Wrangel, an old woman who has, for the previous two decades, worked as an unofficial nurse and layer-out of the dead. Many times George has arrived at the home of a critically ill patient to find her – shawled and silent – waiting by the door, or by the fire, for the inevitable.

They never exchange a word. George knows that she has aborted many women, and on more than one occasion Mrs Wrangel has been present at the birth of a deformed child. These children never live. He knows that if they are severely handicapped Mrs Wrangel will deliver them and let them die. Or she will simply never help them to breathe. He knows why she does it: to help the families. But he wonders if, in all conscience, he could do the same.

When Michael came into the practice his father was, at first, genuinely pleased. He looked forward to their sharing their patients' stories and cases; he anticipated some clash of wills, expecting that Michael would want to bring in new developments. They would have arguments about treatment, drugs; his son would inject new life into the slum practice. George would resist, of course, or at least pretend to . . .

That was how he had imagined it to be. But reality was altogether different. Michael was caring, but aloof; compassionate, but cool. He had none of his father's bluntness, his temper, his railings against fate and at times his patients. There was, George realized with regret, no brutality in Michael.

'Brutality?' Sylvia said baffled. 'What does a doctor want with brutality?'

'At times it's the only thing that gets things done,' George replied shortly. 'A bullying doctor gets a house cleaned, a baby fed right, a man back to work. Sympathy's like castor oil, good in small doses.'

He didn't like to show his impatience with his son; tried hard to conceal it over the following months. But that little malignancy of spirit which had always been between them was omnipresent, and it hobbled both of them. But when the bullish Harry Chadwick came to Aynhams George found himself drawn to the stranger as someone who could finally give him a run for his money. Where Michael was reserved, Harry was outspoken. Where Michael was controlled, Harry was all hot, fevered ambition.

Harry didn't want anything to do with a slum practice; he wanted out of Salford, away from the streets where he had run around, a sore-arsed kid. He wanted to get on and get out – and he had made it clear to everyone that he was on his way up, up, up, in the world. So when Michael left the Manchester Infirmary Harry did what he had always said he would do, he stayed on to train for surgery. Being a slum GP might be enough for the heir of Aynhams, but for Harry Chadwick, no way.

'Meningitis,' Harry said thoughtfully, when the four of them finished dinner one night at Aynhams. 'So that was your baptism of fire, hey, Michael? Meningitis is bad. How many did it kill?'

'Only three – we were lucky,' he replied, staring at him curiously.

'My first big emergency was much more dramatic.'

'I had a feeling it might have been,' Michael responded drily, leaning back in his dining chair to listen.

Gradually, Harry had infiltrated the enclosed world of Aynhams. His initial visit had been awkward, his bluntness causing not a little irritation to Sylvia, George intermittently amused and scandalized by the redheaded stranger. But as time passed, Harry had won them over, his bravado and boastfulness all forgiven.

'I remember last summer well. It was in July,' he said, turning to George. 'I had a car then – but I had to give it up. It was too big.'

'Not for your head, surely.'

Sylvia and Michael exchanged a quick, amused look, but Harry carried on regardless.

'. . . We had a patient who had had his nose burned off in a fire. We made him a new one – well, we tried to, but it didn't take. The rest of his face rejected it.'

'So?'

'Last I heard he blew his nose – and it came off in his handkerchief.'

'Oh Harry!' Sylvia said laughing. 'I don't believe a word of it.'

'God's truth,' he replied, staring at the rapt faces round the table. 'It's all hit and miss, you see. No one really knows that much about plastic surgery yet.' He paused, checking that he had their full attention. 'But I tell you, I'm going to master it. I'll be a famous surgeon one day, with a practice in Harley Street. I'll show all the buggers around here who never thought I'd amount to much –'

'Harry, you know that everyone thought you'd succeed,' George said evenly. 'Stop being paranoid. There must be a shoulder under that chip of yours.'

Harry flushed, suddenly awkward. He admired George, wished – in his quiet moments – that he had had a father like him. A father people respected; not some street fighter from a slum alley.

'I'll be a success.'

'Of course you will,' George argued, adding deftly, 'lifting society women's sagging faces. I heard Lady Caremount's wax injections slipped down from her nose to her chin. Got jowls like a turkey cock now.'

Downing his port quickly, Harry was belligerent.

'A foreign doctor did that job. *I* wouldn't make a mistake like that.'

'Nah!' George said dismissively. 'You'd probably tie her jowls together in a knot and pretend it was a collar.'

Seated at the far end of the table, Michael watched them and saw – not for the first time – that Harry, not he, would have been the perfect son and heir to Aynhams. Harry was as bullish as George, and as certain of his skill; as loud, overbearing and dogmatic. In fact, Michael realized sadly, they were closer than he and his father had ever been.

There was no self-pity in the thought, it simply intrigued him as they began to argue again, Harry's face flushed with alcohol, George retelling the story of how he couldn't fight in the last war because he only had one eye.

'How come?'

'How come *what*?' George asked tipsily.

'How come you only have one eye?'

George could finally see his chance to out-brag Harry, and took it. 'I was shot.'

'Nah!'

He nodded. 'One of my patients was a murderer and when I found him standing over the body of his butchered wife, I tackled him – and he shot me.'

Everyone waited. Harry blinked several times, digesting the story and seeming for an instant to be outshone.

Then, breathing in deeply and straightening himself up in his seat, he said: 'It reminds me of when I confronted a bank robber on Piccadilly . . .'

Smiling, Michael glanced over to his wife. She was dressed in a white blouse and dark skirt, her black hair drawn away from the still calm oval of her face. Her eyes were fixed on Harry, then slowly she turned her head and smiled at her father-in-law.

God, I hope you love me, Michael thought. I hope you love me as I love you.

His glanced moved to Harry and for one breath-snatching moment he found himself imagining Sylvia married to his best friend, the two of them happy at Aynhams . . . Laughing suddenly, Sylvia cupped her chin in her hand and slid her other hand around the stem of her wineglass.

I want to touch you, Michael thought longingly, I want to reach you. What you wanted, I gave you, but was it enough?

Suddenly turning, Sylvia caught her husband's eye. She smiled, then frowned, sensing his unease. For an instant neither of them moved and then she reached out to touch his hand. But she misjudged the action and knocked over her wineglass, the liquid spilling onto the tablecloth and staining it red as blood.

Chapter Six

William Glynn was having nothing of it.

'I'm not bloody closing, so you can get used to the idea!' he snapped at George.

Breathing in with irritation, the latter looked around. 'WILLIAM GLYNN – SURGICAL BOOT MAKER' the sign said over the door, the writing blunt and white. Upright, like its owner. In the window were nearly a dozen photographs and drawings, together with a selection of heavy, metal, corrective boots. Some for amputees, some for club feet. 'Hop-along', they called William behind his back because he wore one of his own appliances to correct a shortened leg. He thought no one knew; but they all mimicked his limp when he walked down St Stephen's Street.

One or another of the Glynns had been on this site for nearly a hundred years, and now the shop was owned by William. Proud as a magpie, he had kept his pre-war moustaches – liked them because they were lush and dark – and when he served his customers he wore a long white apron, his shirtsleeves rolled up. He thought it made him look approachable. As approachable as a butcher.

'You've got to rest, William –'

'And who'd run shop? I've no son to mind the place for me. No offspring to carry on the business when I'm gone.'

'Which might be sooner than you think,' George replied tartly, 'unless you close this place for a week. Go off to Blackpool. Enjoy yourself.'

'Blackpool!' William snapped. 'What the hell good is a place like that? Full of people up to no good.' He leaned over the dark wood counter towards George. 'You should hear what they say about those bed and breakfast places. There's not many married couples go there, I can tell you.'

George wondered how he knew, as William wasn't married and hadn't –as far as George was aware – ever left Salford. But William was a rarity in the area: a male gossip and a quiescent snob. He might have a shop on St Stephen's Street, Greengate, but *his* shop was clean, and bigger than the rest, and *his* grandfather had got a signwriter to put the name over the door. Not some amateur scrawling on the front, like all the others.

'William, take a break, I order you to.'

'And I suppose you'll come in and work here whilst I'm gone?'

'What about your nephew?'

'What about him?'

'Can't he help you out?'

'That lad wouldn't spit on me if I was on fire,' William said sourly, leaning further over the counter. 'I hear that friend of your son's – Harry Chadwick – is doing right well. Qualified as a surgeon. Bloody butcher more like, if he's anything like his father.'

'Tom Chadwick wasn't a doctor –'

'You can say that again!' William retorted heatedly. 'But I bet he put more than a couple of patients your way.'

'This isn't talking about you –'

'I don't want to talk about me.'

'I do, William.'

'They say,' he said, ignoring George and tracing an old scratch on the top of the counter with his fingernail, 'that Harry Chadwick's a right clever bugger now. He weren't so clever when his arse was hanging out of his trousers when he was a kid. And that mother of his –'

'William, are you going to take some time off?' George asked impatiently.

'It's not on.'

'Please yourself.' George picked up his medical bag and headed for the door. 'But don't blame me for the consequences.'

When he got back to Aynhams George was surprised to find Harry sitting in the drawing room talking to a pregnant Sylvia, his hair a burning russet red under the overhead lamp.

'Where's Michael?'

Turning at the sound of his voice, Sylvia raised her eyebrows. 'I thought he was with you.'

'He should have been,' George replied, nodding a greeting to Harry. 'I've got to make another visit and I wanted him to come along.'

'I was just passing –'

'Harry,' George said, interrupting him, 'you *never* just pass by at dinner time. You time it to perfection, just so you can get fed.'

'How little you think of me,' Harry replied, smiling. 'As if I would do such a thing.'

Confidence had sharpened his dress sense and he was less awkward in his movements, but the strange vocal inflection to mask his Salford accent was still only partially successful.

'I told Michael I wanted him to come along,' George went on absently. 'It's a bad case. The worst. Gangrene.'

'I expect he'll be back soon,' Sylvia replied. 'He won't be longer than he need be, wherever he's gone. Give him time.'

'I always give him time,' George responded irritably. 'He's the one who never gives me any consideration.'

'Well, what about Tudge? Couldn't he go with you?'

'I don't want Tudge!' George snapped. 'I want my son – is that too much to expect?'

The tension slapped into the three of them, Harry glancing down at his hands and wondering if he should excuse himself and leave. Embarrassed, Sylvia got up and busied herself with straightening the piles of books and newspapers heaped untidily on a side table. After another moment George sat down heavily on the sofa, hauling his bag up beside him, pointing to it.

'What is that?'

Harry raised his eyebrows: 'A camel?'

'Very amusing,' George answered sourly. '*That* is my stock in trade. My livelihood. My profession. I have carried that bag around with pride for years.'

'So?'

'*So?*' George countered. 'So it means something. It means I take my responsibilities seriously –'

'Oh, for God's sake!' Harry replied, with good-natured exasperation. 'Michael's obviously tied up with a case. He's not out with some woman.'

The shuffling of papers increased suddenly.

'I'm not saying he is!' George retorted. 'I'm saying that he always lets me down.'

'Lets you down!' Harry said, laughing. 'He's your right-hand man.'

Pausing in her tidying, Sylvia kept her back to them and wondered how it was that Harry found it so easy to talk to her father-in-law. Michael could never talk to George like that; could never respond so easily. Not that he was a coward; far from it; he simply could not banter with his father. Life was too serious for Michael ever to be flip.

'You're too hard on him,' Harry said, then wondered if he had gone too far when George stood up abruptly.

'Tell Michael I've gone on my own.'

Sighing, Sylvia turned to her father-in-law. 'Just give him a bit longer. Michael will be here soon.'

'I don't have the time to wait around. I need help now –'

'So let me help,' Harry volunteered, eager to repair the damage. '*I'll* come with you.'

George eyed him suspiciously. 'This is a messy case. A

slum case. Nothing glamorous. No one's going to write this up in any medical journal.'

But Harry was childishly determined to please. 'Oh, come on, let me go with you for the ride,' he smiled. 'I could be useful.'

In silence the two of them piled into George's car, neither speaking by the time they came into the outskirts of Greengate. But as the familiar terraces came into view Harry felt himself tensing, his expression hardening. What the hell was he doing? He didn't want to come back here, he had promised himself he never would: he had made his break, and was steadily making his name at the Manchester Infirmary. In fact, Leonard Cotterill, one of the most innovative exponents of plastic surgery, had singled him out for attention only the other week.

'You'll do well if you apply yourself,' he had advised Harry during an operation which was attended by over a dozen doctors. 'Plastic surgery is the skill of the future. Before long things will be possible that we can only dream about now.' He had paused, stared hard at Harry. 'You've got the ability and the ambition, don't lose sight of what you want.'

So why was he now in the passenger seat of George Cochrane's car visiting the grim row of Thurloe Street?

Parking, George reached for his case and waited for Harry to join him at the door of number 70. The smell, Harry thought with tangible disgust, was the same. It took him back to childhood, to the moist stench of overcrowding and poverty. He could remember his father spitting into his handkerchief, and the freezing cold mornings when Harry set off for school after waking his sister.

'Come on.'

'Aw, leave me alone.'

'Molly, come on.'

The cold in the bedroom was intense; the thin hardboard partition which separated them afforded little privacy.

Moodily she rose, Harry putting his finger to his lips.

'Ssh, Dad's still asleep.'

'Did he win?' she asked, referring to the fight the previous night.

There had been no money on the table, no celebratory shout of triumph when Tom had come home. Only a heavy stomp of his feet on the stairs and the weighty creak as he threw himself onto the bed in the room next door. Many times through the night Harry had heard his father turn and grunt, swearing and sweating in the dark hours.

'No, he didn't win.'

'Harry?' George snapped, breaking into his thoughts. 'Come on, stop daydreaming.'

Reluctantly Harry followed him into the unlit hall of number 70, a dim light coming from a half-open door at the back. On the staircase two dull-eyed children watched them pass, George pushing open the door further and walking in.

''Lo there, Walter.'

A sinewy, curly-haired man was sitting on a makeshift bed beside an unlit fire. On his left was a silent woman, on the right a cupboard full of scraps and drying dog bones. At Walter's feet a greyhound lay still, only its eyes moving as it watched George approach the bed.

'I heard that dog of yours is winning races.'

'Got two firsts,' Walter said, bending over to pet the greyhound's head. ''E'll meck m' fortune yet.'

But Harry wasn't looking at the dog, he was looking at Walter's left leg which had suddenly become visible under his nightshirt as he had moved. The foot was black, flesh soft and ulcerated, the smell rancid in the minuscule room.

Gently George kneeled down and looked at Walter's leg.

'It's no better.'

'Aye, I'd 'ave to agree with yer there.'

'You know what we said, Walter. I'd like you to go to the hospital.'

Impatiently Walter shook his head, pulling his leg up onto the bed beside him. The lamplight caught it, the ulcers bloody, the flesh tight and darkening. Jesus, Harry thought, how could he bear it?

'You'll have to lose the leg,' George said simply. 'Or you'll die. I thought we might be able to save it, but we can't.'

The woman remained silent, her eyes fixed on George.

'We can fix you up with a false leg –'

'From William Glynn?' Walter said drily. 'I hate to think of giving that bugger trade.'

'You'll learn to cope, Walter.'

'It's a good thing it's the dog's what's running and not me,' he replied, turning to his wife. 'Go on, we'll fetch you back when it's done.'

Dumb, she rose and left the room.

George addressed his patient: 'Walter, think about hospital again –'

'Nah, do it 'ere.'

Without a word, George glanced over to Harry, then rummaged in his bag for chloroform.

'We need you to lie down straight on the bed, Walter. Have you got any newspapers?'

'Over there.'

Immediately Harry reached for them and then spread them on the bed under Walter's gangrenous leg. The light was poor, George signalling for the lamp to be brought closer.

'You won't feel a thing, Walter.'

He nodded, but was tight about the lips, losing colour as George poured some chloroform onto a mask and placed it over his patient's face. For an instant there was a look of terror in Walter's eyes and then the lids closed and his breathing regulated.

'Quick, we haven't much time,' George said. 'Hold his leg.'

At once Harry did so, watching as George rinsed his knives in disinfectant and then severed the flesh above the knee. Then, just as quickly, he reached for the surgical saw in his bag and began to saw through the bone. Grimly, Harry held onto the gangrenous leg, Walter's inert body jerking with the sawing motion. This is butchery, Harry thought, unusually queasy, this is a bloodbath. But George was quick and within another minute he had cut off the leg. Carefully he trimmed a flap of tissue he had reserved to cover the stump. Then he cauterized the wound, then stitched the flap in place and dressed the amputation site. Finally he stretched up. His face was oily with sweat.

'That was a good job,' Harry said admiringly.

'But crude,' George replied, picking up his thoughts. 'It's all I can do here, Harry. It's not what I want, but it's all I can do. It's all they let me do.'

'Well, I couldn't do it,' Harry admitted honestly, watching George wrap the amputated leg in the bloodied newspapers. 'Could Michael?'

'I don't know,' George replied flatly. 'I was wondering that myself. That's why I'd asked him to come along with me tonight. I wanted to see how he would react. I thought he'd say that we had to get the patient out of this hellhole and cleaned up; that a surgeon would have to perform the operation in sterile surroundings. He would tell me that medicine is becoming more humane. And in some places, it is. But not here, Harry. Here my patients trust me. No one else. So what I really wanted to know tonight was whether my son would insist on taking Walter Collins to hospital, or whether he would do what I've just done.'

There was a moment's pause before Harry said quietly: 'Would you have thought less of him if he'd refused?'

'I don't know,' George replied evenly, picking up his medical bag and shoving the bundle of newspapers under his other arm. 'And I won't now until the next time.'

Chapter Seven

Surgery was over and now he had time to think. Reaching into his pocket, Michael's fingers closed around the evening newspaper, but didn't draw it out, he didn't want to see the headline 'THREAT OF WAR WITH GERMANY' and consider what it would mean.

If war *did* break out he would have to go and fight. The army always needed doctors, and besides, he had already fought in one war. But he had been much younger then, a single man without a wife or children. Sighing, Michael thought of his two daughters: Mel, born in 1925 and Beth, in 1928. They were so young. He didn't want to leave them. Not for a day, certainly not for months or even years.

He didn't think of his wife in the same way; Sylvia had given him two children, out of affection certainly, but also – he realized uncomfortably – as a part of the unspoken bargain they had made at their marriage, a bargain understood instinctively by both of them. He could not complain about his wife; she was loving, a good support to himself and his father; a splendid nurse, and a beauty. She was, in fact, everything any man could have desired – except for the fact that Michael was never truly sure if she loved him.

Closeness had become almost distasteful after a while. Making love was a release, not a bonding. He had thought, at various times, that he might try to intimate that he knew things between them were not ideal – and yet he never did, realizing what that would do to her. Everything Sylvia held dear would collapse. She would question her status and therefore her security – the bedrock of her life – and morally Michael knew he could never risk it.

Besides, she had never let him down. Other men had wanted her, but Sylvia had never been unfaithful, and neither had he. They were bound by love, certainly, but it was a cold loving, unsteady and frail. Then thankfully love came in another form – their children. The feelings Michael had for his first-born overpowered him.

He felt released: lifelong, unexpressed love pouring out of him onto this dark-haired infant. Mel was born in high summer, coming soft into a slushy, overbloomed world, on an evening still moist with August rain. In the study at Aynhams George and his son had waited for news of the birth, a fellow doctor called in to attend Sylvia upstairs. At around nine, Tudge had come in, his dark clothes sodden from the summer shower.

'Has God blessed you?' he asked Michael.

'Sylvia's not given birth yet, if that's what you mean,' George snapped, rubbing his left ear, his white hair wiry around his face.

'I hope He has mercy on this house,' Tudge went on, his eyes vacant.

For a while George had been wondering if Tudge was losing his reason, his religious fervour increasing manically, his mannerisms bordering on obsession. Not once did Tudge wash his hands before attending a patient, but five or six times, his jacket pockets filled with soap. If the house he was visiting didn't have running water, he went into the street and washed at the pump, the local kids jeering at the spindly dark-coated figure.

'If God wants –'

'Shut up!' George snapped, finally exasperated.

Nodding as though he had expected to be rebuked, Tudge tiptoed out of the room, the front door closing softly behind him.

'Creeping Jesus.'

Michael looked over to his father. 'What?'

'That man is a vile, creeping Jesus,' George repeated, glancing away. 'Do you mind my being here?'

'It's your house –'

'I didn't ask whose bloody house it was!' George barked. 'I asked you if you minded my being here.'

Patiently, Michael took in a breath. His father saw the action and rounded on him.

'How do you keep such control, Michael? I've often wondered that. I mean, apart from the night your mother died, I've never seen you lose your temper.'

The words were unexpected and rocked them both, Michael saying nothing in response.

'Honestly, you can say what you like,' George went on. 'Go on, Michael, have your say. You've been choking on your anger for years.'

But his son wouldn't reply.

'You're a coward –'

At that, Michael rose to his feet in a second, facing his father, his expression threatening.

'I don't want to argue with you now. I don't *ever* want to argue with you. I have nothing to say –'

'Well, *I* have!'

'You always did!' Michael snapped back. 'That was your trouble, you never stopped talking long enough to think.'

'What the bloody hell is that supposed to mean?'

'You swagger around this place,' Michael said bitterly, waving his arm round the room, 'and around your patients like a tinpot god. You've played the part of the all-powerful doctor for so long you can't see how ridiculous you really are.'

Stunned, George stared at his son, both of them breathing heavily, the house silent around them.

'I can't spend all my life apologizing for what happened to your mother –'

'Why not? You failed her.'

'It's not that simple!' George shouted helplessly. 'It's not a matter of my failing her –'

'She died of tuberculosis. You knew she was frail, but you still attended the worst TB cases in your practice. You could have sent someone else, for God's sake,' Michael said, his voice plummeting. 'Dear God, why didn't you send Tudge?'

'I did what I thought was right –'

'You did what you wanted,' Michael retorted coldly. 'You always do.'

'If you hate me so much, why did you come to live with me?'

Slowly Michael looked into his father's face. He was suddenly tired of the ill feeling. It was the wrong time to argue, with his wife about to give birth. But it was always the wrong time.

'Well,' George persisted, 'why *did* you come to live with me? Why *did* you become a doctor?'

The words were out of Michael's mouth before he had time to think. 'I wanted to remind you of what you'd done,' he said without any expression in his voice. 'I wanted you never to forget.'

Gasping, George stared at his son, then stood up and walked to the door.

'In that case you succeeded, Michael, because I never have. And I won't forget what you've said tonight either – not for the rest of my life.'

Upstairs a child cried suddenly. Whilst they had been arguing Melanie Cochrane had been born.

Sylvia came into her new life as a mother as though she had been transformed. Her place was secure; mistress of Aynhams, wife of a doctor, and now a mother. Without realizing it consciously, she altered. No more was she asked to go out on visits with Michael or George; her new motherhood exempted her and she was relieved to avoid the slums, the grinding pessimism of the Salford streets.

So, once Melanie was delivered into the hands of a nanny, Sylvia concentrated her efforts on the other side of Buile Hill, on the town which bordered them, Pendleton. There were plenty of new mothers there; women flattered at the interest the mistress of Aynhams might show in them. 'Isn't she pleasant?' they said to one another. 'And so beautiful.' Sylvia could live with the greenery around Pendleton, the little streets and shops, the people and village atmosphere; all was safe and comfortable – providing she didn't wander too far and breach the boundaries which led to the River Irwell and the dank industry in the valley, or the morose terraces of Salford waiting malignantly only miles away.

But although she felt safe, there was always some suspicion of Sylvia in Pendleton. Yes, she was charming and lovely, everyone agreed, but she was *foreign* – and no one ever forgot that. Sylvia might not realize it, but the bigotry she had dodged all her life was just as prevalent in the green streets of Pendleton as it was in the slums.

Surrounded as she was by the protective grounds of Aynhams, Sylvia found herself becoming more and more disinterested in the practice. She didn't want to think about squalor any more; she wanted to savour what she had, and keep it secure. To that end, she thought of the slums as hungry children come crying at her door. Although she might hear them, she didn't have to answer. Her role in life was as a wife and mother now, and who could blame her if she wanted the best for her children?

Certainly not Michael. If anything he was glad that his wife was no longer overly involved with the practice; he could run it perfectly well with his father and Tudge. He didn't want Sylvia with him. He wanted, foolishly and helplessly, to get closer to his father. But he never did. Instead he watched as Harry came in and out of their lives and usurped his role. Not maliciously, but insidiously, creeping into a corner of George's heart which had been marked out – but never occupied – by his natural son.

It wasn't in Michael's nature to be resentful, but he found himself alternately drawn to, and then irritated by Harry. He was not envious of Harry's skill and burgeoning success, but he was hesitantly jealous of the affection between his friend and his father, and watched them together with a kind of bewildered curiosity. There was no reason to worry about Harry becoming professionally involved with the practice – his ambitions lay elsewhere – but there was something about the ease with which he infiltrated their lives that always disturbed Michael.

Harry, now moving in exalted circles as a plastic surgeon, would come to Aynhams frequently, staying in one of the many spare rooms, his clothes in the wardrobe, a spare razor and comb left on the top of the dressing table. Cologne, imported from the West Indies, left its faint expensive aroma on the room, and the very walls seemed to carry an imprint of Harry's character, totally dissimilar from anywhere else in Aynhams.

It wasn't difficult for Michael to understand Harry's need for a home; after all, hadn't he admitted often how much he had wanted to own, or be the heir of, somewhere like Aynhams? It was his haven, his little pretend, his escape from the memory of the rough kid in clogs running wild on Gladstone Row. But what Michael knew, and Harry had not realized, was that he could never *belong* there. What Harry Chadwick was – tough and ruthless – was a direct *result* of being born and raised in Gladstone Row. Another start in life would have resulted in another man, without the same drive, the same hidden humiliation and determination to escape his past.

But now what would happen? Michael wondered, at last looking again at the headline on the paper. Not another war, please God, he thought, not again. To leave Aynhams, to leave his wife, his children, his home . . . Michael stirred uneasily in his seat. If war did break out they would need doctors, they always did. He would serve, of course. But what about Harry? How would he react to being taken away from the success and glamour of his life? How would he manage the filth of the battlefield, after the gloss of society plastic surgery? Michael was used to poverty and desperation in his patients, Harry wasn't.

If there was another war the world would change. And so would they.

Chapter Eight

'When's Dad coming home?' Mel asked, sitting on the arm of the sofa.

'Soon,' Sylvia replied, picking up some sewing and settling down by the fire.

Her hair was loose around her shoulders, still black, her face serene. Fascinated, Mel looked at her and then remembered her own face, typically English, her hair brown like her father's, her fourteen-year-old body bigger boned than either her mother's or her sister's.

Beth . . . Mel thought of her younger sister and frowned. Beth . . . eleven years old, as dark as her mother, as stunningly pretty as a painting. Sunny, everyone called her, sunny and charming. She would dance for anyone, up on her toes, twirling in party dresses, curtsying at the end to receive her applause. A darling, everyone agreed, a tiny dark angel.

Thoughtfully Mel stared at her feet, her shoes scuffed at the toes. Beth never had scuffed shoes, or a hair out of place. Beth was perfect. Beth was a pain . . .

'So when *is* Dad coming home?'

'As I said – soon,' Sylvia repeated. 'Why don't you read something?'

'Like what?'

'Like a book.'

'I don't like reading.'

'Then draw something.'

'I can't draw.'

Patiently, Sylvia laid down her needlework.

'So what do you want to do?'

'Tell me about India.'

'Please.'

'Tell me about India, *please*.'

Folding her arms and leaning back in her seat, Sylvia began. It was a ritual between them, her elder daughter consumed by the stories of her mother's home country. Repeatedly Sylvia would tell her about the house she had lived in and her parents, describing Poopa, and her mother who had long since died.

'Why doesn't my grandfather come to England?' Mel asked suddenly, her head on one side.

She is so like Michael to look at, Sylvia thought, and so like George in temperament. Fearless, direct – too much so for a girl.

'Poopa doesn't travel. He's never been out of India.'

Mel digested the information thoughtfully.

'Then why don't we go to see him?'

A reasonable question.

'We can't –'

'Why not?'

'Because we can't, that's all.'

Swinging her legs over the arm of the sofa, Mel persisted.

'We could. I heard about a girl at school who went to America.'

'We can't afford it.'

'But everyone says we're rich,' Mel replied firmly.

'We aren't rich, we just live in a big house.'

'But we must be rich to live in a big house.'

Sighing, Sylvia picked up her sewing again. Her daughter could always outmanoeuvre her.

'Is it hot?'

'*What?*'

'India.'

'Of course.'

'What about when it rains?'

'It's cooler then.'

'Cool as it is here?'

'Different.'

'In what way?'

Rapidly becoming exasperated, Sylvia glanced over to her eldest child.

'Where's your sister?'

'In the other room,' Mel said sullenly, unwilling to let Beth into their conversation. 'She's busy.'

'Oh Mel . . .' Sylvia replied, smiling and tapping Mel's knee. 'What a baby you are.'

Irritated, Mel glanced away. 'Tell me about Bombay, Mum. Please.'

'What do you want to know?'

'Everything.'

Sylvia laughed. 'That would take for ever.'

'Can we go – you and me – can we go there one day?'

The request had been unexpected, and yet from the tone of Mel's voice, Sylvia realized it obviously mattered to her.

'Yes, we'll go one day.'

'You promise?'

Staring ahead, Sylvia nodded. 'I promise – one day you and I will go to India.'

'Cross your heart and hope to die?'

'Cross my heart and hope to die.'

She thought that the east tower was perfect; no one went there, it was supposed to be off limits. Mel stared at the rope which hung across the bottom of the stone steps. Why have a tower if you don't use it? She remembered her grandfather telling her how dangerous it was. Monsters live up there, he told her. Monsters who eat little girls. Well, she didn't like to disagree with him, but she had never fallen for that story, even as a child.

Looking round hurriedly, Mel ducked under the rope and climbed the steps silently. The first time she had investigated the tower she had been afraid, but not of monsters, of her grandfather finding out she had disobeyed his instructions. Still wary of his discovering her disobedience, Mel crept noiselessly into the narrow round chamber at the top and then looked out of the window.

The garden seemed a mile below her, the neat houses of Seedley and Pendleton merely patches far beyond the wall which surrounded Aynhams. It looked just the same as ever, even though the country was at war. In the distance the thin white line of a stream trembled in the sunlight, a bird cawing on the ledge outside. It was heaven, Mel decided, luminous with excitement, it was her private heaven. And then she ran her finger over the name scratched on the window in a childish, uneven hand – '*Michael Fields Cochrane*'.

Tracing her father's name with her index finger, Mel smiled, pleased that he had been there before her. She liked to think that she was sharing the tower with him. Didn't mind sharing anything with her father – just as long as she didn't have to share anything with her sister. That she couldn't bear.

A movement below made Mel lean forwards and look down onto the lawn. Her mother was walking with someone – but who was it? Mel leaned further forwards and then frowned when she recognized the figure.

'I don't like him,' she had said vehemently to her mother the previous week. 'I want Dad back.'

'Sssh!' Sylvia had warned her. 'You mustn't be rude. He's bought you a present, and he's very funny.'

'I think he's a bore,' Mel had retorted heatedly, walking off.

Craning further forward, Mel continued to look at her mother and then glanced at her father's name etched on the window.

What Michael had feared, had happened, although when war had broken out, he had not spoken to her about it. Then, late one night, he had found Mel wandering around the house. He had thought at first that she was sleepwalking, but she was just troubled, unable to rest. Taking her to his study, Michael sat next to her on the window seat, the cold moon rising in the garden outside.

'Mel, are you worried about the war?'

'It's a waste of time. And lives.'

He had stared curiously at her. 'Why did you say that?'

'Granddad said it yesterday.'

'Well, whatever he said,' Michael had continued patiently, 'you know that it means I have to go away . . .'

Her face had paled, but she said nothing.

'Mel. Oh Mel,' he murmured helplessly, taking her hand. He shouldn't have favourites, he knew that, but he felt so close to this fearless, outspoken girl.

'You must be brave,' he said to her.

'I don't want to be brave.'

'None of us does. But, you see, I rely on you.' He had squeezed her hand. 'I can go away now and not worry, knowing that my girl's looking after everyone at home.'

'Why can't Granddad go instead of you?'

Trying to keep a straight face, Michael had shaken his head. Mel could always make him laugh, even at the most poignant moments.

'You know your grandfather's too old to go off to war.'

She shrugged and glanced away, fighting tears. 'I just don't understand why you have to go.'

'Because people need me, Mel. They need doctors to look after the wounded.' He paused. 'And I need you to help me.'

Nodding, Mel held on to her father's hand. 'I'll look after everything till you get back. You can count on me.'

'I know that,' Michael said, winking, dry with distress. 'Shall we have a secret code, Mel?'

Her eyes were suddenly alert with interest. 'Like what?'

He thought for a moment then pulled back the curtain and pointed out of the window. Outside it was midnight, a full moon already in place. Clouds, sombre and hesitant, stroked the pale face.

'Look, it's midnight and the man in the moon's smiling.' His mother had told him that years earlier, when she was still well, the year before she died. 'Can you see it, Mel, can you see the man in the moon's smiling?'

Transfixed, his daughter stared upwards and then nodded. 'What does it mean?'

'It means . . .' her father had paused then, hardly daring to speak the words, or think of the morrow when he would leave, '. . . that midnight's smiling, Mel. Tomorrow will be a lucky day.'

They hadn't seen him since, only received letters from the front and descriptions of France. Once he sent a photograph, which Mel put under her pillow, Sylvia following the news every night on the wireless.

It was strange, Mel thought, high in the tower, but it seemed that her grandfather was almost *relieved* that her father was away. He certainly appeared not to miss his son and was more than happy to spend time with his daughter-in-law, talking endlessly about the house.

His practice, having now lost its main doctor, was run by George and Tudge, the two old men taking back the roles they had first adopted decades earlier. Hard of hearing and deeply suspicious of anyone except God, Tudge had become a gloomy figure of ridicule as he walked the Greengate streets, the terraces now bereft of men except for the old and sick.

Suddenly bored with her lookout, and curious to know what Harry Chadwick was up to, Mel descended, and was just entering the hallway as Tudge walked in. He gave her a look which could have turned milk.

'God bless you,' he said hypocritically, putting down his medical bag and feeling in his pocket for soap.

There was a little cloakroom off the hall where the doctors could leave their coats and wash their hands. Tudge drew some water, then soaped each finger individually and then the palms, rinsing them twice before drying them. They were thin and very crinkled, Mel noted, like dead leaves.

'Why aren't you away at the war?' she asked suddenly, although she already knew the answer.

'What?'

'Why aren't you fighting?'

Tudge stared at her incredulously. 'I'm too old.'

'How old are you?'

'Old enough to know that that's an impertinent question!'

Unabashed, Mel followed him into the corridor.

'This war,' she persisted, 'whose side is God on?'

He turned, glowering at her furiously. 'God is on our side!'

'So we'll win?'

Unamused by the precocious girl challenging him, Tudge leaned towards her, his long-gummed smile threatening.

'God is on the side of the righteous. And God hates cheeky girls.'

'Ah, Dr Tudge,' Sylvia said, walking into the hallway, Harry following her. 'Mr Chadwick has come to see us again –'

'Why?' Mel asked suddenly, the adults all turning to look at her in unison.

'Why *what*, Mel?'

She was staring fixedly at Tudge. 'Why does God hate cheeky girls?'

'Because they ask awkward questions He can't answer,' Harry said suddenly, smiling at the child facing him. 'How are you, Mel?'

Her face was set, her hostility apparent.

'OK.'

'Harry's brought you a present –'

'I don't want it.'

'Mel, how dare you be so rude!' Sylvia snapped. 'Apologize to Mr Chadwick at once.'

She remained stubbornly mute.

'Mel, I'm warning you . . .'

'It doesn't matter,' Harry said easily. 'Really, it's not important –'

But Sylvia was adamant. 'You'll apologize, Mel.'

'I won't.'

'You will.'

'I won't,' Mel replied, standing up to her mother and then turning back to Harry. 'Why are you here anyway?'

'Well,' Harry said laughing, 'you're blunt, I'll give you that. Like your grandfather.'

'I'm like my father,' Mel said hotly.

Then Harry understood the reason for her hostility and softened his tone. 'Yes, you're very like your father. That's why I'm here, Mel, to keep an eye on all of you whilst your father's away. He asked me to look out for you.'

But Mel was not so easily cajoled. She said nothing more, but something about her expression told Harry that she was no ordinary fourteen-year-old. She can see through me, he thought with no little humour. It'll be a clever man who can fool her.

He didn't know then that he was predicting the future.

Chapter Nine

'It's the only way we can keep this place running,' Sylvia said to George later that afternoon. Beside her, Harry was smoking in silence. 'It would be a sensible solution for all of us.'

Expressionless, George stared at his daughter-in-law. He couldn't quite make out what he thought about the suggestion. Was Sylvia really trying to help? Or was she – surely not – putting the house and the Cochrane inheritance at risk? Perhaps he was wrong to doubt her, but then again Aynhams wasn't hers. She had married into it, but it didn't belong to her – it belonged to him and to Michael.

Feeling suddenly ashamed of his suspicions, George glanced away, then flinched as he caught sight of the blackout curtains. Even Buile Hill was close enough to Salford and Manchester to attract bombing raids, and there had been many in the previous week. Rumour had it that there would be more, the Germans aiming for the industrial cities, the valley of industry which clung round the banks of the Irwell a perfect target.

His leg suddenly began to jiggle, as it always did when he was thinking. The house had been hopelessly old-fashioned when he first inherited it, not that there hadn't been money enough to maintain it, but his parents had had little interest in the future and lived only for the present. So when George finally took over Aynhams he inherited faulty plumbing, damp walls, outdated lighting and draughty corridors.

The east tower had become structurally unsafe. *East Tower*, George thought to himself, how bloody pretentious when the west tower had been demolished after being damaged in a storm years ago. There *was* only one tower now, the place where Michael used to sneak off as a child, to think. To *think* . . . George snorted inwardly. Michael had done more thinking than a prophet.

'About the house . . .' Sylvia said again, but George wasn't going to have his thoughts interrupted so readily.

He remembered the intricate plans he had been shown of Aynhams – the house set out in an E shape, the gardens arranged formally. Calling in experts, George had bullied the house back to glory, although even after he married Abigail the central and left wings remained closed. 'We don't need them,' he had insisted, 'not unless we have ten children . . .' Well, that wasn't to be, was it? So the wings remained abandoned and closed.

Musty now, George thought. Yes, they must be good and musty, even though the housekeeper aired them a couple of times a year. There were – oh, how many was it? Ten, eleven – no, there were nine bedrooms unused and a vast galleried hall. There were several other smaller rooms, four freezing bathrooms, an unmodernized kitchen – George had had a smart new one installed for convenience in the wing they now lived in – and a whole cluster of extra servants' quarters. George frowned and leaned his head back against the chair. What the hell did anyone want with so many rooms? he wondered. The remainder of the house had always been plenty for his family.

Perhaps there was some wisdom in what Sylvia suggested. After all, if the whole of Aynhams was used it would be safer, for one thing. Over the previous year there had been several break-ins and once a vagrant had been found asleep on a dust-sheet-covered sofa. Not that there was much to steal; George had long ago moved the best furniture into the occupied part of the house . . . but it seemed suddenly depressing to think of all those dark, empty rooms, closed off only feet away from the belly of the family quarters.

87

Blowing a breath from between his lips, George kept his eyes closed, Sylvia exchanging a baffled glance with Harry. Harry had changed very little in the years since they had first met; he was fatter and sleeker, but that befitted the image of the prosperous doctor. Oh, and *how* prosperous Harry Chadwick was; he was respected and feted, his work in the field of plastic surgery a revelation. He had long been an admirer of Harold Delf Gillies in Aldershot, studying his work on the 2,000 facially injured victims of the Battle of the Somme. He had followed everything he could read on Gillies's treatment of burned seamen and visited him often. But although invited to work with Gillies, Harry resisted. As ever he wanted to do everything his own way.

So in the years leading up to the war Harry had refined his art and garnered a vast reputation amongst the élite. Society idolized him; women flew into Manchester from all over Europe and beyond to be operated on by Harry. And he loved it, loved the adulation, the worship from pretty females, the gratitude from burns victims, the idolatry from the parents of disfigured children. He, as no other plastic surgeon before him, realized that the victims of horrific facial disfigurement had to have their looks restored as close as possible to their original features – and he also realized that vain women wanted the attention of the surgeon as much as the attention of a lover.

Not that his fame changed Harry radically: he was as big a braggart and egotist as he had always been. He boasted, he told gossipy, scandalous stories, he flew around the world as few others did, and talked as easily of Paris and Rome as other men spoke of the suburbs. Oh happy, happy Harry, everyone thought, and happy, happy Harry he was – in his consulting rooms or in the operating theatre.

But when he visited Aynhams he felt his confidence stagger like a drunk, and on entering the drive he had the simultaneous emotions of relief and resentment. It was a direct result of his upbringing, Harry realized, his security now provided by his foster family, the Cochranes. Away from them he needed to impress; to strut about in his exclusive Jaguar and his Savile Row suits, smelling of West Indies cologne; but when he came back to Aynhams he reverted to the rough-arsed kid from Gladstone Row. Because although the Cochranes knew all about Harry's past, it didn't matter – with them he was safe.

Harry was also astute enough to know that over the years Michael and he had come to some unspoken understanding; that they were, in fact, each other's alter ego. Michael would talk of the slum practice, and Harry would talk of his glittering life in plastic surgery – and each envied the other. Harry for Michael's family and background; Michael for Harry's glamour and drive.

A deep love developed between the two men, something neither had felt before. Totally dissimilar, they could understand each other perfectly and supplied each other with emotional support. Michael might kid himself that he longed for fame and acclaim, but he valued his privacy more; and Harry might pretend that he wanted a normal stable life, but he was compelled to succeed. In fact, the only thing they both needed was each other; to watch the other's progress, life, achievements, and to wonder – in quiet moments – what it would be like to exchange places.

Naturally, with his ego and wit, Harry soon developed a gift for self-promotion and long before it became fashionable he was wheedling his way into people's minds by familiar sightings in papers and magazines. Immaculate, articulate and brilliant, by the time he was in his late thirties Harry Chadwick had made himself into a medical Goliath, and nothing – and no one – could threaten him.

It looked so effortless from the outside, but the Cochranes knew that Harry – for all his ability – had had to graft hard for his success. For each night out dancing, he spent four in the hospital; for each date with a socialite, he spent many moonlit hours experimenting on skin tissue grafts. He could guffaw his way around and use his lethal, red-haired charm to get anywhere – and anyone – he wanted. But he still thought of Aynhams as home.

Smiling to himself, Harry stared at George, who had apparently fallen asleep in his chair. Wily old fox, Harry thought, amused, he's just faking, sussing out Sylvia's proposition about the house . . . Looking around, Harry's gaze rested on the battered medical bag by the door, and then he thought of Michael in the army.

He could see him as clearly as if he had walked into the room; tall, dark-haired, thoughtful, his voice composed. A very still figure, very calm, very . . . what? Very *loved* . . . Harry breathed in, discomforted, avoiding Sylvia's glance. Well, of course she was beautiful, he wasn't blind, but she was Michael's wife and he never fooled around with other people's wives. That would be too complicated. Besides, he wasn't exactly attracted to Sylvia. He couldn't for the world fathom out why – she was delicious after all; but there was something a little too contrived about her. In fact, Harry couldn't help but wonder if her marriage was as perfect as it seemed. Was her life as the doctor's wife so idyllic? Her role as mistress of Aynhams, local benefactress, and mother of two daughters so sublimely, ecstatically fulfilling?

He doubted it.

George shifted suddenly in his chair.

'Look, Harry, if – *if* – I let you do this, how long would it be for?'

'For as long as the war lasted,' Harry replied, leaning forwards eagerly. 'Aynhams would become the foremost centre for plastic surgery in –'

'Spare me the horseshit,' George said simply, then smiled apologetically at Sylvia. 'If I've got this straight, you want to take over the disused wings here and turn them into a clinic for war casualties –'

'– who require plastic surgery.'

'Not face-lifts, I hope?'

Harry smiled slyly. 'Well, not until they've fully recovered – and then only the pretty ones.'

Laughing, George tapped Harry on the knee. 'Have you looked at the place?'

'Well, no. I mean, I haven't seen it for years.'

'Don't you think you ought to have another look now, Harry?'

The younger man was flushing like a kid, red skin against auburn hair.

'Sylvia said it was plenty big enough –'

'So are the stables, but they wouldn't make a hospital,' George replied, struggling to his feet, his weight telling on him. 'Hadn't you better come and have another look, before we talk about this any further?' He slung his arm around Harry's shoulder. 'It's all rush, rush with you, isn't it? You're so bloody impulsive – not like Michael. Not like Michael at all.'

At the far end of the corridor which ran along the back of the house, past the kitchen, George paused and then drew back the weighty green curtain which covered a carved door. Pulling out his bundle of keys, he unlocked the door and walked through into a narrow corridor beyond, Harry following, Sylvia hanging a little way back.

With every cell she was willing George to agree because the idea of Aynhams being converted into a temporary hospital seemed like the answer to a prayer. Not that she would have admitted it to anyone but she was, in truth, bored.

Since Michael had gone off to war, and George and Tudge had been running the practice, there were fewer calls on their time. And those calls seldom included Sylvia. George insisted that she had enough to do bringing up the girls alone, Tudge was simply dismissive, cold as a corpse. She had gone out with him on one call – had *insisted* – and Tudge had been so bad-tempered he could hardly speak. It was the first, and last time she ever went out with him.

So the aged men continued to run the practice together, reverting to the old days, Sylvia's nursing skills neglected, her vocation now that of a mother. Which had, until recently, been enough for her. But as the months passed Sylvia realized that the role she had so assiduously courted was only partially fulfilling. It was pleasant being treated well, visiting other wives in the village, holding tea parties on the lawn at Aynhams, and, more recently, working for the war effort – but it wasn't enough. She had had a profession, a career, she had been active, responsible – and now what was she? A wife and mother, like so many others.

Her feelings made her guilty, but they didn't go away, and although Sylvia had never thought of herself as ambitious before, she was missing her old life. Harry's talk of the innovative surgical procedures and drugs made her homesick for nursing, the excitement of the new medical procedures making her exclusion from the practice unwelcome.

She missed the patients; even – incredibly – missed the slums. She felt limited, underused. So when Harry turned up with his scheme for a clinic at Aynhams, Sylvia was more than willing to listen. Harry's pitch went like this: he was well known, well respected, and he needed a hospital for his patients, a place of his own where he could operate on war casualties – the disfigured and the burned. A place he could make famous. Besides, there was no way, Harry predicted, that this war would be over by Christmas.

Well, why *not* Aynhams? Sylvia had thought when he first broached the subject with her. George had to agree that the place was partially neglected and wasted and, being a medical man himself, surely he would approve of his home being used for a worthy cause?

Well, of course George could see that, he was no fool; and he could also see that Harry had worked hard on making Sylvia an ally. As they walked down the corridor linking the different wings of the house, George mused to himself. Harry knew Sylvia of old, and was a frequent enough visitor to realize that she was bored. He also knew that she was a trained nurse . . . George smiled to himself. Obviously Harry was as good at professional seduction as he was at emotional.

Pushing open a heavy double door, George lit a candle and walked into the galleried hall.

'No electricity – never needed it here. Got gas,' he said, lighting the lamps on the wall, the colossal room coming into murky focus.

Stunned, Harry looked round. It was better than he had remembered it. Empty, immense, high-ceilinged, the perfect ward to hold twenty or even thirty beds. Windows over seventeen feet high were boarded with shutters, a mammoth fireplace unswept and unused for decades. On the faded, painted walls hung sporting pictures.

'This is . . .' Harry trailed off, uncharacteristically at a loss for words. Aynhams was *perfect*; he could already see the hall transformed into a ward for the patients, could imagine the idyllic surroundings, the gardens where they could convalesce. Hurriedly he moved towards the nearest door and opened it, George smiling wryly to himself.

'The theatre – I mean, the kitchen,' he said, standing in the doorway.

He was teasing Harry deliberately, picking into his thoughts.

The kitchen was very lofty, the old-fashioned cooking range seeming almost small against the vast far wall, a row of iron hooks suspended above on racks. But only the odd utensil or pan remained. The windows, high and well placed, culminated in a vast skylight where the kitchen extended into the yard beyond. Speechless, Harry stared around him. It *was* a kitchen, of course, but there was the room and the potential to make it into a very viable operating theatre.

'Running water?' Harry asked.

George raised his eyebrows. 'What d'you think we are, peasants?'

They exchanged a warm smile, Harry moving on into the corridor beyond the kitchen and beginning to climb the stairs.

'Jesus!' he snapped as he lost his footing in the dark.

Shaking his head, George walked to the bottom of the stairs and looked up, holding a lighted candle above his head.

'Always in a rush, aren't you, Harry? Always in such a bloody rush.'

Borrowing the light, Harry hurriedly lit the gas upstairs and then paused. His face was luminous with enthusiasm, his voice slipping back into its Gladstone Row origins as he rushed from bedroom to bedroom.

'Dear God, George, this is perfect. It's a hundred times better than I remembered.'

Lumbering behind him, the old man kept his face impassive.

'It'll cost money to convert – *if* I agree to letting you use it. And it'll cost a bob or two to run –'

'We can work something out,' Harry said hurriedly.

'We certainly can,' George replied. 'If I let you move into my house and crash about disturbing my peace, I want compensation.'

'I wanted to talk about that.'

'Good,' George said drily, 'that makes two of us.'

Materializing suddenly by her father-in-law's side, Sylvia looked steadily at George.

'Michael would love to think that Aynhams was being used as a hospital.'

The words slid into the old man's ears and sneaked into his consciousness. Well, just what would his son think about it? Perhaps he would be pleased, or then again, maybe Michael wouldn't like the idea of Harry Chadwick invading his territory whilst he was away. Besides, as his father and Harry got on so well, would that worry Michael? Would it make him jealous?

Ashamed of his last thought, George turned his good eye on Harry.

'How much?'

'Huh?'

'You heard.'

Harry grinned broadly. 'Let's talk about it over a drink.'

'Mine, I suppose?'

'Actually no, I've got some fine brandy in the car.'

'You smug bugger!' George said, laughing and clapping Harry on the shoulder. 'You overconfident, egotistical bugger.'

Laughing they walked off, too busy to notice Sylvia standing still and silent at the top of the stairs. Muted moonlight slanted in through the Gothic arch of the landing window and lit her perfect, impassive face. She seemed completely out of place in the cold English house, completely divorced from her surroundings.

So no one, looking at her at that moment, could possibly have suspected the triumph she felt.

Chapter Ten

Ten months later, and the hospital at Aynhams was in full operation.

In the theatre that had once been a kitchen there was silence, no conversation, no music, only the steady in, out, in, out, of the ventilator breathing. At the patient's head sat the anaesthetist, John Wilde, Sylvia standing next to him, Harry on the other side of the operating table. The casualty was very young, sent over from Manchester Infirmary after being invalided home two days earlier, the victim of Luftwaffe bombing over the Channel.

The soldier's face was relaxed for the first time in hours, because he was deeply, benignly, unconscious. Conscious, the pain was so great that he could only roll his head back and forwards against the pillow, his eyes, their eyelids burned away, staring terrified up to the ceiling. His hands too were burned black, the fingers curled inwards towards the palm, incessant ice packs only partially deadening the pain. Morphine couldn't stop it completely either, only for brief snatches and then it came back, worse, always worse.

He would cry for his mother because he was only twenty, Sylvia writing a letter home for him, the soldier's permanently open eyes fixed agonizingly on hers. His tongue had been affected by burns too, but he could still manage to talk, though his head had been swollen to three times its normal size when he was admitted, his coughing waking everyone at night until they moved him into a side ward.

Harry kept him there for observation, in one of the old bedrooms at Aynhams which was now unrecognizable. The soldier's lungs had been affected by smoke inhalation, so

Harry had to be sure that the patient could take an anaesthetic. There was no point trying to repair the man's face if the surgery killed him.

Time shifted into its second speed. Harry had always insisted that time had two rates: fast, as in the operating theatre; and dragging, as in ordinary life. It was dragging now whilst he watched his patient through the door and wondered if the injuries would kill him, or the anaesthetic, or the shock.

After Harry and George had agreed terms, the clinic had opened within weeks. Impossible, people had said, no one can get anything up and running in so short a time. Horseshit, Harry had replied, money can get anything moving. So he invested his own capital and begged and threatened everyone he knew to donate – and make public the fact that he was looking for funds for *our brave boys*. And if anyone resisted, they'd better have a bloody good reason, because Harry didn't take no for an answer. He used his charm and he used his ruthless streak; not employing blackmail, but hinting that someone who had something to hide ought to cough up … It was not a threat, merely an intimation, but it came as a shock to those who had only seen Harry Chadwick's charm, not his street-hard origins.

He enlisted help from the Government too, and because of his status, he was listened to. Money was not plentiful from them, but it came, as it did from virtually everywhere else. On the wireless Harry talked about the burns victims, men sent back from the war mutilated and horribly disfigured. He made their case poignant and heckled for action. He wanted help, support, funds for his patients; he wanted to be heard; he wanted to set up the clinic at Aynhams, and he wanted to do it fast. Fame was tagging along with him for the ride; Harry Chadwick on the warpath, quite literally.

'That's all we can do for him at the moment,' Harry

said, walking away from his patient, Sylvia waiting at the door.

She followed in silence, taking off her rubber gloves as she walked along the corridor with him. It was one thirty in the morning, late hours as usual, patients never keeping to social timetables. Around her she could hear the muted sounds of hospital life; a cough echoing hollow in one of the high-ceilinged wards; a mumble of someone dreaming, and the soft shuffle of rubber-soled nurses' shoes moving across the floor above.

It was strange to think that she was happy for the first time in years – she was home. *Home* . . . Odd, she thought, that she had never thought of India or Aynhams as her real home, but now that Aynhams incorporated the clinic, she had found her true niche. She was someone here, not just by reason of a lucky marriage, but by skill. Harry Chadwick could have had his pick of nurses and staff, but she had – almost from the first – become his confidante and ally. She was his assistant, both in the theatre and out of it. If someone wanted to reach Harry, they had to talk to Sylvia first.

It suited Harry, of course. Sylvia was the respected lady of the house, she was beautiful, a skilled theatre sister and adept socially. And Aynhams wasn't just a clinic, it was a show-place, a heroic shrine dedicated to the war wounded. In papers and magazines Harry Chadwick's stocky frame was often seen, sometimes in operating clothes, sometimes in his newly acquired Blaydon jacket, a pipe now pressed into service as his latest prop. Cigars, Harry reasoned, looked too flash in wartime, only wide boys smoked cigars . . .

The Pathe News ran a number of articles on Aynhams, together with footage of the wards and patients, in amongst the lush environment of Buile Hill. Harry was regarded as an innovator at first, then as a god. Harry Chadwick, taking on the burns cases no one else would touch, restoring the injured back to normality.

At least, that was what the Pathe News said. The truth was somewhat different. No plastic surgeon, no matter how skilled, could totally repair severe burn injuries. In many cases, where the airmen had been trapped in burning planes, their features were burned off. Eyelids, noses and ears were missing, and, in the men not blinded, there was the constant problem of how to keep the eyes moist without the protective covering of the lids. Men as severely injured as this were not the normal casualties of war, they were mutilated externally and internally. Most were also very young, had been ambitious, quick to volunteer for the glamorous life of an airman, hurriedly trained and too inexperienced to be afraid.

But they weren't too young to understand their position when they found themselves invalided out of the air force. It was difficult to explain to a twenty-four-year-old that his face was destroyed – but Harry, in this as in everything else, had his own method.

'You've been badly burned,' he'd start, lighting up his pipe and sitting by the side of the patient's bed.

'How badly?' would – all too often – come the tentative reply.

'You're no beauty any more.'

The bluntness would nearly always cause a smile or a quick comeback.

'You're no beauty either, Mr Chadwick.'

Then the patient would stare at him, willing him to recover something from the wreckage.

'Your hands are no good any more,' Harry would say sometimes, then follow the negative statement with a positive: 'But I can make you a new nose. A better one than you used to have – if your photographs are anything to go by.'

And he was true to his word. The burn injuries were so severe that they were unlike singular repairs of jaw or nose. In these cases the whole face had to be reconstructed. For these terrible whole face mutilations, Harry used the tubed pedicle graft, literally a large piece of skin taken from the patient's body, which stayed attached by a tube – thereby enabling a blood supply to be maintained until a new one was established. Such procedures were ponderous and time-consuming, and there were other drawbacks – like the outbreak of haemolytic streptococci which infected many of the pedicle grafts. After this, Harry changed his technique and the grafts became free placed, without the tube. Although totally lacking in artistic ability, Harry could cut out grafts into perfect shapes with a scalpel free-hand – and earn himself the affectionate nickname of the Theatre Titian.

He learned fast and was gifted enough to assimilate and modify techniques to suit his patients. He was also able to dissociate himself from suffering in order to keep a clear head. Music was played loud and almost incessantly in the day – both to cheer the men's spirits but also to drown out the sounds of screams when the patients had to be immersed in salt baths to have their dressings changed.

Strutting from the theatre at Aynhams to the wards, Harry would bully his patients, understanding instinctively that they wanted to be a part of their own recoveries. Unlike many surgeons, he even permitted patients to watch him as he operated, Sylvia always at his right hand in theatre. His ideas on recovery were radical too. Other doctors would forbid alcohol and smoking, Harry didn't. He reckoned that the patients had come through so much they were entitled to enjoy what pleasures they could. Which is why he made a point of hiring the most beautiful nurses available.

The press were not slow to catch on to this ploy either. Harry might say that it was good for the patients, and it was, but it was also good for his image.

Watching these developments take place over the first six months of the clinic's existence, George was fascinated and not a little impressed. From his point of view, little changed – he still ran his Salford practice with Tudge – whilst only yards away in other wings of the house, Harry Chadwick performed his miracles to the avid interest of the world outside.

As soon as the idea had been mooted about the clinic George had written to Michael. His son had replied promptly. No, he didn't mind that part of Aynhams was being used as a clinic; he thought it was a good idea; and it would give Sylvia an interest whilst he was away. 'Give everyone my regards, and tell Harry that I wish him all the luck in the world.'

Well, I bloody wouldn't! George thought savagely. He had been watching Harry's manoeuvres for a while without saying anything, awed, in a way, that he could get so ambitious a plan into operation so quickly. The money Harry was paying for the use of Aynhams was considerable, but George was uneasy. He had felt, almost at once, that he had lost something; that Harry had somehow managed to take precedence in his home. Even though Harry kept to his part of the house, something of his vibrancy seeped through the walls into George's area. And it rankled.

It also rankled that Sylvia was spending so much time in the clinic, away from her duties as mistress of Aynhams and George's daughter-in-law. Oh, George never for a moment suspected that she would fall in love with Harry, or Harry with her. That would ruin everything – and both of them were surely far too intelligent to scupper their chances. Outsiders might think what they liked about the beautiful exotic theatre sister who worked with Harry Chadwick, the nurse whose husband was away fighting, but George knew they were both too calculating to let passion sway them off course.

But he *did* wonder what Michael thought about it. After all, if a stranger had happened on Aynhams they would have presumed that Sylvia and Harry were married and that Beth and Mel were *their* children. How convenient for Harry, George thought suddenly. He had, without effort, acquired a ready-made family – and yet, if he wanted, he could up and off without remorse. They were, after all, not his responsibility. He might borrow them, but Sylvia was another man's wife and the girls were another man's children.

At the same time that George was musing in his study, Harry was standing by a patient's bed and staring down at the young face. His thoughts shuffled themselves, boxed themselves, then, exasperated, he tried to understand the anger he was feeling.

Michael was entitled to come home, after all. It was his home, his house, his family. It was all his. Not mine, Harry thought. But oh, how I *want* it to be mine. How I want Aynhams, and everything else he has ...

Startled by his thoughts, Harry picked up the patient's chart and began to read. But the figures all disintegrated into one and soon he was staring out of the window, and seeing nothing – except his own stocky, red-headed figure, looking back.

It had been almost too good to be true; he had made his dream happen, made his clinic, and now, only six months since it opened, it was becoming known worldwide. He had made his name and now he had made his medical niche. But he had not made his home.

It was all right pretending, Harry thought infuriated with himself. It was all right bloody pretending, but he knew the truth. Sylvia wasn't his wife and the girls weren't his daughters. He had no right to them. He had his role – that of a favourite uncle – and he should stick to it ... But for once Harry hadn't been forthright, and had allowed the rumours and innuendos to mushroom. Soon everyone was asking the same question: was he having an affair with

Sylvia? He would have nipped such stories in the bud before, but he couldn't. He might not want Sylvia, but he wanted what she represented.

A *wife*. More than that, a gifted, glamorous wife. A wife a famous surgeon could be proud of. A wife too good for a slum doctor . . . Shame made Harry blush, his heart stomping. How could he even think it? How could he? Michael was a just man, a better man than he was in many ways. How could he even consider stealing what was his?

And even if he tried, would he succeed? He wasn't sure about Sylvia, but he knew about the girls. Beth would go with him in an instant; she had trailed him from the first, staring up at him with that unmistakable look of hero worship. She was dainty, pretty and sweet, and when he talked to her she hung on his every word. Beth was to Harry everything he had ever imagined in a daughter: pliable, loving, simple.

But Mel wasn't. Mel was blunt, outspoken, at times downright rude. And as for replacing Michael in Mel's eyes, no chance. She had made that clear from the start.

'What you doing?' she had asked him one morning as Harry prepared to go into theatre.

He was dressed in his greens and was about to scrub up. Mel was leaning on the window sill of the theatre anteroom.

'You shouldn't be here –'

'It's OK if I don't go any further,' she replied with perfect composure. She was right too. 'So, what *are* you doing?'

Harry stared at her; she looked so like Michael – and she was frighteningly mature for a fourteen-year-old.

'An operation –'

'I know that,' Mel replied scathingly. 'I just wondered what kind of operation.'

'I'm trying to repair this patient's jaw. It was smashed.'

She nodded. 'Can I watch?'

'I don't –'

'Dad would have let me.'

Her expression threw down the gauntlet. Did she know that those few words would be the only ones to make him agree? Or was it simply a lucky guess? Harry doubted it. This was one fourteen-year-old who could give anyone a run for their money.

'You'll have to scrub up,' Harry said indulgently, but the words sounded patronizing to his ears and undermined him. What he said next was worse. 'You won't faint now, will you?'

Moving away from the window sill, Mel gave him a look which veered somewhere between pity and amusement.

But for all his misgivings, she was very still during the operation, incredibly so for someone of her age, and she did just what she had said she would – she watched. She did more actually, she *absorbed*. Her dark eyes over the surgical mask took in every movement and every command; and she scrutinized her mother's work with a curious detachment, as though she were watching a stranger. Never once did she get in the way; never once knock anything over, or draw attention to herself. For a girl who was at times clumsy and loud outside, in the operating theatre Mel Cochrane was transformed.

Strangely, as he operated, Harry was aware of Mel as he was seldom aware of anyone. Usually consumed by concentration he would only notice others when he asked for instruments, or spoke to John Wilde about the anaesthetic. Otherwise, he was oblivious. But not this time; this time he was aware of the presence of the girl, and realized that something extraordinary was occurring.

But that had been the first and last time Harry had felt close to Mel. Since then she had watched a number of his operations, but had shown little gratitude, at other times throwing apple cores at him from the top of the east tower. Beth might adore him, as might most of the female population, but Mel was immune to Harry Chadwick. Emotionally vaccinated and morally inoculated against him.

'Dad's coming home,' she told him happily one morning.

For a moment Harry had to fight an impulse to push the apple she was eating down her throat.

'And I'm really looking forward to seeing him,' she went on, stamping on his feelings with a hideously accurate aim. 'He's a hero. Saved many lives, you know.'

What d'you think *I* bloody do? Harry wanted to shout. Murder people?

'He was very brave. Going off to fight . . .' she continued.

The implication was obvious – my father went off to the war, and you stayed home. Coward.

'. . . Tudge says that God will bring him back safely.'

Harry eyed her suspiciously. 'Somehow I didn't think you'd believe in God.'

'I'm not sure if I do, or I don't,' Mel said guilelessly. 'I'm only a girl, after all.'

Oh yeah, Harry thought as he watched her walk away, and I'm a bloody Arab.

The night before Michael's return Harry had finished operating and then eaten dinner with George and Sylvia. He had been muted, almost thoughtful, George watching him curiously. Was he worried about one of his patients? he wondered. No, he would have mentioned it, he always did. So perhaps he was worried about something he *couldn't* talk about – and there was only one subject Harry Chadwick couldn't talk about. His feelings.

Over the top of his coffee cup, George studied Harry's profile. He liked him, had in fact grown fond of him, but he was buggered if he would take Harry's side against his son. His vehemence surprised him; after all, Michael and he had seldom been close, but Michael was blood, and

Harry Chadwick wasn't. He might brag and boast and perform his surgical transformations, but George knew that the thing Harry valued most was what he thought he wanted least – a family. Not that Harry would admit it to himself. He would date every beautiful woman he could find, and dazzle the nurses, but when he closed the heavy door which separated the clinic from the domestic quarters of Aynhams a metamorphosis took place.

'I was wondering . . .' Harry began, then stopped.

'Go on,' George encouraged him.

'I thought I might go away for a few days, down to London to see . . .'

Sylvia was surprised, and showed it. 'But you can't do that, you'd miss Michael.'

He avoided her eyes. 'It would be good for you two to be alone. It's his leave, after all.'

'But he'd love to see what you've done here.' She appealed to her father-in-law for backing. 'Wouldn't he?'

'Harry's got a point,' George said, without looking at either of them. 'I think my son might like to have time alone with his family.'

She frowned, but said nothing in reply.

'Besides,' George went on, 'if Harry's not here, you'll have more time for Michael – not having to be busy assisting him, that is.'

Her face was unreadable, but her voice had an edge to it. 'I don't neglect my family. I don't neglect you or the girls –'

'He didn't say that.'

'Please, Harry, stay out of this!' Sylvia replied tensely, turning back to her father-in-law. 'If you've got any complaints, tell me. Don't brood on them.'

'I never brood on any bloody thing,' George said, finishing his coffee. 'I just speak my mind.'

'To the enlightenment of all of us,' Sylvia replied drily, rising.

In silence, both men watched her and when she'd left the room, Harry whistled between his teeth.

'Wow!'

'She's needled, that's all. She'll come round – if you do the right thing and clear off to London.'

It was Harry's turn to be surprised.

'What?'

'There is only room here for one husband and one father –'

'I never –'

'Harry, shut up and listen to me,' George said simply. 'You have a home here, and you have your clinic here now. But use your bloody head, man, and think. They need time alone.'

'It was *my* idea to go to London.'

'Only because you thought we'd stop you,' George replied deftly, 'and Sylvia would have. But I won't.' Heavily the old man rose to his feet, his bulk making him slow. 'Take some advice from me, Harry, find your own wife and have your own children. These are already spoken for.'

Chapter Eleven

Michael walked into Aynhams like a stranger, wondering for a moment where to put his coat. It was an unpleasant sensation, as though he had no right to be there. He felt out of place, uncomfortable, Sylvia moving towards him with a smile on her face. Immediately he leaned towards her, but she moved, his lips brushing her cheek, not her mouth. Embarrassed, he smiled at her and then thought – for one steely second – that he could see resentment in her eyes.

He had been granted a forty-eight-hour leave, two days to see his wife and children, but he had been delayed and now it was almost two in the morning, and his daughters were in bed asleep. As was his father – George trying in his clumsy way to be discreet and leave them alone. But Michael didn't see it that way, he thought that his father had simply not wanted to greet him and had rather gone to bed than see his son.

It was a chill homecoming.

Awkwardly, Sylvia tried to riddle the fire into life in the kitchen. She had become used to sitting there. It was cosy and now Aynhams' staff had left for well-paid factory jobs and other war work, she was cooking again.

'It's the coal,' she said by way of explanation, 'it's not good and it's damp.'

'Don't bother for my sake,' Michael replied, wondering why his voice sounded so distant. This was his *wife*, for God's sake. 'We might as well go to bed.'

The suggestion rocked both of them; neither longing for the other, the idea of sleeping together unwelcome. Dear God, Michael thought, what's happened to us?

'Are you hungry?' Sylvia asked, the cold overhead light making shadows under her cheekbones. Chillingly beautiful.

'No.'

'Thirsty?'

'Any brandy?' Michael asked, hoping that the drink might take the chill out of his body and his heart.

'I think there's some . . .' Sylvia replied, searching round.

'It doesn't matter. It was only a thought.'

'We do have some. George kept some for emergencies.'

Oh, and this *was* an emergency, Michael thought.

'I read your letters – all about the clinic.'

She nodded, still searching for the brandy he didn't really want.

'Is Harry here?'

'In London,' she answered, turning. 'He sent his regards. Said he might be back in time to see you tomorrow.'

The fire coals shifted, then fell, obliterating the last of the flames. Facing each other, they were as awkward as strangers.

'So, how are you, Michael?'

'Fine. And you?'

'We're all OK here. We missed you.'

'I missed you too,' he replied, without making a move towards her.

'I really should make you something to eat –'

'I don't want it, honestly,' Michael said, wondering what to do, wondering if he could simply go upstairs and slide into bed and go to sleep without having to make love. Because he couldn't do that; he didn't want to, and neither did she. Sad, unbearably so.

'The girls were so excited. They waited up as long as they could –'

'I was delayed.'

'Yes.'

'But I'll see them tomorrow.'

'Yes,' she replied, staring at him.

He was more handsome than she remembered, tall, stunning in his uniform. She should ask him how he *really* was, should hold him and comfort him – but he didn't seem to need it. He didn't seem to need her either.

'Are you tired?'

He nodded. 'You?'

'It's been busy here. I work long hours in the clinic.'

'But you like it?' he asked her, making awkward conversation with the woman he had loved to distraction; the woman who had given birth to his two children.

'Yes,' she replied quietly, 'I like it. I feel as though I'm contributing something.'

'You were always a good nurse.'

Pausing, Michael looked into her face and longed to reach out, to turn back the months and years and be once more in the position of having something to offer her. But that time had passed, she was poised, confident, very much in control, very much beyond him. She could manage their family and a career without him. She no longer needed to set her sights on his name, or his home – she had both. And, he realized helplessly, she no longer needed him.

Oh God, he thought again, why did I come back? *What* did I come back for?

'Daddy?'

He turned hurriedly at the sound of Mel's voice, smiling with relief and reaching for her as she walked into the kitchen.

'Darling,' he said, bending down and kissing her. 'I'm so glad to see you, so very glad.'

Winded, Sylvia turned away.

In the end she pretended to be asleep when Michael finally came to bed. He had been talking to Mel for almost an hour, telling her all about his colleagues and the war, explaining what was happening, describing the conditions

– telling his daughter what he should have told his wife. Mel had listened as though mesmerized, her face fixed on her father's lips, her hands resting in his. Gone was the truculent little monster who persecuted Harry, this was Mel as only Michael knew her. This was his splendid, tough little warrior girl.

'I watched for it, you know,' she told him in a whisper. 'Just tonight, I saw it, so I knew you would be home.'

He knew what she was talking about immediately. He too had seen the moon and silently turned the phrase over and over in his mind. Midnight's smiling, tomorrow will be a lucky day . . . He had thought it was a lie though – until he had seen his daughter, and now, suddenly, it seemed that tomorrow might be sweet after all.

After he finally managed to settle Mel to sleep he tiptoed into the next room and drew back the curtain, the moon-light falling over Beth's sleeping face. So perfect, so utterly sweetly perfect, even in sleep. He loved her, but as he leaned down to kiss her cheek he saw in her features a reflection of Sylvia's face and mentally thanked God for his other child.

George had been determined to make a fuss of his son, but within minutes of their meeting over breakfast, the old awkwardness returned. Brusquely George sliced off the top of his boiled egg and winced at the underdone white.

'Bloody eggs.'

'At least you can get eggs here.'

'Black market. I have no morals,' his father replied, scooping out the jellied white onto the side of his plate.

'How's Tudge?'

'Old and cranky. The bugger'll live for ever.'

'Like you.'

Glancing up, George caught his son's eye and for an instant a warm feeling passed between them.

'I'll show you the clinic after breakfast,' Sylvia said,

as the sound of a door banging broke into the quiet room.

'Seems odd to think of there being a hospital in Aynhams,' Michael said thoughtfully. 'I heard about the work Harry's doing here. It's news, big news.'

Was that jealousy in his voice, George wondered, or simple resignation?

'Is he the same as ever?'

'Worse. Head as big as a horse's arse,' George replied.

'He has a right to some conceit,' Sylvia interjected, 'he does miracles here.'

'I imagine Michael does miracles on the front too,' George said, the rebuke obvious.

Pausing, Sylvia laid down the teapot and stood up. She was pure in her uniform, white from head to toe, a weird pale ghost of a woman.

'I have to get to work –'

'Michael's home,' George said, his tone incredulous. 'You *can't* work today.'

'I have to,' she replied, on the defensive. 'There are things I have to do.'

'Like spending time with your husband –'

'Father, let it rest,' Michael said wearily.

'But –'

'Let it go!' he snapped, unexpectedly angry. 'I'll spend some time with the girls today.'

Without looking at her father-in-law, Sylvia walked out, the connecting door between the family wing and the clinic closing with a dull thud behind her.

Harry had intended to return to Aynhams in time to see Michael, but a few things had cropped up, his train, packed with troops, had been terribly delayed, and in the end he had been too late. When he did get back the only trace of his friend Michael was a completed newspaper crossword and a pair of leather gloves on the kitchen table.

'He'll miss these,' Harry said wistfully as he picked them up and turned them over in his hands.

'There are other things he'll miss more,' George replied curtly.

'I should get back to work –'

'You should be ashamed of yourself.' He was sharp with fury.

'What the hell are you talking about!'

'You know exactly what I mean, Harry, so don't come the innocent with me,' George replied flatly. 'I know your game, so don't try to fool me.'

'I don't know what –'

'You're a hotshot, aren't you? A big man now, on the news, a regular miracle worker. But to me you're still the big-headed, ragged-arsed kid from Gladstone Row.' George's one good eye fixed on Harry menacingly. 'There's more to life than talent – things like integrity and honour. You've got to learn that for yourself, and you will if you've got any bloody sense. But I'd just like to give you one word of warning – don't rock this bloody boat or you'll be the one that drowns.'

'George, listen –'

'No, Harry, you listen to *me*. I might have only one eye, but it works perfectly – and I've got it fixed on you.'

Chapter Twelve

The Battle of Britain had made Harry's name known worldwide. He seemed to be fêted in every publication, and was publicly honoured by the Government. His skill and panache were never in doubt, his innovations in the field of plastic surgery, incredible. It also seemed that he had no fear of failure, his attitude brushing off on the airmen, many of whom would have given up hope without him. He jostled them, told them they were heroes and that, despite the fact that they would never be Adonises, they could get any woman they wanted.

The nurses – who had been instructed to treat the men jocularly as part of the treatment – often fell in love with their charges, the airmen's sorties out on drinking binges tolerated by Harry.

'Jesus, they'll never have a normal life. They probably won't have a normal life span either, after all the anaesthetics. Leave the poor buggers alone to enjoy themselves.'

His colleagues were against him, but that just made Harry more of a renegade. What better than to challenge the establishment and win? Besides, so many people thought doctors distant and patronizing, and here was a man who could work marvels – and who was approachable. Little surprise that Harry was loathed by most of the medical profession; many predicting his downfall after the war. He was having his day now, they said, but wait and see what happened … but the war went on and more airmen were shot down, and the worse cases continued to be sent to Aynhams.

Abroad Michael continued to fight his own war, coming

home on leave to see his family, Sylvia ever more distant, Mel ever more loving, Beth the same as she ever was. He saw, with regret, that his daughters were growing up fast. Without him. He saw the changes as Mel altered from a child into a seventeen-year-old girl, Beth by this time fourteen. The latter was still babied, her sweet nature attracting attention, the wounded servicemen trying to make friends with her. But they only alarmed her; Beth could see their deformities and never beyond that; she was never cruel but she avoided them as much as she could, keeping to the domestic wing and skirting the clinic as a mouse would skirt a cattery.

Mel was the opposite; she had always been involved from the first, and as she grew older she spent more and more time in the clinic. Sylvia encouraged her, wanting her to have a career, to be more than just a wife and mother. If Mel was educated she could escape the trap of dependency – because Beth never would. Sylvia was all too aware of the difference in her daughters and had reconciled herself to it. Besides, it suited her to have Beth as her confidante, her ally. She was more pliable than Mel, more easily led, the gentle pretty girl who was always nearby. Her shadow, Sylvia called her. And, wherever she went, her youngest daughter was sure to follow – whereas with Mel, no one was ever sure where she was.

Throughout her childhood she had been independent, a wanderer, going off on her own to the east tower to read medical books, watching Harry operate in silence, or sometimes just going missing for hours at a time.

'Where have you been?' Sylvia asked her for the umpteenth time. 'We were worried about you.'

Mel looked at her mother in astonishment.

'I was thinking.'

'She gets more like Michael every day,' George had said drily, turning back to his paper.

'Have you been up in the tower again?'

Mel stood up to her mother defiantly.

'It's perfectly safe –'

'It's not safe!' Sylvia replied heatedly. 'That's why it's cordoned off.'

'Father used to go up there.'

'Because your father did it, it doesn't make it all right.'

Oh but it did. Anything Michael did was perfect in Mel's eyes, and Sylvia knew it. She had seen over the years the bond grow between the two and had at first welcomed it, then resented it as she found herself excluded. It did her no good to admit that it was her fault, that she had lost much feeling for her husband, or that, in her involvement in the clinic, she had put Harry's needs first. She knew the truth and yet she was still angered by the shift in status, and uncomfortably aware that she was becoming jealous of her own daughter.

Gradually Michael's leaves had altered in tone. He was no more the reluctant spouse, he was now the loving father, willing to return. And even Harry, never very adept at reading feelings, saw the change.

'So, what d'you think of it?' he asked Michael when he had shown him the new theatre, tacked onto the back of the house.

'A great achievement,' he replied, leaning on the gate which looked out over the pastures attached to Aynhams.

'No hard feelings then?'

Michael's expression was mystified. 'What?'

'About my being here.'

'Why would I resent your being here?'

Harry shifted his feet. God, he had done it again, said the wrong thing.

'I just wondered – Aynhams being your home . . . you know, I wondered if you thought I was taking it over.'

There was a long pause in which the two men studied each other, then Michael turned away. He had been violently jealous of Harry at first, wondering if his position would be usurped, wondering if this famous figure would rob him of his wife and children, let alone stand as an ever-present reminder of his limitations. He was a GP, no more. When the war ended he would return to the Salford practice and treat the same type of people for the same type of ailments which were always prevalent with the poor. He would never be honoured by his country, or fêted for his accomplishments. His was a small donation to the medical kitty; Harry was the banker extraordinary.

Oh yes, it had hurt him at first – it still worried him at times – but gradually Michael had come to realize that – despite what anyone else might suspect – Sylvia was not having and was not going to have an affair with his closest friend. And his father had turned out to be surprisingly loyal. As for the girls, well, Beth might be fond of Harry, but then Beth was fond of everyone. But the one thing Michael had feared above everything had not come to pass – Harry had not taken Mel away from him.

For a long time Michael had thought that Harry might. Not intentionally, but by stealth. She would be watching his operations, after all, and seeing his way of life – that heady belting from Manchester to London, to Aynhams, the press attention, the society invitations. It would have been natural for her to admire him. Her father was away as she was growing up, how easy for her to turn to the ever-present surrogate father, Harry.

But she never forgot that Michael Cochrane was her father, and she never really admired Harry. She admired his courage, his skill, but never ran to greet him the way that she ran to greet her father, and she never laughed with Harry or talked about him when Michael was home.

'He's doing some amazing work,' Michael suggested tentatively, after they were relaxing in the garden, having both watched Harry operate.

Mel had shrugged. 'Sure.'

She was tall now, looked older than her years, her dark

hair full around her face, her frame athletic. Suddenly Michael realized that she would be a handsome woman, not delicately lovely like Beth, but strong, a female to admire and respect. The realization made him catch his breath with pride.

'I've decided that I'm definitely going to be a doctor.'

He stared at her.

'Did you hear me, Dad?'

Nodding, Michael answered her. 'Yes, yes, I heard you. Are you sure that's what you want to do?'

He wondered who had influenced her and felt a dull shudder of doubt. Had it been him? His father? Or Harry?

'I want to be a pathologist.'

He laughed suddenly, making her frown.

'Sorry, darling,' Michael said, 'I wasn't laughing at you, I was just surprised.'

'I don't want to see people suffer, you see,' Mel went on, suddenly very serious. 'But I want to go into medicine – so I thought that pathology would be the right thing to do.'

'It's not a field of medicine women usually go in for.'

'I can do it.'

'I don't doubt that,' Michael replied carefully, 'all I was saying is that there would be a lot of prejudice. There already is – against all women doctors.' He picked at his words. 'You're only young anyway, Mel, you might change your mind –'

'I won't,' she said simply. 'You'll see.'

At that precise moment Harry walked over to them, lit his pipe and blew a cloud of tobacco smoke from between his lips. It made his features blur for an instant, his red hair blazing under the summer sun.

'Ahhhhhh . . .'

Smiling, Michael watched him. 'Mel and I were just talking. She's going to be a doctor.'

'A *pathologist*,' she corrected him.

Grinning, Harry turned to her. 'Well, it was obvious that you'd go into medicine, but pathology's a bloody silly idea –'

'What?' she snapped.

'No real woman wants to be a doctor. You'll never catch a husband if you become a blue stocking, Mel.'

The expression in her eyes hardened. She was nearly as tall as Harry and seemed suddenly to be a woman, not a girl.

'Dad was just saying how prejudiced the medical profession was. He was right, as usual.'

Stung, Harry flashed back at her, 'You're just a girl, what d'you know? You'll end up married like all the rest.'

'My mother's a nurse –'

'Which isn't the same as being a doctor,' Harry replied sharply. 'You shouldn't set your sights too high.'

Mel was glowing with anger. 'If I were a boy you wouldn't be saying this –'

'If you were a boy it would be different,' Harry countered, sucking on his pipe irritably.

'You're a bigot.'

Stunned, Harry turned to Michael. 'D'you see how she talks to me?'

'She's right,' Michael said calmly. 'You *are* a bigot, Harry. You always were. You never thought women should have careers.'

'Oh, they can have careers – until they get married.'

'So what about my mother? She's married and she has a career,' Mel responded. 'You couldn't have managed to run this clinic without her.'

'Your mother is different.'

'Hah!' Mel said shortly, turning away as her father looked warningly at Harry.

'Don't listen to him, Mel. I'm behind you all the way.'

'I only know one female doctor,' Harry said mischievously, provoking her further. 'No one has ever asked her out and she has hair on her top lip. She'll be a spinster all her life.'

Burning with irritation, Mel turned on him. 'But you're not married. Why is it so different for you?'

'I don't want to marry,' Harry replied, suddenly cold.

'Perhaps no one wants to marry *you* –'

'Enough! Enough!' Michael said, coming between the two of them. 'You go and tell your mother we'll be in soon, will you, Mel?'

'I –'

'Go on,' he said, watching her as she walked off.

For a long moment Harry sucked on his pipe, his features unusually stern.

'With the best will in the world, Michael, that girl of yours can be bloody rude.'

'She just speaks her mind.'

'That won't make her popular.'

'I don't think Mel wants to be popular,' Michael said evenly. 'I think she wants to be a success.'

'Charm never went amiss,' Harry replied, taking the pipe out of his mouth and banging it on his palm.

'She really got to you, didn't she?'

'She hit a nerve, yes.'

'About your not being married?'

Harry stared at his pipe fixedly. 'I nearly was. Once.'

'You never said.'

'She dumped me.'

'Oh,' Michael replied simply. 'Did you love her?'

'Of course I bloody loved her, or it wouldn't have hurt so much! But it's a waste of time loving any woman. You can't trust them.'

Glancing away, Michael asked quietly, 'Has there been no one special since?'

'No! And there never will be,' Harry answered, relighting his pipe and blinking through the smoke. He was, Michael realized with astonishment, close to tears.

'You can't trust women,' Harry repeated. 'And clever women are the worst.' His voice had altered, the usual genial tone gone. He was struggling hopelessly to control his feelings. 'I envy you.'

Michael turned to look at him, but said nothing. He couldn't express himself and, as ever, remained mute.

'I envy you your wife and your children and your home,' Harry went on. His emotions had shifted from anguish to anger in an instant. 'You have what I want. Oh, for God's sake, Michael, say something! I'm hung out to dry here and I feel a right jerk.' His voice rose sharply. 'I want what's yours. Go on, break my nose, shout at me, but for Christ's sake, show your bloody feelings for once!'

Flinching, Michael looked at his friend. Then he reached out and touched Harry on the shoulder consolingly before walking away.

It happened when Michael was away. Harry had come back to the clinic at Aynhams at night, driving very slowly in the blackout, a dog crossing his path and making him brake sharply.

'Christ!' he snapped, then breathing in slowly, put the car back into gear and drove on.

He was tired, having been operating in the Manchester Infirmary, and he'd only recently returned from East Grinstead where the plastic surgeon Archibald MacIndoe was working. The two men did not like each other and, even though they respected each other's skill, there was no camaraderie and as soon as he could, Harry left for home. The bombing raids had intensified, Manchester badly hit, the homeless lodging in churches, air-raid shelters and cellars, coming out when the all clear blew. In places the streets were changed beyond recognition, great dark slabs of walls left seemingly unsupported, deep murky trenches of earth torn out by explosions. The landscape of Manchester and Salford was changing: landmarks gone for ever, the local church spire doubled over. It was a bleak omen.

Feeling their age, George and Tudge were called out at all hours, even helping with the digging to rescue trapped families. Only the previous week Harry had seen George reduced to uncharacteristic helplessness when a child they had been trying to rescue for hours was dug out with a broken back. He had delivered the boy only a few years before. It was, he said bleakly, the wrong generation who were being punished.

The mood of the North West altered. It seemed that no family was immune from tragedy; their men killed in action, and at home women and children murdered or mutilated in indiscriminate attacks. Food queues were a common sight, and the water hoses were surrounded by women with buckets collecting what they could. Morose and despairing, George railed against God, and Tudge wisely kept his mouth shut.

They were two tired old men facing impossible odds. Many times Harry had seen George fall asleep at the dinner table, too exhausted to eat. But who else was there? No one younger and fitter. And whilst George daily faced the carnage on the streets, Harry faced the casualties which flocked to Aynhams, the ambulances drawing up at all hours to the hospital entrance, men hurried in with their faces bandaged, or limbs dangling by a strip of flesh. In the face of this slaughter, Sylvia was mutely professional, Beth distant, while Mel watched silently from the sidelines.

Turning over the choke, Harry inched his car forward again and stared ahead at the dark road. Overhead he could hear planes, and the sirens were sounding, but there was nowhere close to take cover. He could imagine the scene at Aynhams, the injured helped under their beds, the lights doused, blinds over every window. There would be no music playing; only this same drone of the plane engines and the wail of the siren.

One of the worst cases had not only been burned, he

was suffering from shell shock, and when the first raids came he was catapulted into madness, his head banging on the pillow, his mouth a wide, screaming hole. Only one person could soothe him, and at the first sound of the siren Mel would help him under his bed and lie next to him, murmuring soothing noises until the all clear sounded.

From a way off Harry could hear a bomb exploding and, realizing that he had to get to cover quickly, he turned towards Salford. There was virtually no one on the streets, only an air-raid warden and several old men running towards a burning house. It seemed, Harry thought later, that he was drawn to Gladstone Row as though magnetized; driving along staring out of the window, the wheels of the car bumping over rubble and dislodged masonry. His sister had long since left Salford for the countryside, but for some undefinable reason Harry drove on towards Gladstone Row and his old home.

But he never made it that far. Instead, parking, he hurried out of his car as another bomb fell, the street reverberating underfoot. His aunt had died ten years before, and Harry had had no reason or desire to visit his roots – until now. Now something was compelling him. Another, nearer, crash made him duck, a bomb landing only a street away.

'Jesus!' he shouted, automatically dipping his head and running down St Stephen's Street. He knew there was a shelter at the end, but before he could reach it a further bomb landed and struck the next street. There was an unearthly silence after the hit, then a rush of air and noise which made him wince, the sky lighting up as the houses caught fire.

It was Gladstone Row.

Harry was running now, his feet slamming on the rubble, his eyes fixed on his old house as he rounded the corner. The dark squat terrace had suffered a direct hit, the two centre houses collapsed like a drunk between their upright neighbours.

'Get out of my way!' an air-raid warden shouted, hurrying past Harry. 'There are people in there.'

Harry followed blindly, and then began to dig with the other man, two other wardens joining them. His hands were soon bloodied, but Harry didn't stop to question what he was doing, he just dug, following the faint sounds of someone trapped under the rubble. He tried to imagine what it was like to be entombed and, inexplicably, saw vividly in a series of flashbacks the drab kitchen of his old house, the steep narrow stairs, the slop stone under the back window.

Sweat ran down his face, his nails torn and bloody as he dug, the light from a nearby fire making dark moving shadows out of the digging men.

'Stop!' one of the wardens said suddenly.

They stopped.

Listened.

Faintly they could hear a woman's voice.

'Right, get on with it. But be careful, she can't have much time left.'

Though unused to taking orders, Harry obeyed without question, looking to the warden for guidance, the woman's voice getting more faint as they lifted the rubble and finally levered a concrete slab off the trapped body. She was lying on her side, her eyes closed, blood coming from her nose. The nightclothes she had been wearing had been torn off by the explosion, her body exposed.

'Too late,' the eldest warden said quietly. 'Funny, I thought she'd make it.'

Staring at the body Harry reeled, the warden looking curiously at him.

'What's up?'

Numbly, he shook his head.

'What's the matter with you?'

But Harry couldn't speak, could only stare at his mother blindly. An image of her on Salford Approach came back to him; he could hear her voice and feel the shame he had felt then. In all the years which had followed she had never – by letter or phone – contacted her only son. But now she was dead and suddenly all the resentment and bitterness he had felt for her were past. Remorse left him limp as a glove.

'Are you all right, mate?'

Without replying, Harry continued to stare at her, then he took off his coat and laid it over his mother's body.

Frowning, the warden said quietly, 'Do you know this woman?'

Harry turned to look at him. The moment dovetailed, turned, threw up a thousand answers and then closed in on itself.

'No . . .' he said finally. '. . . I never knew her.'

Chapter Thirteen

Well, she had been warned, told to expect the prejudice, but Mel had not expected to be so opposed. Her ambition to be an academic pathologist was treated with scorn in some circles, in others by outright ridicule. Women doctors were tolerated, but there was a limit – a woman pathologist was an outrage. She was not inclined to play down her ambitions and was bull-headed, voraciously ambitious.

Intelligent and gifted, she had been accepted readily at Manchester University to read medicine, but her peers found her opinionated and at times, defensive. They were only too aware of her grandfather and father being doctors, and of the part Harry Chadwick had played in her upbringing – and they resented it. They thought, wrongly, that she was lording it over them; the heiress from Aynhams, with powerful friends.

As many had before, they misjudged her, and Mel – in this, as reserved emotionally as her father – did little to change their opinion. She had grown up seeing both sides of the medical world: the poverty of a slum practice, and the breathtaking progress of Harry's work; and had heard all the arguments about the new National Health Service. Medicine – of the best kind – should be available to all, her father had argued, there had been too many deaths due to ignorance and poverty.

Yet most doctors were bitterly opposed to the National Health Service – although the Government, knowing that the pre-war hospital system could never have coped with the casualties of the conflict had created the EMS, the Emergency Medical Service, in 1938. Medical treatment in

Britain was suddenly under scrutiny. As ever, the wealthy could afford the best of treatment, and the very poor could – if they chose – turn to the charitable institutions. But few, as George and Michael knew only too well, ever did.

Some attempts had been made to help people finance their medical fees. In 1911 funds had been set up for working people to contribute from their wages, but the unemployed and the non-employed dependants of workers were excluded from the scheme. They had to find the money to pay for treatment in full or endure a means test to decide if they were needy enough to get free treatment from the municipal medical services.

Finally it was Aneurin Bevan, Minister of Health, who set up the National Health Service and the face of medicine was changed for ever in 1948. As a result there was a new optimism in the hospitals and fresh treatments were challenging the previously held beliefs, so the standards of doctoring rose. For Mel, it was an exhilarating time to train as a doctor, but the new mood of hope went unnoticed by George who, weary from the overbearing trials of the long war, was more than ready to pass over most of his practice to Michael.

It was a Thursday when George collapsed. He had been out on a call in Greengate and returned to Aynhams to find Sylvia in the garden. In an unguarded moment she was smoking, her slender figure sternly white in her sister's uniform. She heard him approach and lifted her hand in greeting. George remembered how a coil of smoke rose from her cigarette into the cloying August air as the pain in his leg intensified. He winced. She stood watching him, puzzled. It seemed to take a long moment for him to fall, and yet in that infinitesimal second George remembered seeing Sylvia throw away her cigarette and begin running towards him. The grass – lush, smelling of earth – took his weight, and as he rolled onto his back he saw a kestrel passing across the countenance of the sky.

He wondered then if he were about to die, and foolishly
– he thought later – stretched his hand upwards towards
the passing bird. After that, he remembered nothing
else.

'He's not going to die,' Harry said later that night. 'Honestly, Michael, it won't kill him. Broken hips don't kill
anyone.'

'He's old, and it's not just a broken hip, he's got an
infection in his leg,' Michael replied evenly, ever the doctor.
'He never said anything to me about having damaged
his calf.' He turned to Harry. 'Did he mention it to
you?'

'No.'

'It looks like an old injury,' Michael went on, his tone
steady. 'God knows how long he's been walking around
on it. He should have had more sense. He should have
retired long ago, but no, he wouldn't hear of it. He'd be
bored, he said. He just *had* to go on.'

'How bad is it?'

'Bad.'

'But treatable?'

Michael considered. 'It should be, but my father's not a
young man and he's exhausted.' Suddenly walking towards
the window, Michael stared out into the garden. 'His age
is against him.'

'But he's tough –'

'He's tired.'

Harry frowned. 'What's that supposed to mean?'

But Michael wasn't saying anything else, and after
another moment excused himself. Harry could hear his
footsteps cross the hall and then there was silence as they
were muffled by the stair carpet. The house seemed very
quiet without George moving around; there were no banging doors, no shouts from the windows, only the far-off
sound of a phone ringing in the clinic.

He was torn then, wondering if he should go to the clinic, but felt compelled instead to climb the staircase up to George's room too.

George was lying in bed, irritable and uncomfortable, his one good eye staring upwards at the rosette of fabric over his head. It was as full blown as a late summer flower, holding up the canopy as it had always done. Groggy with pain George was still alert enough to see Harry come in.

'I broke my bloody hip,' he said by way of greeting.

'I know. Does it hurt?'

'What the hell do you think?'

Having never been ill before George was an irascible patient. Michael glanced over to Harry and raised his eyebrows.

'How long have you had the wound on your leg, Father?'

'A while.'

'It's bad.'

'It feels it,' George replied shortly, then studied his son's face. 'It will get better, won't it?'

There was a plea for reassurance in the words and Michael paused. How ironically things had turned out. Now it was he left in charge of his father's health, just as George had once been responsible for Abigail's.

'It's badly infected. We'll have to wait and see.'

'Wait and see what?' George asked, though his tone was less brusque.

'Wait and see how it heals,' Michael replied. 'I'll treat it but we'll have to give the treatment a chance to work. There's nothing more to be done at the moment.'

George stared at his son for a long silent moment, then he glanced away and stared up at the rosette over his head again.

Although the hip mended slowly, the wound in George's leg festered, and even after repeated treatments, gangrene set in. The only solution was amputation. Michael knew it and so did Harry.

On a late summer afternoon, the two doctors and Sylvia visited George in the still room overlooking the gardens. A recent shower had mottled the bushes outside, birds hurrying to roost, a branch of ivy brushing the window pane as a breeze started up.

'Amputation!' George shouted. 'Go to hell!'

'You know we have to do it,' Michael said evenly, Sylvia silent by the bed. 'It's your only chance.'

'I'm not letting anyone cut bits off me, I want to die whole.'

'If you don't let them amputate, you'll die a lot sooner than you expect.'

'I'm a bloody doctor!' George snapped. 'I *know* what to expect.'

'Michael's right,' Harry said, turning from the window, 'it has to be done.'

'And who asked you to put your two pennies' worth in?' George barked, his head jerking towards Harry. 'I suppose you'd like to be hopping around like a bloody cripple?' He paused, thinking back. 'D'you remember that night we amputated Walter Collins's leg?'

Harry nodded. The same memory had occurred to him.

'He hopped around for three years after that –'

'He *lived* for three years after that,' Michael cut in.

'As a cripple!' George shouted.

It was no good trying to reason with him. George might be in his eighties but he would never accept that he was old. He was not going to be a doddering old man, he told them, and he was damned if he'd end up in a wheelchair.

'Many men of your age are in wheelchairs,' Sylvia said softly.

'Many men of my age are bloody dead!' George hurled back at her. 'That doesn't make the condition desirable.'

Grunting, he moved in the bed again, his hand going to his leg, his teeth biting down hard on his bottom lip. He had seen most things, and witnessed plenty of suffering;

George Cochrane was not about to show himself up.

'I could give you something else for the pain –'

He shot Michael a warning look. 'I can cope with it.'

Turning to Harry, Michael motioned for him to leave the room, Sylvia following him without needing to be asked. When they were alone, Michael sat on the end of his father's bed.

'Watch my bloody leg!' George shouted, leaning back against the pillows and breathing heavily.

'Why are you so stubborn?'

'I want to do it my own way.'

'Do what? Die?'

George opened his one good eye. His face with its heavy jowls looked young for his years, his voice amused.

'You've got a God awful bedside manner, Michael.' But there was no malice in the remark and for an instant George looked at his son and felt an unexpected closeness.

He had, since the end of the war, gradually given over more and more of the practice to Michael, the ever-present Tudge, himself now ancient, working part time, his voice now reedy after a minor stroke. Always the realist, George had laughed about how the two of them looked together, a one-eyed burly doctor with his morbid sidekick. The image made him laugh, but he was secretly proud that he was still working long after most of his colleagues had either retired or died.

His patients needed him, George insisted at first, they knew him, they would talk to him; they knew he wouldn't bugger them about. But gradually the irregular hours wore him down, and a few times he had returned home late after calls and sat, breathing heavily, in a chair before getting up enough strength to heave himself to bed. He had a duty to his patients, he'd told Michael, he had a duty to serve and save.

'You have a duty to save yourself too,' his son had replied. 'You've done enough.'

Oh, but it was never enough, was it? George thought now, staring at his son as he sat on the edge of the bed. No amount of medical successes could ever compensate for the most tragic failure of his life – the death of Abigail. I tried my best for her, George thought to himself, I did everything I could. And yet you blamed me for her loss. You *still* blame me.

'Father, you know what we have to do,' Michael said quietly. 'We have to amputate.'

The old doctor's good eye fixed on his son. 'No.'

'We have to, or you'll die.'

George continued to stare at him and then finally glanced away. The bedroom had never changed; it was the same now as it had been when Abigail was alive. Only time had made any alteration, the sun fading the edges of the curtains and lifting the colour out of the rug by the window.

'Michael . . .'

'Yes, what is it?'

'I want the truth,' George said firmly. 'If they do amputate my leg it won't save me, will it? You and I both know that. The gangrene's spreading too fast, no one can stop it now. I don't want to die like that, Michael,' he said with perfect composure. 'I don't want Sylvia to change stinking filthy dressings, I don't want you to have to dope me more and more to stop the pain, and hack off bits of me until there's bugger all left.'

'Father –'

He put up his hands to prevent Michael from continuing. 'It would be a hideous death, and everyone – not least of all me – would suffer. It would drag on and on, the girls would see me waste away, and so would you. I would be useless, dependent, with no hope. If I were a horse, you'd put me out of my misery.'

Sighing, Michael said, 'You might do better than you think –'

'Don't lie to me!' George snapped. 'We're both doctors

and I don't need your horseshit.' He paused, dropped his voice, his breathing heavy. 'There's another way. Quick, clean.'

Michael stared at his father without speaking.

'You know what I mean. You can do it. Do it for me, Michael, please.'

'Do what?' he asked hoarsely, knowing exactly what his father meant and yet praying that he was mistaken.

'Finish me off.'

Silence. The clock in the hallway chimed the hour. Five o'clock, Michael counting the beats. One, two, three, four, five . . . Outside, he could hear the sound of activity from the other wing, an ambulance arriving with another patient. The clinic had not closed after the war, indeed it had expanded, the airmen needing numerous further operations, as did the civilians who had been burned in bombing raids. The hospital was going to be there for ever, Michael realized. Things change, people come and people go, houses alter, we live, we adapt. We die.

'I can't,' he told his father at last.

'You can,' George replied, reaching for his son's hand. But Michael hurriedly withdrew it and glanced away. 'Oh, come on, lad, get a grip. You're no coward –'

To the amazement of both, Michael laughed.

'Did I say something funny?'

'I was just wondering,' Michael replied, 'if you never get tired of goading me.'

A smile flickered between them.

'Well,' George said at last, 'you know how to stop it.'

Another minute passed in silence, the clock outside ticking by the moments.

'I can't do it,' Michael repeated finally, turning back to his father. 'I couldn't live with myself if I did.'

'I'm giving you permission –'

'I would still be killing you!'

'Jesus, Michael!' George bellowed. 'I want you to!'

'It would be immoral –'

'You don't believe in God.'

Incredulous, Michael shook his head. 'God has nothing to do with this. It would be impossible for me to commit such an act. You are my father . . .' the word moved between them, trailing unanticipated tenderness.

'But I would do it for you.'

'Yes, yes, you would,' Michael agreed, 'and I admire you for that. But I'm not you.'

'You can say that again.'

Once more, Michael smiled. The clock was still audible, ticking loudly, counting out their conversation against the passing of time.

'It would be a kindness to me,' George said at last. 'I know we haven't been close, and I know I have no right to ask you to do this for me – but, damn it, I *am* asking.' His legs moved fitfully under the sheet. 'I can't die in bits, Michael, not with all the smell and mess of it. It would minimize me, make me lose face in your eyes.'

'That's not the point. The act of killing would be mine. It would be murder –'

'It would be a merciful release,' George countered, then struggled to sit up against his pillows. 'I am so tired, Michael. I want to go, I want to be with your mother. Yes, your *mother* – the woman I failed. You worry about your conscience, well try living with that all your life. You try coping with that guilt, knowing that every hour of every day your son blames you for his mother's death.' Exhausted, he slumped back against the pillows, Michael silent. 'Does nothing reach you? Nothing ruffle your feathers? *Nothing?* I know you feel, I know you feel things deeply, but you don't ever show it. Why is that?' George asked, genuinely mystified. 'Why? I've tried so hard to get to know you, Michael, but you never let me in, did you?'

'It doesn't matter now –'

'Oh, yes it does,' George disagreed. 'It matters because

there is no real bond between us, because if there was you would help me now. You would do it for me, out of love.' He paused, embarrassed by the word. 'Out of *love* for me. But because you don't really care about me – I mean no more than any other patient – you can refuse to help me, as you would be justified in doing with any other patient.'

Michael's voice was low, controlled. 'I can't do it, whatever you say –'

'Then leave the stuff out for me and I'll do it myself!' George barked hoarsely. 'Don't make me beg you. Please, don't make me do that.'

'You're my father –'

'Yes, I'm your bloody father! I gave you life – and now I give you permission to take my life. Quid pro quo, Michael, quid pro quo.'

Defiantly, his hand reached out again towards his son, and this time, Michael took it.

Chapter Fourteen

It was, Sylvia would realize later, the excuse she needed to leave Michael. The morning after he and his son had talked, George worsened suddenly and despite every attempt to save him, he had died. It was very quick, Michael standing by his father's bedside and administering the dose he knew would kill him. Then he sat down and reached for George's hand, taking his pulse as he did so. The pulse was slow, strong, George watching his son's face.

'I'm not afraid.'

Silence.

'Michael, I said I wasn't afraid.'

'I am.'

George could feel his son's hand around his own and felt for an instant a closeness between them which was unbearably sad. This was how it could have been, he thought. Dear God, what we wasted, what we lost . . .

'Father?'

'I'm still here.'

Against his better judgement, Michael smiled.

'That's right, you smile,' George told him gently. 'It's all a bloody joke anyway.' His hand gripped his son's, his eyes closing. His pulse was slowing, his breathing laboured. A lonely, lingering minute passed before his father suddenly opened his eyes again and looked at his son.

'Thank you,' he said simply.

George Cochrane was dead.

Surprised by the speed of her father-in-law's death, Sylvia questioned her husband and was told that George had suffered an unexpected heart attack. Tudge, now well past his best, had agreed. It had seemed strange to her, but old men did die suddenly; they did have heart attacks; and they frequently lost the will to live. But George? Never. He might lose the will to live a full life, but he would never lose the will to fight – unless his will to die was stronger.

She knew that he had hated the progress of his illness, knew that he resented being anything other than the blustering medical man, looked up to and respected. He couldn't have borne to see himself fail, to witness in himself what he had seen so many times in his patients – the corruption of life which comes with a slow undignified death. But a heart attack so soon after being told the extent of his illness? It was too convenient, too perfectly neat.

Suspicion coiled inside her and as she watched her husband Sylvia became convinced that he had ended his father's life. Which was, to her, incredible. She didn't think Michael had had it in him, for one thing, and for another, having been brought up by a doctor father, married to a doctor and having lived for many years with George, she found it hard to condone the deliberate ending of another person's life. It was, in fact, one of the few things she had retained from her Indian childhood – a belief in the soul and a fear of meddling with God.

Besides, she missed the old man. He had, she felt, betrayed her by dying, and now that her own father was dead she felt orphaned, and worst, excluded. George hadn't asked *her* to help him, and it was obvious why: Sylvia would never have condoned it, would never have aided him to die; but she resented the fact that – after all she and the old man had shared together – he had, in the end, turned to his distant son.

Suddenly there seemed very little left for Sylvia at Aynhams and she was coldly restless. Her marriage had been staggering along since before the war, her children were grown, and now that old George was gone she looked ahead and saw only year after year of life with a reticent man. The thought winded her. So, ever opportunistic, Sylvia seized her chance and took the mercy killing of George as her way of killing off her marriage.

Glancing out of the window, she could see Michael pacing the garden, avoiding Harry and walking round and round the little white pavilion at the end of the lawn. Nearby she could see a patient in a wheelchair, wrapped up against the September breeze, and another sitting on a bench, but Michael seemed immune to them. He was immersed in his own thoughts, as ever.

At which point had it all gone wrong? she wondered. Did he guess that she never really loved him? Yet surely he must have known how much she respected and was grateful to him? But then again, maybe Michael didn't want gratitude ... She would, she realized finally, never know. It was, like so many other things close to her husband, off bounds to anyone. But maybe not to Mel ... Thinking of her elder daughter, Sylvia tried uselessly to fight a feeling of threat. Mel and she were reasonably close, she told herself, they talked, they even still dreamed of visiting India together; she had no real reason for her jealousy. But jealous she was, and sighing, she turned away from the window.

Everywhere seemed very cold, very empty suddenly. Nothing she touched felt hers any longer. The feeling had been slow to gain momentum, but gradually she had felt more comfortable in the clinic, keeping more to Harry's side of the house than the family quarters. She had found that walking the wards was more satisfying than tending to the house, and that even the gentle pressure of Beth could only tempt her back intermittently.

Unconsciously she found she had thrown in her lot with Harry, because he needed her and was forced to respect her skill. Without her, the clinic would never have been the success it was; Sylvia was the one who had done the accounts, hassled the workmen and taken the pressure off

Harry's shoulders. Without her, he would have been brow-beaten by bureaucracy, hounded by minutiae – all of which Sylvia had controlled seemingly effortlessly. And even Harry, chauvinistic and bigoted to the end, thanked her for it.

But they never became sexually involved. That would have been too easy. Not that Sylvia hadn't thought about it. When Michael first returned from the war with all his chill politeness in place she *had* toyed with the idea of having an affair with his friend. Would it make him jealous? Would it shake him out of his emotional lethargy? But in the end Sylvia decided against it – she neither wanted Harry nor the untidiness such sex would unleash. How could she work next to him in the theatre if they were lovers? How could she concentrate?

Because, Sylvia was finally realizing, her emphasis had shifted. Her first thought should have been for her husband and her children, but it wasn't – it was for the tension of long, concentrated hours at the operating table, the excitement of an operation which had gone well, the slow repair of mutilated faces and bodies, the inching back to humanity which she had watched for so long – and in which she had played a vital part.

She was *important* to the clinic, important to the patients, important to the men who cried out in the night and clung to her hand. She could write their letters home and comfort them when fiancées and wives abandoned them; she could listen without judgement to their anger and self-pity; she could treat them and clean them and never once feel disgust *because they needed her*.

As her family no longer did. Anger welled up in Sylvia with a terrible force; anger kept suppressed for years, since childhood, the old clammy feeling of rejection making her sweat. At first it had been her race which had excluded her and now it was her family.

She had no place here any more, she decided ruthlessly.

She had to get out; and now she had the excuse she needed.

'Sylvia?'

She spun round at the sound of her husband's voice.

She was, he realized, rigid with fury.

'You killed your father, didn't you?'

He wouldn't, couldn't, answer her.

'Well, *did* you?'

'He was very sick –'

'He was your father!' Sylvia snapped, walking over to Michael and pausing only a foot away. It was the closest they had been for months, sleeping as they did in separate beds, giving each other room as they moved about the house.

'He asked me to help him –'

'You had no right.'

Now it was Michael's turn to be angry. He had suffered bleak, dark, corrosive guilt since George had died, had hoped – pointlessly, it now seemed – to find some comfort in his wife. But there was none forthcoming. He felt in that instant emptied of any emotion – guilt, love or hope. There was nothing, only a freezing chill of aloneness which settled over him and made his heart sting.

'I did what I thought was right –'

She leaned forwards, her face close to his. He remembered how he had loved her once and wanted to put his hand over her mouth, to soothe her, to stop the words coming which would finish them for ever.

'Sylvia, listen to me.'

But she was beyond reason. To her he appeared rigid, uncertain, and she misread his confusion as dismissal. The one thing she feared above all was happening again – she was being rejected.

'How could you kill your own father? It's beyond belief. I can't understand you, I never could.'

The emphasis had shifted, the argument no longer about George, but about their marriage.

'I've told you, I did what I thought was best –'

'Oh, you always do that, don't you, Michael?'

The bitterness shook him. 'What's *that* supposed to mean?'

Exasperated, she threw her hands up in the air. 'I can't talk to you. I never really could.' Blindly she glanced round, frustration making her reckless. 'I can't stay here any more.'

The admission came not as a shock to her, but as a profound and soothing relief.

'I have to go away.' Brusquely she moved away from him, keeping a yard of space between them. It might just as well have been a continent.

'Be reasonable. You can't go away, Sylvia. Your home is here.'

'This is *not* my home!' she replied shortly, her anger coming sweet; revenge, honey on her tongue. This was the way to punish him. This was the way to make him feel something. 'Aynhams is *your* home, I was only ever a lodger here.'

'That isn't true, and you know it,' Michael replied wearily.

But in truth he was past fighting and he suddenly wanted her to go, her dark luminous beauty turned off, temptation for ever out of his reach. For once he was about to lose control, as angry as she was; enraged that she had taken his name and home and never once given herself in return. If he could, Michael thought, remember one recent incident of affection, one loving look they had exchanged, one instant of moist, fulfilling passion – then he would have forgiven her. But there had been no warmth for years.

'If you want to go, I won't stop you.'

The chill of his words made Sylvia rock for an instant on her feet, her mother's voice coming back to her: *I worry about Sylvia. Who will have her? Who will marry her . . . ?* She was going to be thrown out, dismissed, to fend for herself. But hadn't that been what she wanted, to leave?

Wasn't that why she had goaded her husband so far? And yet now, suddenly, she was terrified.

But she wouldn't show it.

'What about the girls?' she asked, her voice husky, her mouth dry.

Jesus, Michael thought, what are we doing? But the words had taken on their own momentum and now even the unthinkable was being discussed.

'They stay with me.'

'They are my children –'

'They are *our* children,' Michael corrected her. 'If you stay here you can have them with you. If you go, they stay with me.'

She had pushed him too far and knew it. She had taken his reticence as weakness and had never understood that when he was finally provoked into action, Michael would be intractable. A moment passed, Sylvia trying to control her thoughts. Maybe she should retreat, even try to laugh it off. Married couples argued all the time, didn't they? And then they made up? Oh, but *they* couldn't retreat to a warm bed and forget. They couldn't even touch hands.

'Well?' Michael prompted her.

Immediately Sylvia's head went up, pride making her stubborn, pride forcing her out of the house and away from her children. I can start again, she told herself defiantly. I can do anything I want. I've done the impossible before and I will again . . .

'I'll go tomorrow.'

I'll go tomorrow.

Nodding, Michael turned away, then turned back. For an instant they looked at each other as both remembered the past, then hesitantly Michael reached out for his wife. But the fury that George had seen all too clearly in his daughter-in-law made Sylvia brush her husband away – and in that one moment she lost her status, her family, and her home.

PART TWO

In real life, I never chanced to see
The woman who was loved, and did not know it,
And observation proves this fact to me:
No man can love a woman and not show it.

E. W. Wilcox, 1850–1919

Chapter Fifteen

It amazed Mel that her sister could take the news so calmly. She herself had been so angry, so bewildered – how could her mother leave? How could she up and go without even saying goodbye? It was unbelievable, they were her children. Her daughters.

'Do you realize what's happened?'

Beth looked over to her sister. Was she as placid as she seemed?

'Mother's gone.'

'She's left for good,' Mel replied shortly. 'She's not coming back.'

Understanding filtered across Beth's oval face, but no tears came. She had followed her mother around persistently, had been her shadow; she had chatted to Sylvia about everything she did – school, friends, everything. Often Mel would hear them talking together in the evenings, or she would watch them return from trips into Manchester, Beth giddy with some treat or other, Sylvia luminously proud of her pretty daughter.

So how could she be so calm now, now that their mother had gone? Mel wondered, jumping at the sound of the front door closing. And what would they do now? What would her father do? The answer was obvious. She was in her twenties; she would look after her sister and father. She had finished her initial medical training and was to continue at medical school, to specialize in pathology, so Beth would have to be more capable.

It was odd but the thought of looking after her sister and father pleased Mel. With her mother gone she would have Michael to herself; she could talk to him about the practice, the clinic next door, make up for the war years when he'd been away.

'Mother might come back,' Beth said suddenly.

'No, she won't,' Mel replied, unexpectedly cruel.

She had loved her mother well enough, but there had never been a real closeness. Beth had always been the favourite.

'She *might* come back,' her sister repeated, twenty, stunning, her hair drawn back into a ponytail. 'I miss her.'

'I know,' Mel said sympathetically, 'but we have to look after ourselves now.'

'And Dad.'

'Yes,' Mel agreed, 'and Dad.'

It was past midnight when Mel finally got out of bed and turned on the light. She couldn't sleep, and realized to her surprise that she longed for her mother. Quietly she moved out into the hallway and made her way to Sylvia's bedroom. Her parents had slept apart for several years, so her father would never even hear her from down the corridor. Without making a sound, she turned the door handle and entered.

Sylvia's bed was made. She had been tidy and efficient to the last. It reminded Mel of one of the beds in the clinic, remade after someone had died. Slowly she walked over to the closet and pulled open the door, an inside light flicking on to illuminate her mother's few remaining clothes, empty hangers swinging from the rail beside them, the shelf above stripped bare.

You never said goodbye, Mel thought incredulously, her hands pulling open a drawer and lingering for a moment on one of her mother's belts. Then suddenly she remembered something and moved back to the wardrobe, searching for her mother's nursing uniform. It had gone.

Hurriedly Mel searched through the remainder of her mother's cupboards and then, exasperated, pulled everything in them onto the floor. The photographs of her and Beth as children were still there, as were the children's odd shoes, the baby ribbons, the teething ring Beth had been given by George. In amongst the pile she found her own school reports and a Christmas card she had made from paper, cotton wool providing a beard for Santa Claus. Beth's christening gown was there too.

Sylvia had taken nothing of her children with her.

For a long time Mel sat looking at the mementoes of their childhood. Their mother had gone without saying goodbye. She hadn't even taken a keepsake. She had just left – and left her children behind her.

Enraged, Mel got to her feet and then idiotically began to kick at the heap on the floor, the baby clothes, notes and photographs scattering around the room, the ribbons ground underfoot. It was an act of madness, she would admit later, but unbearable hurt motivated her. Gathering together her mother's bedding and the few remaining clothes Mel walked through Aynhams and then pushed open the connecting door to the clinic. The place was in semi-darkness, nightlights showing dimly beneath the doors as she made her way down into the cellars and weaved between the sacks of refuse waiting to be burned.

The vast black incinerator was hot, the heat scalding her face as Mel opened the door and stared in. Coals, white and red, boiled with savagery, the smoke coming thick from the chimney as she loaded her mother's things into the fire and cried as she watched them burn.

There had been many people who had prophesied that when the war ended the clinic at Aynhams would gradually drop into disuse. After all, there would be no more burned airmen on whom Harry Chadwick could accomplish miracles. But they were wrong; wars may come, and wars may go, but burns, crashes and mutilations continued endlessly – as did the cosmetic surgery. So the makeshift clinic which had grown up to serve the war wounded thrived, its reputation becoming world known, a medical lighthouse tucked into the élite pocket of Buile Hill.

'What a bloody mess,' Harry said simply, sitting down in his operating clothes and putting his feet on the kitchen table. Opposite him, Michael was eating a piece of toast. 'I see it's not affected your appetite any.'

'I have work to do,' Michael replied calmly. 'I have patients who need me. I can't afford to brood.'

'You want that bit?' Harry asked, taking a slice of Michael's toast and chewing it greedily. 'Heard anything from her?'

'Who?'

'Who d'you bloody think? Sylvia.'

'No. What about you?'

'Nothing,' Harry said, marmalade sticking to his upper lip. 'She left the records all tidy, though –'

'Oh good, I'm really pleased for you.'

Harry winced. 'I meant –'

'She left the bed made too. I suppose that's a point in her favour as well.'

'Oh shit,' Harry mumbled, changing the subject. 'I suppose you heard about the *auto-da-fé* last night?'

Frowning, Michael looked up. 'The what?'

'The ritual burning – oh, you hadn't heard.'

'What happened?'

'Apparently the boiler man saw your elder daughter cram some things into the incinerator last night, and when he went to investigate it seems that she had torched Sylvia's clothes.' Harry paused. 'Sorry, I thought you would have known.'

'No, I feel sure it would have stuck in my memory if I had,' Michael replied grimly, wiping his mouth and standing up. 'I was wondering, do you think I should get a housekeeper in?'

'Not unless you want to end up in the incinerator yourself.'

'What's that supposed to mean?'

'That Mel wouldn't take too kindly to a stranger,' Harry explained. 'If I were you, I'd let her take over the reins here. She can do it, no problem – and it might work off some of that excess energy of hers.'

'You're not too fond of Mel, are you?'

Harry smiled. 'You're wrong, I have great admiration for her, she's one on her own. But people like Mel make waves and they can get into trouble. They have no fear and that frightens other people. Your daughter could go one of two ways – she'll either self-destruct or she'll amaze us all.'

Absorbed with his own thoughts, Michael parked George's old car and sat staring out of the window. The street was virtually empty, rain hustling people indoors, a corner shop closed, its gaslamp hanging broken from the wall outside. Here, there was small evidence of rebuilding, and some places – where the bombs had fallen – were laid waste, mounds of dirty rubble where the kids played, an old church – its roof fallen in – used as a flop house for tramps. A little way further off, a UCP tripe shop had opened, and a few doors down the main street a tobacconist's shop sported a wooden Indian on its doorstep, the legend 'CAP-STAN FULL STRENGTH' hanging round its neck.

Turning into Jubilee Place, Michael grimaced at the irony of the name. Here the houses were amongst the poorest in Salford, notorious for their violent fights, an influx of immigrants after the war giving the tenants an excuse for spasmodic viciousness. And yet Michael, like his father before him, never considered that he might be injured himself. Instead he walked ahead purposefully, without hesitation, nodding to an old patient who was sitting outside on his doorstep.

'Bloody foul weather, innit?'

'Better indoors and that's a fact, Mr Loomis.'

The rain had temporarily ceased. A couple of lads were hanging about the corner with a mongrel dog.

'How's yer wife?'

Had they heard about Sylvia's departure, Michael wondered, or was it a general enquiry?

'Gone, Mr Loomis.'

The old man stared up at him, rubbing his finger along his bare gums, his eyes quick with interest.

'Gone where?'

'I don't know. She left me,' Michael said simply, peculiarly relieved to admit such devastating news, to have it out in the open. His privacy, usually so jealously guarded, was suddenly up for grabs. He felt reckless, unlike himself.

'Sorry to 'ear that, Doctor,' Mr Loomis said genuinely, shifting over on the doorstep to make room. ''Ere, sit with me for a bit.'

Surprised, Michael found himself putting down his bag and taking the makeshift seat. The house behind them was quiet: Mr Loomis's wife had died long ago and there was only the gloomy sound of a cat mewling in the darkness.

'What 'bout yer girls?'

'With me,' Michael replied, taking out a packet of cigarettes and offering the old man one.

He took it gratefully and lit up, inhaling the good tobacco.

'Been a sod of a year for yer, in't it? What with yer father dying and now this.' The old man paused, coughed, then pointed across the empty street. 'The Barnets flitted last night. Up and went without a word. No one even 'eard 'em. Best to bugger off before the bailiffs turn you out.'

Michael stared across to the emptied house, the front door slightly open although the daylight made little impression on the darkness behind.

'People have their troubles.'

'They do, Doctor,' Mr Loomis agreed. 'We all do, no matter who we are.'

It was his way of consoling him, Michael realized grate-fully, his way of saying that life goes on.

'Shame it weren't that sow-faced bugger Tudge who left,' Mr Loomis continued, inhaling again. 'For all his bloody religion God doesn't seem keen to tek 'im on.'

Smiling, Michael turned to the old man. 'Dr Tudge does his best.'

''E's not liked though. Never were – not like yer old man. Now 'e were a good doctor. Rough like, not one to mince 'is words, but you could rely on 'im. I were right sorry to 'ear 'e'd died.'

Silently, Michael turned away. The rain had begun again, but tentatively, hardly reaching the two men on the door-step. At the end of the street the lads dispersed. A woman in a headscarf came past with a bag of washing. Michael nodded in recognition, but the woman moved on quickly without acknowledging him.

The previous summer there had been a heatwave in late September, the streets rancid, dogs fighting, the unwelcome heat and crowded conditions making sleep impossible. Her husband had been laid off from work and had brooded for days around the house, his temper and frustration growing in strength as the heat built up.

It had been a Saturday when the woman returned from the market, her husband waiting for her. She had – the neighbours said – tried to ignore him and carry on with her housework, but around six, when the sun was still sweating down, he had picked up the iron she was using and pressed it against her cheek, holding it there long enough for the skin to pucker and blister as she screamed.

'Will you stay 'ere?'

Michael looked at the old man in surprise. 'Of course, why would I leave?'

'I just wondered like, what with your wife gone off. I thought mebbe you'd go after 'er.'

'No,' Michael said, rising to his feet. 'I won't ever go after her.'

'What 'bout that big shot up at yer place?' Mr Loomis said, changing the subject. 'That red-'eaded swank.'

'Harry, Harry Chadwick.'

'That's 'im,' Mr Loomis agreed. 'Made a right name for 'imself, 'e has. Saw a picture of 'im in the paper with some blonde – looked like the cock of the walk, 'e did. Strutting 'is stuff. Right clever, what 'e does – I'll give 'im that – but 'e's an 'ead on 'im big as a brick outhouse.'

Everyone knew Harry, Michael thought, suddenly seeing his friend through the eyes of outsiders – a flashy, cocky upstart – and for an instant he wondered how his daughters viewed him.

'Rumour is that 'e's got a place big as a palace on t'coast,' Mr Loomis went on, eager to know the details.

'I believe he has a place, yes,' Michael said cautiously, and then realized, with surprise, that he had never been invited there.

Oh, it was true that Harry spent little time away from Aynhams, living in a couple of rooms he had apportioned for himself next to the clinic, but when he did go away, where did he stay? He had mentioned some flat in the centre of Manchester and a house on the coast between Southport and Lytham St Annes, but he had never described them, or shown off photographs. He had kept that part of his life secret, and until then Michael had never thought of it.

'Seems odd . . .'

'What does?' Michael asked, looking curiously at the old man.

'You and 'im living in Aynhams with yer girls and no missus now.'

The words struck home with all the force of a hammer blow and, turning his collar up against the sudden rain, Michael hurried on, deep in thought.

Chapter Sixteen

'I don't want to,' Beth said quietly, pushing her long dark hair back from her face. 'You do it.'

Angrily snatching the vegetables from her sister's hands, Mel began to chop them on the board. She was late in from a lecture, a pile of work to be done this evening, now lying malignant and untouched on the kitchen table. Studying and keeping house were not as easy as it had first seemed and Beth was little help. She had been undecided about a career, toying with several ideas, but not fixing seriously on anything for long.

'You should do more around the house,' Mel said impatiently. 'I can't do everything.'

'But you like looking after us,' Beth replied sweetly. 'You know you do.'

This transparent ploy did not fool Mel. She knew that her sister was kind and good-tempered – but she also realized that Beth could be superficial and at times reluctant to feel deeply. Perhaps she had inherited that trait from their mother, Mel thought – not from their father certainly. Beth made all the right noises and assumed all the appropriate expressions, but there was this little wilderness of spirit inside her sister which only Mel saw and wondered about.

It was incredible, but since Sylvia had left, Beth had seldom mentioned her; there was no anger, no sense of rejection, just acceptance. Still being cared for by someone seemed to be all that truly mattered to her; the caring, not the carer. Mel might rage about her mother's behaviour and still ache with loss a year later, but Beth's tranquillity was intact.

Again, Mel looked over to the pile of books on the table, then turned back to the vegetables. She could hear the sound of an ambulance as it pulled into the back of Aynhams and longed to escape to the clinic – but instead she was making dinner. As she always did. No good leaving it for Beth, she couldn't – or was it wouldn't? – do it, and their father had to be looked after.

When I'm fully qualified, Mel told herself, I'll get away from here and make my name. She thought of Harry's jibes and then remembered her father's constant support – *You can do it, Mel. You know that. Use your brains and your courage and the rest will follow.*

But would it? Mel eyed the books again, then suddenly walked out of the kitchen and pushed open the connecting door which led down a corridor to the clinic. There, she moved past the main ward and on towards the operating theatre, standing in the anteroom and looking through a circular viewing hole in the door.

Harry had only just returned from a lecture tour in India, his face still slightly reddened from the hot sun, his hair luminously fiery where it poked out of the surgical cap. The operation was one he had talked about the previous night to Michael, an airman undergoing his fifth attempt to have his eyelids repaired with grafts.

Stuart Hunter was the airman's name, Mel remembered, and he was only two years older than she was . . . Steadily she watched Harry's hands working around the patient's eyes, the respirator breathing in, out, in, out, as the anaesthetist, John Wilde, caught sight of her and winked. Smiling, Mel waved to him and then turned and leaned her back against the door.

She loved every morsel of the clinic; loved it with such a passion that each movement, each noise, was etched in her memory and replayed over and over in her head. It was only to be expected – she had been brought up in a medical family – but this was more, Mel realized. She had

a *longing* for the profession. She wanted only one thing –
to qualify as a pathologist. She would accept nothing less,
and nothing, *nothing*, would stop her.

Unless she stopped herself . . . Wearily Mel thought of
the books on the kitchen table and the meal waiting to be
made and remembered the argument she had had earlier.
If only she had kept her temper, if only. There had been
three doctors, all talking about her mother and repeating
an old piece of gossip – that Sylvia Cochrane had run
away because her love affair with Harry Chadwick hadn't
worked out.

It was rubbish – Mel knew that – and yet it hadn't
stopped her from lashing out. This was not the first
occasion she had been in this situation, only this time she
had overstepped the mark and made herself enemies –
something, with her background, her gender and her hot
temper, she didn't need.

The operating theatre door opened beside her, making
her jump. Harry gave her an amused look.

'What's happened now?'

'Why should anything have happened?' Mel countered
briskly.

'Because you look sick,' he said, moving past her.

In silence she followed him to the restroom and watched
as he pulled off his operating gown. Underneath he wore
sporting trousers and a dark shirt.

'You look like a gangster,' Mel said, leaning against the
door.

'What d'you know about gangsters?'

'I watch the films.'

He pulled a mock impressed expression. 'Wow! . . . So,
what *is* the matter?'

'Nothing.'

'Oh yes there is. You always hang around like a fly
around a dung heap when something's up. So tell me.'

'I'm fed up.'

'Any particular reason?'

'I don't fit in at the Infirmary –'

'Oh, come on, Mel –'

'– and I'm running behind with my studies because I don't have the time to work, because I'm looking after the house and everyone in it.'

Harry paused, tie in one hand, and shoes in the other.

'I thought you were doing well.'

'I was – until lately. Suddenly I'm slipping behind.'

'Then apply yourself.'

'*Apply myself?* That's what I'm trying to do.'

'So do it.'

'In case you haven't noticed, I have other calls on my time,' Mel said coldly. 'I don't see you with an iron in your hand.'

He was patently baffled. 'What's that supposed to mean?'

'It means that I have to do all the donkey work here, and I don't see anyone else helping.'

Harry winced.

'You should try it for a while,' Mel continued furiously. 'You should try doing your own work *and* doing all the cooking, cleaning and washing –'

'Then don't do it.'

'Oh really?' she countered. 'And then who'll do it? The tooth fairy?'

Hurriedly Harry tied his tie. 'So ask your father to get a housekeeper in.'

'We don't need a housekeeper – and no one wants to be in service these days anyway,' Mel countered. 'We just need everyone to pull together. You never wash up.'

'What!' Harry was aghast.

'You eat the food I make when you're here and then you walk off and let me clear up after you.'

'Don't nag.'

'I'm not nagging!' Mel snapped. 'But it's not fair, no one expects a man to do anything.'

'I'm busy –'

'I'm busy too, just in case you haven't noticed.'

Ill at ease, Harry tied up the laces on his shoes.

'Talk to your father.'

'I don't want to worry him.'

'So why worry me?'

'You can take it,' Mel said simply. 'He won't understand, Harry; this is the one thing my father *won't* understand.'

He agreed with her. Since Sylvia had left Michael had been a tolerant and affectionate single parent. He had spoiled Beth and encouraged Mel, although at times he had sought refuge in the clinic when his daughters had discussed some personal matter. It made Harry smile. Michael was a doctor, used to hearing about all types of female disorders – but whereas that was acceptable with strangers, it was strictly off limits with his daughters.

Boyfriends had the same effect. It was Harry who heard about Mel's first crush, and Harry who gave her advice about how to treat men: *badly*. They competed for the girls' affections constantly, but whereas Beth was won over by the last one she spoke to, Mel, always strong-minded, was liable to side with whoever put forward the best argument.

And usually it was Michael who won, because Mel loved her father so much. Enviously Harry thought of the way the two of them walked around the garden, or when they came in talking animatedly about some case Michael had taken his daughter out on. Her intelligence was potent, exceptional, and since her mother's departure she had eagerly accompanied her father on some of his evening calls. As blunt as George Cochrane had been, Mel was, however, also clever enough to know when to keep quiet and could learn with a complete and impressive absorption.

She should be sailing through her exams, Harry thought,

suddenly impatient. It was ridiculous that she was worried about running the house when she should be concentrating on her training at the Infirmary.

'Talk to your father,' he said again.

'I can't, Harry. He wouldn't know what to do. Besides, it would look as though I couldn't cope and I don't want him to think that.'

'So talk to your sister.'

'That would be a fat lot of good!' Mel replied, looking straight at Harry. 'Why don't you talk to her?'

Silently Harry studied the young woman in front of him. She could be difficult, that was true, and temperamental; but she was also smart and quick-witted and funny when she chose. More than that, Mel was, although few others recognized it, considerably kinder than her sister. Now twenty-one, Beth had matured into a powerful beauty, very like the exotic Sylvia – and she had also her mother's steely streak, a resilience of nature which was not entirely admirable.

Her dislike of the clinic had mellowed. She now visited the wards quite regularly – although Harry wondered if that was due to a new interest in medicine, or men. Certainly she enchanted the patients, talking to them and listening patiently, but always avoiding unpleasantness as a woman in an evening dress would avoid a dirt track. She had told Harry only the previous week that she had finally decided that she would become a nurse. Not a doctor, Harry noticed, a *nurse*.

Why? To stay close to what she knew without forcing herself out into the chilly world of the GP or the surgeon? Or because she could, in this way, emulate her absent mother and, indirectly, slide into the vacant place left by Sylvia? If she did train as a nurse Beth would always find work at the clinic in Aynhams; she would never have to go far, and before long which young casualty might wish to stay with her, not as a patient, but as a husband?

Harry sighed, still looking at Mel but thinking about her sister. Michael loved Beth, but he had never really encouraged her; he knew instinctively that her ambition was limited and that the thing she most wished to secure was safety. And safety, to Beth, meant Aynhams. It also meant money.

Surprisingly, Harry couldn't decide whether he admired Beth's love of the house, or not. Certainly she had been encouraged in her appreciation by her mother: *This is your home. You must always remember that*. But had she also indirectly inherited Sylvia's sombre insecurity? Or was she simply avaricious?

Mel stirred, interrupting his thoughts.

'Well, *will* you talk to Beth?'

'I don't think –'

'If you don't I'm sorry but I'm not going to look after you any more,' Mel replied shortly. 'If the situations were reversed, you wouldn't do it.'

Harry was outraged. 'That's not the point!'

'Oh, but it is!' Mel snapped back. 'A man wouldn't dream of being a dogsbody. If I were a boy no one would expect me to run the house as well as study.'

Harry's tone was heated. 'But you're not a boy –'

'No! More's the pity,' Mel responded bitterly, lapsing into silence.

Miffed, Harry pulled on his jacket. He hated to be involved in family arguments – they blotted the rosy picture he had of domestic life, and yet he could, grudgingly, see Mel's point of view. Sylvia had been gone for over a year; during which time her eldest daughter had looked after her family, and, fully qualified, begun specializing in pathology.

Difficult as it was for him, Harry tried to imagine himself in the same position and then felt guilty remembering how often he had come over from the clinic and found a sandwich ready made for him. Little things suddenly rankled on his conscience: the bath he forgot to clean out, the shirt he begged to have ironed at the last moment . . .

'I'll talk to your sister . . .'

Mel glanced at him.

'. . . I'm not saying it'll do any good . . .'

Mel shot him a warning glance.

'. . . but I *will* do it.'

It seemed for a moment that she might thank him, but when no gratitude was forthcoming Harry found himself struggling for words. Damn, he thought, Mel Cochrane was the only woman on earth who could make him feel uncomfortable.

'I should have seen how hard it was for you, Mel,' he said awkwardly. 'We all should have done.'

She nodded, pushing back her hair from her face.

'It's time Beth had a taste of domestic life.' Her expression was steely. 'Oh, and another thing, Harry, when I do finally escape the housework, I'm *never* going back to it.'

'You will when you marry –'

'Oh no,' she replied firmly, 'I love my father and I'll do it to help him out, but I won't do it for any other man.'

He smiled wryly. 'Wait till you fall in love. You'll see things differently then.'

'You mean I'll want the kitchen stove and clematis round the door?' She smiled back at him. 'I don't think so, Harry. I don't think I'm cut out for the role of housewife – even part time. You see, I want the life you've got. I want the freedom, the success, the independence.'

'It has a price of its own,' Harry said softly.

'Maybe it does,' Mel replied. 'But I won't let any man on earth stop me from getting it.'

Chapter Seventeen

Beth had landed what she wanted – her father's medical partner, Daniel Ellis. Theirs had been a perfectly organized romance, as obvious as day following night. They would meet, they would fall in love, they would marry – it was inevitable.

For a while after George's death, Michael had used locums – then Daniel Ellis had applied for the position of junior partner. A young man, newly qualified, with an easy manner and ability to work hard, Daniel was soon accepted both at the surgery and Aynhams. Since 1948 Michael's surgery had been established in Greengate, just off St Stephen's Street, well within the densest populated area of Salford, still a deprived area in need of rebuilding from the bombing. Michael took morning surgery every day and went on his rounds every afternoon. Emergencies only came through to Aynhams in the evening, when he would turn out in his Austin car and head down from Buile Hill to the Salford streets. Uncomplicated and friendly, Daniel was the perfect foil to Michael's reserved nature and the two men worked effortlessly together.

But there was something missing. No banging doors, no hectoring, no blast of energy which had once been so much a part of the practice. Daniel Ellis was no George Cochrane – but then, who could be?

'In six months those two will be engaged.'

Harry ducked out from under the bonnet of his car and glanced at Mel, frowning.

'Which two?'

'My sister and Daniel.'

'Horseshit.'

Smiling, Mel leaned against the car wing.

'I bet you a fiver.'

He pulled a face. 'Jesus, you must be sure.'

'It would be perfect,' Mel went on. 'Daniel's attractive, the right age, the right profession, and he would be able to share the practice with Dad as equal partners in time. Besides, he's pleasant.'

Wiping his hands on a rag, Harry stared at her. 'If he's so bloody wonderful, why don't you make a play for him?'

'Not my type. Far too uncomplicated.'

As Mel had predicted, six months later Beth announced her engagement to Daniel. They would marry soon, she told her sister over the phone. 'And I want you to be my maid of honour.'

'Oh God, it's not going to be a big do, is it?'

'Not really,' Beth replied lightly, 'about fifty people, and a reception to follow at Aynhams. I'll wear white, of course.'

And look beautiful, of course.

'Do you love him?'

'Of course I do!' Beth replied, laughing. Uncomplicated, easy – *could* anything or anybody be that easy?

It was the summer of a love affair and a marriage, and it was stiflingly hot; hardly the weather for either. All about the peripheries of Aynhams the walls were overhung with trees and drooping, wildly scented bushes, beneath which moss and ivy grew in moist and secret layers. The white pavilion in the garden was crowned with jasmine and cool inside, smelling darkly of perfume, a woman standing motionless at the entrance.

In her hand were her car keys, her wedding hat taken off, her hair hanging moist on the back of her neck.

'That was stupid,' Mel said, turning to the man behind,

unseen in the gloom of the pavilion. 'But romantic,' she added, staring out towards the house.

The wedding party had returned from the church some time ago and now the afternoon was drawing to a close, the heat-sweet shadows making furry outlines around the house, the guests inside talking and drinking, others wandering onto the terrace which surrounded the house, fanning their hands uselessly in front of their faces. Everything was drowsy with heat, music soft, the notes sodden, voluptuous, the empty discarded glasses outside drawing late insects.

Smiling at the touch to her shoulder Mel rested her head against the man's hand. They had made love quickly and tenderly at the back of the pavilion; hurriedly, urgently, because before long Cy would have to leave again, return to Africa, to the Ivory Coast. His skin, dark enough to betray his Moorish ancestors, was even darker in the half-light, his fingers resting tenderly against the dark hollow of Mel's neck.

I'd like to bring someone home for you to meet, she had told her father before Beth's wedding, *someone special to me*. He had felt a mixture of fear and pleasure in her words. Over the years Michael had never asked his elder daughter about her love life, had been too discreet to intrude. Beth had introduced one timid boyfriend, but Mel had never brought anyone home before. He took it as an omen; was this man different? Special enough to warrant his approval?

He's coloured, Dad, she had added simply, turning to look at her father. *African.* What had he thought at that moment? Mel wondered. Whatever it was, he hadn't shown by a look or a word that he might disapprove. *A doctor . . . Good*, was all he said, *we could do with another doctor in the family.* She never told him that Cy was married, that he was separated from his wife, but that she had refused to divorce him. She told him the positive things instead. About Cy's work, his ability, his kindness.

Nuzzling her cheek against Cy's hand, Mel closed her eyes. Her study of pathology at Manchester Infirmary was nearing an end, and she was hoping to be taken on permanently in the department; but her ambition was still greeted in many places by ridicule. Women weren't cut out to be pathologists, the Principal of the Manchester Infirmary had told her when she'd first applied to the Pathology Department; it wasn't a female discipline. And her tutor, Dr Bolting, had, of course, agreed . . .

'Is there anything to say that I can't train in pathology?' Mel had countered.

'No, nothing . . .'

'Then that's settled,' she had declared. 'That's what I intend to do.'

How easy it sounded, Mel thought, when you thought of it like that. So uncomplicated, so tidy. But that wasn't the truth, it had been a stern progress, and at times, bitter. More bitter than anyone knew. Indeed at one point during the first year of her training she had suddenly succumbed to a depression which was at once terrifying and unexpected. Every word or look she took as a criticism; every action she made she believed spied upon. The truth was that she was tired, and prone to that deep purple depression from which her grandfather had suffered after the death of his wife. But Mel, too proud to admit her fears, struggled on, sleeping little, overworking, constantly proving herself and battling.

One particular event always stuck in her mind from that time. The doctors had been working late on a dissection and she had stayed on after everyone else had gone home. The body she was working on was that of a man in his sixties and on the table beside her was another body covered in a sheet. She had wanted to test her ambition, to find out if pathology was really the discipline she wanted to follow, and had taken the opportunity to consider what it would be like working in such surroundings full time.

Time slunk past heavily, the mortuary cold in winter, the windows blanked by night, the fluorescent lighting overhead bleak and chilling. It made the flesh of the corpse look blue, darkly purple underneath where the blood had settled after death. Mel studied the incision down the chest wall and through the abdomen, then glanced at the organs which had been taken out and weighed. On the opposite wall the clock read eight thirty and from outside in the alleyway she could hear nurses calling good night.

Immersed in the dissection of the man's heart Mel was suddenly uneasy, thinking she heard a sound behind her. Turning she saw nothing, but found herself breathing more rapidly and repeatedly glancing to the door. Then, just as she was about to weigh the heart she heard another movement and turned to see the sheet rising on the body laid out on the next examination table.

It had been a joke, of course, played on her by one of her male colleagues, but instead of laughing Mel found herself breathless and clammy with shock, driving back to Aynhams that night and sitting for a long time alone on the terrace. The bigotry her father had warned her about was costing her more than she realized. It had materialized almost immediately and never lessened, embodied in the dour figure of Dr Lance Bolting looming over her from the start.

He was a sour elderly man who had worked throughout the war in Manchester, identifying, amongst the usual mortalities, the myriad bomb victims – mostly women and children. He had found such work so harrowing that he had become hardened to the daily tally of premature deaths. He was taciturn, brusque – and against women in the medical profession, let alone women in pathology.

He had expounded his views frequently, often within Mel's hearing.

'How could a woman behave against nature?' he'd

asked. 'It's not natural for a female to work in amongst death.'

It did Mel no good that she was amongst the more proficient junior doctors of her year, in fact it counted against her as Bolting had little to criticize. Daily he watched her for mistakes with a greedy eye, longing to vindicate his bigotry. And daily Mel struggled with her own feelings of anxiety.

'Cut deeper,' he would insist. 'After all, they can't feel it any more.'

But although Mel knew that, she was aware from the first that this body was someone's mother, father, or child. This corpse had once breathed, eaten, laughed, loved. It had *been*, it had lived. So how could she reduce it by a lack of compassion? How could she carve it and dissect it without remembering always that the mortuary was the last place it would rest before the grave?

It had little to do with religion, but a great deal to do with compassion. After she had made a stand about the housework, Mel had decided it would be better for her to live away from Aynhams, although she visited home regularly after taking on a flat in the city. She liked the distance, the apartness from her family, it helped her to study, she said. But there was more to it than that, she no longer felt that she had a place at Aynhams. Not in the house or in the clinic. And that had added to her feeling of isolation.

Time and distance had altered the status between the two sisters. Training as a nurse, Beth had done what everyone expected her to do, and was due, after she qualified, to begin work in Harry's clinic. She was to be a ward nurse, not a theatre nurse – her ambition never extending her abilities.

But what *were* those? Mel wondered. Was she as limited as she liked to make out, pretending that it was a miracle if she qualified, asking her father and Harry for advice with even the most trivial of matters? Or was she simply staking her claim, being dependent and needy for them?

But if so, where had she got it from? The answer was simple: their mother – from whom they had heard nothing save the second-hand news that she was working as a theatre sister in London at the Fulham General. And yet Sylvia had never been dependent, far from it. So why was Beth so clinging? Perhaps, Mel thought, it was subconscious; if she was childlike, she would not be abandoned again. No one would reject her if she stayed at home, amongst those she knew, and those she could count on to protect her.

And as Beth became more dependent, Mel became more independent. After the departure of her mother she had decided that there was no one on whom she could completely rely. Oh, she knew that her father would never let her down, but there was that need inside her which insisted that she make her own way. If she looked after herself, she could always rely on herself.

So now Mel travelled between Manchester Infirmary and Aynhams, watching the changes from a distance – the death of old Tudge, the introduction of Daniel Ellis as her father's new partner, and the love which developed between her sister and Daniel. As for Harry, he didn't change much, his reputation just became more powerful, his operating techniques copied round the globe. He travelled extensively and lectured, putting on weight and the type of *gravitas* that he thought a middle-aged mentor should assume.

'You look tired,' he said to Mel, one weekend as she visited home not long after the incident in the mortuary.

'I've been working hard,' she replied, but her tone was unlike her and alerted him.

'Things tough?'

'What d'you think?' she responded, suddenly sitting down and closing her eyes. He had an overwhelming impression of sadness, something unexpected in her.

'Can I help?'

She opened her eyes and stared ahead; he could sense that she was fighting tears.

'I feel so alone.'

He knew the sensation and knew what it cost her to admit it.

'You chose a difficult profession. You knew it'd be hard, Mel. You're fair game, and as a woman you have to be twice as good and twice as tough as the men.'

'I don't know if I am,' she replied quietly.

'Good enough or tough enough?'

'Tough enough,' she answered, turning to him. 'I don't sleep so well any more. Things get on my nerves.'

'You need something to take your mind off your work,' Harry said flatly. 'Find a man.'

There was a long pause.

'Oh . . .' Harry said simply. 'Is this part of the problem?'

Still Mel said nothing.

'Trouble with the heart?'

'Is that anything to do with you?'

'No.'

She laughed suddenly. 'Why don't *you* get married, Harry?'

'No woman would want me full time.'

'No woman could *stand* you full time,' she replied, looking back to the house. 'You *should* marry, have lots of little geniuses.'

He relaxed suddenly. This was more like the Mel he knew, the two of them exchanging the banter he enjoyed so much.

'I can't see myself as a daddy, can you?'

'I can't see myself as a mummy,' she replied. 'I can't even see myself as a wife.'

'You've always said that, but you'll change. One day you'll be a qualified pathologist in the mortuary, filleting someone, and there he'll be – the man who'll make your heart beat faster.'

'Just as long as it's not the one on the slab,' Mel answered, smiling and staring ahead.

'So who is he?'

'A doctor.'

'That's a change.'

Mel smiled.

'Where does he come from?'

'The Ivory Coast.'

'Oh, so he's not a redhead then?'

Laughing, Mel stood up, linked arms with Harry and began walking across the lawn.

'Is he handsome?'

'Very – not that he could touch you, Harry.'

'Who could?' he replied, pursuing the topic. 'Your age?'

'A bit older. Well, quite a bit older.'

'Ambitious?'

'Very.'

'Talented?'

Mel turned suddenly. 'What is this, twenty questions?'

'I'm interested, that's all.'

'You're nosy, you mean.'

Harry was intrigued. The Ivory Coast ... well, if Mel was going to pick anyone it wouldn't be a GP from the suburbs and that was for sure. But someone coloured? That was asking for trouble; wasn't her life difficult enough without the scandal of this love affair if it became public? Her career might be ruined before it had a chance to begin.

He could imagine the gossip; the way such information would work against her. Her male colleagues would talk about her, and as for her superiors – Harry winced – how would the note 'Had affair with coloured doctor' look on her Personnel file? Perhaps Mel's upbringing had been too unconventional for her own good, he thought suddenly, wanting to speak out, to warn her. Of what, he couldn't quite say, but he wanted to put some kind of protection around her. Others might think she was tough, a real hard piece, but Harry knew otherwise. Mel Cochrane was hard only because she was afraid to show weakness.

Next to him, Mel was silent, the faint drift of her perfume coming on a half-hearted breeze. Pathology was too dark a science for most men, let alone women, and the mortuary at the Manchester Infirmary was a bleak place. Harry knew it and avoided it, the murky clank of the double doors closing at the entrance, the same constant chill, the white tiled walls and sterile examination tables. It could make his flesh creep even to hear the sound of the fridge drawers being opened, a tagged foot appearing from under the edge of the sheet.

Once he had had one of his patients undergo post mortem by Dr Bolting, and had watched the pathologist in his greens dissect the cold tissue, working briskly and efficiently in the high-walled echoing space. But what was the point? Harry had wondered then and still wondered now. The patients were dead; life was over. No pathologist could make them better, improve them, fight to restore them. The skill was a dead end.

Mel was the first to speak again.

'I suppose you think I'm mad falling in love with Cy? I suppose you think it will all end in tears?'

He smiled, squeezed her arm.

'Probably, what doesn't?'

'God,' Mel replied laughing, 'an optimist to the last!'

But as she said it Harry could feel her relax, the overhang of her unease lifting. He was glad of it; glad to see her recover herself, even if the reason was partially selfish. Harry needed Mel to remain unchanged; needed her to be unimpressed by him, even dismissive at times. After a career which encouraged adulation, he relied on her forthrightness, her candour – which he got from no one else.

Admittedly Michael was never in awe of him, far from it, but he was never truly at ease with Harry, and as for Beth, she always treated him like a god. A friendly one, but a god all the same. But when it came to Mel Harry knew that she looked on him not as a father, not as an elder brother, nor as a friend. More as a competitor. She liked him with caution; but respected him totally. Not that she would ever admit it: she would merely quote him, or listen to what his opinion was on this matter or other, and shelve away his cleverness for future reference.

And yet in general medicine it was Michael who was the more gifted. He might be reticent, almost aloof, but he felt another's anguish as his own – and that was something Harry never did. Michael Cochrane was kind naturally, because kindness became him.

Sighing, Mel's thoughts came back to the present and she glanced over to Cy, listening to the sounds of the wedding party coming sweet and distant over the garden. She *was* afraid that the news would come out that she was seeing a coloured, married doctor, but in the end the only person's opinion she really valued was her father's.

She could remember pipping her car horn as she drove up the drive, Michael turning, her hands clutching the wheel as he saw Cy sitting beside her. He had been waiting for her and listening for the sound of her car and when he saw her he stepped forward, never betraying in his expression or his voice the shock that Cy's appearance must have been to him.

As for herself, Mel was becoming used to the quick intake of breath, the stares, as the two of them went out together. There was a stigma attached to coloured people, the popular belief being that they should *stick to their own kind, and not touch our girls*. As they walked down the streets, people pointed, and in shops salesgirls were frequently rude. They made her feel angry, defensive, although Mel's first thought was always for Cy, not herself.

She didn't need any more bigotry, but Mel was never cowardly or short of courage. After all, it wasn't as though her romance had been planned, as though she had intended to outrage everyone. Oh yes, Mel was well aware that her outspokenness and ability had made her enemies, and – even as a student – she would stand up to anyone and hold her corner. Such defiance never went unnoticed; some predicted a bright future, others prophesied something darker for a woman who was too sure of herself. But Mel wasn't overconfident, she was simply determined never to show her weaknesses again, and, like her mother before her, she could be awesomely tough.

It was at a medical conference that Mel met Cy Tolash. She had been listening to a lecture of his and was impressed. Some of her colleagues had also attended the lecture but it was only Mel who plucked up enough courage to approach him afterwards. They got on immediately, Cy patient with the new doctor, Mel, as ever, eager to learn. Well, an hour passed and then another, and the conversation was too good to bring to a close, so they went for a coffee . . .

And then, much later, they went for a walk, and then the following morning Cy phoned her at her flat and said that he was returning to the Ivory Coast, but that he would like to see her again when he returned to London. Without a moment's hesitation, Mel had agreed, knowing full well that she was once more embarking on a very rough road.

But what was the choice? The few other men she had gone out with had been amusing or attentive, but a frisson, a spark, had eluded her. She had even begun to doubt that she would ever experience it – and then, unexpectedly and suddenly, she could feel her pulse quicken and her voice lighten when she spoke to Cy, her smile a little too ready, her body movements a little too sensual. And that was it. Hell, she thought to herself, this is *it*. This is finally *it*.

Well, it would be, wouldn't it? she thought immediately afterwards. I would want a man who lived abroad, a man who was totally dissimilar from those I meet in

Manchester, a man who was tall and striking and *black* ... But hadn't her mother, that distant and imposing figure, been half Indian? Hadn't her parents been of mixed race? Yes, Mel thought to herself, and hadn't their relationship been a disaster? But was that due to their backgrounds, or something else?

She would never know the answer to that question, because her father, for all her probing, would never tell her why Sylvia had left. It had been obvious for a long time that the marriage was failing – even as a child Mel had felt that unsteady insecurity which heralds a break. The silences, the avoided eye contact, the short replies – all had added up to present a barren failure of communication. Her mother had loved them separately from their father; their father had loved them separately from their mother – they were divided from the first to the last.

But what act of malice or violence had prompted the final end to the marriage? Mel wondered now, her gaze travelling over Aynhams and lingering for an instant on her mother's bedroom window. What had finished it off? *Who* had finished it off?

'What are you thinking about?' Cy asked, his lips pressing briefly against her neck.

'My mother.'

His own parents were ill-educated, ambitious for this handsome, gifted son. They had worked hard to send him to school and university and he had rewarded them by becoming exactly what they had hoped for. Cy was, to them, the living outcome of a dream.

'Do you think of her much?'

'Every day,' Mel said honestly. 'At first I expected a letter, at least a present at Christmas – not for the gift, but because it would have been an excuse for her to get in touch. But there's been nothing.' She continued to stare at the window on the upper floor. 'She used to tell me about India, promised we would go there together someday.

When I think of her I think of someone beautiful in a nurse's uniform pushing open the dividing door between the family side of the house and the clinic. She wore white at work; white uniform; white cap . . .' her voice trailed off. 'I found out where she was working last year.'

Cy slid his arm around her shoulder, listening.

'At the Fulham General in London. I nearly asked a colleague to look her up for me, but then I decided against it.' She breathed in deeply. 'It was when Beth got engaged to Daniel. I thought that was something she should know.'

Not that Beth seemed at all concerned about whether her mother knew or not; she was happy with her lot and apparently more than willing to let Mel be the shining light.

'Everyone always knew you'd go far,' she said one weekend when Mel had come home to Aynhams.

'Why?' Mel replied.

Beth's long, oblique eyes – so like their mother's – flickered for an instant. She didn't like to be pushed, Mel realized.

'Why did everyone always think I would go far?' she repeated stubbornly.

'Because you were smart,' Beth replied, turning away and busying herself with some food.

Her figure was slight, weighing no more than a hundred and ten pounds, her dark hair waving around her shoulders. It was easy to see why Daniel would find her lovely, easy to see how she could soothe him and offer no challenge. But had nothing of Sylvia's strength and passion passed into Beth's genes? Mel wondered.

Apparently not, and yet at times there was a look, a certain coolness about the eyes which only Mel saw. It was ephemeral, and obvious to no one else, but to her it was a potent reminder that this sister – this happy, uncomplicated sister – had the potential to be cruel.

Shaking her head at the thought, Mel turned and laid

her hand against Cy's cheek. The light was fading kindly in the pavilion, the smell of the overhanging jasmine drowsy and erotic in its seductive pull. Suddenly another thought entered her mind – with a breaking sense of hopelessness – that she would *never* marry Cy. His wife would stand between them always, and if Mel stayed with him year after year would follow and she would never be able to say the words her sister had said that afternoon, or exchange the vows, or take her husband's hand. Because that was some other woman's privilege.

'I love you,' she said helplessly, and he, in return, stroked her forehead and leaned his head against hers, without speaking, knowing too the enormity of their loss.

Chapter Eighteen

After the war much of Manchester Infirmary had been rebuilt, the knot of corridors renovated, others tacked on to the main body of the hospital, several modern new theatres replacing the old ones. Above ground, the Out Patients Department sported glass doors and a wide open modernized area, contrasting starkly with the sombreness of the panelled entrance hall. Uniforms, updated and shortened, gave the nurses an approachable look. Yet although innovations of the new National Health charges had caused splits in the Government, Wilson and Bevan resigning, in the hospitals the mood was optimistic and untroubled.

All over England the first labour-saving devices were beginning to emerge, although there were still shortages. The war had changed everyone and everything, from the clothes people were wearing to the films being made. Now there were no more war films, instead there was a run of light-hearted stories and musicals causing queues round blocks across England.

But not everything had changed. There was still one place, reached only by a web of corridors, a place cool and still, a place unchanged for over a hundred and fifty years: the mortuary of the Manchester Infirmary. If you take the route from reception there are forty steps down. At the bottom you reach a tiled passageway and have to walk for several yards until you can turn again. There you can either move to your right – which leads to several narrow offices – or to your left – which leads to the mortuary itself.

There is a coldness here which the electric fire in the main office does little to penetrate, and the fluorescent light overhead is always turned on, even on the brightest of days. For many years Dr Lance Bolting had sat here; a thin, acerbic figure, morose after the early death of his wife. He had taught many students and had bitterly opposed the teaching of pathology to women, but time and progress had overruled him and now Dr Bolting was about to retire.

His petty spites would go with him, together with his antique clock; he might, if he had a mind to it, think of his bigotry and bile as the minutes ticked past. But Mel doubted it, standing in front of the desk and watching him on the evening he was due to leave the hospital for ever.

She had waited for this day for a long time and as she looked at the old man she could remember all too clearly what he had put her through.

'Well, what *is* this muscle called?' he had asked her sharply once, his instrument holding up the leg muscle, the gaggle of students – all male apart from Mel – watching in trepidation. 'Come on, come on, Dr Cochrane, even a *woman* can remember the basics, surely?'

Even a woman.

There had been many other times, other indignities; like the occasion that Mel had walked into the hospital canteen and, seeing her colleagues seated with Bolting, had moved over to join them. As she sat down, Bolting had paused extravagantly and looked over to her.

'That place is taken, young lady.'

'By whom?'

His eyes had hardened, but she had stood her ground.

'Why can't I sit here?'

'Because I,' Bolting had said maliciously, 'only eat with the brightest students.'

He had terrorized her; unsettled her, at times even frightened her. She, who was used to being accepted by the most brilliant men, like Harry Chadwick. Oh Harry might joke about women doctors, but he had encouraged her in his own way and as for her father – he had always made her believe in herself. He had made her believe that she could achieve *anything*.

So when she came up against Lance Bolting, Mel found herself undermined, her certainty shaken. Within weeks of his tutelage, she was making stupid mistakes, and the more her colleagues laughed at her, and pitied her, the more clumsy she became. Having begun to train in pathology as one of the brightest medical students of her year, Mel rapidly found herself trailing behind, the constant barrage of verbal intimidation wearing her down. Answers to simple questions eluded her, Latin names for diseases were wiped from her mind under Bolting's malicious and sadistic gaze.

'You have to fight back,' Harry said flatly.

'It's not that easy, and you know it,' Michael had replied, pouring all three of them a drink and returning to his seat in the study at Aynhams. 'A bullying teacher can ruin a student's career.' His voice was steady, thoughtful, as he turned back to his daughter. 'You could report it to the Principal –'

'No. Bolting would get to hear about it, and that would make things worse,' Mel said wearily.

'Then you could go and have a talk with him yourself,' Harry suggested, stretching his legs out in front of the fire.

'I tried that – he said he hadn't the time for chitchat.'

'I told you at the outset that it would be hard,' Michael said, staring at his daughter.

She looked tired, her movements weary. Not with studying – Mel was never tired with mental work – but she was emotionally exhausted, and, Michael realized with surprise, close to tears.

'There is another way to escape Bolting. You could always apply to another hospital.'

'And let him win?' she snapped, Harry exchanging a quick smile with her father.

'Or you could poison the old bastard. After all, you're

in the right place to hide the body,' Michael added, laughing, and then reaching for Mel's hand. 'I know how hard it is for you. But you've got to remember *why* Bolting does it – because you threaten him. You've just been appointed to the permanent staff, in time he knows you'll make it to the top job, Head of Pathology – and where will he be then? Long since retired.' Michael paused, to let the words take effect. 'Bolting's one of the old school, who believe that women should stay out of medicine altogether, and then you came along, the brilliant young doctor, the one who everyone knows will get right to the top . . .'

Mel was holding on to her father's hand tightly, like a child.

'. . . Bolting can't take that, because he knows that his little kingdom will belong to you one day. A woman. He looks at you and knows that you're capable of sitting in *his* chair, and having *his* power. He looks at you and sees his nemesis.'

Mesmerized, Harry had watched Michael talk to his daughter, and felt the extraordinary bond between them: Michael's words – spoken without emotion – restoring his child's confidence with every syllable uttered. It was then that Harry realized the true power of family; the bond between parent and child; the blood energy which defies logic and inspires miracles.

'Bolting wants you to fail,' Michael went on, 'to be beaten – and you will be, Mel. If you let this man win, you'll let him take away your destiny. If you let him defeat you, you'll lose your self-respect and your rightful place in life . . .'

She had glanced down, then nodded once.

'. . . It's tough, because only a few *can* survive what you have to go through, Mel. It's tough – but it's not impossible.'

It's tough – but it's not impossible.

No, it wasn't, Mel thought as she watched Bolting sitting at his desk for the last time. They had held a party for him, with some food and drink laid out on one of the dissecting tables – mortuary humour at its best – and the old man had shuffled about, moist-eyed, thanking everyone and glancing about him like a prisoner about to be led to his execution.

Which, in a way, he was. Only Bolting's execution didn't consist of a gun shot, or a length of rope, his was the slow counting down of time in his cramped flat – from which the hospital was always tantalizingly within sight. He would live his remaining years alone, watching the familiar building and longing for it as an alcoholic longs for a drink. He would see other doctors enter the place which he had entered for decades and would ache as he thought of other hands touching *his* desk and *his* equipment. He would feel useless, excluded, beaten – which was his perfect punishment.

'I suppose I should congratulate you,' Bolting said, his voice querulous as he glanced briefly at Mel. 'Although I never thought you'd actually make it to the permanent staff. I just hope you don't dishonour the hospital,' he added, rising to his feet and picking up his medical case.

Was he tipsy, Mel wondered. Or just shaky with emotion? For an instant he seemed about to fall and grasped the side of the desk for support, Mel automatically extending her hand and then withdrawing it. This had been the man who had refused to let her sit one of the pathology papers because she had been two minutes late. Two minutes late – due to a trapped lift – *two minutes late . . .* and he had disqualified her, making Mel sit the examination again – six months later. Making her fall behind her peers; belittling her.

She had said nothing, but that had been the point at which steel entered her backbone, and she had sworn that however long it took, one day she would have Bolting's job. His chair, his office, his status.

And now that she was on the permanent staff at the Infirmary, it would all come to pass.

'If anyone needs me . . .' Bolting began, suddenly vulnerable as he looked to Mel for pity.

With another person she would have faltered, but not this man. He had almost broken her, and she was not about to forget.

'Then we'll get in touch, Dr Bolting,' she replied, opening the door for him and standing back to let him pass for the last time.

He moved forward gingerly, as if afraid to fall, then paused for an instant at the threshold. Mel would wonder for years afterwards why she did it, but without thinking she patted the old man gently once on the shoulder and then moved away.

From the kitchen window Beth could see her husband prune the apple tree and watched as he took off his jacket and carefully folded it before placing it over a nearby branch. Everything was just as she expected it to be: Daniel was kind and she was happy being Mrs Ellis. So happy, in fact, that she only nursed part time in the clinic and looked after the house instead.

She had insisted on some changes – after all, it was a while since anything had been altered at Aynhams. Michael, eager that his daughter and her husband have a part of the house to call their own, gave them the top floor, except for Mel's old room, limiting his own rooms and study to the ground floor. He teased them that they would soon need the extra room for children, and never once considered that he might marry again.

'Sylvia and I aren't even divorced. I couldn't marry, even if I wanted to. Which I don't,' he told Harry when he brought the subject up one evening.

'Well, I still say you should get out more.'

'I like it here,' Michael answered, looking into the fire and thinking of one of his patients.

He was very glad of Daniel, of his kindness, his affability.

He was an attractive young man, but without passion, Michael thought, without sexuality of any kind. A brotherly man – probably even if you were married to him. People could talk to Daniel, especially people in the practice.

It was strange, but since Beth's marriage, Michael had begun to think about his father again, even missing him. Sometimes, when he was alone and it was late, he thought about George's death, about the pulse fading under his fingertips, that slow slide away from life. Sometimes he dreamed of his father and of the old days, walking with him down the Salford alleys and ginnels which no longer existed. It had been a lamp-lit world, cruel and short-lived for many, and the doctors had had little then with which to fight disease. But it had all seemed so *worthwhile*.

Michael stirred. His father was dead, Beth was married, and Mel was away for most of the time – only Harry was left. Harry Chadwick, of all people.

'What the hell are you smiling at?'

Glancing over to Harry, Michael shook his head. 'I was just thinking, here we are sitting round the fire like a couple of old maids.' He laughed, rubbing his chin with his left hand. 'Oh God, Harry, if your public could see you now. Some lady-killer you turned out to be.'

Slumping further into his chair, Harry grunted, then undid the buttons on his tight waistcoat and unfastened his shirt cuffs. Bloody fashion, he thought, waisted jackets fit to cut off the blood to your balls. Nonchalantly, he then slid off his polished brogues and let his features relax . . . God, he loved it here, it was the only safe place on earth. No cameras, no operations, no press, no women. Just a big fire in a battered old grate, the wind snoring outside the windows.

Dozing, he closed his eyes. If he had never come to Aynhams, what would have happened to him? A breakdown, Harry answered himself, he would have had a nervous breakdown, ended up a drunk, or with some avaricious tart.

His mouth fell open, a snore beginning. Aynhams, red-bricked, tall on a hill, warm inside; Aynhams, with his clinic next door and his flat above; Aynhams, where he didn't have to be amusing or pressurized.

He had what he wanted: a home and family which he could borrow when he needed to. Love without responsibility; a home without ties; a place to which he could return always, a place to hide. No one, Harry thought distantly, could ever penetrate Aynhams, no man, no woman, could ever reach into this house and pluck him away. Like a child he could play outside and run home when it was dark.

No other home had ever interested him. No hearth offered by a besotted girlfriend, no children which would have been so eagerly borne. Even his other properties meant little; the impressive showcase near Lytham and the bachelor pad in Manchester were only watering holes, stop-offs, without any tugs to his heart. Harry was interested only in his work, his patients, and in the triumphant achievement which was Harry Chadwick. When he had finished dazzling in foreign countries, or after giving lectures, he could turn his car for Aynhams and know – with blissful certainty – that he would never permit *anyone* to intrude on these few sacred acres.

So, whilst his patients slumbered on the other side of the dividing wall, and Michael stared thoughtfully into the fireside beside him, Harry Chadwick slipped into sleep as soundlessly and easily as a child.

Chapter Nineteen

Years come, and years go, some make little impression, others seem magical. Some are malignant. After Mel achieved a permanent position at the Manchester Infirmary, Cy came to England and told her – without preamble – that he wanted children. Only he wanted children with his name, borne by his wife.

That was March. In May, Daniel had a fall, nothing dramatic, just a minor tumble off the terrace at Aynhams. By October, he was diagnosed as suffering from an incurable wasting disease.

The bad years were coming in fast.

Mel was watching her sister curiously.

'How are you coping?'

'I manage,' Beth replied, busying herself in the kitchen, a saucepan of vegetables bubbling on the stove. 'Daniel isn't that bad yet; he can still get about.'

She said it calmly, as though she was talking about something irrelevant. Her husband was seriously ill, the safe cocoon of her life was being threatened. No more would she be protected and cosseted, now it was Beth's turn to care – for how long, no one knew. Daniel might deteriorate rapidly, or he might continue in reasonable health for a while. Certainly he had made it clear that he intended to practise for as long as he was able.

The people in Pendleton admired Beth for what she was doing; indeed, everyone did. They talked about how brave she was and smiled at her on the street. Even in the worst areas of Greengate Michael was repeatedly asked for news of how Daniel was faring. It wasn't right, people said, it was a lousy thing to happen to a lovely young couple like that.

Glancing into the room beyond, Mel could see her brother-in-law in an easy chair and stared at the back of his head. Daniel was watching television and laughing, one hand resting on the arm of the chair. The disease had made no mark on his body yet, his face unlined. He looked young for his age, his fair hair curly, his eyes clear – but for how long, Mel wondered. How long before the disease aged him, made an old man out of him?

Over Daniel's head she could see a photograph of her father and wondered if his son-in-law's illness was the real reason behind his sudden withdrawal. Reticent Michael had always been, but now he was closed off, even to Mel. Certainly exhaustion was playing its part. The practice – which had seemed to be in such safe hands with Daniel before the illness had struck – was now producing a gruelling workload.

'Dad not home yet?'

'No. I never know what time he's coming in any more,' Beth replied idly, stirring the pot of vegetables.

It was late, Daniel couldn't sleep, so she was cooking him something. Vegetables were supposed to be good for him, Beth told her sister as she prepared them, vegetables and vitamins and all manner of other diets and remedies she had read about.

That had surprised Mel. She had expected – perhaps unfairly – that her sister would fold at the news of Daniel's illness, or that she would turn to their father for support, but she didn't. Instead, Beth investigated the disease and made all kinds of enquiries and set about purposefully trying to find a way to help her husband. Was she fooling herself, Mel wondered, or did she really think she could delay the inevitable? And with *what*? Vegetables?

'Have you still heard nothing from Cy?'

The name bubbled between them.

'Nothing,' Mel replied at last. 'I don't suppose I will now. It's over.'

'Poor thing,' Beth said simply, smiling over her shoulder. 'You'll meet someone else.'

She was being kind, but somehow her very kindness irritated Mel, although she was ashamed to admit it. After all, Beth was suffering too, finding out about pain herself now: Mel might have suffered the loss of her lover, but her sister was going to watch the steady slipping away of her husband. Her loss would not be savage or quick; it would be bitter and prolonged, stretched out, with plenty of time to grieve as Daniel changed and died, piece by piece.

Suddenly Mel wished that their positions were reversed; that Cy was ill and dependent on her. In such a way she could have kept him. She could have looked after him, held on to him . . . Angrily, she dismissed the thought. Outside she could hear one of her father's dogs barking and walked over to the kitchen window, pulling back the blind. The moon was hung low over the gardens, barely leapfrogging the high trees.

'What time is it?'

Beth glanced at her watch. 'Midnight.'

'Midnight . . .' Mel repeated, staring at the clouds moving across the blank white face. 'The man in the moon's smiling.'

Frowning, Beth glanced over to her sister: 'What?'

'Don't you remember? *Midnight's smiling. Tomorrow will be a lucky day.*' Sighing, Mel let the blind drop back over the window. 'Somehow I doubt it.'

'I don't,' Beth replied simply, her tone light. 'I think that tomorrow might be very lucky indeed. I'm pregnant, Mel. I'm having a baby. Daniel and I are having a baby.'

Chapter Twenty

Five years later, and Salford was changing, if only super-
ficially.

A pall hung over the city, the town dull under a sheeting
of rain cloud. On St Stephen's Street the old medical appli-
ance shop had gone, a bookie's in its place, and where the
bombed ruins of Gladstone Row had stewed was now a
library. The terraced streets were disappearing fast, modern
flats being put up in their places, the old cobbled ginnels
concreted over, cars and vans parked bumper to bumper.
But it was still a depressed place, still prone to crime, to
violence, to a viciousness which seemed bred into some of
the very people who populated it.

It had been a Monday when the news first broke; it
was whispered, repeated, then the afternoon report came
through, billboarded on the newsstands. 'SALFORD
CHILD MURDERS – SUSPECTS HELD.' Coming
out of the surgery, Michael bought a paper, taking it back
indoors to read. After a few moments he could hear the
first patients arriving for the evening surgery.

'. . . I know 'er mother. I don't believe it. You can't, can
you? I mean, she seemed right normal.'

'She married that bloke down Featherstone Row. You
know, his father had the pub over at Broughton.'

'I can't believe it,' the woman repeated again, 'not of
someone I know. Gives you the creeps . . .'

Michael turned back to the paper. The bodies of four
children had been found in various makeshift graves
around Salford, three suspects arrested and charged with
their murders. One of the streets where a body was found

was Harris Alley, a narrow cutting between houses, most of which had been boarded up and deserted since the war. The place had become notorious for drunks and tramps sleeping rough, but not for murder. Not for child murder.

Reading on, Michael suddenly came across a name he knew personally, and stared blindly at the page. He had treated the child for chickenpox years earlier; the boy's parents had split up and he was living with his aunt, running wild. In fact, Michael remembered, the child was like Harry would have been. Only in Harry's day it was safe on the streets; this child had been murdered.

Michael felt suddenly queasy. In amongst the streets he had walked for years – the streets George Cochrane had walked before him – there had been a man and two women who had killed children. He might, without realizing it, have stood next to them in a shop, or crossed them on the street. He might have touched the same door handle or been caught in the same shower of rain. They had been moving around the Salford streets in amongst normal people, acting and looking like them, undetected, unknown – and yet somehow Michael wasn't surprised. He had felt long ago that Salford was a bleak place; he had once said that God had no place there, and he had been right.

Putting down the newspaper Michael stared out of the window. The block of shops opposite looked squat and depressed, the Belisha beacon a leering orb of yellow in the oppressive gloom. Salford, so often despised and ignored, would suddenly be known by everyone. England and the world would talk about it, would learn its layout, would know the names of its narrow, interlocking streets. Newspapers and television would throw up every unphotogenic corner and every taciturn citizen.

And, in the middle of it all, would be his daughter.

'. . . so I said, if you want to do it, get the hell on with it. What is that? A bloody scalpel! I didn't ask for a scalpel, girl. Wake up! . . . Then the old man said that he might reconsider . . .' Harry glanced at the scrub nurse. 'Are you with us or not today?'

'Sorry, sir.'

He raised his eyes over his surgical mask impatiently and then continued, the patient anaesthetized on the operating table in front of him. He was doing one of his normal procedures, and was working on autopilot, his thoughts elsewhere as he talked. At the head of the table John Wilde, the anaesthetist, listened, amused, laughing at the appropriate places, one eye always on the respirator gauge.

Harry never changed. Just got a little more bluster, a little more fame, a little more extravagant in his gestures. He was a good teacher, a mite acid at times, but thorough and popular with his students. Dipping down suddenly, Harry stared at the patient's face and declared himself satisfied. Then John motioned to the door of the operating theatre where Mel stood watching.

'Well, well, well,' Harry began, 'it would seem that we have a very illustrious visitor today.' Happily he waved and then concluded his stitching of the wound, Mel smiling as he finally walked out into the antechamber.

''Lo there. You look good,' he said admiringly.

She pecked him lightly on the cheek. 'I heard about the gong. Well done, *sir*.'

'Did you hear about the murders?'

'Who hasn't heard?'

'It would be Salford, of all places,' Harry replied, walking into the restroom and taking off his operating gown.

A few months earlier he had decided that he wanted to be fit and had taken up golf, then squash, then swimming. None of which suited him. In the end, he had convinced himself that a little extra weight made a man look prosperous . . . Wincing, Harry pulled on his tight suit jacket.

'Is your tailor blind, or what?' Mel asked, folding her arms and leaning against the door.

'You could do with a few pounds *on*,' he retorted, pointing at her. 'I've seen better legs on a chicken.'

'Enough compliments, Harry, I wanted to talk to you.'

''Bout what?'

'The murders.'

He glanced at her and then took her arm, steering her out into the garden. The white pavilion was still there, Mel turning away hurriedly from the old memory it never failed to provoke: Cy Tolash, now the father of two sons . . .

'What's up?'

'I've been asked to work as the pathologist on them. It's my first really big case, one that will grab the public's attention.' She paused. 'I can't talk to Dad about it. He wouldn't understand. Besides, he's worried about Daniel and the practice, it wouldn't be fair to off-load on him.'

Harry raised his eyebrows. 'But it's fair to off-load on me?'

'You can handle it,' Mel answered, walking to a bench and sitting down, Harry joining her, the sound of a child's play coming sweet on the still air. 'Edward . . .' she said simply. 'He's growing.'

'They do.'

Nodding, she said nothing in reply. Edward, the son of Beth and Daniel, had come like a good spirit into the Cochrane household. Conceived before Daniel had been severely disabled by his illness, the boy had become the focus of everyone's life. For Michael, he was the reason to continue, for Beth, he was the proof of her love for her husband, and for Mel he was the child she could borrow, the one unspoiled, perfect creature in her life.

Many times during her medical progress, she had thought of Edward, putting his photograph on her desk and thinking, sometimes, if she was low, about Cy Tolash. If she had met a man like Daniel, instead of Cy, then Edward might have been *her* child – but it hadn't worked out that way. Mel had loved Cy, and, after losing him, no man had ever really interested her again.

She had had lovers, naturally. But there was always a suspicion that they might leave, and so Mel never allowed herself to get too close or become too vulnerable. Then, if they went – as her mother and Cy had done – the damage would be limited. Only in her work did she find complete absorption, her concentration awesome. Within a relatively short time no one could match her in her field, and soon her competitors became her followers, Michael's belief in her vindicated as Mel became one of three pathologists working for both the Home Office and the Manchester Infirmary.

She had no fear whatsoever of death. Since the first time she had entered the mortuary and watched Lance Bolting dissect an old woman who had died of carbon monoxide poisoning, Mel had felt only respect for her charges. Others might make mortuary jokes, but never in her presence. She was formidable, she was handsome, she was one on her own.

It came as something of a surprise to Harry. He had always expected Mel to do well, but her burgeoning success left him not a little jealous and now that she had been chosen to work on the child murder cases he could see – only too clearly – her sudden ascent to the limelight. He used to tease her that anyone could be a good pathologist – after all, what mistakes could you make, the patient was already bloody dead! But he was curiously impressed, despite himself. After all, Michael was a good GP, but now that the National Health Service had provided everyone with care, who needed slum doctors any more? The days of George Cochrane walking with a lantern down Sladen Alley were over. There were no longer epidemics nor grand disasters.

There were only personalities. Heart surgeons, brain surgeons, plastic surgeons, like himself. Men who had built up careers which put them in positions of unassailable power; doctors and surgeons who had become – through unspeakably hard work and egoism – demigods.

But Mel wasn't a man, and she wasn't out to court publicity. She was – as her grandfather had been – a doctor first and last. Only she doctored the dead.

'So what's the problem?' Harry asked her, his thoughts coming back to the present. He tried to sound nonchalant, but he was all too aware that she was nervous about this case.

She was dressed in navy-blue slacks and a white silk shirt, a pair of dark sunglasses shading her eyes. In the sunshine she could have passed for a glamorous girlfriend of some important businessman.

'I loathe it.'

'Loathe what?'

'Acting as the pathologist on these murder cases.'

A little way away she could hear Edward laugh, a loose balloon floating high over their heads.

'But you're the best there is, otherwise they wouldn't have asked you to do it.'

She turned to him, taking off her glasses. Dark purple shadows shaded her eyes, the signs of lack of sleep all too obvious.

'I saw the first murdered child. It was something I'll never forget.'

Disturbed, Harry glanced down at his hands. There had been details of the murders in the papers, children tortured and then butchered. Other details had been withheld, a man in custody, two women held with him, the *Manchester Guardian* refraining from publishing the worst horrors. But the rumours had still circulated about the atrocities inflicted, rumours which had been dismissed by some as sensationalism.

Another, more senior, male pathologist should have covered the murders, but he was on sick leave when the news came through, and so Mel had been called in to do a post mortem on the body of the first child, then the second. Then the other two they found.

Her hands shaking, Mel stared at the sunglasses on her lap. Edward was still laughing behind the high trees which surrounded them.

'I thought I could handle anything. But not this,' she paused, her voice slowed. To control panic, or the impulse to cry, Harry wondered. 'I look at these bodies and wonder how anyone can do something so . . .' The word slid from her grasp. 'Is it madness? Or just evil? I want to know. I want to understand.' She saw her reflection in her glasses. 'Nietzsche said – when you look into the abyss, take care that the abyss looks not also into you.'

Harry touched her hand. 'You're one of the good guys. Evil doesn't rub off.'

'My mother phoned me,' Mel said suddenly. Harry stared at her in disbelief. 'She said that she had read about me in the papers and that she was proud of me . . .' Slowly Mel turned to look at Harry. 'D'you think that if I'd turned out to be a movie star she would have said the same?'

He shrugged, genuinely dumbfounded. 'I don't know what to say.'

'Thank God for that.'

The balloon was trailing over their heads, Edward still laughing and making whooping noises. Suddenly Beth called out to him and a moment later Mel could hear the sound of Daniel's wheelchair being pushed over the gravel.

'How can I help?' Harry asked, studying Mel's profile and seeing nothing of Sylvia in the troubled face.

'You can't help,' Mel answered him, 'no one can . . . God!' she snapped suddenly. 'Why did I go into this bloody profession?'

'Because you were meant to.'

'*Meant to?* What does that mean, Harry? Were the murderers meant to kill? Or the victims – were they meant to die? I see so much death. Every day. All types of people, all types of ways to die. I work alone and in quiet – and it suits me. I like to take time to find out what happened. Sometimes I even whisper to the body – *what happened to you? Tell me, help me to find out.* Crazy, hey?' She smiled to herself, feeling distanced from the man who sat next to her. 'I've seen dead babies and foetuses and people who were relieved to die. But I've never before seen hatred in a body.'

He listened in silence.

'I think that's something I'll never forget,' Mel said, rising to her feet. 'Listen, Edward's laughing again.'

For a moment all they could hear was the sound of the child over the garden wall.

'Thanks, Harry.'

'What for?'

'Saying nothing of any help whatsoever,' Mel replied, laughing.

'It's something I've been doing for years. It's my greatest talent.'

Slowly Mel moved towards the walled garden, Harry falling into step with her.

'If anything happened to Edward –'

'It won't.'

'But if anything *did*, Harry –'

She was prevented from continuing by the appearance of Beth at the gate, waving to her, Mel walking towards her sister without looking back.

Chapter Twenty-one

With her male assistant next to her, Mel looked carefully at the child's body, trying to assess every relevant detail. She knew the boy had been strangled, but she had to be careful not to concentrate so much on the obvious that she missed something of importance. As there were no witnesses to either sight or sound of the murder the time of death was wide open.

Gently Mel felt the limbs and muscles around the jaw. Rigor mortis was present. She knew that as it occurred within a few hours and could last from between one and a half to two days it was only a guideline to the time of death. The time span depended on internal factors such as the muscular activity before or even after the time of death, and there was always the temperature to take into account.

Carefully Mel felt the skin. The body in average conditions felt cold around twelve hours after death. She coughed suddenly, then turned back to her secretary and continued to dictate. She was impassive, doing everything as she had been taught, as she had done so many times before – only this time it was harder to stay detached. This was a murdered child and she had seen too many over the previous three days. Carefully Mel looked under the boy's fingernails and scraped out what appeared to be blood and skin. Then she gave it to her assistant who bagged it and labelled it for the police.

Aware that her heart was not racing and that there was no increase in her pulse, Mel knew she had a tight grip on her emotions now. This was not the ugliest sight she had seen recently. In one of the anterooms off the main examination chamber there was another smaller room in which infectious or decomposing bodies were kept. Like the one brought in the previous day. Found under floorboards in a house off Lyman Street, this child had been dead for some time. Until its examination even its sex remained undetermined.

Meticulously Mel X-rayed the head of the child in front of her and then examined the brain and the injuries around the face. After she had finished, a mortuary technician – under her guidance – reconstructed the face and body of the child to avoid any further grief to the relatives. In the end he looked as though he was asleep.

Cloth and other material fibres were also duly bagged and labelled. Taking a sample of the child's blood, Mel then examined the internal organs, after which she photographed several bruises to the skin around the breastbone and lower back. As she had requested, her assistant had combed the child's hair for possible hair samples from the murderer, and then after Mel had dictated every detail she covered the body with a sheet. It would now be stored away in one of the refrigerator units against the far wall, the boy's left foot tagged with his name and age.

Mel knew that in Salford a family waited to give their child a decent burial, but she also knew that the body could not be released until it was certain that no additional examinations needed to be undergone. So the child would have to wait in the mortuary refrigerator for days or even weeks – sometimes it could be months – until it was released for burial.

Silently, Mel took off her green overalls and pushed open the side door of the mortuary which led into a backyard where the bins were kept. Leaning against one, she lit a cigarette and then suddenly realized how much her hands were shaking.

*   *   *

'England's Loveliest Pathologist' – the headline blazed up from the table next to Daniel on the terrace, Mel wincing as she laid her glass on the paper over her photograph. Harry was talking on the phone inside, Beth fussing around Edward.

Suddenly Daniel slumped to one side in his wheelchair. Mel was on her feet in an instant, but her sister was there before her, settling Daniel comfortably and then taking the seat next to her sister.

'It's getting cold, autumn's coming.'

Mel nodded, staring at Beth for a long moment under the low sunshine. She was coping admirably – everyone said so – always patient, loving, never complaining. Daniel's illness seemed somehow to have ennobled her, made her almost saintly. Musing, Mel watched as her sister then took hold of her son and pulled Edward onto her lap, her hands clasped tightly around the little boy.

Well, what could you expect, people asked. Poor woman's bound to be overpossessive of the little one, what with her husband being so ill ... It was natural, Mel thought, mothers were supposed to love their children. But to this extent? Beth worshipped Edward, made a little god out of him. *Edward did this, Edward did that* ...

'He's doing so well at nursery,' Beth said suddenly, 'though I can't believe that next year he'll be at proper school.'

'In Pendleton?'

Beth nodded, still looking at her son, still admiring him.

Beside her Daniel made a sudden sucking sound, then swallowed awkwardly, his head tipped back against the wheelchair. The comparison between the child and his father was blatant, poignant.

'Do you need anything?' Mel asked, waiting patiently for Daniel to answer.

He struggled with the words, his once young face contorted, his mouth working hard to make up the syllables.

What did her sister think, Mel wondered, when she lay next to this man who had once been attractive? Did she remember their making love? Their wedding, the myriad times Daniel had taken her hand or bent to kiss her? Didn't she feel any bitterness for this mutilated life? A future blighted? A career ended?

Apparently not.

'I'm . . . fine . . .' Daniel said at last, smiling, then jerking his head towards his wife.

Instantly, Beth smiled in return.

I couldn't have done this, Mel realized. I couldn't have been loving and patient like this. I would have been raging against God, against life. I would have hated everyone . . . Jesus, she thought looking at her sister, how *does* she do it?

'We read about you in the paper,' Beth said instantly. 'They did a profile in the *Manchester Guardian*. They're talking about you everywhere.'

Mel smiled automatically, not knowing what to say. Their lives were so dissimilar, so distant from one another, what points of real comparison were there? And yet Mel still came home almost every weekend, and she listened to Beth talk about Daniel, just as her sister listened to her talk about her career. Two different women, with two different lives . . . And yet we support each other, Mel realized. At long last we have some kind of bond.

'Dad read it to us,' Beth went on, still talking about the article. 'He was so proud.'

I would have been jealous, Mel thought. I would never have been so magnanimous about you. Sorry, Beth, sorry. Sorry for all the times I doubted you and thought you hard. Sorry for all the mean suspicions. Sorry, sorry.

Manchester had never been a place she had really liked. Not that it was as bad as Salford – God, that was a dump. The weather had been quite reasonable in London, but the further Sylvia had travelled the worse it had become. And now, as the train pulled into Manchester Victoria, it was raining. As ever.

Picking up her handbag, Sylvia got off the train and walked to the barrier, looking for a taxi outside, but when she saw the queue she decided to walk. The Manchester streets were familiar, Kendal Milne looming majestically over Deansgate, the sooty buildings which marked the rag trade industry rising dourly against the inky sky.

She walked quickly, without glancing round, her figure as slender as it had ever been. Weaving confidently between pedestrians and crossing streets blithely, Sylvia glided, until finally she stopped outside a delicatessen and looked into the lighted window.

Her beauty was all it had ever been, a passerby flinching at the sheer impact of her physical appearance. But Sylvia was unaware, and mesmerized, studied the food in the window. She was well into middle age and yet she was almost unchanged, unmarked by time. Something rare had happened to her; something which happened to very few: for a time Sylvia had found her place in life, and had thrived there.

Away from Aynhams and her familial ties she had managed to hold on to her beauty. There was nothing of regret in her face: rather there was an extraordinary youth which denied children or responsibilities. Her ruthlessness – glimpsed by George so long ago – was firmly and immovably in place. She had made her decision to leave and had never regretted it. Until now. For years there had been no guilt, no turning back, no return. Until now.

Finally Sylvia managed at last to hail a taxi and slid into the back seat. Only then did her heart rate pick up, and by the time they pulled up outside the Manchester Infirmary she was morbidly pale. Paying the driver, she paused for an instant in some unexpected sunshine and then moved towards the entrance doors. Well used to hospitals, she read the signs and worked her way through the green

painted corridors, past banging radiators and tall conden-
sation-drenched windows. Finally, at the sign which read
'Mortuary', she turned and moved towards the door which
faced her at the end of a long and dismal corridor.

There was no one about, although she could hear voices
coming from behind a closed door. Carefully Sylvia read
the next signs, paused outside the door marked 'Pathology
Department', then knocked.

'Come in.'

Mel was sitting with her back to the door, talking on
the phone, and swivelled her chair round as Sylvia entered.
Starting in surprise, Mel said simply, 'I'll call you back,'
and put down the phone.

'Mel.'

'Mother.'

'I came to see you.'

'Why?' Mel asked bluntly, as her mother moved over to
a seat on the other side of her daughter's desk and sat
down.

She looked well rested, well nourished, and totally untroubled. This was her *mother*, Mel thought, trying to
remember her childhood, trying to recall the anguish of
being deserted. She could see the flames in the incinerator
glowing white hot around her mother's dresses and smell
the acrid smoke, but there was no pleasure in the memory,
and her petty act of revenge had had no effect on Sylvia.
The smoke trail had not led her home, or instilled any
feeling of guilt. She was not ashamed of having left her
family, and the realization was, to Mel, something worse
than the act of abandonment itself.

'How are you?'

Her face was quietly lovely. God, Mel thought, I hadn't
remembered just what a beautiful woman you are.

'What do you want, Mother?'

Her dark eyes flickered only momentarily before she
answered, 'I was reading about you in the papers. You've

done very well, you've achieved a lot.' There was a long pause, Sylvia glancing at her daughter's left hand. 'Are you married?'

'No.'

'Children?'

'No,' Mel replied, astonished by the interrogation.

She should have been the one asking the questions. Why did you leave? How could you do it? How could you just walk out and never come back? How, you bitch. *How?*

'What about Beth?'

'What about her?' Mel replied coldly.

'Is she married?'

'Her husband was the answer to her dreams,' Mel said coolly. 'Daniel Ellis, a young doctor who became my father's partner. They were meant for each other.'

'So what happened?'

'Daniel has a wasting disease. He's no longer a real husband to my sister and my father's working all day and most of the night trying to run the practice alone.' She paused, venom on her tongue. 'You *do* remember the practice, don't you?'

Sylvia's eyes hardened. 'Don't take that tone with me! I am your mother –'

'I think we're a little bit past that, don't you?' Mel replied, ignoring the phone when it rang again. 'You're no mother to me.'

'I suppose I should have expected a reaction like that from you –'

'Yes, I always was the difficult one, wasn't I? The one who spoke her mind. Funny thing is, I don't have anything left to say now. I thought I would – but I don't.'

'How's your father?' Sylvia asked, her tone defiant, refusing to be cowed.

'Overworked, as I said,' Mel replied impatiently. 'Look, if you want to know, why don't you ask him? There's a phone at Aynhams.'

'You're not making this very easy –'

'I don't intend to!' Mel snapped. 'You didn't make it easy when you left. I was the one who had to finish bringing up my sister and look after my father. I was the one who had to look after the house and do my studies at the same time. You weren't around; you didn't even bother to leave a note of explanation –'

'I was angry.'

'*You* were angry!' Mel shouted, then dropped her voice and leaned back in her chair. '*You were angry* – I wonder how angry my father was to be humiliated like that.'

'The marriage had been over for a long time.'

'That doesn't make it right,' Mel retorted hotly. 'You owed him something. Some respect, at least.'

'Respect!' Sylvia replied, her tone incredulous. 'Respect! I don't respect your father.'

'You should. He's a good man.'

Sylvia's face darkened with rage, her hands clenched on the arms of the chair. 'You always worshipped him, didn't you, Mel? Always thought he was perfect. Always took his side. The noble Dr Cochrane working with the poor. That reserved, sensitive soul –'

'That's enough!' Mel shouted.

'No, no, it isn't!' her mother replied loudly, leaning forwards. 'Do you know why I left your father?'

'I don't want to know,' Mel lied.

'I think you do,' her mother replied, the words tickling her tongue. 'I left him because he killed your grandfather.'

Mel was on her feet at once. 'You're a liar! You left because you wanted to get away. My grandfather died of natural causes and you know it.'

'Your grandfather,' Sylvia said chillingly, 'died of an overdose, administered by your father. I suspected the speed of George's death, and when I confronted him your father admitted it.'

On the corridor outside Mel could hear a trolley pass.

The wheels made a clanking sound on the concrete floor.

'He killed his own father,' Sylvia emphasized, her voice dropping, dipping down into calm again. 'Our marriage had been failing for a long time, neither of us was happy, but when your father did that I couldn't stay. You do see that, don't you, Mel? How could I stay with a man who could do such a thing to his own father?'

The trolley had passed by now, the doors beyond falling closed with a soft thud.

Shaken, Mel sat down, her eyes fixing blindly ahead. 'How could you?'

Baffled, her mother stared at her. 'How could I –'

'How could you tell me?' Mel repeated, looking at her mother with real loathing. 'How could you come here after all these years and try to excuse your actions by telling me that it was all my father's fault?' Her voice shook, lost its footing for an instant. 'How could you try to ingratiate yourself by betraying him?'

'Betraying him!' Sylvia snapped, the Madonna-smooth face enraged, her features unflattered by anger. 'He killed –'

'My father did what he thought was right! He did it to help my grandfather – and it couldn't have been easy for him. And you knew that. You knew it would play on his mind, that he would feel terrible guilt – but you still left. Why? Because of your principles? I doubt it!' Mel said savagely. 'You simply saw it as an excuse and you took it. And now you want to turn me against my father to assuage your own conscience –'

'I want to come back,' Sylvia said hoarsely, interrupting her daughter.

'Like hell you will!' Mel retorted, getting to her feet again and towering over her mother. 'If you even go near my father you'll have me to deal with.'

'I *am* your mother –'

'And I am your daughter,' Mel countered. 'I know you,

Mother, I understand you. He's had enough, let him be. Dad's made a life for himself and he's at peace. Don't hurt him again. Please, don't hurt him again.'

If he could just find an old stalwart to share the workload ... Michael thought as he drew up outside a new block of flats. Even someone like Tudge could help him now. He was tired, not that he was going to admit it, but he needed someone to share the burden. Locums had come and gone, no one wanting to stay permanently at the practice, young doctors using the Salford experience as a stopping-off post on the way to somewhere better. No one wanted to stay.

If only Daniel hadn't been taken ill, Michael thought. They had worked so well together – Daniel easy, with that kind of affable charm which soothes patients. The future had seemed to be for once beautifully mapped out. Then Daniel had become ill ... He had to be very careful at home, Michael realized, had to pretend that he was coping fine alone and that he was expecting his son-in-law to return to the practice when he had recovered.

It was a game, and they both knew it. But somehow everyone needed to pretend that Daniel's disease was something temporary, when, with every day that followed, it was patently obvious that he was failing. His balance had been the first thing to go, then his speech, then, cruelly, his ability to walk. Finding it difficult to communicate even minor needs, Daniel was tied to his wheelchair, his eyes fixing on his son avidly.

The child was, Michael realized, what kept him alive. That, and Beth's unceasing care. At night she had to turn her husband and clean him, and often Michael would hear her footsteps walking overhead in the early hours. But she never complained, never bemoaned her lot, accepted everything and daily became more and more besotted with her son. It was to be expected – Edward was the ever-present reminder of what her husband had been, a constant reiteration of the love she had shared with Daniel. No wonder she adored her son, no wonder she clung to him so possessively.

By this time Michael was inside the block of flats and attempting the stairs. Sighing, he leaned against the banister. It was getting more and more tiring to climb the steps, he thought, breathing heavily as he reached the second floor. Who needed flats like this? Whose idea was it to knock down all the terraces and build these modernized cages? Shifting his medical bag from one hand to the other, he walked on, looking for flat number 15, then knocked.

After a moment an old man answered, peering through the glass pane at the top of the door. On seeing Michael he smiled and slid back the chain, moving to let the doctor pass. It was a cold night and Michael's coat was steaming as he walked into the centre of the cramped room, a budgerigar whistling a greeting from a cage in the corner.

'Coming up for Christmas, Doctor,' the old man said. 'Spending it at home, are you?'

'As always,' Michael replied, taking the stethoscope out of his case and laying it on the old man's chest.

'How's that son-in-law of yours?'

'Not too good, Mr Kershaw.'

'Shame that, you two being in the same business like. He made a good partner for you.'

'Breathe in.'

The old man did so, Michael listening to his chest.

'How are the pains?'

'Bad when I walk any distance. Bad on the stairs too.'

'Take them more slowly.'

He gave Michael a dry look.

'Aren't the tablets helping?'

'Better than the other ones,' Mr Kershaw agreed. 'How's that grandson of yours?'

For the first time since he had come in, Michael smiled. 'Edward's fine. Thank you for asking.'

'We follow the news 'bout your girl, the doctor lass. You must be proud of her,' the old man went on. 'Shame she didn't go into the practice with you, though.'

Yes, Michael thought, he would have liked that. But Mel was too brilliant to be a GP, too ambitious. He thought of her and imagined how they could have done their rounds together. The nights would have seemed that much shorter with his daughter around. She would have made him laugh, and when he was tired he could have trusted her to take over. It would have been perfect, Michael thought, straightening up.

'Taken all in all though, the pain's only really bad when I go upstairs,' the old man continued. 'I get tired then, and that's when it gets you the worst.'

Yes, Michael thought, briefly touching his own chest around the heart. That *is* when it gets you the worst.

Chapter Twenty-two

One man and two women had been charged with the murders of six children. The accused had all come from Salford, one woman having been born in Haswell Street, a dingy terrace which was part of Michael's patch. When he read her name in the paper he remembered that his father had once treated the woman's mother. For what, he couldn't recall.

The case was set to be tried in the New Year, Mel having undertaken post mortems on all the bodies, her evidence due to be heard at the trial, along with all the other expert witnesses. She had performed her job professionally and with rigid detachment, refusing newspaper interviews and only mentioning the case when she visited Aynhams – which she did more and more as the evidence mounted.

The sheer darkness of the murders, together with her anxiety about her father's workload, the threat of her mother's return to Aynhams, about which only Mel knew, and Daniel's decline, made her moody, unwilling to socialize as the winter nights drew on towards Christmas and party invitations began to arrive with the usual flurry of medical mail. She would, she promised herself, just go home for the holiday, sit in front of the fire and eat and drink. When she was tired she would go to her room, which had never changed since childhood, Beth not wanting to trespass on her sister's territory, and draw the pale curtains and sleep in the same bed where she had once planned her brilliant career.

Rising to her feet, Mel glanced out of the window and up into the street beyond. From the mortuary's basement level she could only see feet passing and then noticed the first flecks of snow landing soft and clean against the dark brickwork of the sill. It was late, well after nine, and she was the only person still here, the other pathologist having left earlier, the attendants fighting their slow way home through Christmas traffic.

Wearily, Mel closed her eyes. She might let herself sleep for just a moment, just a moment . . . Overhead the sounds of a man shouting came down to her, followed by the heavy clatter of a steel dish hitting the floor. Then quiet. After another moment she felt her muscles relaxing and willed herself to wake, but it was too late and an instant later, Mel was deeply asleep.

Obviously she hadn't heard him come in, he thought, watching Mel as she slept, his coat damp from the sudden snowfall. He should wake her, but then again, she was tired, it was a kindness to let her sleep. Her face, seen in rest, seemed different to him, the animation and intelligence turned off, and he had the peculiar sensation of looking at someone who was at the same time both familiar and perfectly strange.

Her good looks did not surprise him; he had been aware of those for a long time, but when she slept Mel seemed curiously vulnerable, the stern, gold-plated lettering of her name on the desk – 'Dr M. Cochrane' – seeming totally at odds with the young woman asleep.

He had come on a whim, expecting to see her as he always did; busy, competent, alert. Not as a fragile woman, sleeping alone in an office chair in a cluttered office next door to the Infirmary mortuary.

'Who is it?' Mel said, snapping suddenly awake and sitting up. At once her expression altered from surprise to wary pleasure. 'Harry – what the hell are you doing here?'

'I was in town for a lecture,' he said, smiling, 'and then when it finished I thought I'd take you out to dinner.'

'No girlfriend in tow?'

He pulled a face. 'I need stimulating company.'

'That's what I mean,' Mel said drily, 'no girlfriend in tow?'

She was laughing with him, pushing her hair back from her face and pulling her jacket around her. Suddenly cold, she shivered and then blew on her hands.

He had seen her perform the same gesture innumerable times. As a child she would waylay her sister around the corner of the house with snowballs and then let fly, blowing on her hands to warm them afterwards. Once he had seen her do the same standing in a Salford cinema queue and more recently Mel had blown on her hands to warm them just before she had smoothed down Daniel's hair. Only a small detail, but a kindness none the less.

'Well, *what* about dinner?' he asked, glancing towards the window. 'Or would you rather we stayed here and got snowed in?'

'Sounds wonderful,' Mel replied, pulling on her coat.

'What? The dinner, or being snowed in?'

'Depends where you're taking me,' she replied, clicking off the light as they left.

He had parked his car in the underground car park behind Deansgate, Mel insisting that they could walk to the restaurant, the snow falling more heavily as they made their way towards Lloyd Street. She was telling him about Sylvia, then about her father, talking hurriedly as though she had been waiting a long time to confide. And Harry listened, glancing in shop windows from time to time and checking his reflection automatically, his pigskin gloves keeping his cherished hands warmed.

It had been an impulse to look up Mel, but he had a suspicion that she might be in need of a friend, and knew only too well how debilitating public scrutiny could be for someone essentially private. The media had been avidly interested in Mel. She was a novelty, a sign of the changing times, a young woman called upon to give expert evidence on a series of the most horrifying crimes ever perpetrated. Everyone wanted to know how she dressed, how she sounded, what her background was, her marital status, her love life. They wanted to set her up as an icon – a single woman taking on the might of a male-dominated profession, a woman coping with horrors few men could tolerate.

And for once her father couldn't understand. Michael's practice in Salford was too far removed from his daughter's high-profile career; his patients needs and illnesses were commonplace, his surgery never attracting the world's press. Michael might talk of her, and be proud of her, but what did he – in St Stephen's Street, Salford – know of the pressures? The few streets which he walked were familiar to him – even rebuilt after the war, they were still the same gridding of roads he had always known. He still treated the same families, and used the same words and actions he had always done.

But with the murders had come a different life for Mel, and only Harry could fully understand the pressure she was under. Much as she might run home to Aynhams to escape, there was no one there who truly understood. Apart from him. At long last she was finding out what he had known for years: that to be the best was to be set apart.

'We're here,' Harry said finally, holding open the restaurant door for Mel to enter, her presence immediately noticed by the maître d'.

'Dr Cochrane,' he said delightedly, then stared at the man by her side. 'And Mr Chadwick. It's been a long time.'

'I have a poor appetite,' Harry replied wryly, falling into step behind Mel as they were shown to a secluded table by the window. Silently, she slid into her seat and then peered out, her index finger tracing the word Christmas on the steamy window.

'Looking forward to it?' Harry asked, ordering wine without needing to see the list.

'Looking forward to the rest,' she replied. 'You coming to spend Christmas at Aynhams?'

'Don't I always?'

She nodded, suddenly longing for the countryside, far away from Manchester where the snow-flattered streets would be black-slushed by morning, the sky leaden, gloomy, oppressive over the short days. What she wouldn't give to leave that very evening, to drive out of the city and make for home. It would be a quiet drive, maybe snow would fall, maybe not. On the hour she would listen to the radio news and as Buile Hill came into view she would tense herself, waiting for that first ecstatic glimpse of home.

'. . . Hey, Mel? Mel?'

She smiled, dragging herself back to the present.

'Where were you?'

'Aynhams.'

He raised his full glass to hers in a mutual salute: 'Aynhams.'

In silence they drank, both longing for the same sweet sanctuary of home.

The doorbell rang just after ten that night. Michael turned off the television and rose to his feet.

'I'll get it,' he said to Beth, who was sitting beside Daniel, their own rooms deserted, Beth in need of company now that her son was in bed.

Yawning, Michael walked to the door and opened it. The snow had fallen over the front lawn and driveway making a white landscape, the slight figure on the doorstep as insubstantial as a shadow.

'Michael?'

He flinched at the sound of his wife's voice and automatically closed the door behind him. Softly the snow fell on both of them.

'Sylvia,' he said stupidly, 'what is it?'

Her eyes ranged over the front of the house, then drifted

towards the far wing where the clinic lights blazed out from the ward windows.

'Nothing changes,' she said quietly. 'Can I come in?'

Her very presence threatened him.

'Do you think that's a good idea?'

Searching her husband's face Sylvia found it, as ever, unreadable.

'Please, Michael, let me in.'

A moment passed and then he moved back, opening the door for her to enter. She sighed – he heard her – as she moved into the hall and studied the surroundings hungrily. When they had first married she had had the same look, the same incredulity at her good fortune.

'It's still beautiful.'

Shrugging, Michael longed suddenly for old George to be there; wondered what his father would think. *Bloody hell, boy, this is a turn up for the book.*

'I heard about Beth's husband. Mel told me.'

Suspicion slid down between them like the blade of a guillotine. Why hadn't Mel told him? Why hadn't she – who told him everything – mentioned that she had seen her mother?

'When did you see Mel?'

She laughed, turned her oval face upwards towards his. Her beauty pulverized him.

'You're so cautious, Michael. Why does it matter when I saw Mel? She's my daughter, after all.'

Behind him, Michael could hear Beth moving around and willed her to stay in the sitting room, but almost as he thought it she opened the door and walked out, her footfall soft in slippers.

'Beth,' Sylvia said simply.

He turned then, looked at his daughter and then at his wife and had the peculiar sensation of seeing two people in one.

'Daniel's ready for bed,' Beth said simply, ignoring her

mother and turning to her father. 'Will you help me to get him upstairs?'

She had wrong-footed both of them by her calm, by that nasty placidity which was somehow more disturbing than anger.

Sylvia stared bleakly at her daughter. 'Don't you have anything to say to me?'

Beth's face was as still as a mill pond. 'Not really ... Are you staying?'

Eagerly Sylvia looked to her husband. 'Am I?'

Michael was confused, suddenly anxious to wake up, to see the whole ludicrous episode as nothing more than a dream. But although he waited for an instant there was no shift in consciousness – it was all too painfully real. He had never been adept at showing his feelings and now it was too late for him to change; he had no talent for outrage, for fury, he was simply tired and strangely embarrassed.

'Do you *want* to stay?'

'I want to come back, yes,' Sylvia replied, without moving. There was no plea in it, no apology. Just a statement of fact.

You've got to hand it to her, George would have said, *she's a tough bird and no mistake.*

'I thought you were in London,' Michael blustered. 'I thought you were happy there.'

'I was for a while,' Sylvia admitted. 'But I've changed, Michael. I want to come home, to be with you and the family. I want to make it up to you.' She glanced at her daughter imploringly. 'I could help you, Beth, I could help you nurse Daniel –'

'I can manage,' she replied without emotion.

Rebuffed, Sylvia turned back to her husband. 'I could help you too, Michael. You need help, now that Daniel's ill. The practice could use a nurse.'

So she *had* been talking to Mel, Michael thought, otherwise how could she know so much about their lives?

Confused, he glanced away, searching for anything to take his eye amongst the familiar objects.

'I *could* make it up to you,' Sylvia continued, her voice mellow, an echo from a past too distant to remember clearly.

She had to persuade him, she knew that, she *had* to get back. Her time was over in London, she was no longer young, no longer freshly attractive. Soon she would be unable to bargain with her looks, to wheedle attention by her appeal. Her ambition had long since been sated; there was only so much fulfilment in being a theatre sister, and independence was only a temporary joy. As the years had passed Sylvia had seen the beauty – which had brought her lovers and protection – begin to falter, and now she was uncomfortably aware that she had to do something to secure her future.

'Why come back now?' Michael asked her coolly.

'I missed you,' she replied so smoothly that she almost convinced herself of the lie.

'After so long?'

Panic winded her suddenly. Where would she go if she couldn't come home? To die after a lonely old age? Without family, without status. Her savings gone. Many things had made her leave – wilfulness, boredom, ambition – and George's death had been an all-too-convenient excuse to desert her marriage. At first she had been giddy with free-dom, had seen whom she wanted and run her own life without having to consider anyone else. No children, no husband, just herself to indulge and amuse.

But after a while it paled, and again Sylvia found herself longing to jump over the high fence into another life.

'We've managed without you for a long time,' Michael said, his tone even.

'But I'm sorry, so sorry for what I did to you,' Sylvia replied. 'Michael, let me come back. *Please*.'

Baffled, he looked to his daughter, but Beth immediately

turned away. God, he thought angrily, why wasn't Mel here? Mel would know what to do . . . What would be the point of letting Sylvia return? Their marriage had always been unstable, his love for her far stronger than the love she bore him . . . if it was love at all. He doubted it; thought that she had been merely grateful; thankful that he had given her a name, a home, status. She had been a foreigner when she came to Salford with only her beauty to set her apart; he had saved her, given her the position in life she had craved. But even her need for security hadn't been enough to hold them together. In the end Sylvia had left him, and their children, walked away from her allotted role when he needed her most. She hadn't understood his part in George's death. At the time when he had hoped for some understanding she had rejected him. And now she wanted to come back.

It was madness, complete madness.

Without answering, Michael studied his wife's face. You're still lovely, but you're older – how lonely your future must look to you now that younger, prettier women have overtaken you . . . He could see in Sylvia a mirror of his own fears – and, much to his astonishment, he pitied her.

'Sylvia, it wouldn't work. I can't risk it –'

'Risk *what*?' she asked pleadingly, touching his arm and stirring some dim memory of desire.

He was weakening, she could sense it.

'I won't hurt you again, I promise, Michael. I promise you I'll make up for the past.'

He was tired. He was lonely. His guard was down. If George had been there he would have raged at his daughter-in-law, torn her to shreds and made her crawl, but his father *wasn't* there and Michael had never been able to display his feelings. And besides, even as he recognized his stupidity, he still gave into it.

Just as she knew he would.

*   *   *

At the same time that her mother and father were trying to salvage their marriage, Mel was eating dinner with Harry, and arguing with him.

'I don't think that you know what you're talking about!' she snapped, downing the last of her wine and holding out her glass for a refill. 'You've always been a smug bugger, Harry.'

'I've always stood up to you, you mean,' he retorted, getting warm under the collar himself, 'and I've been the only one who has.'

She was clinking her nails against the glass, her face slightly flushed. The argument had begun over some simple principle of medicine, both insisting they were right and both refusing to back down. The other diners had already left, the evening dipping into night as they stayed and argued the toss.

'The problem is,' Mel said, narrowing her eyes, 'that you can't bear to think of a woman being smarter than you.'

'Because I've never met one.'

She was on her feet immediately, pulling on her coat and calling for the bill.

'I'll pay,' Harry said sourly, thrusting some notes at the waiter and hurrying after Mel to the door.

The snow had banked up against the windows and was over an inch deep on the street outside. Momentarily hesitating, Harry followed Mel, catching up with her just as she slipped turning the corner.

'Damn it!' she snapped, landing heavily on one knee, Harry bending down towards her. 'Go away! I don't need your help!'

'Oh, grow up –'

'I don't want help from you!' she repeated fiercely, trying to get up, her leather-soled shoes losing their grip on the snowy street.

Angrily, Harry hauled her to her feet and then turned her towards him.

'You are *so* stubborn,' he hissed, staring at her face as Mel breathed quickly, her skin pink with alcohol and exertion.

He could feel her arm under his grip and found himself suddenly transfixed by the sheen of her skin under the streetlamp. Cold to the bone, Mel shivered, the sensation passing like a shadow over both of them as Harry pulled her towards him.

His mouth searched for hers, his hands moving inside her coat, against her breasts, along the line of her thigh, Mel kissing him hungrily, her tongue finding his, her hands pressed against the small of his back. He moaned and clung to her, tugging off his gloves and stroking her face with his bare hands, leading her along the pavement and towards the car park. Without speaking they moved up the concrete stairs, feeding on each other greedily, breaths coming fast as they found their way to his car.

Neither of them remembered the short drive to her flat, and by the time they reached the bed inside they were naked, the lights turned off, the snow falling whitely outside.

Chapter Twenty-three

'Dr Cochrane! Dr Cochrane!' Reluctantly Mel turned, the journalist running towards her. 'I just want a moment to ask you about the murders –'

'I have nothing to say.'

'But –'

Mel raised her hands to fend off further demands. 'I have nothing to say,' she repeated. 'You shouldn't be in this part of the hospital.'

The woman held her ground. 'I just thought that you might –'

'No,' Mel said, showing the woman to the door which separated the mortuary from the main body of the hospital. 'I have nothing whatsoever to say now, or at any time in the future. Goodbye.'

Returning to her office, Mel closed the door and sat down heavily. At first there had been only a little interest in her, just a couple of newspaper stories, but as more and more victims had been found the press had become very curious about the pathologist who was in charge of the case. Mel's background and appearance were widely commented on, her photograph displayed next to the suspects, her calm face a startling contrast to the dark features of the accused. And with the exposure, came the loss of privacy, Mel followed and photographed, the pressure increasing daily. She knew she had to perform well, it was a major case, and a very public one, a case on which her future would depend, and the intrusive press attention unsettled her badly.

The trial had been scheduled for New Year, but in the

end it was postponed, the investigations dragging on and on, a further body being found.

Mel had been called out very early, before dawn, the first birds making winter calls into the freezing air. Blowing on her hands, she had stood in the grim Salford alleyway, Gordon Cutting, and waited for the police to finish sealing off the crime scene. The previous night she had done a post mortem on a widow of ninety, carefully dictating her notes and then pulling the sheet over the body. Ninety was a good age to die.

Seven wasn't ... Her ears were burning with the cold, her legs numb as she waited. After another few minutes one of the policemen gave her a coffee in the cup off the top of his Thermos flask, the steam rising hotly into the damp Northern air. Gordon Cutting lay between two terraces, long since boarded up. Many years before Mel remembered how she and her father had visited one of the houses to treat a stab wound. The man had been monosyllabic, frightened.

There was no man any more. No tenants, no families. Nothing. Except boarded-up houses, row on row, bombed out, still waiting to be demolished, the sites to be rebuilt. It was a neglected, dead place. Mel looked ahead down the narrow alleyway. A skip full of rubble and a dead Christmas tree stood next to a collection of dustbins and a pile of filthy sacking.

A dog had found the body, and tried to dig it out, but it was jammed between the skip and the wall. His owner had whistled for him repeatedly, and then finally gone over to see what his dog was barking about. The man was still hanging around. He didn't look sick, or even curious, just oddly blank-faced. Slowly the daylight had winched itself over the tops of the terraces, drizzle darkening the police tape as Mel turned off her torch.

'Looks like another one,' the policeman in charge had told her. 'A kiddie.'

Pulling on her surgical gloves, Mel nodded, and then crouched down beside the dead child.

'Can't be more than six,' the officer had gone on. 'How long has he been here?'

'She.'

'What?'

Mel glanced up. 'It's – it *was* – a little girl.'

The policeman had fallen silent then, rain falling on his uniform, the cobbles of Gordon Cutting darkening with the shower. Gently Mel examined the child and then signalled for her attendants to put the body in the hearse bound for the mortuary. Far away she could hear the sound of a car backfiring.

The trial had been reset for April. That was wrong, Mel thought. April was spring, how much more fitting for the trial to be held in winter when it was bleak, without the blind rush of warming earth and optimistic flowers. Her hair was wet with rain, her skin damp, the policeman watching her and wondering how a woman could look at a kiddie in that state without crying.

It was as though his wife had never been away, Michael thought incredulously. He had woken the previous night to hear the toilet flushing and started, before remembering that Sylvia was home. His wife had returned. Softly he then heard her feet pad back to her room and the muted hum of a radio playing into the dark. Sylvia had never been a good sleeper.

For a moment he was tempted to go to her, but resisted. If he did, it would result in embarrassment for both of them. Sylvia didn't want *him*, she wanted to be Mrs Cochrane again, and everything that implied. Sighing, he rolled over onto his back and stared up at the ceiling, a feeling of emptiness welling up inside him.

Who were these two strangers in his house, he wondered. He didn't have any real closeness to Beth – he never had

had – and since the onset of Daniel's illness she was more preoccupied than ever. And as for Sylvia – who was she really? What did he know about the years in which she had been away? What had she done, said, felt? Whom had she talked to and loved?

Loved. Had she loved someone? Michael's heart beat uncomfortably at the thought. Had she slept with some man, or some *men*? Quickly he closed his eyes. He would never ask her, because he wouldn't be able to. He might ache to know, but what words would he use? What words *could* he use? She had come back, that was the main thing.

But was it what he really wanted? If he hadn't been so tired, so preoccupied, so lonely, would he have allowed it? If Mel had been living at home, would he? Ah, but if Mel had been living at home he would never have been lonely in the first place.

Sylvia's radio was playing Beethoven, some dismal piece which made Michael think of his father. In the end George had died so easily. There had been no embarrassing last-minute confessions, no pleas for understanding, no apologies. No clutching of his son's hand, just a resonant final breath. For a time Michael had sat looking at his father's body and willing George to move again, to push himself up on his elbow and bellow to him, *You're bloody useless, I can't rely on you to do anything right* . . .

But he didn't, he remained inert. Finished. And there was no way Michael could call him back.

All the anger he had felt at the death of his mother was over. He couldn't blame his father any more, couldn't use him as a spur to his own ambitions and feelings of revenge. And why? Because George had – his son realized with the benefit of age and hindsight – done his best.

As I have, Michael thought, as I have. I wanted to punish my father, becoming a doctor to prove that I was the better man; that I would never have let my mother die. *I* would have saved her . . . He smiled hopelessly into the darkness.

I would save *everyone*. But who did *I* save? My patients, yes. But in the end, with stupefying irony, I killed my own father. How pointless all the anger had been, Michael thought. Nothing had turned out as he had expected. He had forgiven his father. And now his wife was back.

It hadn't been easy to tell Mel the news when he phoned her.

'What!'

'Your mother's come home.'

'Why?'

'She wanted to. She thought it was time to make amends.'

There was a long pause on the line. He wanted to say something else, but he couldn't, his reserve making communication impossible, even with Mel.

'I don't think it's a good idea, Dad.'

'She's different –'

'No, she's not,' Mel replied shortly. 'No one ever is. They might say they are, but they're not. I don't want her to hurt you again.'

'No.'

'Don't let her.'

'No.'

The usual weekend visits from Mel had stopped from that day onwards. No more blaring of her car horn as she came up the drive on Friday nights, no more hurried synopses of her work whilst she rummaged through the fridge for food. No more of her huge energy and life. She had withdrawn. In the middle of the greatest career challenge of her life, she had turned away. And it was only then that Michael realized why – she felt excluded.

Oh no, Mel, Michael thought powerlessly, alone in the dark. Not you. Never you. You're always first with me, you should know that. Always the one who was closest to me, who understood me best . . .

Wearily, he turned over in bed again, but couldn't sleep.

His ally was gone, and he felt surrounded by strangers, as helpless and abandoned as a child.

'What the bloody hell are you playing at!' Harry roared, throwing the surgical instrument across the operating theatre. 'You're nothing but a bloody amateur!'

Wincing, John Wilde watched him at the head of the operating table. What the hell was wrong with Harry? Oh yes, he could be temperamental, but since Christmas he'd been impossible, exploding at everyone, being demanding, critical, even cruel at times. Was he ill?

'What the bloody hell are you staring at?' Harry snapped. John glanced down at the patient hurriedly. 'Keep your eyes on your work – I can't watch all of you.'

Furiously Harry then turned his attention back to the patient, breathing in to steady himself. This was bloody ridiculous! He was losing his grip, out of sodding control. It had to stop . . . Idly he flexed his hands and then made the incision from ear to jawline. Thank God he had his work, he thought, otherwise he'd be one jump ahead of the butterfly nets by now. All he had to do was to submerge himself and he'd get over it. He always had before; no women ever *really* got to him.

But this wasn't a woman, this was Mel. This was the girl he had watched grow up, the one for whom he had prophesied great things; the one he had relied on to keep him on his toes. Mel Cochrane, blunt, smart-mouthed – and his best friend's daughter.

'Christ!' Harry said under his breath.

The scrub nurse glanced over to him anxiously. 'What is it?'

'Nothing, nothing!' Harry barked. 'I was just thinking aloud.'

He could only be grateful for one thing – that old George wasn't alive. If he had found out what had happened . . . Bloody hell, Harry thought blindly, what was I thinking of? No idiot fouls their own doorstep. No moron sleeps with their best friend's daughter. How could I have been so stupid?

Aynhams was his refuge, the one place on earth where he was safe, where no one could get him – until now.

Now the house seemed to throb with reminders. He saw Mel at the operating theatre window, in her father's study, in the kitchen, the garden – even coming out of the bloody toilet, for God's sake! Her photograph was everywhere, and when Harry looked up he could remember her lobbing apple cores at him from the east tower when she was a kid. She had been an impossible child, clumsy, outspoken, rude – and yet much as Harry fought to remember the past, all he could really see was Mel lying on her bed, her arms stretched towards him.

'Shit . . .' Harry moaned to himself, his hands working deftly on the patient's face. 'Shit, shit, shit.'

Daniel was watching his mother-in-law with fascination, his head lolling to one side as he moved, Edward playing on the floor in front of him. So this was Sylvia, he thought, dribbling from the side of his mouth, his arms jerking uncontrollably. This was the mother of his wife . . . His eyes followed the slim figure around, then flicked over to the door as Beth walked in.

He grunted slightly in welcome and she turned, smiling as though he had said something articulate, clever. He loved her madly for that; for her kindness, her gift of compassion. Without her, he would have given up long ago; without his wife and his son he would have lost heart. His right leg trembled suddenly from a nervous sensation. Beth was beside him immediately, straightening him up in the wheelchair before he turned his attention to his son.

That was a fine achievement, Daniel thought. For all the rest which had gone wrong, for all the hideous squalor of his illness and dependency, he had sired a perfect child.

Swallowing with difficulty, Daniel tried to reach out to his son, but his arms only jerked uselessly, his right foot tapping a mad rhythm against the steel slat of the wheelchair. He could cry, he thought with mounting frustration, he wanted to cry...

She was there in an instant, her hand against his cheek, her lips next to his ear. Softly Beth murmured to him, stroking his forehead, his eyes closing as the anger thawed under her touch. He had her, he told himself, he still had her – and now she had help.

It had worried him for a long time. How could his wife cope with his illness as he grew worse? But his prayers had been unexpectedly answered. Sylvia had returned, and, unless he was mistaken, she was more than eager to make amends.

Chapter Twenty-four

It was useless trying to deceive herself, Mel realized, she might use the excuse of her mother's return for not visiting Aynhams but in reality she was ashamed. How could she face her father when she was having an affair with his best friend? How could she try to explain to the one man who had excused her everything – *Sorry, but I'm having an affair with Harry. You do understand, Dad, don't you?*

How could he? Why *should* he? He had loved Harry as a brother, he had given over his house to him. Harry's clinic was under his roof, his clothes in a room especially kept for him. For year after year Harry Chadwick had shared Aynhams with the only man who had loved him. And understood him.

But Mel knew her father would never understand this. No words, no explanations would do. Harry had betrayed him; and she – his beloved daughter – had betrayed him too. Their love affair was furtive, a secret that had to remain so for ever. Melanie Cochrane, who had judged her mother so harshly, Melanie Cochrane, who wielded such power in her profession and in court, was lying and deceiving herself and the man she loved above all others, her father.

It made her love for Harry all the more urgent. If they loved each other completely, genuinely, then surely that might excuse them? Please God, she thought, don't just let it be an affair, something cheap. Let him love me, let me love him. Let it be strong enough to endure and then maybe, just maybe, one day I can tell my father and he'll understand.

But she still couldn't look Michael in the face, and missed him constantly, trying to console herself with the fact that her mother was home. Her father wasn't lonely, she told herself, he probably wasn't even missing her. But the lies sounded sour to her and although she longed to confide her phone calls home were brief, her father repeating the invitation endlessly: *Come home soon, I miss you. Come home. Mel, come home.*

Slowly and insidiously Sylvia had infiltrated herself back into Aynhams. By offering Beth help with Daniel, she was soon invaluable, and if her daughter had been up tending her husband during the night, Sylvia was the one to take Edward to school in the morning. The news of her return had rocked the nobs of Buile Hill and the upright little town of Pendleton. No one had ever expected Sylvia Cochrane to return. They would snub her, they said to each other, taking the moral high ground. If poor Dr Cochrane was a fool to take her back, they didn't have to follow his example.

But they reckoned without Sylvia's steel. For weeks they ignored her and to their amazement she, in turn, ignored them. Instead she walked the streets of the town and did her shopping and collected Edward from primary school. And she never apologized or explained.

They had expected her to be cowed, but she wasn't, and so gradually Sylvia was tolerated again – never accepted, but she didn't care about that for she had never been accepted before. All she wanted, she had: her family, her home, and her status back. It was true that her relationship with Beth was strained, but her daughter was relying on her mother more and more. Soon their differences would be forgotten, Sylvia was sure about that.

But the one thing she wasn't sure about was Mel. Her elder daughter had always been an unknown quantity. Mel wouldn't fall for her mother's pleas for reconciliation, nor for her persuasive arguments. Mel was angry – angry for the past, and for the present – because now she had been ousted as chief recipient of her father's love. Sylvia had usurped her daughter both physically and emotionally and Mel was not about to forgive that.

But had she *really* usurped her? Sylvia wondered. Were Mel's long absences from Aynhams a rebuke to her parents, or was there another reason? The murder trial couldn't be her excuse – Mel had always talked to her father about work before. So what was it? Sylvia asked herself. Mel loved her father too deeply to avoid him just because her mother was home. No, this estrangement was too extreme to be so easily explained. There was something else.

I know my child, Sylvia thought, I know her and I know that she is hiding something. And what it is, I intend to find out.

'I can't imagine what the families of those children are going through. I don't want to imagine it,' Mel said as she walked into Harry's flat and sat down. 'At night I close my eyes and see the bodies.' Her voice was dispassionate, controlled. 'I wish someone else had been the pathologist. I'm ashamed to say it, but I wish someone else had had to deal with it. I won't ever forget what I've seen, Harry. I can't ever forget it.'

The drawing room of the apartment was warm and expensively furnished, oil paintings on the walls, the view overlooking central Manchester. On the table beside her was a photograph of Harry with the Queen, and another of Aynhams, spectacular under a heavy snowfall.

He was pouring them both a drink.

'We have to talk –'

'My God,' Mel said, catching sight of another photograph of Harry with Elizabeth Taylor, 'is she a patient?'

'Very funny,' he replied, sitting down on the settee.

He was dressed formally, having just come back from a

black tie affair at the Midland Hotel. His hair, turning grey at the temples, was still thick, his face cheating his age. If she had passed him in the street, Mel thought, she would have thought him no more than fifty.

'We're making a mistake, Harry . . .'

He stared into his drink.

'. . . You know we are.'

'How's the case coming on?' he asked, changing the subject.

'Due to come to trial in April,' Mel replied. 'They found another body, a boy this time.'

'I heard.'

'Shocking . . .' she said softly. 'They had used a mask on the child to prevent him from crying out.'

'Jesus.'

There was a long pause, then Harry reached out and took Mel's hand. 'Sorry.'

'These things happen,' she replied distantly. 'Oh, how they keep happening.'

'Is there anything I can do?'

'No,' she said simply. 'Just listen.'

Her hand was still lying in his; for another instant he hesitated and then touched her cheek.

'You're doing very well. Everyone admires you.' His fingers lingered around her temples.

'I keep thinking about those children –'

'You can't afford to, Mel, you have to give evidence. You have to be dispassionate. Impartial.'

'I know that!' she snapped, Harry's hand moving down her neck tenderly. 'I know my job.'

'Then do it,' he said simply, leaning over and kissing her neck.

'Harry, we can't –'

'Can't what?' he murmured.

'We can't go on with this. You're old enough to be my father, for God's sake.'

He drew back immediately. 'You know, that is the kind of remark which could make a man impotent.'

'Is that a problem with you, Harry?' she asked mockingly, keeping her tone light although her heart was leaden.

Make love to me, she thought, make me forget what I'm doing, what I've seen. Make me forget.

His mouth moved momentarily over hers before he suddenly pulled away again.

'Are you nervous?'

'Why?' she asked, baffled. 'We've done this before.'

'Not about sex, about the trial!'

'I don't want to talk about it,' Mel replied, sighing and leaning back against the cushions of the settee. 'Harry, don't.'

He was unfastening the zip on her skirt, his breathing accelerating.

'Harry, don't,' she repeated, urgently reaching for his tie and unfastening it. 'I have to go back to work.'

'Later.'

'No,' she said, undoing his shirt buttons. 'I have to go now.'

'Later,' he repeated, pulling off her blouse and bra and leaning over her. 'You know, you can always ask my advice.'

'What on? Time-keeping?' Mel replied, moving position until she was under him. Slowly she stared at his bare chest. 'You're in good shape – for an old man.'

'It's all the plastic surgery I've done on myself,' Harry replied, his lips moving to her breasts. 'When I have an hour to spare I just tighten the odd pectoral.' His lips lingered over hers, then slowly he traced his tongue over her diaphragm.

'Harry, don't,' Mel said, closing her eyes. 'Don't. Please.'

Baffled, he stared at her. 'Don't what?'

'Don't stop,' she said huskily. 'Please, don't stop.'

*   *   *

Alone in the kitchen at Aynhams Beth stared at the table top. Daniel and Edward had been fed, her mother was waiting to eat when her father came home. She had been a good help, willing to sit with Daniel or take Edward to school, willing to help ... Beth's hands stretched out on the bare wood, her fingers splayed. Slowly she traced the markings in the wood and then, equally slowly, she scratched at it with her fingernails.

'You must be so pleased to have your mother back. With the situation what it is,' someone had said to her cautiously the previous afternoon. 'You've done so well on your own, Beth, and now you've got the help you deserve.'

Another woman had come up to her in the greengrocer's.

'I can't tell you how much we admire you and the way you've coped. Your mother came home just at the right time, didn't she?'

From the other room Beth could hear the evening news. There was mention of the murder case and the pathologist: Mel's voice coming over clearly ... Suddenly Beth realized that she missed her sister; wanted her there; wanted to hear her news. Wanted, she thought unexpectedly, to question her about her life. What do you do, Mel? Who do you see? Who do you love?

She was greedy to know all at once. Avaricious for news – how did her sister live? How had her mother lived for all those years she had been away? How *did* other women live who weren't bound up with illness and responsibility? How could *she* have lived if she had been Mel?

I want to know what you do, Beth thought hungrily, I want to know. I want to know. How do you live without a husband and child? Without sickness? Without responsibility? How do you live just for yourself? And how does all that glory feel?

'Beth?'

She turned at the sound of her mother's voice, her expression softening into a smile.

But Sylvia had been watching her daughter for a long time from the door and had seen in Beth that hunger which she recognized all too well. She might fool the grocer, the doctor, and her father, Sylvia thought, but not me. I know you, Beth, I know you because you are a part of me.

And it was the part she feared.

Three months passed in as many seconds, Mel staying away from Aynhams and talking to her sister and father by phone. Not once did she speak to her mother. Daniel did not improve, or deteriorate, and Edward attended school in Pendleton, bringing home hand-made cards and letters written to Mel, which the teacher had helped him with. It was like writing to a celebrity, she told her husband that night, like writing to the prime minister.

As for Michael, he continued to run the Salford practice alone. At the weekends he employed locums, but otherwise he coped unaccompanied. He wanted to. Not just because he was a conscientious doctor, but because he wanted to spend time away from home.

On many occasions Sylvia had asked to help him, as she used to do in the old days, but he had always made excuses – *I can cope, I'll be back soon. No, you help Beth instead . . .*

The truth was that he found her company cheerless. There was no real feeling between them, not even that of friendship, and as he grew older Michael discovered that the only real peace he felt was when he was with his patients.

By now Salford had changed visually out of all recognition: the bombed sites had mostly been rebuilt, the inner part of the town restored. But to what? After the slums had come stocky little estates, but no change in the feeling of the place. That was still bleak, still pocketed with violence. And the murders had done nothing to lift the atmosphere.

Grim black-and-white photographs on the front of the newspapers confirmed what everyone felt – Salford was a place without heart. The faces of the accused corroborated it too. Dull, white faces, with hard eyes which had in them the shadow of the tenement, the long dark alleyways, the ill-lit squalor of Haslam Street and Gladstone Row. People looked at the photographs of the accused and the streets where they lived and were afraid of them. Afraid of the poverty, the grinding savagery which had come to fruition in the glut of child murders.

The families George had treated for TB, and all manner of illnesses caused by lack of hygiene and sanitation, had spawned their inevitable offspring and as he walked around at night Michael had noticed with helplessness that – even amongst the new houses and flats – the same hollow emptiness remained.

Now the council estates were pitted with gangs, stone-faced youths hanging round street corners, some no more than kids. At first Michael had called in the social services to look after some family or other, but as time went by he realized that he was one of the few that people would talk to. He had been around a long time; he was accepted.

So the most covert of men became the father confessor to all the misplaced, desperate and abused amongst his patients. Maybe it was Michael's very reserve which compelled them to ask him for help; maybe his lack of pity was more tolerable than the bleating of some university-trained bureaucrat. Whatever it was, Michael found that his St Stephen's Street practice gradually became a system of emotional, as well as medical, support.

After the murders, Halsall Street had been demolished, Gordon Cutting changing its name, although no one went down there at night and a few flowers were left daily at the grim entrance. Where Michael's father had once gone on foot with a lantern, down cobbled alleys and along the roughest patches of Salford docks, Michael now drove.

Though before long the streetlights had been broken and the same desolation lay wedged over the dark town.

A desolation which had intensified with the news of the murders. No paper, no television programme, no magazine, seemed to be exempt from it. The fact that the accused were a Salford man and two Salford women made the guilt universal to the town. People spoke about knowing the families, others denied ever having known them, and Michael remembered his father describing one of the accused's mother as being 'a bint, God help anyone she comes into contact with.'

George had known from instinct, from experience, from walking those streets for sixty years. He had known automatically whom to trust and whom to doubt. As he reached the turning into Wardourn Alley Michael wished that his father were beside him. *I wasted so much time being angry with him. Blaming him. I lost so much time with him . . .* Michael's footsteps halted suddenly.

I won't make the same mistake with Mel, he thought. I won't lose her because I was stubborn.

His spirits lifted suddenly. Things were not as bad as he had feared. He had a family, a profession, a daughter who adored him, and one close friend. Walking on, Michael thought of Harry and wondered why he hadn't been to Aynhams for a while. Admittedly the clinic was now being run by an administrator, and used by a number of other plastic surgeons, either as their main base or as a supplementary clinic. Harry didn't need to be there constantly, but he usually came once a fortnight. Sometimes more often. But not lately . . .

Michael paused, looked up at the sky. Spring would be coming soon, spring and the lighter nights and warmer days. He would welcome it. Aynhams looked beautiful in spring. He might suggest that Mel came home for a rest before the trial began; he might even try to effect a reconciliation between Sylvia and her daughter. Besides, there was always Edward to use as an excuse. How could Mel keep away from her adored nephew?

He would ask Harry to come as well – get everyone together. It would be like old times, in a way. It would be as if nothing had changed. Yes, Michael thought happily, it would be good for everyone to see each other again.

Chapter Twenty-five

'You *are* joking?' Mel said, pulling on Harry's towelling robe and wrapping it around her. 'I know Dad wants to see us both, but we can't go back to Aynhams.'

'Well, not together, but separately we could.'

Her eyes fixed on Harry. 'On the other hand, why *not* together? I mean, we *are* having an affair, aren't we? Why can't we go together?'

'Be reasonable,' he replied wearily. 'How can we?'

'I could say you were the man in my life,' she replied lightly, almost as though she were serious, 'and my father could then throw you out of Aynhams and close the clinic.'

'You could marry me, I suppose.'

Stunned, Mel stared at the man sitting at the end of the bed. Marriage – was he joking? Marry Harry? The words sounded funny – *Marry Harry* – and stupidly, she laughed.

'Am I to take that as a no?' he asked coldly.

'I wasn't laughing at you,' Mel replied, sliding over to him and putting her head on his shoulder. 'But how *could* I marry you?'

He had obviously had second thoughts himself and was anxious to retract. 'It was a stupid idea, forget it.'

'No, now come on,' she coaxed him, 'think about it seriously. We can't get married, we can't even let on that we're involved.' She touched his cheek. 'Harry, don't get mad at me.'

'It was a stupid idea,' he repeated, getting to his feet. 'I don't know what came over me.'

He was moving away hurriedly, almost as though he were putting distance between himself and his words. The sudden coldness surprised Mel; surely she hadn't hurt his feelings? Surely he knew she was talking sense? She was glowing from the unanticipated proposal. He must love her, she thought, he *must*. Harry never got serious about women. Never. So he must love her to have proposed.

She loved him, after all . . . Didn't think she would, knew too much about him to think it was anything more than an affair, was for a while too angry with herself to consider any real future with Harry Chadwick. Besides, even if she had fully trusted him, could she really commit herself to marrying him? How could she tell her family – her father especially. What could she say?

Her gaze followed Harry around the bedroom. They had been lovers for months, both independent, both strong-willed, both highly charged. Both also had well-developed egos – which was why they understood each other so perfectly. Only Harry could comprehend the pressure Mel was under; only Mel could fully understand his ambition. Neither wanted to be tied down, neither wanted marriage.

At least, neither had seemed to want commitment until now. Now Harry had asked her to marry him; now he had declared his feelings . . . Her heart rate accelerated. Maybe she could risk it, maybe she could. And then she realized – incredulously – that she *wanted* to be married to Harry Chadwick. She had never dared to articulate the thought, or even fully consider it before, but now he had spoken out Mel wanted him with an urgency which threatened to overwhelm her.

The time had come. The time had *finally* come.

'Harry . . .' she said quietly, '. . . I'm pregnant.'

He turned slowly, then picked up his clothes and walked into the bathroom. Stunned, Mel slid off the bed and dressed, her hands shaking as she fastened the buttons on her jacket. She didn't understand: he had asked her to marry him; he had shown he loved her, so what was the difference now that he knew she was pregnant?

For a long time after she was dressed Mel sat waiting for Harry to come out of the bathroom. She heard the cistern flush, and the sound of a running shower, then the drone of his razor as he shaved. Staring at the door she felt a fierce desire to hammer on it, to shout at him, even to physically hit him, but she couldn't, she was numb.

Finally Harry emerged. He looked, Mel realized, suddenly older. Dear God, she thought, he's aged. The shock has literally aged him.

'Do you want a lift?'

'To the hospital or out of the window?' Mel asked, trying the joke for size.

It didn't fit.

'I'm going past the hospital,' Harry replied, walking to the door.

She ran up behind him, scared now, frightened that she had – within the space of half an hour – lost him.

'Harry, what is it?'

'What d'you think?' he replied incredulously. 'I don't want children. I never have. We should have been more careful . . . Mel, I'm sorry, really sorry. But I can't have children.'

'You're not having it, Harry,' she replied, her tone icy. 'You've done your bit.'

Angrily she walked towards the lift, expecting him to follow, but he didn't, he simply watched her go.

Mel didn't go to Aynhams before the trial. And neither did Harry. He phoned her a couple of times to talk about 'things' and suggested that an abortion would solve their problem: 'We could go back to where we were, Mel. It would be the best for everyone . . .' She had put the phone down on him and then rested her head on her hands, the door of her office locked. He had understood her better than anyone – even her own father. Harry knew everything about her, every quirk, every failing, every strength. They were perfectly matched; perfectly attuned; perfectly alike. Except for the fact that he didn't want children, and she did.

What the hell! Mel thought to herself, then felt the old clammy sensation of panic overwhelm her again. How much do I love him? she asked herself. Enough to go against my principles? Enough to abort a child I never thought I would have? And if I did, and the affair broke up, who is to say I would meet someone else and get pregnant again? Who could I ever meet who would compare with Harry?

She had loved twice in her life. Cy she had lost because he wanted children; now she might well lose Harry for the same reason, only this time it was *her* choice.

A knock on the door startled her.

'Dr Cochrane? You have to leave now to get to the court on time.'

Wearily Mel rose to her feet. The nausea had passed, morning sickness now lasting well into the afternoon, and slowly she moved towards the door. Oh God, she thought, suddenly vulnerable and afraid, I miss my father. I can't talk to him and I need him so much.

'Dr Cochrane?'

'Coming,' Mel said, straightening up and walking into the corridor.

'Good luck.'

Which was precisely what she needed.

You didn't know someone as well as he knew his daughter without realizing there was something wrong, Michael thought, putting down the phone. When he had talked to her Mel had sounded tired, but in control, answering questions about the trial and assuring him that she was coping. But when he asked her to come home for the weekend she had blustered about having work to do, then rung off hurriedly.

Was it simply the trial? Admittedly the evidence was

horrific, but there had been something more than just nerves behind Mel's voice, some little shadow of that child he had once known; the one who pretended to be so tough, and was so often hurt.

Oh Mel, Michael thought, don't make me guess – you know how bad I am at that. Let me help you. Tell me what's wrong. Tell me what I can do for you. Talk to me. Talk to me.

PART THREE

The world is a comedy to those that think, a tragedy to those that feel.

Horace Walpole, 1717–1797

If thy heart fails thee, climb not at all.

Elizabeth I, 1533–1603

Chapter Twenty-six

No, it wasn't true, was Mel's first reaction. It couldn't be, it couldn't. She had come across the information by accident when she was looking up some detail for the trial. It had leaped up at her from the medical reference book and dug its teeth into her flesh, refusing to let go. Dear God, Mel thought again, it can't be. It can't . . . Heavily she rose to her feet and paced the office. Fifteen feet one way, twelve the other. What should she do? Confront her sister? Well, what was the choice? Her stomach was swelling slightly, her pregnancy becoming obvious. In life and on the television.

Her father had phoned then to ask her why she hadn't confided in him.

'I don't care if you're having a baby, Mel. You should realize that it doesn't matter to me. All that matters is you and now you need support. Come home.'

Her voice had wavered.

'You don't want to know who the father is?'

'If you had wanted me to know, you would have told me.'

Her eyes filled. Damn it, she was so emotional now, hormones, all those bloody hormones making a fool of her, making her vulnerable. The secret was out, everyone suddenly knew that the unmarried Dr Cochrane was pregnant. Unmarried and pregnant. Male colleagues nudged each other as they passed, acquaintances either ignoring the pregnancy or making an issue out of it.

'How brave of you, Mel, to have a baby alone.'

'Does the father know?'

'Who is the father?'

'A single mother – how daring. And you famous as well. I have to say I admire your guts.'

It had even been mentioned in the paper, the pathologist on the infamous murder trial being pregnant causing something of a stir – especially as the case was about child murder. Did it make her an impartial witness, someone asked.

'You're having a baby, aren't you?'

'Actually I've got a bad case of wind,' Mel had replied drily.

Harry had laughed when he saw the remark written up in the paper. But what could he do? He didn't want children. But he wanted her. But how much? His confusion rocked him. He missed her, even wondered if he *could* be a father, after all. But a moment later, he dismissed the idea. He had never wanted heirs; had been astonished when he asked Mel to marry him – that had gone against all his instincts. But then Mel wasn't like any other woman. Mel was a one-off. Mel was . . . Mel.

Many times he had wanted to phone her, or drop by her office. But what would he say? 'I miss you?' What would that mean to her? What would that sort out? Not the baby, or their relationship. So he left it hanging, not knowing what to do – and thereby doing nothing. But God, how he admired her. Standing up to everyone – in the courtroom and out of it. Look at me, her expression said, I don't have to hide from any of you.

And she didn't, but now, on top of all the other problems Mel had found out something which was so huge, so damaging, it hung in her mind like a death sentence. She couldn't dislodge it, or forget it. She had seen it and nothing would ever be the same again.

Laboriously Mel made her way towards the front steps. On the terrace the worn iron swing rocked listlessly in the breeze, two drinking glasses left empty on the table next to it. She thought back suddenly to the time she had sat with her father on the swinging hammock, watching stars, and remembered how he had looked up to the moon.

Midnight's smiling, tomorrow will be a lucky day.

How long is it since I told you that I loved you? Mel wondered. I hope it wasn't too long ago . . .

She paused on the gravel. The lights were on all over Aynhams, night coming in slow, surprisingly hot. She thought of her father walking up the drive with his medical bag, of the sweets in his jacket pocket, of the finished crosswords in the evening paper and the sadness he carried with him always.

He was everywhere, and nowhere. Faded film of her childhood, shot in fast forward. Hold it, Mel thought, grabbing at the memory, hold it there . . . Her father turned, pulled a mock solemn face at her . . . What will you say? she wondered blindly. What will you say now? . . . Another light went on in a window upstairs. Her old bedroom, looking out over the front garden. It was on that window ledge that she had scratched her initials years ago, and a heart with the name of a boy in it. Mel tried, but she couldn't remember the boy's name . . . Her mother had scolded her and she had deserved it. She had never been the easy one, the agreeable one. Not like Beth.

The name rattled in her chest. *Beth.* The loving wife, caring for her disabled husband and looking after their adored son. Little Edward, coming into their lives to compensate for the debilitating illness which had stopped his father in his tracks. Little Edward, idolized by his mother, running amok from this part of the house to the clinic, the hospital extension jutting out belligerently over the wide lawn.

She could remember all too easily her sister at Edward's age. Three years younger than her, smooth-faced, hair in a ponytail, dressed in yellow like a little golden sprite. She used to sit on the terrace drinking lemonade, still, very still, hardly childlike ever.

Beth had never teased anyone, had never been cruel. Had never said anything brusque or showed unkindness. But Mel had. Patients had petted Beth, and she had looked at them with those great wide eyes. How many times had her sister been cosseted and adored whilst Mel herself sat on the steps kicking the gravel and trying to remember the medical names in her father's books? Hardly anyone had taken her seriously then.

Mel wants to be a doctor? Never. She hasn't the temperament, Beth is the caring one.

The sound of a television knocked Mel's thoughts back to the present. The night was sticky, her hair clinging to her neck, her ankles swollen. She hadn't realized what it would be like to be pregnant; the heavy breasts, the sullen sickness stalking her from morning to night, the heat making her queasy in the mortuary. She had never been nauseated before; even when bodies had come in decomposed. Even when she had been called out to the first mutilated child's body, the birds singing, the winter cold misting the air as she spoke. Even then she hadn't felt the sickness she felt now.

But now this child inside her was making her weak; pulling all her strength away from her. She even found herself wounded by barbs she would once have ignored. Gossiped about, leered over, pointed out – she had stepped over it all – until this child took possession of her body, clinging to her womb and making her clumsy, too heavy to step over anything any more.

The television noises pooled out into the stifling air. Somewhere a car horn sounded, then canned laughter came out of the window. Slowly, Mel took the steps one by one, her hand pausing over the front door handle. Perhaps she should just walk away, pretend she didn't know . . .

But she couldn't. She had been duped, that was the worst of it. Even worse than Harry rejecting the baby and leaving her; even worse than all the bigoted prejudice she had experienced at work; even worse than the sight of the murdered children she had to examine.

So leave, she told herself. Walk away. Go on, get back in the car and drive off. The road's waiting, no one will ever know ... Oh, but *she* would know, wouldn't she? Distressed and uncomfortable in the cloying atmosphere, Mel leaned against the door frame. Don't ever see your sister again, she urged herself. Keep away. Why face what will surely be a confession of guilt? Why risk more trouble, more distress? But she couldn't let it be.

She thought suddenly of Daniel. Where was he now? Sitting in his usual place in front of the television, no doubt. Dressed in cotton, cool against his skin. Beth was good about details like that, knew she had to keep her husband comfortable, now that he couldn't do anything to help himself. He had lost the use of his neck muscles now: his head rolled, he dribbled. Once he had been attractive, walking down those same steps with her father, going out on a call. And once she saw him cry when one of his patients died. Mel had watched him through the serving hatch; he had been fine one minute, then he suddenly doubled over at the stomach, contracted with grief.

He didn't contract any more now. Couldn't move. Lost his sensations one by one, was losing his way. His life had narrowed down to a few rooms, a wheelchair, and the television – and the sweet continual service of his wife. People loved Beth for that. Talked about her devotion: ... *such a pretty young woman too, so sad. She should be having the time of her life now, having more kiddies and everything. Just look at the way she nurses her husband, it's wonderful* ... and Beth had accepted the praise modestly. Any wife would have done the same, wouldn't they?

When Edward was born everyone was ecstatic. *She deserved some luck*, their neighbours said. *A baby will take her mind off her troubles.* Daniel had deteriorated soon after; but he would hold on, whether he wanted to or not.

His disease was like that; it hobbled him, left him physically penniless, looking down the pauper years to come. Did he know then what his prognosis was? Mel wondered. Of course he did. Daniel was a doctor, after all. So did he despair? Did he want to die? She didn't think so. She had seen some life in him, certainly a look of pleasure every time he saw his son.

It was a particular look from way inside him – a look of hope. Edward was the future; Daniel might be crippled, dying, but Edward was healthy. Edward had his life to live, his chance of happiness. Edward had the means to let Daniel walk again, talk again, live again – because Edward was his son.

Mel stiffened at the thought and then pushed open the front door and walked in. It was hot inside, even though the windows were open, the television blinking in a corner of the sitting room, a vase of dying flowers dropping their heads in the twilight. Heavily, Mel walked across the hall, meaning to go upstairs to find Beth in her own part of the house, and then paused, seeing Daniel just where she had expected – Edward asleep on the settee next to him. She had never noted a likeness between the two, but that hadn't seemed strange, just something she had never thought about before.

Unwillingly, she struggled to remember what Beth had said after her son was born.

'I think he's more like me than Daniel.'

It was true. She hadn't lied about that.

At that time Daniel could still talk and was luminous with pleasure.

'I'm glad he's got your looks, Beth. I just hope he's as smart as I am.'

Had he really been light-hearted once? Mel wondered incredulously, looking at the back of Daniel's head slumped to one side.

A noise startled her suddenly, the sound of a tap being

turned on in the kitchen. Slowly, Mel moved towards the sound, her feet, in their flat shoes, silent on the carpet. Beth was moving around busily, bending down to empty the tidy bin, her hair piled high on her head, her arms beginning to tan. She was even humming to herself and was so engrossed that she jumped and dropped the bag when she saw Mel.

'God, you startled me!'

'Sorry.'

Immediately she smiled that lazy, kind smile. No, Mel thought, it can't be true. It *can't* be. You can't have fooled all of us for so long.

'It's good to see you. We were all worried about you,' Beth said kindly, glancing down at her sister's stomach. 'How goes it?'

'Difficult.'

She looked sympathetic.

Hypocrite, Mel thought, smiling, lying hypocrite.

'I wanted to talk to you, Beth.'

Unconcerned she nodded, picking up the bin bag again and walking to the door. 'OK, I won't be a minute.'

Outside, Mel could hear a dustbin lid being lifted then dropped. The smell of blossom filled the air suddenly, almost sour.

'So what can I do to help?' Beth asked, walking back into the kitchen and sitting down.

What can I do to help? She helped everyone, Mel thought. Helped the patients, helped her husband.

'I found out something recently,' Mel began, then groped for a seat suddenly.

The kitchen was too hot, sticky with the overheated night, and her nausea was returning. Hurriedly she dabbed at her forehead with the back of her hand. Was it the baby, or something else entirely?

Without being asked, Beth flicked on the fan and poured her sister a glass of water, bending over Mel anxiously.

'Are you OK?' she asked kindly. 'Whatever made you drive from Manchester so late at night – especially in your condition?'

For a prolonged moment Mel stared at her sister before answering.

'Listen, Beth, I was doing some research and I came across something about Daniel's illness . . .'

Interested, her sister leaned forwards across the table. The hairs on her arms were pale, the fan overhead humming like a metal insect.

'And?'

'I found something which worried me . . .'

Beth frowned, concerned. Tell me all about it, her look said, let me help.

It can't be true! Mel thought again. You can't have lied for years. Not you, not you . . .

'Daniel's sterile.'

For an instant Beth's eyes flickered, then she glanced down at her hands.

'Don't you think that I don't know that?'

Caught off guard, Mel frowned.

'He's been sterile for two years,' Beth went on. 'We haven't made love – in any way – for that long.'

She said the lie with such conviction that for an instant Mel almost believed it.

'Beth,' she said at last, 'you know as well as I do that Daniel has been sterile for much longer than two years.'

Her sister's eyes fixed on hers. They dilated, the look altering from interest to hard suspicion. Someone's slipped into her seat and taken Beth away, Mel thought madly. Her sister had gone, there was a stranger looking at her now.

'Well?'

The one word took a dive at Mel, her stomach dragging at her, her back aching.

Oh God, she thought, I don't feel well. I shouldn't have made this drive, I shouldn't have come here. What good will it do anyone to know the truth?

But she had to know; couldn't let the matter rest, couldn't allow it to go on any longer.

'Beth, Daniel had been sterile since the onset of his illness.'

Nothing. No response. Only that cold look in the eyes watching her.

'Daniel's been sterile for over six years,' Mel continued angrily, feeling her sister's gaze boring into her skull. *'Edward is five years old.'*

The fan moved indolently overhead, pushing the mushy air. Behind Beth, the cold tap dripped sullenly, a dishcloth hanging on its hook by the sink.

'Edward is five,' she repeated.

With one quick movement, Beth pushed away her chair and stood up. Slowly she moved round the kitchen and then leaned against the sink with her arms folded. Her face was grim with anger.

I never knew you, Mel thought helplessly, I never knew you at all.

'Who is Edward's father?'

Laughing, Beth scratched the top of her left arm. 'You're hardly the one to lecture me on morals, walking around with a kid due and no father in sight –'

Mel's face flushed with rage. 'I've never pretended to be anything I'm not!' she snapped. 'I didn't lie to people and let them think I was a bloody martyr –'

'So what do you expect – a medal?' Beth's voice had hardened, compassion turning to dust. She had been found out and was spiteful with guilt.

'You bitch!' Mel shouted. 'You let everyone think that Daniel was Edward's father.'

'Keep your voice down!' Beth hissed. 'I don't want them to hear.'

'I'm not surprised,' Mel countered. 'I can imagine what it would do to Daniel if he found out –'

'Which he won't,' Beth replied serenely. 'Because you're not going to tell him.'

'No, I won't,' Mel admitted, 'but not for your sake, for his. You deceived that man –'

'What was I supposed to do?' Beth replied fiercely, 'live the rest of my life without sex? Nurse him and look after him and lie next to him without ever making love again?' She was flushed with resentment. 'I was tired of being the good girl, the sympathetic one, the kind one. Whilst you played around I had to stay here and nurse my husband.' Her voice dropped, slid into its usual coaxing tone. *I'll look after you, darling ... Oh, it's nothing, I love my husband ...* What else could I do? Any woman would have done the same.'

She stared boldly into Mel's appalled face. 'Wasn't I allowed some fun? *Wasn't I?* Or was I supposed to have no sex drive at all? It didn't even last – it was just a fling, nothing else. But it gave me Edward. Oh, for God's sake, Mel!' she snapped. 'Was I really expected to stay the little Madonna, doing eternal good works? The poor young wife with the handicapped husband?' She was hoarse with malice now. 'You got out – I didn't. I had to stay here and listen day in and day out to, *Clever Mel, funny Mel. Look at Mel in the paper – isn't she doing well? Aren't you proud of your sister?*'

She was jealous! Mel realized. This woman of whom she had always been envious for her popularity, her kindness, her family – she was envious of *her*.

'It was always Mel,' Beth went on blindly, pushing away from the sink and leaning over the table towards her sister. 'Mel this, Mel that – God, how I came to hate you.' She pointed abruptly to her sister's stomach. 'You'll soon see what all this caring's like when you come to have that kid. Not that you have a husband to worry about. But then a husband can be useful to deflect suspicion, if nothing else.'

Mel had struck her before she had even thought about it, Beth's face reddening from the unexpected blow.

'You lying, hypocritical bitch!' Mel snapped. 'You sneaking, underhand cow.' She stared incredulously at her sister, the fan humming senselessly overhead. 'You know, until now I couldn't believe it. All the way up here I kept thinking that there had to be an answer, that you would explain it to me somehow.' She shook her head. 'Dear God, I admired you – so many people did. I respected you.'

Glancing away impatiently, Beth slumped back into her seat, her feet stretched out in front of her. She was breathing quickly, a vein pulsing over the fine skin at the base of her neck.

'I want to know who Edward's father is,' Mel said coldly. 'One of the patients? There have always been plenty of men around – was it one of them? Beth! *Was it one of them?*'

She said nothing, remained silent.

'Tell me!' Mel snapped, her hand banging down onto the table beside her sister. 'Tell me who it is!'

There was a dead silence. Outside, a fox barked in the field beyond, a car passing, its headlights falling on the windows for a second. Only the fan stirred in the liquid stillness, the pale green blinds flapping listlessly, a pair of silver spoons lying discarded on the draining board.

A memory came into life suddenly – their father stuffing a turkey at Christmas, the year before their mother left home. Another memory followed on, a hand at the window knocking on the pane: Daniel when he was fit, pressing his nose against the glass and holding up his medical bag. Newly promoted, newly wed.

So many ghosts, so much goodness, all gone.

Her voice low, Mel continued to stare at her sister. 'Who was Edward's father?'

A moment passed. Paused. Moved on.

'Beth, for God's sake – who was he?'

'You wouldn't believe me if I told you.'

'Oh, I'd believe you. I'd believe anything now.'

'Let it rest,' Beth said flatly. 'Mother will be back soon.'

'I don't care about that, I want an answer to my question.'

But Beth was being stubborn. 'She'll be back any minute now, and you know you don't want to run into her.'

'Beth,' Mel repeated warningly, 'tell me.'

'Why? It would do you no good to know. I've told you, it was hardly the love of my life, just a fling. He doesn't even know that Edward's his child.'

The heat was pulling at the creased silk of Mel's suit and dragging on her body. Even her hands felt swollen, plump-skinned.

'Tell me who is Edward's father!'

'You'd be shocked.'

'I doubt it!' Mel replied angrily. 'Nothing *could* shock me now. For the last time – who is Edward's father?'

'Harry,' Beth said finally. 'Edward's father is Harry. Harry Chadwick.'

Mel didn't see it coming, not for an instant. Didn't even feel the knowledge making an impact on her brain. The name just sank into her head, the words soggy, blurred. And then suddenly they registered – the pain coming like a siren, the name turned over and over in the fan above her head.

Chapter Twenty-seven

Summer of 1957 came in slow after the first steaming days, Michael finding a new partner for the practice and allowing him to undertake some of the evening call-outs.

Troubled, Sylvia was lying awake in the bedroom along the corridor from her husband. She heard him go to his room after eleven and the sounds of him preparing for bed. Above her, she could hear Beth wheel Daniel's chair across the floor. Why hadn't they changed over? she thought. Why didn't they occupy the ground floor instead of having a lift installed to the first storey? It would have made far more sense.

But she wouldn't say anything; she didn't feel as though she could interfere. She had no rights. Funny that, Sylvia thought. Once I ran this whole house and the clinic. Once I had control everywhere, now I am simply a lodger, with limited influence. It wasn't what she had expected; she had thought that bit by bit Michael and she would be reunited; she would go out on calls with him again and keep house, edging back into her previous role. But that role had been unexpectedly usurped; Beth was the one in charge now.

Sylvia didn't like it; didn't like it one bit. Nothing was going the way she had hoped and Michael was no closer to her despite her efforts. Stupidly she had thought that when he employed Dr Clements it was to secure some more time at home, but she had been wrong, Michael was simply exhausted, nothing more. He wanted peace, not a reconciliation.

Of Mel, nothing had been seen. Apparently since the spring she had become estranged from her sister too and only wrote to her father, the letters arriving at the weekend, Michael taking them with him without a word when he went to work. No one asked what was in them. Not Sylvia, not Beth. No one brought up the subject, although it was simple arithmetic to work out that Mel was due to give birth in September.

Of course Sylvia could ask her husband about it. She should have been able to; Mel was her daughter as well as his. But somehow she didn't dare. Michael loved Mel; there was no point in Sylvia ever trying to insinuate herself into that relationship ... Turning on the bedside light, Sylvia sat up and glanced at the mirror on the wardrobe door, sliding her nightdress over her head and studying her reflection. Thoughtfully, she then brushed her hair and cleaned her teeth, then slipped on her towelling robe and made her way down the corridor to her husband's room.

The house was silent, then above her Daniel coughed, the sound echoing in the empty hallway. Then silence again. Noiselessly, Sylvia moved toward Michael's room and paused outside. Should she knock? Oh God, she was his *wife*, why should she knock? Slowly she turned the door handle and walked in. He was lying on his side, apparently asleep as she moved over to the bed and looked down at him.

With what little light there was she studied his features and noticed the regular breathing of sleep, then she took off her towelling robe and slid into the bed beside him. He stirred, she took his hand and laid it against her bare thigh. He moved, said something inaudible and turned onto his back. Slowly Sylvia slid her hand between his legs.

He woke to the touch and remained still, staring at her dusky shape against the white sheet, her hands working over his body. Shaking with a mixture of frustration and desire he tried to push her away and then suddenly clung to her, pulling her body towards his frantically in mute and desperate longing.

*   *   *

It was the last post mortem she would do, Mel promised herself – no more until after the baby was born. She had done everything a mother was supposed to do, eaten well, rested when she could, and undergone every available test. She hoped that the baby was a girl. A boy would need a father more, would need someone to emulate, look up to. A girl could follow her mother's lead . . . As she had followed Sylvia? Mel thought impatiently, taking off her surgical cap and gloves and dropping them into the metal waste bin.

Now that it was finally over, the three accused found guilty and sentenced to life imprisonment, Mel could admit just how much the trial had taken out of her. Day after day she had waited to give evidence, then when she *was* called she had frequently been subjected to a barrage of questions from the defence lawyer. Was she sure about the injuries? How much experience had she had in cases such as these? Did she realize what her testimony would mean to the accused? Yes, she realized, just as Mel had realized that every day she gave witness the parents of the murdered children watched her from the public gallery.

She had always avoided their eyes, because she didn't want to see the longing there; the plea for revenge. Instead she had given her evidence coolly and refused the offer of a chair. Obviously pregnant, Mel had never allowed herself to be swayed by emotion; to think of the child she carried undergoing the same fate as the dead children. Her composure had impressed everyone who watched her, but in the evenings, when she left for home, Mel's control faltered and when no message or letter came from Harry she retreated within herself.

The phone rang, but it was work, or her father. Never the call she hoped for. Letters came and were duly answered, the Principal of the Manchester Infirmary commended her on her evidence, as did the police, but inside her there was a loss so raw and unfathomable that it left her emptied of feeling. All she clung to was the thought of her child, of the baby she carried. Of the baby which had cost her so much.

There had been no end of gossip, even a bet running in the doctors' restroom as to the father of Mel's child. Many thought it might well be Cy Tolash – after all they had had a hot thing going for a while, and he had been back in England. Others decided it was some young inexperienced doctor just starting up, someone who didn't want the responsibility of a wife and family. All agreed that it would be a tough job finding out – the lady in question wasn't exactly forthcoming on the subject.

But they had to admire the way Mel had behaved. From her demeanour no one would have expected that here was a high-profile pathologist who was unmarried and about to give birth without a partner anywhere in sight. Oh, they said, it was very liberal, very independent. But there was still a stigma attached to being an unmarried mother, even for someone in Mel's position. The reasoning went this way: how come she couldn't get the father to marry her? She was a successful woman with money. Maybe he was married; maybe he had dumped her. Either way, they all agreed, it was a humiliation and no mistake.

Then something very strange happened. The trial had been over for some weeks, the press turning their attention elsewhere, the suspects' grainy photographs no longer appearing on front pages. The attention which had stalked Mel had also moved on, and yet, now that everything was still again, she suddenly experienced a numbing depression. All the details and horrors of the children's injuries came back to her in dreams; as did the faces of the accused. She could hear their voices and replayed the way the two female suspects had exchanged glances when Mel was giving her evidence.

She had been so professional, so contained, that the emotion of the experience had passed her by – until now. Now

Mel knew that she had looked evil in the face, and realized – for the first time in her life – that she had seen something of which she was truly afraid.

It was at this time that the Principal of the Infirmary had called Mel in to see him. After congratulating her once more on her evidence at the murder trial, he turned the conversation round to children, without directly mentioning the fact that she was unwieldy and seven months pregnant. There had never been a case like this before, he thought with curling embarrassment, usually the pathologists were whey-faced male doctors in late middle age, not heavily pregnant, good-looking women who had caught the attention of the media.

He wanted to know if Mel wished to take pregnancy leave. Only a few weeks, Mel replied. Fine, he said, fine . . . And that was it. Mel walked out deep in thought. She would have to hire a nanny, she realized suddenly, someone competent so that she could carry on with her career. There was no possible way she could give up work, she needed the money to support herself and the child now. And she needed the stimulation.

If only things had been different, Mel thought longingly, if only she had never read that piece about Daniel's illness and discovered Beth's betrayal. If only everything had stayed as it was before. Then she could have gone home to Aynhams, could even have left the baby with Beth and her father, getting a local nanny to help out. Her child would have had the same upbringing as she had; it would have had room to breathe, to grow, to flourish – as Edward was flourishing.

A jolt of unexpected envy irritated her and, annoyed, Mel snapped closed her medical case and left the mortuary, walking through the rain to her car and turning on the engine. It was a Friday night. In the past she used to go home on Fridays, to forget work and her colleagues. She could relax at Aynhams, talk to her father, talk to her sister . . .

But she couldn't talk to Beth any more, couldn't even look at her. Beth had lied to all of them – and worse, much worse, *her sister had given birth to Harry Chadwick's child*. Harry had never said anything about an affair with Beth. Never a word. He had lived and worked at Aynhams and had been having an affair with Beth, and then he had had an affair with her.

It was all so sordid, Mel thought listlessly. Beth had even referred to her liaison with Harry as a 'fling', something quick and obviously of no importance. It might be of no importance to Beth *but it mattered to her*. Mel rubbed her temples vigorously. It had been a joke, her thinking that she was the love of his life. Harry Chadwick was just a user – and how flattering to his ego to think that he had seduced the two daughters of his best friend. And how stupid of her to be taken in by him. After all she knew, after all she had seen over the years, to be used and then rejected was almost unbearable.

And there was no one to whom she could turn for comfort. Certainly not her father, from whom she had to hide the truth for ever, nor her sister, of course – and as for her mother: she had never confided in Sylvia. And even if she did confide in someone, what would be the point? They would only tell her what she already knew – that it was wrong, all wrong. Wrong to be fooled by Harry, and wrong to have deceived her father.

But she couldn't forget it or put it behind her, because she was carrying Harry's baby. There would be no tidy ending; this child was to be a permanent reminder of what she had done. Gingerly, Mel touched her stomach with her fingertips. Harry had slept with her sister, *possibly loved her sister*. Mel closed her eyes against the thought. Harry was the father of her nephew. But did he really not know? she wondered for the thousandth time. Beth might tell her that Harry had no idea, but had he never wondered, never guessed that Edward might be his son?

She tried to think back to the times she had seen Harry and Edward together – had there been any special bond, any extra attention that Harry had lavished on the child? Nothing that she could recall, but then Harry was always generous with presents, affection. He would spoil the little boy, but then he would have spoiled any little boy. He was good with children, was Harry . . . And he was good with women, all kinds of women, young, middle-aged, single, married. Even women who were the daughters of his best friend.

Her hand slammed down suddenly on the car horn, making a passerby jump at the noise. What a bloody mess it was. She couldn't even look her father in the face any more. And she could never tell him who her baby's father was. She couldn't tell him who Edward's father was either. It would crucify him. Jesus, you were busy, Harry! she thought bitterly. Two sisters in one family. That was going it, even for you.

Her hatred was dark inside her: it drew on every evil thought and intention she had considered over the sleepless nights since her argument with Beth. Harry Chadwick had left her with his child. He had deserted her because she was carrying *his* child. God, didn't he realize that she could ruin him? One word from her, one tearful confession to her father, and Michael would have the clinic closed and Harry barred from Aynhams for ever. Her father was an honourable man, he would never forgive his oldest friend for such treachery.

And if Mel *did* expose Harry, Beth might be tempted, but she could never tell their father the truth about Edward. A confession like that would ruin her. It would also destroy Daniel, and smash the legend of Saint Beth into a thousand pieces. Gone would be the martyr; gone would be the sacrificing wife; Beth would be exposed for what she was – and she would never allow that.

After all, Harry had served her sister's purpose. Mel

doubted that Beth had loved him, he had simply provided her with sex and a child she could adore. He had done her a favour, in fact. At least, that was the way Beth would see it. But *she* couldn't. Mel could only think of Harry sleeping with both of them simply in order to notch up two other conquests.

No, that couldn't be true! she thought, straightening up and glancing out of the window. The wind had blown a piece of the *Manchester Guardian* across her windscreen, a photograph of a child catching her eye. How could Harry have even suggested that she abort their child? Didn't he know anything about her? Didn't he realize that after she had examined the bodies of murdered and tortured children she would never consider taking her child's life, even in embryo?

She could *ruin* him, Mel thought again, a feeling of rage crushing her. Remorse followed immediately, complete with a sense of absolute loneliness. Oh God, I don't want to ruin him. I want him back, I want him here, I want him with me when I give birth to his child ... Her eyes fixed on the windscreen wipers, fighting tears.

She couldn't go home, she couldn't ask anyone for help. She was alone, completely and utterly alone.

And she was very scared.

Chapter Twenty-eight

Two years passed, and on her son's birthday, Beth threw a party for him and his friends at Aynhams. Edward was dark as his mother and grandmother, a strong child, well-muscled, fit; his family's lodestone; his father's link to life. Daniel had lost all power of speech by this time so now Edward spoke for him, his mother encouraging the closeness between the two.

There were many children in the garden, presents scattered under a large sun umbrella, a table laden with food and cold drinks, balloons bobbing in the slight breeze. Hearing the noise, several of the patients in the clinic stared out of the window towards the party taking place on the grass, and amongst them stood a familiar figure, red hair almost completely grey, his stocky figure filling out the white doctor's coat.

Harry had been to South Africa for the summer months, and had already made arrangements to visit Russia at Christmas, returning to Aynhams in the New Year. His rooms had remained unchanged, his clothes – of course updated – still hanging in the closet, his watch and glasses laid on the table beside his bed at night.

He crept back slowly after the affair with Mel. Came back inch by inch, Beth making no reference to the argument with her sister and no mention of their past liaison. Michael was so grateful that his old friend had come home. He wondered aloud why he had seen so little of him, and Harry pleaded a heavy workload.

'Don't be a stranger, don't go off again,' Michael had

said, touching Harry on the shoulder. 'We like having you around.'

We. Harry noticed that the pronoun had changed. Not I, *we.* Michael had been lonely for years and when Mel drifted away, he had been so empty that suddenly it didn't seem impossible to let Sylvia back in. Triumphant, she slithered back into her old life. Her status was restored; she made love to her husband; she made him whole again. She pretended that he was the only man she had ever loved, and he pretended to believe her. Why? Because he needed to.

A figure suddenly approached Harry – Dr Clements coming across the grass. Nothing like old Tudge, he was young and lively, stopping to pick up one of the children's balls and throwing it over the stable wall. Harry noticed – not for the first time – that he was a little like Michael, and a lot like Daniel used to be. The St Stephen's Street practice was busy. The energetic Simon Clements had introduced new drugs and attended many lectures to hear about medical procedures. He's keen and quick, Harry thought, and he doesn't mind the long hours.

Yet everyone who was present at the party was aware that there were two people absent. Mel and her daughter, Sydeney. Baby photographs had been exchanged between father and daughter, pictures passed over to Sylvia and then on to Beth. They all wrote to congratulate her, and to press her to visit. But she never came to Aynhams. She stayed away, in Manchester, then when Sydeney was nine months old she moved out of the city to the coast, taking a house in Southport. A house with a high stone wall around it and a view of the sea from the bedroom windows.

People talked about her. She was well known, called upon to give evidence at other murder trials and undertaking more post mortems than most other pathologists in the North West. Her workload was formidable because she was ambitious and because she was trying to prove something – that she needed no one. That she could survive by herself, with only her child for company. That way Mel could no longer be hurt. That way she would be safe.

But she *was* hurt every time her father sent her photographs of Edward. She saw him in the house her daughter should be enjoying, she saw him indulged, petted, growing stronger day by day on a diet of adoration. Beth allowed her mother, father and husband to believe that they loved Daniel's child, and she probably even grew to believe it herself, sometimes – if no one reminded her of the reality.

And who would? Not me, Mel thought, and she was the only one who knew. So Beth was safe, she had pulled off her deception with aplomb and had also scored well over her sister. Now that Mel was estranged from the family, Beth was the admired one, the loved one, the loyal one. How cruel of Mel to stay away, she said at times, how could she not let us get to know her child?

Always clever where her own interests were concerned, Beth became even more cunning, hiding her feelings with immaculate ease. No one but her sister really knew her, and Mel was a long way away. Deftly, she sowed the seeds in tidy, poisonous rows over the years.

'I miss Mel so much,' she said to her mother, 'she should be home. She should let bygones be bygones.'

Sylvia nodded. 'I know she'll never forgive me for what I did – but why is she angry with you?'

Beth smiled her angel smile. 'I think the baby's father let her down so badly she can't face us. I think she's ashamed.'

'Did she ever tell you who he was?'

'No,' Beth replied honestly. 'I think she wanted him to marry her, but he wouldn't. I think that's why she's so bitter.'

'But we'd understand –'

'I know,' Beth went on sympathetically, 'but Mel was always touchy, always oversensitive. I suppose she feels embarrassed . . . I don't know for sure. But I miss her.'

Such perfect slices of spite Beth served up over the years, keeping her anger to herself as she shored up the evidence against her sister. It's so easy, she thought. After all, Mel had always been the difficult one, the odd one out. Everyone knew that. So Beth continued to watch her son grow up knowing that one day he would inherit Aynhams. Edward was the grandson, son and heir. It was Edward, *Harry Chadwick's child*, who would inherit the house. And so, by proxy, Harry Chadwick would have his wish granted. The sore-arsed kid from Gladstone Row who had peered over the wall at Aynhams so many years ago, would, through his own son, inherit the place he had so coveted.

Meanwhile Mel went to her rooms in the Manchester Infirmary after leaving Sydney in the care of Mrs Morris – a widow in her fifties – and undertook her post mortems on all manner of bodies, after all manner of deaths. Sometimes she realized with bitterness that one of Harry's children had everything by stealth, and that the other was isolated, apart. She knew it as surely as she knew that she couldn't usurp Edward's position by exposing her sister. What would be the point? Daniel would crumple with the news, and her parents would never be able to view their younger daughter and grandson in the same light again. So who would benefit? Only Mel, and only for a brief flicker of revenge.

So she kept quiet for over two years and burned with injustice. She didn't want to wish ill on her nephew, but she wanted her daughter to have everything he had, in equal measure. She wanted fairness, she wanted to confront Harry, and her sister, to damage them as she had been damaged. To demand explanations, confessions, amends.

But all she could so was to watch from a distance and smart with resentment on the part of her child. She wanted to go home, and she wanted to take her child home – but she could never go home again. And that was something far worse than any pain. So Mel blocked it out, and held her child at night and promised Sydney all manner of magical things for the future. And meanwhile Harry sent money every Christmas to help with the upkeep of his daughter. And every New Year Mel put the money in a savings fund for Sydney when she reached eighteen.

Then one day Mel noticed that her daughter showed all the signs that she would be tall. Already her hair was dark red, and about her mouth was always some look of Harry.

Chapter Twenty-nine

It was just beginning to get dark, Edward's birthday party still in full swing, the September warm keeping the leaves long on the trees. Muted shadows played across the sloping lawn, a bird landing on the roof of the little white pavilion: and from the window of the east tower Edward looked out, as his aunt and grandfather had done before him.

Smiling, Edward stared down at his friends on the lawn. No one had missed him yet. Soon they would, and then they'd all come looking for him. Leaning out of the window he thought of the scolding he had had from his mother that morning.

'No one goes up into the tower,' she had said. 'I know you've been up there, Edward, the lock's been forced.'

A long time ago Michael had fixed a padlock there to prevent anyone climbing the rickety steps. The tower was unsafe: when anyone had the time to think about it they promised they would restore it, but now there were other calls on their time, like the practice, looking after Edward and nursing Daniel. So they ignored it. No one needed the old tower. It was off bounds, set aside, cut off.

But Edward didn't listen. He had been spoiled and knew that he would always be forgiven for any minor trans-gression – especially on his birthday. Besides, he liked the tower, liked the idea of being apart from the rest of the house; away from his parents, his grandparents, and the noise from the clinic beyond the adjoining wall. Up in the tower he could escape, do what he wanted without anyone watching him. Because they *did* all watch him; especially Daniel.

He had become used to having a sick father, defending Daniel if anyone at school mocked him; even taking over some of the minor tasks of looking after him. Feeding was no trouble to Edward, neither was pushing his father's chair out onto the terrace when the sun was warm. He might look at other boys' fathers and wonder what it would have been like to have an active parent, but Edward was phlegmatic, not given to introspection. Or rebellion.

Except in little matters – like the tower. That small part of Aynhams was his, his alone. He needed it, needed somewhere apart from adults and sickness. The small space above the stone steps was the perfect haven, an area given over to his fantasies, a place to be himself. No one could get to Edward there, no one could spoil him, or fuss him, or ask him to do things for them. He was apart, stealing little pockets of time.

He would play up there, and listen to the radio Michael had bought for his last birthday and mime to the music, playing an imaginary guitar as he had seen Elvis Presley do on the television, his school tie taken off, his feet – in socks only – quiet, so that no one could hear him from below. Throwing his head around and strutting on the dusty floor he was famous, he was happy. They might think he was going to be a doctor when he grew up, but Edward had other ideas. He was going to be a star, he was going to sing, leave Aynhams, go to London, or – his head spun with the magic of the thought – America. He was going to be famous.

Smiling to himself, Edward moved away from the window. They still hadn't noticed he had gone yet; some of his friends were playing football, and one of them had climbed up to the top of the apple tree in the centre of the lawn. Luminously, the balloons glowed their bubble-gum colours in the fading light.

He had sneaked away after he had cut his birthday cake and crept along the back corridor to the foot of the tower steps. Listening carefully, Edward could hear voices, but they were coming from the garden, and, believing himself safe, he had produced the borrowed key, unfastened the new padlock and pushed open the door.

Pulling it closed behind him Edward had then climbed the uneven steps to the tower room above. He wasn't going to be a singing star today, he was going to be a football hero. He had been watching Billy Wright on the TV and was mesmerized, taking off his shoes and pretending to kick a ball around.

In his mind he could hear the roar of the crowd, thousands rising to their feet as he scored, Edward hurling his hands in the air and running round the tower room. His feet slid over the floor quicker and quicker, his feet slippy in their socks, making trail marks through the dust, his eyes closed. The air in the tower room was stuffy, clogged with stale sunlight, but Edward heard and saw nothing – only himself scoring and taking the adulation of the crowd.

He was completely absorbed. He was *there*, a football hero, the sounds of the stadium and the ball going through the goal posts real to him. Again, Edward replayed the point of real triumph – another goal! The crowd were going mad now. No one had ever seen anyone as good as this before! Throwing up his arms, Edward's head went back, the hairs prickling on the back of his neck as he ran round and round the circular room, his feet travelling fast, very fast, towards the top of the stone steps now only inches away.

Out in the garden Beth had suddenly noticed her son's absence and turned round, looking for him. She saw all the other boys, swinging from the trees, kicking a football, but no Edward. Idly she wandered down the lawn looking for the birthday boy, shadows lengthening across the grass, the coolness making mossy darkness under the trees. Her glance rested on each child for an instant, ticking them off mentally, walking further away from the house as – up in the east tower – Edward scored his imaginary goals.

He was oblivious. He was *in* his dream, could see it, feel it, and wanted to hold on to the moment as long as he could. So he kept his eyes closed as he ran, his mind swollen with sound and sight and fantasies, his brain seething with excitement and euphoria.

Then, suddenly, his left foot caught the top step and his ankle turned over, Edward's eyes snapping open as he felt himself propelled down the first few steps, his head striking the stone wall at the first bend. He felt no pain, just wondered how he would explain what he had been doing up in the tower. Then he felt his head strike another step and tried to scramble for a foothold, his arms flailing round, his hands fixing on nothing. The third blow was the worst. It broke his nose, blood coming into his throat as he lost consciousness. And still he continued to fall.

His body finally came to land against the bottom door – thirty-five steps below.

It was Michael who found him. He noticed the padlock of the tower had been removed and opened the door, his grandson's body falling out at his feet. Panicked, he kneeled down and frantically felt for a pulse, then checked and rechecked Edward for signs of life. A little way off he could hear Beth calling for her son, and remained for a while kneeling beside Edward unable to move, unable to comprehend what had happened.

A few further minutes passed, Beth's voice rising higher, irritation muted. She had expected her son to have reappeared by now and suspected that he had sneaked off to his room without telling her. In another moment, Michael knew she would mount the stairs and walk into Edward's bedroom.

Helplessly Michael felt for his grandson's pulse again, but there was nothing. The child was lying awkwardly on the floor, his legs splayed over the last two steps. Gently

Michael pulled his grandson towards him until his whole body was lying on the carpet of the hallway. It looked less horrific that way. He then cradled the boy's head in his arms and waited for Beth to find them.

She was calling out frequently now. 'Edward, Edward . . .'

She would be expecting to hear his reply, or his footsteps hurrying towards her . . . In Michael's arms Edward lay immobile and pale, his lips slightly open, his gaze fixed on nothing. His hands shaking, Michael closed his grandson's eyes, smoothed his hair, and pulled his jumper straight.

And waited.

Beth's footsteps had ceased overhead. Now she was coming downstairs; before long she would move into the back passageway and see them. Michael held his breath. Waited. He wondered if he should call out. Warn her. Tell her. But she would know soon enough. Her feet moved quickly now, her heels tapping on the wooden floor. She had passed from the main house and was opening the first door into the back corridor.

For a second Michael nearly lifted up Edward's body and hid it. He could pretend that nothing had happened; postpone the moment when his daughter would see her dead child. But instead Michael remained where he was, holding Edward and waiting for the inevitable opening of the last door. When Beth walked through that door she would see them. She would know.

One, two, three footsteps. Her voice was closer, louder, her feet pausing only momentarily as she turned the handle of the door and opened it.

Mel left Manchester as soon as her father told her the news, only detouring to collect Sydney who was with Mrs Morris in Southport. Hurriedly helping her into the car, she saw her daughter's dark eyes fixed curiously on her.

'We're going on a trip,' Mel explained, wondering what

to say next, '. . . to see your granddad.' Quickly she climbed into the driver's seat and started the engine. 'He needs us now.'

Pulling out into the traffic, Mel's eyes fixed intently on the road ahead. Edward, dead. No, it wasn't possible, he was only a little boy. He couldn't be dead. She blinked against a sudden rain storm, turning on the windscreen wipers. Oh God, Beth, she thought. Dear God, what will she be thinking? Glancing into the mirror, Mel checked her daughter's reflection. Sydeney was asleep.

Her sister's child was dead. *Edward was dead* . . . She tried to imagine how it would feel to lose her child and couldn't, *wouldn't*, pursue the feeling. Who cared about the past now? Her sister needed her, she was going home. Beth, Beth, Beth, nothing you did deserved this. No one deserves this.

The rain belted down on the windscreen suddenly. Slow down, Mel told herself. You don't need to have an accident. Arriving ten minutes earlier won't bring Edward back . . . Oh Christ, she thought, *nothing* would ever bring Edward back. She had been jealous of him, of her own nephew, bitter that he had everything. She had been estranged from her family for years because of her sister's treachery. And what good had it done anyone? Edward was dead, there was no reason to resent the child any more, no reason to be envious of him or his mother.

Her foot lifted on the accelerator, Mel glancing at her daughter again. If anything happened to you I couldn't live, I couldn't breathe, she thought. Her eyes flicked back to the road. How would Daniel take the news? Her parents? How would *Edward's father* take the news?

Angrily, Mel increased her speed once again. What did it matter what Harry thought? Maybe he would never know he was Edward's father. Dear God, why was she thinking of Harry at a time like this? She should be thinking of her sister, the woman she had loathed for years. The woman who had betrayed them all. Lied to them all. The woman who had lived her life pretending to be something she wasn't.

So was this a punishment? Mel thought. Surely to God, no. Nothing any woman did was worth such a penalty.

The rain came down harder, Mel changing gear thinking of Beth. How would she take the news? And how could she genuinely grieve with Daniel, knowing that Edward wasn't his son? How could she keep that secret now? And what would she *do* now? What was there left for her to look forward to?

Still sleeping, Sydeney sat on the back seat, Mel stealing glances at her child. Please God, let nothing happen to my daughter, please God let nothing happen to her ... The lanes narrowed after Mel left the main road, turning her car towards the familiar landscape of home. I've wanted to come back for so long, she thought, but I never thought it would be such a return ... Hurriedly, she drove through Pendleton and then moved into Buile Hill, Aynhams imposing, rain settling on her windows; the sun making a wicked rainbow over her chimneys.

As he had done so often in the past, Michael was standing in the drive waiting for her, and as she pulled up he wrenched open the car door and reached for his daughter.

'Dad, sorry, sorry,' Mel said blankly, holding on to him. 'I'm so sorry.'

'I knew you'd come home,' he said, then glanced over her shoulder, looking into the back seat of the car. His eyes fixed on the child sitting there and he seemed to falter, to hesitate.

'This is Sydeney,' Mel said, taking her daughter from the back seat and passing her to her father.

He took her eagerly, stared into her yawning face, then glanced over to Mel.

'Don't ever go away again, will you?'

She shook her head, then slowly followed him into the death house.

She should eat, everyone said so, but Beth wouldn't. Neither would she wash, nor change, nor comb her hair. Instead she stayed sitting on her bed, immobile, everything forgotten, even Daniel. In fact, she now ignored her husband. He was abandoned, his needs neglected, the force of Edward's loss crippling his wife as surely as his disease had hobbled him.

'What about your husband?' Sylvia prompted her.

Beth's eyes flared. '*What* about him? I've looked after him for years, I can't do it any more. I don't *want* to do it any more. There's no point –'

She wanted to scream until she was hoarse, until her throat bled. She wanted to tear at her father's face, his impassive eyes, to shout, *Why didn't you get the tower fixed? Why? Why? Why?* But she didn't, she didn't say very much of anything, just kept seeing the body of her son lying in the passageway in his grandfather's arms.

Boys are always falling, she had thought at first when she saw him. But they never hurt themselves. He must be stunned.

'Come on, Edward, time to say goodbye to your friends.'

But he hadn't been stunned, he had been dead. Killed by that bloody tower. And she was alone now, wasn't she? She was stuck with her useless husband and the only thing which mattered to her was dead. Her hand went up to her mouth, her teeth biting into the flesh. She couldn't *stand* this, she *couldn't*. She was going to go mad . . . Her breathing accelerated frantically as she looked round the bedroom, her eyes felt charred with disbelief.

They had made love in here, had conceived Edward in here. She hadn't loved Harry, but she had enjoyed him, and she had been very grateful for the child he gave her. It had seemed to work out so perfectly; she had the son and heir to Aynhams and her future was secure. She hadn't needed to tell Harry, she had let him think that Daniel was Edward's father – just as she had let everyone else draw the same conclusion. And Harry had never suspected a thing. In fact, if it hadn't been for her sister, no one would ever have known.

Her sister . . . Beth's nails tugged at the bedspread. Her sister . . . Mel would have everything now, she had the child, she had the career, she had the upper hand . . .

Frantically Beth's eyes closed, her teeth clenched. She would just keep her eyes closed and think back to the morning, that was all. And would picture Edward and hear his voice and imagine him back. And everything would be fine. It would be OK, just as it always was . . . But Edward didn't come back: he wasn't even alive in Beth's thoughts any more. He was lying dead on the floor in the passageway. He was lying dead and all her hopes were crushed under him.

'How is she?' Mel asked her mother as she walked in.

Without showing any surprise, Sylvia answered, 'Not well. She's taken it badly.' She turned to her husband and looked at the child in his arms. 'Is this your daughter, Mel?'

She nodded, 'This is Sydeney.'

'Unusual name.'

'It's French,' Mel said awkwardly, her mother watching her. 'I'm sorry –'

'It wasn't your fault.'

'I meant that I was sorry for all the bad feeling over the years,' Mel explained with difficulty. 'It doesn't seem to matter any more – not after something like this.'

She was formidable, Sylvia realized as she looked at her daughter. Tall, athletically built, perfectly coiffed and manicured, Mel bore no resemblance at all to the prickly, clumsy child she had once been. Her life and reputation had honed her, her voice, her movements, her presence, were all impressively polished. Incredible, Sylvia thought, how could I have produced such a child and not realized her worth? Was I so blinded by Beth's light-weight charm that I overlooked the value of this girl?

'It's good to have you home, Mel.'

Before she could answer, a voice interrupted them.

'Mel,' Beth said simply. 'Behold, the returning prodigal.'

Her bitterness winded all of them as she moved towards her father, her dead eyes fixing on the child in his arms.

'So this is the little bastard, is it?'

Wincing, Mel took in her breath. For an instant she nearly responded in kind – *Well, you're the expert on bastards, aren't you, Beth?* – but she couldn't. Her sister was obviously vitriolic with grief, aching to fight.

'Beth, I'm so sorry –'

'Liar!' she snapped back, her hair falling lankly around her cheeks, two bright patches of colour under her eyes. She was circling Mel like a fox circling its prey, Michael passing Sydeney over to his wife and then moving between his two daughters.

'Stop it. Beth, calm down, let me give you something –'

'I don't want anything! I just want my son back!' she shouted, walking away from them all and running up the stairs.

'I'll go after her,' Mel said hurriedly to her father. 'Can you look after Sydeney for me?'

'Maybe I should go with you –'

'No, leave us alone for a while, please.'

Nodding, Michael moved off, Mel just reaching the head of the stairs when the front door opened and a man walked in. For a long suspended moment Mel watched him, then she swallowed and called down to him.

'Harry.'

He turned at the sound of her voice, staring up at her.

'I heard about Edward,' he said by way of greeting. 'Jesus, how's she taking it?'

There was no enquiry after Mel, or their child, this was Beth's time. Strange, Mel thought, but I don't even feel jealous.

'She's bad, Harry. Very distraught.'

'I'll give her something –'

'She doesn't want it.'

'She doesn't want what?' Beth asked, moving into the corridor, glancing at her sister and then looking over the banister rail. 'Well, hello, Harry,' she said, her voice thick with bile. 'How are you?'

'Beth, I don't know what to say –'

'That's a first,' Beth replied, her usual sweetness completely obliterated. 'You usually know *exactly* what to say.'

He had begun to walk up the stairs towards her, his expensive coat creased from the long car ride.

'Beth, let me help,' he said, putting out his hand to her.

'You've given me all the help I need!' Beth snapped, 'I don't need any more *help* from you.'

He frowned, obviously puzzled. What was she talking about? The past? And if so, why was she angry about an old affair? Why did that suddenly matter after what had just happened?

Watching them both, Mel knew in that moment that something dreadful was going to happen. She knew it and yet she couldn't stop it. It had developed a momentum of its own and would play itself out.

'Beth, come on, calm down –'

'I have lost my son!' she shouted. 'I have lost my son!'

He still didn't realize what she was talking about and walked into it blindly. 'I know that. I'm so sorry, Beth.'

'You're *sorry*!' she said, barking the word at him. 'How sorry are you, Harry?'

He frowned, still baffled. 'I don't know what you mean –'

'Don't you? Well, you *should* be sorry,' Beth went on, leaning towards him, a ghastly look of pleasure on her face. 'You should be very sorry for my loss, because it affects you too, Harry, and you know how badly you take anything which affects you –'

Hurriedly Mel moved towards her sister and took her arm, but Beth shook her off violently.

'Why are you trying to stop me?' she asked. 'You were the one who knew all along, Mel. You were the one who was so outraged by my behaviour – although God knows why, when you were having your own bastard.'

Harry was silent, watching Mel's face, waiting for her response.

'Beth, calm down –'

'I don't want to calm down!' she hissed. 'I'm through with being calm and pleasant and loving. It's over, Mel. I'm not pretending any more. I thought you'd approve –'

'This isn't the time –'

'For what?' Harry asked, worried now, knowing that there was something malignant waiting for him.

'For the truth,' Beth replied, turning round to face him, her eyes hard with revenge. 'Edward wasn't Daniel's son, Harry. He was yours.'

He heard the words and then flinched as though she had pushed him. His mouth opened but nothing came out and blindly he backed away, running down the stairs towards the door. It was only as he pulled it open that Harry realized someone was watching him.

From under the turn of the stairs Michael had been listening to every word.

Chapter Thirty

'What have you done?' Michael asked, his voice menacingly quiet. 'You were my friend, Harry. What have you done?'

Harry was breathing heavily through his mouth, looking helplessly at Michael as he walked over to him.

'Michael –'

'What kind of man are you?'

'Michael, let me explain –'

'I don't want to hear it,' he replied quietly. 'I don't think I could take it in.' Slowly he glanced up to his two daughters at the head of the stairs. 'Edward was *Harry's* son?'

Beth nodded, running her tongue over her dry lips.

'He was?' Michael repeated, as though he were willing it not to be true. 'Daniel wasn't Edward's father?'

'No. Daniel has been sterile ever since his illness began,' Beth replied, her voice defiant.

Slowly, Michael glanced back to Harry, his expression blank, unreadable. He had loved this man who had betrayed him; he had welcomed Harry into his family; he had grown older with him; shared with him; always had a seat at his table waiting for him. And how had this friend repaid him? By seducing his daughter.

Oh, but it was worse than that, Mel thought looking at her father, reading his expression, you only know half of the story.

'Harry, *why*? Why did you do it?'

'I –'

'Why *my* daughter? You could have had any woman, why her? Why *my* child? In *my* house?' His voice was faltering with disbelief, the betrayal almost too much for him to comprehend. 'I thought of you as a brother, Harry. How could you do this?'

Cornered, Harry turned and looked up to Mel, still standing at the head of the stairs. His expression was unlike anything she had seen before; he was ashamed and suddenly aware of the magnitude of his actions. A strange, hurried feeling passed between them as Harry looked at her, memorizing her face; and in that one instant Mel realized that Harry Chadwick had loved her and still loved her.

At another time she would have gone to him. He would have gone to her, but it was too late. All Harry wanted to do now was to behave honourably. He felt cheap beside Michael, shoddy and loud-mouthed, a braggart who, for all his talent and success, could never match the integrity of the man he had duped. There was no excuse he could offer, and now all Harry wanted to do was to take the beating which was coming to him.

'Sydeney is my child too,' he said simply.

Mel closed her eyes and gripped the banister rail.

Michael's expression faltered, then he glanced away.

Beth laughed. *Laughed.*

'My grandchildren? Both my grandchildren?' Michael said blindly. 'You are the father of my grandchildren?'

'It never should have happened –' Harry began, but Michael raised his hands as if to avoid any further words.

'No,' he said simply, 'no.'

Harry's face had lost its bluster. Instead he was tormented, all too aware of the pain he had inflicted on the man he had loved as a brother. He watched Michael move towards him and stiffened, almost willing the blow which was sure to follow; but Michael didn't hit him. He just stared at Harry and then weaved past him, blundering out into the garden beyond.

* * *

No one would ever forget the night which followed. Rumours about it filtered around Pendleton, Salford and beyond, the details – known or imagined – embellished and embroidered by each telling. On Buile Hill, Aynhams had been shielded by trees, no sound of argument reaching beyond the perimeter wall. For all that anyone outside knew, nothing seemed very different – until the news began to spread about the death of Edward. It passed from mouth to mouth like buckets of water passed hand to hand at a fire. Shocked reactions mingled with simple disbelief. No, Edward couldn't be dead; he was only a child. Surely they meant Daniel. His father was the sick one.

Oh God, was their next thought, how would Beth take the news? And how would Dr and Mrs Cochrane be able to bear the loss of their grandchild? It was too much, they went on, they'd had some rough breaks in life, and Mel wasn't around any more ... They talked that night about loss and pity and they never knew until afterwards just what had really gone on.

Michael waited until it was dark, until the light had disappeared, then he came out of the white pavilion and walked across the lawn towards Aynhams. But instead of going in at the front doors he turned and moved to the clinic entrance. There was a light on, night staff coming in to watch the patients through the dark hours. Frowning, he skirted the side of the extension and then unlocked one of the doors to the old cellars. Inside, he moved carefully around the basement under the clinic, looking for what he wanted, finally making his way up the cellar steps to the operating theatres above.

He had lived for so long as the reserved Michael Cochrane; had controlled his feelings, had underplayed his emotions so much that at times he had wondered if he would ever feel anything again. Or if there would always be that gap between him and the trauma he encountered. But with the death of Edward there was pain. It began as Michael cradled his grandson and it pushed the cool composure out of his brain and left every nerve screaming. He wanted to beg his daughter for forgiveness. He told himself repeatedly that it was his fault, he should have had the tower mended or demolished. It should never have been left, just waiting for a tragedy to happen.

The fury of his rage and grief seemed to fill Michael's gut and burn in his throat. Nothing he could say, nothing he could do, could ever lessen the pain, the loss of a child. The loss of his daughter's one hope in a life which had been crippled; for she, as much as her husband, was handicapped.

He had watched her over the years and been proud of her compassion, of her willingness to nurse Daniel. Her beauty and kindness had been awesome to him, and he could see no echo of Sylvia in her. But he had been wrong again. His daughter had lied to him and to everyone else. She had played a role, and taken credit for being someone she was not. Her husband, whom she attended so lovingly, she had duped, and worse, she had allowed all of them to think that Edward – that precious, wanted child – had been Daniel's.

And all the time he had been Harry Chadwick's son . . . Michael caught himself breathing rapidly, sweat running down his face and back. He, who was never ill, felt as though he had a fever, his tongue dry, his ears buzzing. The scene in front of him blurred for an instant before righting itself, the walls dipping dizzily away from him. If I fall, Michael thought, I will die here. My heart will give out . . . He thought of his father and could hear George's voice: *For God's sake, lose your temper, Michael. You never lose control, do you?*

Oh, but he had. Slowly Michael felt his way along, his figure stooped over. Anyone seeing him would not have recognized him, not his posture or his expression, which was anguished, his mind replaying a scene he could not dismiss – his beloved daughter Mel, with Harry Chadwick.

He could see her talking to him, touching his arm, offering Harry – of all men – her love. He had not only made love to his daughter, but turned her against her father, and for that, he would be punished. Michael paused, leaned against the wall and punched at his stomach with his clenched fists. He would kill him, he would kill Harry. He would stab him and turn the blade inside his gut to make him feel something of the pain Michael was feeling now. He would cut out his eyes, would castrate him, would stop him from ever touching his daughters again or siring children.

He would stop Harry Chadwick. Michael was breathing rapidly. He thought that, maybe, just maybe, he was mad, and felt in those dark minutes as though he could do anything, as if the world and its morals and restrictions were apart from him. He had stepped across a line which separated reason from chaos, and there was no desire to go back. Carefully he felt his way along, using the wall as a guide, although there was some light coming through the small round windows of the operating theatre doors.

There would be no operations that night. Michael knew exactly what went on in the clinic; he had seen its inception, its growth, the immense stature it achieved over the years. He was one of the few who could remember Aynhams without the clinic, in those long ago days when he and Harry had been friends. In the days before wives and children. In the sweet unsullied past.

But there was no past any more. Only the present, and the present was terrible. Michael had lost his daughters. Not, as he had feared during the war, to Harry Chadwick, the surrogate father, but to Harry Chadwick, the lover. Chadwick had made liars out of them, had forced them to hide the truth from their father, had made them strangers. More Sylvia's children, than his.

For an instant Michael covered his face, and realized to his astonishment, that he was crying. The tears tasted salty against his tongue, but with them came no release, only heightened torment as he thought of Harry. He had lost the man he thought of as his brother; he had lost his friend. After all the years of enjoying that security in his life; that constant, valued ally, he had never once suspected that he might lose him.

How did you look me in the eye and betray me? How could you? Michael wondered blindly. Would I have done the same to you? Would I have abused your friendship, your home? When is it ever enough for you, Harry? You envied me as a child and I understood that. Later, I shared what I had with you – but it wasn't enough, was it? You had to take my children too.

The operating theatre was empty when Michael finally reached it, the only light coming through from the corridor outside. He could remember the excitement when it had been built; could remember the pictures which followed on the Pathe News; the Battle of Britain heroes, burned beyond recognition; the Aynhams nurses, chosen for their good looks; the hum and buzz of excitement which transmitted itself through newspapers and magazines and radio.

Britain was winning; we were showing the Germans that they couldn't beat us. The clinic had become a symbol of triumph. Nowhere else in the world was as famous, nowhere else was as respected, or as beautiful, standing as it did amongst the lush oasis of Buile Hill, the dank city of Manchester lurking beyond. He had been proud to be a part of history, to live here, to walk the land and call it home.

And now that was all shattered, as effectively as Greengate after the bombing. His home, his world, was crushed, as empty as a turned-out pocket. And there was only one person to blame.

Moving into the middle of the operating theatre Michael

raised the wood axe in his hand, bringing it down with all the force he could summon. The table reverberated with the blow but remained intact, Michael turning and smashing the arc lights, the overhead lights, and then kicking over the instrument trolley, scalpels and knives skittering across the polished floor. His strength was formidable, blow after blow raining down, spittle forming at the sides of his mouth, as he began smashing the wall tiles, the pristine, sterilized theatre cluttered with debris, the crashes of the axe eerily loud.

He was killing the clinic; killing the thing that Harry loved best. Killing Harry, because *this place was Harry Chadwick*. This was Harry's dream, Harry's ego made real. No child, no woman, could ever usurp the clinic in Harry's heart. Breathlessly, Michael kept smashing into the tiles on the walls, then on the floor, destroying the very objects which had once sustained life.

All through his long career he had had tried to save lives, but it had been a false ambition. He had blamed his own father for his mother's death and in the end he had been the one to kill George. He had tried to keep faith with his beliefs and had found the world disinterested and that his patients loved him no more for his integrity.

Suddenly Michael could hear feet running in the corridor and turned to see several staff members looking in at the windows and rattling the locked door. But he didn't stop, his rage – now that he had finally found it – giving him the energy to destroy the clinic, to lay waste to something good – because everything good in his life had been soiled.

He was sobbing out loud now, swinging the axe, his body dripping with sweat, his eyes unfocused, the sounds of his screams and blows echoing godlessly in the corridors and travelling through the door connecting the clinic to the house.

Perhaps he might even have died there; died beating his fury and hurt into the walls as he ground the smashed tiles and glass under foot. He might have exhausted himself and lost all reason as the operating theatre was destroyed by his hand: he might have suffered a stroke, had not one person had the courage to walk in.

Calmly Sylvia unlocked the door with a spare key. Slowly she moved into the wrecked theatre and watched the man in front of her lift the axe again.

'Michael.'

He stopped, then turned and stared at his wife's slight shape in the semidark. All his life he had never shown his true feelings; all his life he had suppressed his emotions and struggled uselessly to make his actions match his passions. And now every injury, every hurt, every sense of betrayal had been perfectly articulated – not in words, but in the destruction of the clinic. He had nothing left to say.

'Michael, stop,' she said quietly, knowing that they were watched. 'Stop this now.'

He stared at her as though he had not seen her before; his eyes blank with shock.

'Michael,' she repeated, 'come away. Come away.' Her hand went out in the dim light, her palm turned upwards. 'Come home.'

He woke as though he had been sleeping, turning round and staring at the chaos he had produced. Nothing was left unmarked. Nothing Harry had ever touched was whole. Nothing he had valued remained. His friend had taken his daughters, had used them, had been the father of their children. Edward was dead, but more than that, Edward had been Harry's child, as was Sydney.

'Why?' Michael asked hopelessly. But he wasn't talking to his wife, he was talking to his absent friend.

Why did you cheat me? I let you into my life and into my family, Michael thought brokenly, I loved you, Harry. And you betrayed me. You took everything I had, my home, my family; you even grafted your clinic onto my house, living with us, putting secrets between us, the brilliant cuckoo who had finally overtaken the nest.

'Where is he?'

'Harry's gone,' Sylvia replied evenly. 'He's gone.'

Her husband's face was terrifying.

'I should have killed him.'

Chapter Thirty-one

In the week which followed the builders repaired the operating theatre and restored it to what it was, but Harry never came back. His clothes were packed up by Sylvia and sent to his flat in Manchester, his books likewise. The consulting room and office he had used in the clinic were repossessed by other doctors, new doctors who were now practising at Aynhams in Harry's place, their patients being operated on by Harry's instruments.

His name was never mentioned at Aynhams. To all intents and purposes there was no longer any link between the Cochranes and Harry Chadwick.

Three days after his death on 8 September, Edward was buried at St Anne's, Pendleton. A queasy peace settled between Michael and Sylvia, Beth returning to the care of her husband. After the death of Edward, Daniel seemed to shrivel, his racked frame curling up like a leaf on a winter bonfire. He no longer tried to communicate, but there was a peculiar animation in his eyes which Mel noticed and which unsettled her. He would watch Beth with a certain look, and although his face had been rendered expressionless by the disease, there was malice in his eyes.

Dear God, did he overhear the argument that night? Mel wondered. Does he now know that Edward was not his son? Silently she watched Daniel fix his eyes on Beth. There *was* something different, Mel told herself, she wasn't imagining it. *He knew*.

And now what would happen? Would he give up? Or linger, holding on deliberately to punish his wife, to force her to become the person she had pretended to be for so long? And then, as Mel watched them, she saw Beth suddenly turn and catch her husband's stare. She smiled automatically, then seemed to falter, turning away from Daniel and gazing for a blind moment at the wall ahead.

Mel stayed a few weeks at Aynhams with Sydney, telling herself it was good for her daughter to be with the grandparents she'd been denied until now. But she was lying to herself – the reason she really wanted Sydney at Aynhams was because everyone needed her daughter to fill the vacuum left by Edward, to make sense out of the senseless.

Michael recovered his composure, and never mentioned what had happened. He was a loving and attentive father and grandfather, but at heart he was as remote and unreachable as a ghost.

No one understood the anguish Harry had experienced after the death of Edward. His had been a triple blow: the death of a son he had not known existed; the realization of his full betrayal of Michael; and the destruction of his operating theatre and expulsion from the clinic.

Only Harry knew what despair had driven Michael to destroy the theatre. He was a doctor; he of all people would have striven to save, not destroy, the clinic. But Michael's profession had meant nothing that night; all that had mattered then was the knowledge that his friend, the only man he had ever loved, had betrayed him. The grandchild he had loved as Daniel's son, the child who had so tragically died – as if that hadn't been enough – was not who Michael thought he was. He was an interloper, a changeling. Daniel was not his father, Harry was. Harry, his friend, his ally, the man who had looked out for his family whilst he was away during the war.

Michael would be sure to wonder how long his love affair with Beth had gone on – when it had started. Then he would wonder about Mel – whether the sisters knew about each other's involvement with Harry – whether they were in cahoots. He would feel excluded, betrayed, bewildered; would look at his daughters and wonder how they could have kept so many secrets for so long. He would suspect them, and what was worse, he would suffer for doubting them. He would hurt, Harry realized with appalling anguish.

Oh God, Michael, Harry thought, I never meant to hurt you. I never meant to hurt anyone. I was just selfish, egocentric. Beth and I had a brief affair: she was unhappy, upset about Daniel, and one night we got talking and that was it. It only happened once. Only once. Neither of us mentioned it again, and after a while I thought she had forgotten it. I never made the connection with Edward. How could I? She never told me. If she had told me it would have been different . . .

Oh really? Harry's mind ran on. Why would it have been different? What would he have done differently? Married Beth? She was already married, so what else could he have done? Acknowledged Edward as his son? Well, even if he had wanted to, how could he? Daniel believed that he was the child's father – how could he take away the only thing Daniel had left? So how would it have been different if he had known?

Trying to control his burning conscience, Harry paced his flat, then picked up a patient's file from his desk, only to put it down again immediately. There was no escape this time, he was finally going to have to face up to what he had done. He had to think about it now; he had to realize what he had done and account for it.

His expulsion from Aynhams was a body blow. His confidence had dissolved as soon as his books and clothes had been returned to him the night after Michael destroyed the clinic. Without a note. Warmth and love cut off. And who could blame the Cochranes? He had deserved it. He had abused their love, their trust. He had shown himself for what he really was: a coarse, slum kid with no morals and no heart. Closing his eyes, Harry thought of Michael and missed him, pretended he was talking to him, sitting in front of the log fire at Aynhams, the wind blowing round the cold October night. He said mentally what he couldn't say in person. In the weeks before, his telephone calls had been cut off, his letters unanswered. So now he talked as though Michael were sitting in front of him.

Michael, listen to me, I'm sorry. I know that's not enough, but I am so sorry. I've missed you so much, miss Aynhams, Sylvia, the girls, my clinic which you bloody near wrecked. That was my little kingdom, Michael. You know that, that was why you smashed up the operating theatre. It served two purposes at the same time – one, I couldn't operate there, and two, you knew I would never dare return. It was bloody effective too.

If you had hit me, I could have hit back, we could have quarrelled and argued and in time you would have forgiven me – I know you would, you think not, but you loved me, Michael. You would have let me come home one day. We have too much shared history between us to remain enemies. I remember your father, Sylvia leaving, the girls growing up – yes, Michael, the girls. I know what you're wondering, but no, I never touched either of them until they were consenting adults. I would never have done anything like that. But you're not sure any more, are you? You thought you knew me before, and look how I turned out. So I'll tell you the truth, Michael, here and now. All of it, every bit.

I loved Mel. I still do. She was all I wanted in a partner – funny, intelligent, good-looking, tough – remember how she used to talk back to me when she was just a kid? No one else ever stood up to me like Mel – no one else dared. But she wasn't afraid of any bugger. How can I tell you this next part? I can't, but I have to – when Mel became pregnant with my child I asked her to abort it.

Harry swallowed, his eyes still closed, imagining Michael's face.

I said we could go on as usual if she got rid of the child. I even asked her to marry me . . . When she refused to have an abortion, she also refused to have anything more to do with me.

Opening his eyes, Harry stared ahead, a feeling of homesickness overwhelming him, even though his exile had only been a matter of weeks. He *longed* to return to Aynhams, to the one and only security he had known, but they wouldn't have him. The common kid rejected by the nobs. Only the common kid deserved it. His home – the only real home Harry had ever had – was off limits to him and he was cut loose. And he couldn't even blame them.

He had worked like a lunatic throughout the remainder of September, tiring himself out, falling into bed in the early hours. But when he closed his eyes sleep didn't come. All he could see were pictures, portraits of Michael, Mel and Edward. He struggled to remember the child, *his child*, tried to conjure up an image of him. But it was too hazy, too indistinct to hold on to. He had been dark, but what else? Just a child, someone to spoil – but Edward hadn't been just a child, he had been *his* child. And now that child was dead, buried in Pendleton.

Harry had been to visit the grave although he had not dared to show up at the funeral. Flowers had been banked high, the cards still legible. One said, 'To Edward, our darling son. Love from Mummy and Daddy.'

It was a grim punishment, Harry thought, remembering, and justified. *I didn't want the child Mel carried and I never knew my son. Serves me right. Serves me right that now I have neither. I don't have a home or a family.* He swallowed, closing his eyes again and continuing to talk to Michael in his head.

I never forget you, or Aynhams. I never forget that the only time I was ever truly loved and accepted was there.

Aynhams was my sanctuary and I would never allow anyone – especially any woman – to encroach. In a way I
suppose that was another reason why I loved Mel. She
didn't have to force her way in; she was already there.

Why can't we talk, Michael? I don't suppose you and
Mel have ever discussed this. I don't suppose you have ever
talked to Beth about me – it wouldn't be like you to pry,
would it? I bet you'd have said that it was all in the past,
forgotten, and never to refer to it again – but you think
about it, don't you? I know you do, I know you miss me.
I was a good friend to you, Michael. I betrayed you, but
I never set out to injure you. It was never deliberate, never
planned.

You and your family are so ... extraordinary ... I
wanted so much to be a part of it. First, when I met George,
and then when I opened the clinic, Sylvia running the show
whilst you were in the army. I pretended they were mine,
Michael. Your old man knew that, he sensed it, and gave
me the gypsies' warning. He told me to find my own wife
and children, because yours were already spoken for. I was
angry with him – but only because he knew what was in
my heart.

I've envied you always, Michael. Funny that – everyone
else envied me, but I was jealous of you, I wanted to be
you, to have what you had, to be quiet and gracious – but
I never was. I was a braggart, a loud mouth, a glad-hander.
I was never in your league. You outflanked me, Michael,
you outclassed me, and in the end you won.

I'm the outsider now, for ever. I can't come back to
Aynhams and I can't even contact my daughter – yes, I do
think about her, Michael. I wonder how she looks and
how she sounds. I was never fanciful before. I also think
about Edward. It's difficult grieving for a son who died
before you had the chance to get to know him as your own
child.

But it serves me right – wasn't I the one who said I never

wanted a wife and children? Well, I got my wish, didn't I? Mel doesn't want to know me, and as for my children, one is dead and the other one is estranged from me.

Keep it that way, Michael. I'm not worth much – the bluster's fine for me, the success and the attention are great. It's all ephemeral bullshit. But I can't do real life. I can't, never could. I would mess it up, whether I wanted to, or not.

Do you feel old, Michael? I do. Now, at this moment I would give anything to pick up the phone and talk to you. My bloody feet ache and I've got haemorrhoids – Jesus, not such a smart arse now, am I? We're old, we should be friends again. I want to sit by that fire and hang my clothes up in that cupboard. I want to see the grass turn from dull green to malachite in summer and I want to see you.

Look after our girls, Michael, and look after yourself.

Preoccupied, Mel pushed the file aside in her office and rummaged for a packet of cigarettes she kept hidden. Greedily she lit one and breathed in, staring at the reversed letters of her name on the glass door opposite.

DR M. COCHRANE

PATHOLOGY DEPARTMENT

It looked like jibberish, the wrong way round. Closing one eye, Mel stared at the letters and tried to make a seven-letter word from them, then exasperated, inhaled again and stared at the phone instead. She might phone her father and ask about Sydeney, talk about trivia to her mother and then enquire after Beth, reassuring them that she would be home – as always – on Friday night.

Or then again she might call a friend and go out to lunch. Or then again she might call no one and sit in her office eating a sandwich she didn't want. What did it matter what she did? She was just going through the motions, living in limbo, the huge empty place in all their lives growing greater by the day.

We all miss him, Mel thought incredulously. We all hate him and want to punish him – oh, but how we miss him. How we all think of you, Harry. Without our mentioning your name how constantly present you are in all our lives. Every corner of Aynhams has some memory of you; at every sound from the clinic and every opening door we expect to see you.

And I still love you . . . Slowly Mel rose to her feet and gazed out of the window of her office. I *will* get over this, she told herself, it *will* stop hurting one day. One morning I'll wake up without thinking of you, without wanting you. One afternoon some other man will make me laugh and his touch, scent, voice will replace yours. One evening our daughter will look more like me than her father. One day I will hear your name and feel nothing.

It *will* end, she thought – then closed her eyes against the lie.

Frowning, Beth moved to the back door, her clothes creased, her hair greasy, unwashed. Daniel was now bed-ridden in the sitting room next door to the kitchen. He could no longer speak and merely stared through the door, following his wife everywhere with his eyes.

'I'm making some soup,' she said tentatively. 'You like soup, don't you, Daniel?'

He stared at her without trying to speak.

'Chicken soup,' Beth went on, her voice edgy.

He *knew*, so why was she still pretending to be the loving selfless wife? He *knew*. A void opened up inside her; as distant as her reflection in her husband's eyes. She couldn't cry, couldn't talk about Edward, couldn't grieve. She could only make soup. Soup after soup, meal after meal, down all the hours, the days, the months. Until he died, or she died. Until she stopped moving and working and thinking.

'I'll bring it in on a tray, Daniel,' she said, half mad with frustration. 'We'll have it watching television. That would be nice, wouldn't it? Wouldn't it?'

His eyes fixed on hers, his expression unreadable. At times he would jerk, his body sliding down in the wheel-chair until she straightened him. He now had a band around his head attached to the top of the chair to keep his head upright. Beth stared at him; he looked like a tor-ture victim, trussed up, ready to be mutilated.

His eyes were still on hers.

It was a mistake, I know, I know. I shouldn't have done it. But you were sick when I wanted a man, and Harry was there . . . It was only once . . . You see, I missed you so much, Daniel. You were so fit once, tapping on the window and holding up your medical bag the day you were made partner in the practice. You had hair which used to lie damp against the back of your neck, and a birthmark on your right thigh. You were real. Once.

'Don't look at me like that!' Beth snapped, then – slowly and patiently – she began to feed her husband.

Chapter Thirty-two

The bush was deep in the soil, well rooted, as Michael tried to dig it out, darkness all around him. It was madness to garden at night, but he had to do *something*. Breathing heavily, Michael paused and wiped his hands on an old handkerchief, turning to look up at the house. On the right-hand side the lighted clinic entrance was just visible behind hedges, and on the left the double entrance doors of the house were half open, the sweet autumn air nuzzling into the stuffy rooms.

Upstairs Michael could see a figure move past a window. Sylvia? Probably. Too tall for Beth. Slowly he counted the lighted windows and then paused by the last one on the ground floor. His father's old study. Well, Michael thought, I wonder what you would say if you were alive? What would you have done? He picked up the shovel again and pushed it into the dark, moist earth. What would you have done?

You always said Harry was a hard man, like old Tom Chadwick. A street fighter. You even tried to warn him off, didn't you? But you loved him. As we all did . . . Angrily, Michael pushed the spade back into the dark earth. God damn you, Harry, I miss you. I miss my friend. And Mel misses you, I know that. She's longing for you, Harry. As you long for her. Because you do, don't you? I could see it in your eyes the night Edward died.

I want you away from her, but I can't stop it, can I, Harry? We can ignore you and never mention your name, but you're here everyday, as is your child. I want to see you ruined, beaten. I want to see you dead. I want . . .

Michael paused, his hands shaking . . . I want you to come back.

Then suddenly the moon shifted out from behind the trees, Michael staring upwards as the clouds moved over its face. Against all logic, he took it as an omen, a symbol.

Midnight's smiling, tomorrow will be a lucky day.

Bloody rain, Sylvia thought, what else? Hurriedly she walked under the entrance of the Paddington Infirmary and shook the water off her umbrella, leaving it by the door as she walked in. She couldn't stand the silences at home any longer; the long pauses; the awkwardness between them all. Beth wouldn't meet her eyes, and Mel was distant. And as for Michael, well, she never really knew what her husband was thinking.

But she knew what she thought and walked purposefully towards the London lecture theatre, sliding into a vacant seat at the back, her eyes fixed on the familiar figure on the podium.

She was pleased to see that Harry looked older, tired. Not that it showed in his voice – that was as forceful as ever, the peculiar intonation unchanged. He hadn't been near the Aynhams clinic for weeks, had even avoided the Manchester Infirmary, obviously anxious not to run into Mel. Instead Harry had lectured abroad and had only now returned to England, staying in London to give a speech to a convention of plastic surgeons.

Watching him, Sylvia thought back. I remember you when you first came to Aynhams, Harry. Full of ambition, fuelled up with your own importance. I remember when you opened the clinic and the years which followed when I ran it for you. We had some laughs then, Harry.

Only the previous night she had been looking at the old photographs of the Battle of Britain fighters who had been brought to Aynhams mutilated and burned. The men – in all stages of surgery – had been smiling into the camera, most of them bandaged, good-looking nurses standing guard over them, the vast bulk of Aynhams like a movie backdrop behind them all. And in the middle, seated, was Harry. Harry with his pipe, with his presence, his confidence. Look at me, he seemed to be saying. I did the impossible, this is my work, my patients. Look at what I've achieved.

Other photographs showed pictures of her daughters growing up, Beth still and pretty, Mel putting out her tongue to the camera, and later on there was a picture torn in half of Sylvia and Michael. Torn, but not thrown away. Had Michael done it, or Mel? Sylvia wondered, putting the two pieces together and sticking it with Sellotape.

Of course Michael hadn't talked about the death of Edward or the revelations which followed, although he knew full well that his wife had overheard everything. Instead, after he had wrecked the clinic, he fell silent; apparently his violent fury had expended itself and he had nothing left to express. Instead he reverted to the Michael of old. And yet many times Sylvia caught her husband looking at his daughters, or watching Sydeney, and she wondered what he was thinking.

At first she had felt an anger in him, but as the weeks passed the feeling was replaced by something altogether different, regret. Without discussing it, everyone had come to the same conclusion: all their lives had been affected by Harry Chadwick, he had caused irreparable damage, and yet one simple fact remained – without him they were all adrift.

Oh, do get on with it! Sylvia thought impatiently as Harry finished his lecture and took his applause. Then she waited until the audience had left and only she remained. He was collecting up his papers and hadn't noticed her – until she walked down to the podium and approached him.

'That was a good talk.'

He dropped his papers at the shock of seeing her, bending down and scurrying to pick them up.

'Sylvia. I wasn't expecting to see you.'

She laughed. 'No, I don't suppose you were.'

'How is everybody?' he asked awkwardly, flushing.

She had the upper hand, and knew it. 'I bet you're wondering what I'm doing here, aren't you?'

'I'm sorry.'

'For what?'

'Everything.'

'Oh,' said Sylvia airily. 'That's a big word, "everything". But even four syllables can hardly encompass the damage you've caused.'

'I meant I was sorry . . .' he faltered, struggled for words. 'I wrote –'

'I tore up the letters.'

'And phoned –'

'That was good of you, Harry. Unfortunately no one wanted to speak to you.'

'So why are you here now?' he asked, recovering some composure.

'I'm worried about Beth,' Sylvia said, ignoring the question. 'She's had a difficult life. Which is strange, considering she had such a charmed childhood. Now Mel was *always* difficult, prickly, awkward, we expected her to have a fight on her hands.' Sylvia paused. 'You might not realize this, but I love them both very much. I suppose you think that's strange. After all, I did leave them when they were young. I wasn't a model mother.' Her glance ran over the papers in Harry's hands. 'I care about my husband too. He doesn't love me, but then that's a side issue. I just don't want to see him suffer any more.'

Harry was silent, listening.

'It's a funny thing about getting older. You realize the true value of things. Emotion doesn't get in the way the same.'

'I don't understand.'

'You will,' Sylvia replied, taking a seat on the front row of the auditorium and crossing her legs. 'When I was young I wanted nothing more than to be married to an Englishman – me, of mixed race, marrying an Englishman! No one thought I could do it, but I did. I did care about Michael when I married him. But not enough. After all, I did leave him. I was selfish for a very long time. In fact, I'm an expert on selfishness,' Sylvia said, smiling, her eyes unfathomable. 'I'm selfish and tough, so I can easily recognize those qualities in others. Like you, Harry.'

'Now, look here –'

'I like this lecture theatre,' Sylvia replied coolly, looking round, 'all enclosed and safe. It reminds me of a cave. I like places where you can hide. People *should* hide more – especially when they have secrets to protect.'

Flushing, Harry stared at her.

'But then subtlety was never your strong suit, was it?'

'Nor yours.'

She laughed again. 'Mel still cries for you.'

His mouth dried. 'How d'you know that? She'd never talk to you.'

'She didn't. I eavesdrop. That's what people do when other people don't confide in them.'

'You always were hard –'

'And you were always a braggart, a liar, and a chancer, Harry. Not evil, not bad, just selfish, hard, unfeeling. Harry feels for Harry, no one else. You never considered your actions, you were always in too much of a hurry, too much of a rush to make your name . . .' She paused again. 'You were fun, though. When we were young, you used to stay at Aynhams and talk to old George: I'd hear you laughing and telling jokes. We were happy. *You* were happy then. You belonged there. I don't suppose you've ever belonged anywhere else.'

She had hit a nerve and knew it. Harry glanced away.

'I miss Aynhams. I miss all of you,' he said hoarsely. 'I've buggered everything up, Sylvia. All of it. I never knew about Edward, I never knew he was my son until after he had died. I think about him every day, I can't get him out of my mind.'

'Neither can Beth,' Sylvia replied mercilessly.

He flinched. 'I lost my son before I ever knew I had him, and now Mel's keeping my daughter away from me.' He was talking in a rush, his accent slipping, the Gladstone Row voice coming out. 'Help me, Sylvia, help me to do something right. I want to make it up to Mel and Sydeney. I want to look after them.'

When he had finished, she clapped. The sound was hard and echoed in the auditorium. Harry flushed again.

'Oh, well done, well done. That was quite a speech,' she said icily. 'A little too much vibrato on the top notes, but otherwise very convincing.'

'You bitch –'

She was on her feet instantly, moving over to him and staring him in the face.

'Now you listen to me, little man,' she said warningly. 'If you hadn't been brilliant no one would have given you a second look; you'd have stayed in Gladstone Row with your snotty nose and your arse hanging out of your trousers. You're common, Harry, an upstart. And I should know. Don't call me names, I've been called them all before, and by bigger men than you.'

He faltered, shaken by her fury. She was, Harry realized, utterly ruthless.

'Don't bleat on to me about your lost child. You never wanted children, Harry, so don't go all sentimental on me now. You had no conscience when you slept with my daughters, and you had no conscience when you asked Mel to abort your child. She carried that baby and gave birth to it alone. Without you. And as if that wasn't enough, she was so ashamed of what she'd done that she avoided even seeing her father. You drove a wedge between them that injured the finest man you'll ever meet.' Angrily she gripped Harry's arm. 'You want to make amends? Well, you will, you bastard. You'll make amends for the rest of your life.'

'She won't talk to me,' Harry said sharply. 'Mel won't even take my calls. And neither will Michael.'

'So go and see her. And go and see Michael. It's been weeks, Harry. That's too long.'

'What if they won't see me?'

'Michael will,' Sylvia said firmly, letting go of his arm, her voice calm again. 'And he'll forgive you – because you're his past, the brother he never had. He'll forgive you because he has to. You two are getting old, he needs you more than he needs anyone. And you need him.'

'And Mel?'

Sylvia smiled shrewdly. 'Mel's another matter. I'll try and plead your case, but I don't know if it will do any good. We were never that close.'

'Sylvia, I –'

'Oh, save the hearts and flowers, Harry,' she said dismissively. 'It serves my purpose too, you know.'

Mel was still in her green overalls when her mother phoned. Sitting down she listened to what Sylvia had to say without interrupting and then pulled off her green surgical cap.

'How's Sydeney?'

'Did you hear what I said, Mel?'

'Tell her I'll be home on Friday.'

Sylvia took in a deep breath. 'Harry wants –'

'I don't care what Harry wants. And if you talk to him again you can tell him that.'

Walking down St Stephen's Street Michael stopped and stared at the site where the old tobacconist's had been. It was newly opened as a hairdresser's, with photographs of the latest London styles in the window. Glamorous poses, glamorous faces, out of place in Salford. He paused at the trafficlights and then crossed over, avoiding a puddle as he passed by what used to be Gordon Cutting. The alleyway was boarded off, wooden planks crossing the entrance, graffiti scrawled in letters a foot high: 'MANCHESTER UNITED RULES OK'.

Next to his car was an old van; a boy of about fourteen was kicking a football against the wall of a derelict house. Michael had just one call left to make and then he would go home to Aynhams. A curl of smoke came out of one of the chimneys in the distance, October showing its teeth after the clammy September heat.

As he walked along, Michael suddenly remembered the leaflet in his pocket and pulled it out to read about a new drug for bronchitis. He would phone the drug company in the morning and get some samples. Winter was coming, there was always bronchitis in Salford when the weather closed in.

Absorbed, he walked along reading, only glancing up as he crossed the roads, but otherwise so engrossed that when a man bumped into him Michael jumped.

'Sorry . . .' he said automatically, and then stopped, staring at the figure in front of him. *'Harry?'*

'You had your head in a book the day we met,' he said quietly. 'It was about VD –'

'I'm on a case, Harry, I can't talk.'

'I'll come with you,' he said hurriedly, falling into step with Michael. 'I once went out with your father.'

'The gangrene case.'

Eagerly, Harry nodded. 'That's the one. George amputated the man's leg there and then. I'd never seen anything like it before.'

Pushing the leaflet he had been reading into his pocket, Michael walked on in silence. He had tried to imagine what it would be like to see Harry again. What he would say, feel. He thought he might hit him or ignore him, but now that Harry was here all Michael could see was the young man he had first known. The one he had liked, the one he missed.

He tried to conjure up some of the anger he had felt the night he had ruined the operating theatre; tried to ignite the same madness, the same drive to destroy – but it wasn't there. He had wanted to kill this man, *he had wanted Harry Chadwick dead*. But now that he was here, he wanted only the past. And the past included Harry.

'Can I come with you?'

Michael stared ahead. This man had deceived him and caused immense suffering; but he had also inspired happiness and hope. His drive, his energy, had fuelled Michael; they had led separate lives, but each had been privy to the other's. Their bond was stronger than a blood tie, it was need.

'Michael, please . . . can I come with you?'

The sky was dimming, streetlights going on. Soon it would be dark, the streets hostile. Suddenly Michael was tired of being alone, and nodding, walked with his friend into the night.

Chapter Thirty-three

On 9 October Harry wrote to Mel again. The letter was rerouted from the Infirmary marked 'Return to sender'. He phoned that morning four times, and each time Mel's secretary told him that she wasn't there. Or she was out to lunch. Or in a meeting. Or in the mortuary. She was busy, sorry. Sorry, she was busy.

At three o'clock in the afternoon he ordered flowers from a shop in Deansgate, then, just as he was about to pay, he cancelled them. Mel wouldn't give a damn about flowers. He thought about sending a message to say that one of her colleagues wanted to meet her for dinner to talk business. But he knew she wouldn't fall for it. By five he was desperate and wondered if having himself admitted with a heart attack might do the trick. Then he realized that he was doing and thinking all the things she expected of him: being cheap, being aggressive, being flash.

So what *could* he do? Harry stared up at the hospital from the street outside. It was difficult to be sincere, he realized, he had been superficial and selfish for so long. What did real people do? What did other men who loved women do to win them back?

And then something occurred to Harry which had never occurred to him before – that Mel might not want him back. *Jesus, she might really not want him back*. He had never considered that cold fact; had always thought that he could return to her one day and that she would accept him. But what if she didn't? What if his arrogance had blinded him to the obvious – Mel Cochrane no longer loved him or wanted him back in her life.

Swallowing, Harry stared ahead. He was suddenly aware of a sensation he had not felt since childhood – fear. He was groggy with anxiety, damp-palmed. He had never thought he could lose, not in his profession, or his private life. After all, everyone knew that he was invincible, powerful. But now he was terrified.

Don't shut me out, he thought helplessly. Please Mel, don't shut me out. Homesickness – deep in the heart – threatened to overwhelm him. His legs were unsteady, his pulse accelerating. All his success and money meant nothing now; he was back in Gladstone Row, the rough kid who stole flowers from the rich man's garden.

Suddenly even to look at Mel Cochrane and expect her to want *him* was ridiculous. He had nothing to offer her. She had her own success, her own money, her own integrity. She had their child, and she had more courage than he would ever possess.

Rain started, and fell heavily on his hair, darkening the shoulders of his coat as he stood there. Passersby stared at him, but he didn't notice, he was simply trying to find his way out of a labyrinth he had built around himself. Give me the words, he pleaded, tell me what to do. Tell me how to get her back.

He had to see her *now*. He had to speak to her *now*. This was the time, there could be no further delay. His heart was racing, his stomach turning over. Dear God, was this love? This terrifying passion? This incapacitating fear of rejection? Of the loved one slipping out of the grasp? Was this what women in the past had felt about him? This awful sickness, loss of control? Is this what Mel had once felt for him?

Harry walked on, stumbling for an instant before righting himself. Had she felt the same terror when she told him she was having his child? . . . His breaths came quickly. And what had he done? He had told her to have an abortion. When she had laid herself open, he had crucified her. And now he was the one being crucified.

Slowly Harry walked into the hospital and followed the signs to the mortuary. He no longer felt in control, no longer cared about his image or his pride. The corridors widened, narrowed, and then he came face to face with the door marked 'Dr M. Cochrane' and, without thinking, without giving himself time to back off, he walked in.

She was sitting behind her desk, her assistant seated opposite, another pathologist beside him. As the door opened, she looked up expectantly and then her face hardened. Her expression winded him.

'I'm in a meeting –'

'We have to talk,' Harry said blindly, the two men in the room exchanging glances.

Mel's voice was hostile, unyielding. 'I have nothing to say.'

'But I have –'

'So write me a letter!'

'I have, you never answer them!' Harry snapped back, turning to the embarrassed men sitting rigidly in their seats. 'Would you excuse us?'

They stood up.

'Sit down,' Mel said coldly. 'Mr Chadwick is just leaving.'

They sat down.

Harry stood his ground, glancing away from Mel to the men again.

'Just give me five minutes –'

Up they stood again.

'Stay where you are!' Mel hissed, the men sitting down immediately, startled.

Dear God, Harry thought, this is ludicrous.

'All right,' he said evenly, 'they can stay. But I'm still going to have my say.'

Mel's eyes were flinty. 'Not here.'

'Where then?'

'Nowhere. You had your chance, it's over.'

'You don't mean that.'

Staring awkwardly out of the window, Mel's assistant could feel his face flushing, his voice tentative, as he suggested, 'Look, maybe we *should* come back later –'

'No,' Mel countered, 'Mr Chadwick only ever likes to talk when it suits him. And now, because it suits him, he thinks that I should interrupt my work and give him my full attention.' She leaned back in her seat. God, Harry thought, she looks incredible. 'Mr Chadwick has trouble with words, you see, gentlemen. He can only use certain parts of the English language. He also has trouble forming sentences – unless they begin with the letter I.'

'I want you –'

'Do you see what I mean, gentlemen?' Mel said acidly. 'A perfect example.'

A sudden gust of wind blew the rain against the window. Mel stood up and pulled it closed. A few drops of water had settled on the white paint of the sill.

'I want you back.'

' "I" again,' Mel said, folding her arms and staring across the room to where Harry stood in the doorway.

She had expected him to return one day, but not like this. She had expected flowers, or some showy plea for reconciliation, not Harry coming love-struck and gauche, showing himself up publicly.

I've cried for you on and off for years, she thought. For so long I waited for you and every man had your face, your voice, your mannerisms. I was sick for you, and sick without you; you were so much a part of me that you could have been my own reflection in a mirror. But I won't give in. I won't let you tread on me and leave me and pick holes in me. I won't let myself lose control and pride in myself because of my love for you. Never, never again.

'Mel, I have to talk to you alone.'

'No, Harry. I won't ever talk to you alone.'

He swallowed, and then said quietly, 'You can keep our

daughter away from me, you can keep yourself away from me, you can ignore me and hate me, but you can't stop me.' He stared at her, the two doctors in the room listening avidly. 'You can't stop me wanting you and waiting for you. You can't stop me looking at you and thinking of you. You can't stop me regretting every moment what I've done to you . . .'

Mel's eyes fixed on him.

He was talking from the heart. It was killing him but he was opening himself up, knowing that people were listening, knowing that they would gossip and poke fun at him for it. She knew how much his position meant to him – the slum kid made good – and now he was jeopardizing everything, being totally honest for once. It made him suddenly a brave man.

'Harry, stop –'

'No,' he said simply, 'I'm not going to stop. Never. If you never take me back, I'll not stop. I've got nothing to give you, Mel, that you don't already have. I can offer you nothing that some other man couldn't match or beat. You deserve better than me.' His eyes searched her face. 'You deserve someone who'll love you and appreciate you. Someone kind, thoughtful, honourable . . . but he won't be me, Mel. He won't be able to think and live without you; but he won't be me –'

Putting her hands up Mel's voice faltered as she said, 'Harry, don't say any more –'

But he wasn't going to stop. 'You and I are meant, Mel. Neither of us is ever going to have the normal marriage, the normal home, the normal family. You want to do things your way, so do I. You want to lead, so do I. You want to be top dog. So do I.' His voice rose suddenly. 'Think, Mel! I understand you, for Christ's sake. No one on earth understands you like I do.'

He moved towards her, Mel turning to the two men still in the room.

'Would you leave us, please?'

Reluctantly, they left, Harry watching the door close behind them.

'I suppose you realize that you've just made a horse's arse out of yourself?' Mel said quietly.

Gently, he stroked her cheek. 'I meant every word I said –'

She ducked out from his touch and moved to the window. 'It's raining.'

He frowned, wrong-footed. 'What do you expect? It's Manchester.'

Slowly she traced her finger down the window. 'My father said that you and he were reconciled.'

'Are you pleased?'

'My father is, so I'm pleased for him.'

'Honestly?'

She turned to look at him. 'No, Harry, *honestly* I'm wary of you. I wonder when you'll let him down again. I wonder how long it will be before you get bored. If you get what you want now, how long will the feeling of triumph last?'

Her bitterness caught him off guard.

'This isn't about winning –'

'Everything you do is about winning!' Mel replied hotly. 'You can't bear the idea of losing anything. You want me back now because I've turned my back on you. You want your daughter because your son is dead. You want, you want, you want. You want what is yours, not what you've earned.'

'If I got what I'd earned, I'd have nothing.'

Mel smiled faintly. 'Now you're learning, Harry. Now you're finally beginning to understand.'

'So what do I have to do?' he asked her helplessly.

'Nothing.'

'*Nothing?*'

'Nothing,' Mel repeated. 'There is nothing *to* do, because

it was all done a long time ago. When we met it started, and when we die, it will finish.' She leaned towards him and brushed the rain off his hair. 'And in between, we come and go.'

'So you won't marry me?'

She laughed gently. 'No.'

'Or live with me?'

'No,' she repeated, looking up at him. 'I won't give you unlimited access to my career, my child, or my house. Only to my heart – and that should be enough.'

'You win,' he said, taking her into his arms.

'About time, Harry,' she replied. 'About time.'